Mine Forever

No me without you

Sexy M.F. Series Book III

by

Lisa Mackay

(V7)

POD

ISBN-13: 9781913279028

THANK YOU

To all my wonderful readers.

*

To Jan, for inspiring me to do better.

*

To my lovely parents for everything they do and are.

*

To Ruelle – I get to love you.
To Spencer Combs (ft Holly Maher) – You are mine.
Beautiful songs, perfect lyrics – Available on iTunes.

*

To my beloved sister, Tracy. Always in my thoughts.
Love you more x

*

Finally, to our own imagination, may it never fail us!
May we always find our Sexy M.F. but if not…
May we always have books.
Them's the rules.
X:-)

CONTENTS

Lisa Mackay

PLEASE NOTE

To any non-UK readers,
I have included a glossary at the back of this book
to explain some of the British terminology
which you may not be familiar with.
Cheers! (Thanks)

FOREVER, YOU PROMISED ME FOREVER

My shattered heart still beats, but has no reason to go on.
My eyes still seek you out, and yet I know that you are gone.
If all is lost and broken, then why bother with endeavour?
You promised me the world, my love, you promised me forever.
And though the darkness claims my soul, torturing my mind.
Its brutal force a test of will, so painful and unkind.
But know my heart will find you, I'll reclaim my stolen treasure.
Because my love, you are my life, you promised me forever.

"It's time Vivienne."

"No… I'm not ready to say goodbye."

"I know, poppet, I know." Jan wraps a comforting arm around my shoulders giving me a gentle, reassuring squeeze. I wish it was enough.

My tear blurred eyes gaze down at my engagement ring. The lustre and hypnotic brilliance of its flawless stone, glints with the memories of the moment he'd proposed. *You promised me forever, Max. You promised.*

"Miss Vivienne… We'd better go, we don't want to be late for the service."

My aching heart twists violently in my chest, and I don't

even try to stop the tears from flowing. I'd cry him a river if it would bring him back. *You promised me forever.*

Jan hugs me, kissing the top of my head. "Vincent, just give us a minute or two, would you? I'll bring Vivienne down in a moment."

As Vinnie leaves, Jan releases me from her comforting hold and reaches for my hand. Her soft fingers tenderly rubbing the back of it in a gesture of affection, silently conveying that she understands my pain. As the tears spill over my lashes, dripping down to the silk fabric of my black dress, I stare down at the growing circles of dampness in my lap. My heart hurts with an aching emptiness. Where it once had a reason to beat, bursting at the seams with love and joy, it now lies dormant in my chest, crippled by inexorable loss, savagely shattering it into a million pieces.

Without Max, I feel utterly destroyed. I'm lost without him. My eyes mourn the loss of his handsome face. In sleep, my fingers still seek his warm silken skin, and my body constantly craves the contact of his powerful arms around me. The pain of his absence grows deeper and darker with each passing day, and I know, for me, life will never be the same again.

No me without you… I miss you.

Instinctively, I circle my hand over my belly, over our precious nuggets. The last thing Max did before he was taken from me, was to rub his hand over my belly and kiss me tenderly on the lips. The feel of his kiss still lingers on my mouth, and his scent has long been embedded in my skin.

As constant as the contact between us was, it always had the same intoxicating effect. I ached for his touch. My body craved it. And when it came, it would always charge my skin with a tantalising, all-consuming electricity, filling me with want and need to be possessed by him in every way.

Max was a force of nature. Strong, sometimes overwhelming, but always impossible to ignore. Designed by angels, Max was perfection. He'd been lovingly crafted with all the requisite contours of masculine beauty. Every edge, curve, and detail of his gorgeous face and sinfully sexy body had been carved with love and a deep understanding that his external magnificence was merely a mirror reflecting the kind and beautiful soul within.

How could I have known that would be the last time I'd ever see his gorgeous face. That it would be our last kiss, our last touch, our last embrace. To never be able to gaze into the bluest eyes I'd ever seen, or to feel them burn me with the depth of his love, is a deprivation I know I'll never survive. How could I? His love was an opiate, and I was completely and irrevocably hooked, like an addict.

If I'd known he was going to be cruelly ripped away from me, I'd have held on to him for dear life and fought till my last breath to keep him.

"Come on, Vivienne. We'd better go," Jan whispers, softly. "They'll be waiting for us."

She gently manoeuvres me onto my feet, blotting the tears from my cheeks with her handkerchief. With a heavy heart, I lean on Jan's arm as we leave the penthouse to make our way downstairs.

The lobby, normally bustling with activity, is eerily still and deathly quiet. Everyone bowing their heads or averting their eyes as we pass. Even the street outside the Foxx-Tech building, usually busy with people and noisy with traffic, seems subdued as Jan and I make our way to the first of six black limousines waiting at the kerb.

With a reassuring smile, Vinnie opens our door, then closes it softly once we're inside. Taking Sylvie's hand in mine, we sit in silence all the way to the church. Each of us in mourning, each silently bearing the weight of our own grief.

~

The man was loved, that's clear to see. It's painfully evident on the faces of those who have come to pay their respects. So many people. So many hearts that he had touched. He touched my heart too, so deeply.

The day he offered to walk me down the aisle in place of my own father, will be a day I'll never forget, and a memory I'll cherish forever. I cared for William very much, I'll miss him terribly.

He may not have been Max's biological father, but they certainly shared a kindness of heart and an immense capacity to love.

Sadness mutes the church. As we sit in silence waiting for the service to begin, my mind wanders back to that fateful night. It's never far from my thoughts, the events are on a constant, painful replay in my mind, bringing me back to the moment when my heart was torn apart.

During the chaotic hours that had followed Max's abduction, things seemed to go from bad to worse in the blink of an eye. Already fragile, the news that Monica had taken his son, affected William more than any of us could have anticipated. He collapsed in shock, grasping at his chest short of breath.

Sylvie tried to make him go to the hospital but he refused point blank. He didn't want to leave until there was news about Max, his beloved son.

Knowing William needed urgent medical attention, Vinnie called for an ambulance anyway, but by the time the paramedics arrived, William had suffered a major heart attack and had slipped into a coma.

They rushed him to the hospital and did everything they could to save him, but sadly, he never regained consciousness and died three days later, not knowing the fate of his son.

That was almost two weeks ago.

Since Max's abduction, I've suffered every painful minute of every painful day, agonising over what could have happened to him. There's been no word and no answers. Is he alive? Is he safe? Will he ever come back to me?

For me, the pain of losing Max is an unbearable torture, breaking my spirit and crushing my soul. I can only imagine how Sylvie must be feeling right now. Her son has been suddenly and cruelly ripped from our lives by his crazy ex-girlfriend, and now she's lost her husband too.

William and Sylvie had been together all their adult lives. They were made for each other, two halves of one whole.

Their love had been tested through many hard times and personal tragedies. The worst of which, the tragic deaths of their natural born sons. But they were a team, a partnership, bound by love and a deep mutual respect which kept them strong. Kept them together.

But now, like me, Sylvie's lost her soul mate. In a cruel twist of fate, we're gathered in the church mourning the loss of a husband, father, and friend. With heavy hearts and tears in our eyes we've come to say goodbye to this wonderful man.

William's favourite song begins to resonate around the echoing stone walls of the church, bringing me back to the present. 'Old blue eyes' crooning a standard from the classic American songbook, softly breaks into the respectful silence.

Sylvie gasps, drawing her handkerchief up to her mouth, sobbing beside me. I squeeze her frail, trembling hand, choking back the ever tightening lump in my throat as we turn to watch William's coffin being carried into the church.

Suddenly, my heart stops and my whole world seems to tilt on its axis as my wide eyes land on Max's devastatingly handsome face. The face I've longed for. The face that has been painfully absent from my life for far too long.

But it isn't Max. It's Cole, his twin brother.

I knew he would be here for his father's funeral, but the shock of seeing Max's double is almost too much to bear. My eyes follow him into the church as he helps to carry his father's coffin toward the alter. I can't look away, my eyes are conditioned to seek out his face and now that they have, it's impossible not to stare.

His hard set jaw clenches as he swallows his pain. His lush lips pressed together to hold in the sounds of his grief, the sounds that men prefer not to emit in public.. His nostrils flare in his blade straight nose. Watery pools of crystal blue beneath a troubled brow, stare straight ahead full of sadness. Even his tall masculine frame sheathed in an expensive suit, bears remarkable likeness to the body I'm so familiar with.

I can't stop myself from wanting to look at him. I need to look at him. Every edge and plane of his handsome face is identical to the face of the man I love. It's remarkable how alike they are to look at, and yet how different they are in character and personality.

As I drink him in, it makes the ache in my heart even more unbearable, and yet I can't take my eyes off him.

~

Almost everyone who came to the church, has come to the wake. There are so many people, many of which I've never met before.

It's stifling to be surrounded by Sylvie's family and friends. They're very kind and mean well, but I've become so used to the self-imposed solitude in the last couple of weeks that I can't handle it, so I quietly remove myself from their company and go outside for some fresh air. Some space.

"Vivienne, do you mind if I join you?" Jan asks hesitantly.

I nod, then we silently continue to walk in the gardens of Sylvie and William's home. Neither of us really wanting to speak.

I wanted to walk down to the lake where Max had brought me before. For me, anywhere we had spent time alone still holds his essence, giving me comfort. I needed to find somewhere peaceful and calm, I can't handle the crowds and the constant questions everyone seems hell bent on asking me. And if I told them how I really felt, they'd put me on suicide watch for sure.

When we arrive at the water's edge, I stare out at the still, glass-like surface of the lake and bend down to pick up a small, flat pebble. I had watched Max throw them into the lake the last time he had brought me here, when his mother had introduced me to the family. His pebbles had delicately skimmed and bounced across the surface in a graceful dance before diving noiselessly into the water. Mine just sink immediately with a pitiful splash, as if even the pebble has lost the will to live.

"Vivienne, are you sure I can't convince you to stay here in London?"

Shaking my head, I throw another pebble into the water.

"No. I need to be back in France, looking for him. I can feel him, Jan. I know he's out there somewhere. He needs me."

Dark and frightening thoughts of Max at the mercy of Monica, swirl around in my brain, quickening my heartbeat and churning my stomach.

Jan's soft hand rests on my shoulder. "Vincent's doing everything he can to find him, but Monica's left no trace, and those two waiters have simply vanished. It's been two weeks and there's no—"

I spin around glaring at her, cutting her off mid-sentence. Negativity and pessimism are two things I can't deal with right now. Even the police think the time for Max's safe return has passed, but I can't cope with anyone else feeling the same way. I won't give up hope. Hope is all I have.

"He's still alive, Jan. I know he is. And I'm not going to stop looking for him until I find him."

Her sad, watery eyes drift over my face. "I know," she sighs softly. Lowering her gaze, she begins to fidget. It's not a characteristic I recognise in her.

"Vivienne… Sylvie has asked Cole to manage the business, until Max returns, of course. She wants him to stay at the penthouse so he can be near the office, and also… to look after you."

A burst of anger pulses through me. "I don't need looking after!"

Without flinching at my rudeness, she smiles sympathetically, searching my face with her sad eyes. "Vivienne, Sylvie has lost her son and her husband, she doesn't want to lose you too."

Tears fill my eyes and I crumple to the floor in a sobbing heap. "I need him, Jan. We need him." I run my hands over my belly as the racking sobs take over my body. "I want him back. I miss him so much."

"Oh, Vivienne…" Jan kneels down beside me, her comforting arms around my shoulders.

If only that was enough.

~

Fiona had come to the funeral service, but thankfully she hadn't come to the wake. It bothered me to see her so upset during the funeral. Her tears were for Max, not William, and I wanted to slap her for it.

I had avoided her at the church, but I knew if I was to find myself alone with her here at the wake, we'd end up having words. I dislike her intensely, and in the state I'm in, with all my emotions lying close to the surface, I knew it wouldn't take much for me to lose my cool.

Since Max was taken, I've preferred to spend my time alone. Solitude can be strangely comforting, and the kindness and sympathy I've received, makes it harder to deal with.

I've managed to avoid Mary's intolerable and probing questions, but I know it's only a matter of time before she'll corner me somewhere and begin her interrogation. Gossip is something she thrives on.

I've stayed at the wake for as long as I can bear. Sylvie is surrounded by people who love and care for her, so I don't feel too bad making an early exit.

PLEASE DON'T MAKE ME LIVE WITHOUT YOU

As John drives me home to the penthouse, I run my hand along the empty seat next to me. The loss of him is suffocating. I can't get used to all the empty spaces since Max has been gone, I hate them in fact. They only serve to fuel the painful memories of that terrible night which constantly invade my mind, breaking my heart all over again.

Life without Max isn't a life at all, it's just a necessary existence because, as I've been told constantly by well wishers, life goes on. But how can it when the light of your life has been extinguished. How can I ever recover from losing the man who is, my everything.

Max possessed me in every way possible, invading my heart, mind, body and soul with his unique and indelible presence. But now he's gone, and all I have are the echoes and memories ingrained and entrenched, like a brand seared into my soul.

On the journey back to the penthouse, my mind wanders back, as it does so often, to the night he disappeared. What had started out as a beautiful day with Lucy and Dan's wedding, ended in tragedy and heartbreak for us all.

After finding out that Max had been abducted by Monica,

all hell broke loose. I became inconsolable, screaming and crying and demanding that someone should find him and bring him back. I'd never felt pain like it.

William collapsed at the news and was rushed to the hospital. John called Trencher to start a search for Max. And then the Police and a forensic team arrived, detaining everyone until their statements had been taken. A long and drawn out process considering the language barrier.

Poor Lucy, I felt so sorry for her. Still in her beautiful wedding gown, she ended her wedding day comforting me, yelling at the police to stop asking stupid questions, and to get out there and find the crazy bitch who had done this.

She was my rock for those first few hours. Without her, I would have gone insane.

She taped the torn fragments of my babies scan back together, and held me for hours while I cried my heart out. In the blink of an eye, Lucy and Dan's fairy-tale wedding had suddenly become an horrific nightmare. One I could never wake from until Max was found.

In the early hours of the following morning, we were finally released by the police. All of us tired, weary, and still dressed in our finery from the night before.

Vinnie organised the transport to take the guests back to the hotel, and Benny had been tasked to fly them all back to London in the afternoon. And once the guests had left, the yacht felt like a ghost ship. The mood was sombre and nobody spoke a word.

While the forensic team continued to gather their information, Lucy and Dan stayed behind on the yacht with John, while Jan, Vinnie, and I, went to the hospital to see William, and to support Sylvie in what must have been her darkest hour.

Everything felt so completely and utterly fucked-up.

In the hospital, I held Sylvie's hand at William's bedside as she reminisced about their life together. They'd had such an intense and abiding love. They'd known pain and suffering at the loss of their two sons Andrew and Joseph, but the way she spoke about Max and Cole, it sounded like adopting them had more than made up for the loss of their own sons.

Sylvie was a strong woman, the powerhouse of the Foxx family, but as she held onto William's hand, willing him to live, she looked broken, frail, and completely lost without him. I knew exactly how she felt.

I couldn't sit still for long. Every nerve ending was screaming out for me to move. I had to be doing something. I wanted to be out there looking for Max. I needed him. He needed me.

The police seemed so unhurried in their investigations, and the fact that I couldn't understand the language made it worse. Every time I had checked my phone, the disappointment that no one had called, or text with any new information, was driving me mad.

After a couple of hours, Jan offered to sit with Sylvie, so I went outside to get some fresh air. My mind was all over the place.

I remember pacing up and down the pavement at the front entrance of the hospital in my long burgundy bridesmaid gown. I could feel people staring at me. My mascara was smudged underneath my red-rimmed eyes, and I'm sure I must have looked a sight, but all I could think about was William and Max. The lives of two of the most important people in my life were suddenly and cruelly in the gravest of danger.

I don't know how long I was out there for, but when Vinnie walked out of the sliding doors, I remember stumbling to a halt when I caught sight of him. He looked ashen. So sad and weary, like he had the weight of the world on his shoulders.

I walked over to him. With tears in our eyes we stared at each other for a long moment, and then he opened his arms and held me in a bear hug that almost knocked the wind out of me. I held on to him for dear life, sobbing my heart out. He'd been a life support for Max, and now he was my shoulder to cry on.

None of this seemed real. Max was gone, and William's life

hung in the balance. How had any of this happened? How could Monica have got so close?

Vinnie sighed heavily, releasing me from his crushing hug. "Oh, Miss Vivienne. I'm so, so, sorry. I should have known Monica would do something like this. She's hurt the people I care about most in this world. If I ever get my hands on that bitch, I'll fucking kill her!"

I knew Vinnie meant every word, and the pain in his voice hurt me deeply.

I began to feel a strange sense of guilt. We all knew she was capable of this, and of all people, I had first hand experience of Monica's rage and tenacity, and yet, I had let my guard down, I hadn't seen her coming.

We sat on the wooden bench by the hospital entrance. I stared down at Vinnie's hands as he clenched and released his chunky fists. The winged dagger, tattooed on the back of his hand, stretching and shrinking as he did so. I listened as Vinnie vented his feelings about Monica, and then, with emotional reverence, he spoke about William and Max. They really were like family to him.

As we sat there talking, it occurred to me that this was Lucy and Dan's first day as a married couple. It hurt me. They were supposed to be spending it like every other newly-wed couple should, blissfully happy, enjoying their romantic honeymoon on the yacht. But now, the yacht had become a crime scene.

Vinnie had come to their rescue, as he does so well. He'd arranged for them to stay at Max's penthouse suite at the Hotel Martinez for the remainder of their honeymoon, but how could they possibly enjoy themselves after their wedding day had ended so tragically.

As Vinnie and I sat outside the hospital in a moment of silence, my mind wandered back to the night before, when Max had asked me to dance with him. He had held me in his arms looking down at me with love bursting from his eyes. His eyes were amazing. Bluer than the turquoise shallows of a coral reef, those eyes had hypnotised me, pulling me in until I was lost inside them. He had a way of telling me everything he was feeling through his eyes. And they could sear my skin with desire, just as easily as they could caress it with love.

As we danced, he told me of his plans to fly me off to some secret place where we would be married. I remember feeling so excited and happy. We were both happy.

Everything was perfect. He was the man of my dreams, the love of my life. No one had ever made me feel like he did. His love was deep, unconditional, and at times overwhelming. He had taken my heart and given his in return. I was privileged to own it, and I would cherish his love for as long as I lived.

The look in his scorching eyes had burned into my soul with love and longing. Losing myself in his gaze was an established effect that I couldn't control and never wanted to change.

At the time, Max hadn't elaborated on his plans for our wedding, choosing instead to keep it a secret. I was happy to let him surprise me. He knows me so well that I knew, wherever we went, whatever he had planned, it would always be perfect.

Of course, Vinnie knew what his plans were. As Vinnie divulged the details of Max's wedding plans, he squeezed my hand a little tighter and his voice was full of emotion. He told me that Max had arranged to fly us out to his private island in the Caribbean, 'Paradiso Volpe.'

We were supposed to be staying there for seven days, just the two of us. Hearing Vinnie say that, made my heart flutter. With our busy schedules, time alone was precious for Max and I. The thought of spending a whole uninterrupted week in the arms of my gorgeous lover would have been enough, but that was just the beginning.

For the second week, Max had arranged for all our friends and loved ones to be flown in for our romantic, sun-kissed wedding on the beach. Vinnie surprised me when he told me that with Lucy and Davis' help, Max had secretly designed my bridal gown. He'd also designed our custom made wedding bands, which Vinnie was supposed to present to us on our wedding day as his best man.

As he spoke of it, Vinnie became tearful. It hurt me to see him so distressed, but since Max's abduction, we've all been teetering on an emotional knife-edge.

It all sounded so idyllic. William was going to give me away, and Lucy was going to be my maid of honour. Max had even made provision for my mother to be there, if at all possible.

As Vinnie explained all the secret details of our romantic wedding, I couldn't believe that I had been so oblivious to it all. It sounded so perfect. Max had given it so much thought, and nobody, not even Clive, had uttered a single word.

But in the blink of an eye, everything had changed. My beloved groom had been cruelly taken from me, and wherever he may be, my heart had gone with him.

Vinnie and I sat in silence for a few minutes, both of us exhausted and emotional. My brain taunted me with snapshots of what our wedding in paradise may have looked like, and as the images began to fade, I felt even more alone, even more destroyed.

Vinnie reached into his pocket, hesitantly producing a flat, red velvet jewellery box. My breath caught as I stared down at it through tear blurred eyes.

"He was going to give this to you on your wedding day." Vinnie's voice was choked up, and my throat tightened as fresh tears blurred my vision.

Tentatively, he offered me the box, but I felt so emotional, so raw, and I knew whatever lay within the red velvet box would only break my heart even more.

Laying my hand over Vinnie's, giving him a soft squeeze, I gently pushed it away, refusing to accept the gift. Swallowing the lump in my throat and attempting a smile, I looked Vinnie in the eye. "You look after it for him," I'd said, choking back the tears. "He can give it to me when he comes home."

Hesitantly, and with the saddest eyes, Vinnie returned the box to his pocket.

"Yeah… You're right, Miss. He'd like that."

~

When we arrive at the penthouse, John delivers me to the door of F1. I feel drained from reliving all the recent events since Max's abduction.

"Is there anything I can do for you, Ma'am?" he asks softly as I open the door to the penthouse.

"No. Thanks John. I'll call you when I'm ready to leave."

He says nothing more, but waits for me to go inside before he leaves. His concerned eyes stay on mine until the door closes between us. I know he's worried about me, everyone is, but I just want to be by myself.

As I stand alone in the hallway, echoes of Max bounce from every surface of the penthouse. Our home. But now just an empty shell, where memories of our time together fly through my mind, crushing my heart.

Shrugging out of my coat, I let it fall where I'm standing, then I sling my bag on the bottom step of the staircase and wander into the dark living room. The vast panoramic windows twinkle with the city lights beyond. Walking over to them, I lean my forehead against the cool glass as my tears blur the scenery. "Oh, Max… Please don't make me live without you."

I'm physically and emotionally exhausted, but I need to pack a bag and head back to France. I'd only come home to attend William's funeral. I need to get back there, so I can keep looking for him. I'll never stop.

The police have been kind, and they assure me they are doing everything they can to find him, but so far they've come up with nothing, and as the time passes they seem less inclined to believe Max will be found. I can't put any credence in their way of thinking. I won't give up. I have to find him. I need to find him. Someone must have seen or heard something.

In the days and weeks that had followed Max's abduction, and against everyone's advice, I stayed in France. I couldn't bear the thought of leaving, knowing Max was out there somewhere, waiting for someone to help him. Waiting for me to find him.

Monica's one crazy fucked-up bitch, but I couldn't believe

she would really want to hurt him. She'd want to keep him for herself, but surely she'd want to keep him safe. Alive at least.

But where? She's a fugitive, wanted for the murders of Charlie, Steve, and that poor woman in Portsmouth, where the hell could she hide?

For the first few days, as the forensic team had taken over the yacht, busily gathering their information, I had kept myself locked in my room at the hotel. I didn't want to see or talk to anyone, not even Lucy. I was a wreck. I couldn't stop crying. I just wanted to be on my own.

Once the police had finished with the yacht, I moved back on board, but the voracious pack of journalists and photographers swarming around the marina, made it impossible to move until they were given a statement. Vinnie and Trencher arranged a press conference and helped me through it. After that, it all seemed to calm down and I was able to move about more freely.

Every day I had gone out with photographs of Max and Monica. I had asked in every bar, restaurant, hotel, and shop. I had stopped people in the street. I even pestered sunbathers on the beach, anyone who would listen to me. But as the days passed, it was becoming more and more hopeless. No one had seen or heard anything that night.

The French police informed me that the marina's c.c.t.v. cameras nearest our yacht, had been smashed. The cameras on board had also been disabled minutes before the abduction with some kind of spray on solvent.

The night it happened, the two waiters that Sasha had hired at short notice had also disappeared. They must have been involved, and even though I looked at the face of the waiter who had spilt the water over Max, I couldn't for the life of me remember what he looked like. The only descriptions any of us could offer for the missing waiters, were two men of average height and build, short dark hair, dark eyes, tanned skin, both with foreign accents, but none of us knew for sure whether they were French.

It's shameful to realise how unobservant we become to

people in uniform. They'd wandered around the yacht, mingling with the guests, serving us with a smile, and yet they were invisible, just wallpaper. A damning indictment of our indifference to the service industry.

Ed and I had trawled through all our photographs and video footage of the wedding in the hopes of finding them, but everyone photographed was accounted for. Whoever had organised this, had been incredibly careful, and it was planned and executed with meticulous stealth and detail.

It was then that I realised how much I had underestimated Monica.

The blood on the cabin door was tested and found to be Max's blood. Drops were also found on the deck and down the gangway, but the trail ended abruptly a few feet away from the yacht, signifying that he had probably been bundled into a car on the pier and driven away.

Vinnie and Trencher had tried to find the missing waiters, but their identities were false and their phones had been disconnected, there was no trace of them at all.

When it was time for Lucy and Dan to leave France, after their ill-fated honeymoon was over, Lucy offered to stay with me, but I insisted they go home. They both had businesses to run and lives to live.

Casper and Ed assured me they would take care of everything back at my office, but at that point, I couldn't care less. Finding Max and bringing him home was the only thing I could focus on.

With a deep sigh, I drag myself away from the window, retrieve my coat from the floor, my bag from the step, and then I head upstairs to shower, change, and pack a bag. The sooner I get back to France and keep searching, the better I'll feel.

As I climb the stairs, my phone rings, but I don't want to speak to anyone right now. I take it out to check who's calling in case it's Benny, he needs to know when I'll be arriving at the airport. My heart sinks when I see it's Mike calling, so I just let it go to answer-phone. I'm sure Lucy and Dan will have told him what happened, and if not, it's been all over the papers. He's called several times, but I can't talk to him right now. I can't talk to anyone.

As I enter the bedroom, I kick off my shoes and unzip my dress, letting it fall from my shoulders. Stepping out of it, I leave it in a puddle of black silk on the bedroom floor. I begin to unhook my bra, but when I hear the shower running in the bathroom, my whole body freezes. "Max?"

My heart beats frantically in my chest, wild butterflies now swirling in my stomach, my mouth is dry, and my lungs are empty. "Max!" I sprint to the bathroom door and barge my way through it, then judder to a standstill. Agony makes me fold, my arms curling around my stomach trying to hold me together.

Cole is standing naked in the shower. He jumps when he sees me, trying to cover himself with his hands. "Jesus! Vivienne, I'm sorry. I thought you were still at the wake," he splutters, turning his hips away from me. I stand there, wide eyed and motionless, tears flooding down my cheeks. I can't take my eyes off him, he's the absolute image of Max. The hair, the body, the face, everything. The only difference is the M.F. tattoo missing from his chest, and the whip marks and scars across his back and forearms.

Cole stares at me with a furrowed brow. "I'm sorry. I just needed… Ah, there were no towels in the guest room and I didn't expect you back yet… Vivienne?… Shit!"

I open my eyes to the light on the bedroom ceiling. Turning my head, I see the empty space on Max's side of the bed.

"Vivienne, I'm sorry. I didn't mean to upset you." His velvety, husky voice is so familiar and it makes my heart crack wide open.

Lifting my head from the pillow, I see Cole pacing at the foot of the bed. He's naked apart from a towel wrapped low around his hips. Rivulets of water bead and roll down his impressive pecs, then bobble over his tightly packed abdominals, dripping down his well-defined V, before disappearing into the towel. And when he drags his hand through his wavy black hair, eyeing me with a concerned frown like Max always does when he's nervous, he just seems so familiar. He is Max, at least he looks and sounds like him.

My eyes drag all over his strong, defined body. The body I've come to know every inch of. The body I've held, stroked, and kissed a million times. My skin heats and butterflies fill my belly in reaction to the glorious sight before me.

Cole doesn't have the M.F. tattoo on his chest, but his face, his body, the curve in his eyebrow, his nervous expression, even his raspy voice, it's all Max.

Tears pool in my eyes as my heart twists in my chest. "What happened?" My voice is croaky and tight.

Cole throws me a nervous sideways glance then he stops pacing, resting his hands on his hips. "You passed out. I'm sorry, Vivienne, I shouldn't have…" He looks down at the floor, pausing to let out a deep sigh.

Shaking my head clear, I push myself up to a sitting position. Looking down at myself, I realise I'm semi naked in only my underwear, so I grab Max's pillow to cover myself. His scent wafts up from the pillow, twisting my heart even more.

When I'm covered, Cole gingerly raises his eyes back to mine. The eyes of my lover gaze down at me through the duplicate body of a relative stranger.

"No, it's okay, Cole. It's not your fault. It's just… You look like Max."

He frowns then shrugs. "That's the irony of twins, I guess."

I can't stop staring at him. Every fibre of my being wants him to be Max.

Cole breaks the eye contact, nervously shifting on his feet as an awkward silence stretches out between us. "Ah, I'll get dressed and leave you alone."

Utterly mesmerised, I watch him walk back into the bathroom. They even have the same swagger in a towel.

Butterflies are swirling in my belly, my heart is fluttering in my chest, and my breathing has even become ragged and shallow. My body is reacting in its usual way to the sight of Max. It's a preconditioned response to his innate possession and control of all my senses.

But he's not Max. Just a cruel reminder of the man I can't live without.

When Cole closes the door behind him, I sit there staring at it, then my eyes flood with tears and I sob into Max's pillow. I've cried rivers of tears but they won't bring him back, and I hate it when I allow myself to wallow in self-pity. Max needs me.

Come on, Viv. Get your sad arse out of this bed and go and find him.

Dragging myself up, I walk to the dressing room to find my robe. My stomach sinks as my watery eyes land on Max's clothes hanging neatly in his side of the dressing room, then they search out the long, red evening gown I had worn the night of our engagement. So many happy memories flood my brain creating a deep ache in my broken heart.

The sound of the bathroom door opening, jolts me out of those wonderful memories.

When Cole emerges from the bathroom he's fully dressed. Unintentionally, I drink him in. His tall, lean, masculine body, dressed in t-shirt and jeans, is as easy on the eye as his brother's. And why wouldn't it be? Cole is an identical copy of Max. He even has the same predatory walk.

Why couldn't you be Max.

He seems uncomfortable that I'm just staring at him but I can't seem to stop myself. Eyeing me warily, he starts edging toward the door. "Ah, Mom said I could use the penthouse as a base, but if it's going to be difficult for you, I can find somewhere else to stay."

I force myself to snap out of it and pull myself together, it's becoming weird. "No. No, it's okay, I'll get Jan to make up the guest room for you." I turn away, I can't look at him anymore, his likeness to Max is too strong, too painful.

"I sure could use a drink right now, care to join me?" he asks softly.

I don't think there has ever been a time when I could use a

drink more. "I'll be down in a minute."

Once I've showered, changed, and packed a bag for France, I make my way down to the living room. Cole's voice has me turning to face him as he walks in from the terrace. He looks down at my suitcase with a worried frown. "Where are you going? Please don't leave on my account."

Pff, don't flatter yourself. "I'm not. I'm going back to France."

"Alone?"

"No. John will be with me."

"No, I meant... shouldn't you stay here, with people who can take care of you?"

I ignore his question. I don't need taking care of, I need my fiancé. I need to keep busy. I need to find him.

Cole moves to the sofa and sits back in the cushions. Draping an arm along the back, he rests his right ankle on his left knee.

Jeez, he even sits like Max.

I walk to the opposite sofa and stare at the glass of wine that Cole had thoughtfully poured for me and left on the coffee table. How I wish I could drink it to numb myself against the aching loss crippling me from within. But I haven't had any alcohol since I found out I was pregnant, and I'm not going to start now.

"Will you be staying at the chateau?" he asks, sipping his Scotch.

Raising my eyes to his, I almost flinch. I can't get used to seeing his handsome face. I crave it. Every time I look at him it hurts a little more, but I can't drag my eyes away. I need to see his face, I long to see it, but it's a bittersweet torture.

"Ah, no. Vinnie said the chateau hasn't been opened up yet." My eyes slide down to my knotted fingers twisting and fidgeting in my lap. "I'll be staying on the yacht."

Cole sits forward, resting his elbows on his knees. "You're probably better off on the yacht. The chateau is a huge, drafty, sixteenth century mansion, but it hasn't been used for months. You'd need to get the housekeeper in at least a week beforehand just to air it out."

A beat of awkward silence ensues. We'd only met once before and that was very brief. Charlie's funeral was the last, and only time I had spoken with Cole. I don't know what to say. It's difficult not to stare at him, but staring without talking is just weird, so I rack my brain for conversation until the obvious slips into my head.

"I'm sorry about your father. William was a lovely man, he was always very kind to me." I struggle to hold back the tears which have suddenly sprung into my eyes.

Cole looks into his glass, absently swirling the amber liquid inside it. "Yeah…he was." Knocking back the rest of his Scotch, he places his empty glass on the table beside his chair. The sadness at his loss clearly showing on his face. His eyes glisten, his jaw is clenching.

Part of me feels sorry for him. He's lost his mother, two fathers, and a son in his short life, but part of me still hates him for blaming Max for the death of their natural parents.

"I hope you won't blame your brother for William's death too." My cheeks heat with a blush. I feel ashamed of myself. I didn't mean to say it out loud, it just came out.

His wide eyes dart up to mine. He knows what I'm referring to, and to his credit, he looks ashamed. "I'm sorry," he murmurs, looking away.

"It's not me you should be apologising to."

His eyes dart back to mine. Neither of us speaks for a moment, but I can't bring myself to release him from his guilt. As far as I'm concerned, his behaviour toward his brother when their parents died, is unforgivable.

Taking in a deep breath, I dig my phone out of my bag. I need to call Benny and John to make my arrangements for the flight back to France.

"How long will you be away?" Cole asks with a raspy voice.

My throat tightens as I stare down at my phone, Max's beautiful face smiling back at me. "For as long as it takes."

I can feel Cole's eyes on me, but I daren't look at him. I'm so close to bursting into tears right now.

"Is there anything I can do?" he asks softly.

A puff of sarcastic air huffs out of me. I look up, staring directly into his eyes. "You can take care of your brother's business. Until he comes home." Emotion removes the intended defiance from my tone and I have to force myself not to cry.

He frowns and nods then looks down at his fidgeting hands.

Once I've spoken to Benny, I call John, arranging to meet him in the lobby in five minutes. Replacing my phone in my bag, I stand and straighten my skirt.

"Jan will take care of you, she has my number if you need to contact me." I begin to walk over to my suitcase.

"Vivienne…"

His soft familiar voice stops me in my tracks, evoking all the usual feelings and responses. I turn to face him. I would have turned to face him anyway before I left even if he hadn't called out my name. I just needed one last look at his handsome face even though it haunts me inside.

"You're an incredible woman. Max is a very lucky guy… If you need me for anything, anything at all, I'm here for you."

Tears prick my eyes. The expression on his face is so familiar and inviting.

"And don't worry, I won't let my brother down. Not this time."

The lump in my throat chokes off any chance of me responding, so I force a tearful smile and turn away.

~

On the flight back to France, all I could see in my mind was Max's face, or rather, Cole's face. It's strange, but even though I knew it wasn't Max, when I'd looked into Cole's eyes, I got the same butterflies in my stomach, and the same feeling of being drawn in. The feeling that makes me sway a little as his innate magnetism pulls me in.

I know it's just my vulnerability causing my reaction, but it's uncanny how alike they are. Identical doesn't even come close.

John is travelling with me, he hasn't left my side since

Max's disappearance, and he knows me well enough to know when I want to talk, and when I need to be alone. He's become to me, what Vinnie is to Max. Someone I can trust, who will take care of me without the need to ask or explain.

Once I'm settled in on the yacht and I've had a few more tears on my own in the cabin, I pull myself together and head up to the office to print out some more 'missing' posters.

In the morning, John and I are going to hand them out in every bar, shop, and cafe in the marina. Giving them to anyone who will take one in the neighbouring towns too.

I check the answer-phone, but there are no new messages. It's late, so once I've printed out another batch of posters, I make my way back to the cabin.

Hugging Max's pillow to my chest, I curl around it in a tight ball, letting the tears flow freely. I'm not one for crying in public, but when I'm alone, I can't seem to stop.

Breathing in his scent, I stare up at the photograph of us alongside the scan of our babies. A deep feeling of dread soaks into me as I gaze at his handsome face. Sleeping alone without his arms wrapped around me, and his hot breath against my cheek, feels so utterly wrong. Max would always have his hands on me whether we were in bed, or eating a meal with friends. It was a characteristic I had noticed right from the start of our relationship. It was as if he couldn't be near me without touching me, and I felt the same way.

Sometimes, in the beginning, I had thought he was doing it as a display of ownership or possession, but the more I got to know him, I realised it was just that he craved the connection. And so did I.

Please don't make me live without you.

MISSING FOXX

"Do you love me?"
"With all my heart."
"Do you trust me?"
"You know I do."
"Then that's all you need, baby. Until forever."
"I love you, Max."
"Love you more, baby."

I reach out to lay my hand on his chest, but I can't find him. Even before I open my sleepy eyes, I realise I won't find him. I've been dreaming again. I've dreamt about Max every single night. The pure contentment I had felt only moments ago, vanishes, only to be replaced with the dread and emptiness that I've felt every morning since he disappeared.

As usual, I find myself standing in the shower crying my eyes out. It's become somewhat of a ritual. I'm grieving. But I prefer to do my crying alone.

Once I'm dressed and ready to face the world, I gaze at Max's photograph on the bedside table. "I'll find you, Max. I promise. If it takes forever, I'll find you."

I meet John for breakfast up on the sun deck. Sasha brings me some tea and asks me what I would like for breakfast, but I haven't had much of an appetite recently and I don't feel like eating, much to John and Sasha's disapproval.

To ward off the brightness, I pull my sunglasses down from the top of my head. My eyes are sore from the constant crying and sleepless nights.

To break the awkward silence, I decide to tell John of my latest plans for the day ahead. "I asked Sylvie if she would sanction a reward, and she's kindly agreed, so I've added that to the posters today. And I'll be doing a recording at the local radio, and T.V. stations this morning."

"That's great. A reward will definitely help," John says, digging into his waffles, eggs, and bacon. That man can eat.

Staring into my tea cup, I release a deep sigh. "I hope so. And I hope it'll bring those two waiters out of the woodwork. I'd gladly give them every penny just to get him back."

John pauses after loading up another forkful. "Ma'am, you really should eat some breakfast."

I force a smile. "I will. I'll grab something while I'm out."

I know I should eat for the babies, but my appetite has completely vanished.

As I watch John polishing off his breakfast at an alarming rate, I notice he's wearing a wedding ring. I've never noticed it before. I'm ashamed to admit that I'd never even bothered to ask him about his personal life.

"John, are you married?"

He smiles, a big beaming smile which lights up his eyes and broadens his tanned cheeks. "Yes, Ma'am. Julie and I have been married for five and half years," he says, proudly.

I feel embarrassed that I've never taken the time to ask him. "I didn't realise."

He shrugs and looks down at his wedding ring. "Yeah, I don't usually wear it when I'm working, but I like to wear it when we're apart for any length of time."

How sweet. I take a sip of my tea, but it's still too hot. "Doesn't Julie mind you being away from home so much?"

Tilting his head on a smirk, he shrugs. "She knows how it is."

I feel myself frowning at his glib remark. I had never

thought of John as a male chauvinist, but that comment bugs me. I'm just about to say something when thankfully he continues, stopping me from putting my foot in it.

"She's currently one of your Royal family's personal bodyguards," he says, wiping his mouth with his napkin. His face lights up with pride, his lips curling into a satisfied smile.

I'm a little taken aback, she must be quite a woman and not the fluffy housewife I had wrongly pictured in my mind.

I attempt another sip at my hot tea, then place the cup back in its saucer. "Don't you worry about her being in that line of work?"

"Hell no," he smirks. "That woman kicks ass. She could kick my ass for sure."

That puts a grin on my face. "I'd like to meet her some day, she sounds like my kind of woman."

After John finishes his breakfast, including the second helping and two rounds of toast, he drives me to the local radio station. I'm scheduled to record an appeal, and as I have no idea how long it will take, I ask John to drop me off so he can put up some more 'missing' posters around the town. It's been a thankless task so far, but I refuse to give up.

After I've recorded a piece for the radio, I walk to the T.V. station a few streets away. They're letting me record an appeal for Max that will air on every regional news channel across the country. I'm doing everything I possibly can to highlight his disappearance. Someone must have seen or heard something, and I'm hoping the reward will jog their memory.

As I leave the television studio and make my way back to the marina, I call John for an update. "Hi, how did you get on?"

"Well," he starts, sounding promisingly enthusiastic. "I've run out of posters so I'm on my way back to the yacht to get some more. Where are you?"

"I've just finished recording my appeal for the news. I'm heading back to the yacht myself, but I'm going to stop for something to eat on the way. Would you like to join me?"

"No, Ma'am. I'll take a rain-check if you don't mind.

Vinnie's got some new leads to follow on the missing waiters, so I'd like to get on with that, if that's okay?"

"Yes, of course. Good luck." *Please let it be a positive lead this time.* After so many dead ends, I've learnt not to get my hopes up too soon.

As I wander along the far side of the marina in the late afternoon heat, I spot a sign on one of the bar awnings. 'Coeur Du Mer.' The name seems familiar but I'm not sure why.

"Vivienne!"

Startled, I look to my left. "Mike! What are you doing here?"

Mike emerges from the bar striding toward me with a tray of drinks in his hand. Looking tanned and handsome in black trousers and a white shirt, he pecks me on the cheek. "Take a seat, I'll be right over."

I watch him skillfully deliver a tray full of drinks to one of the tables on the open terrace. The giggling girls gaze up at him in adoration of his good looks and toned physique. His cheeky smile clinches the deal causing another twitter of giggles before he leaves them with a saucy wink.

I take a seat at one of the tables in the shade fanning my face with the menu, it's so bloody hot this afternoon.

On route, Mike hands his tray to one of the other waiters and walks over to me, bending down to kiss me on the cheek. "I thought you'd gone back to London."

As he takes a seat opposite me, I quickly glance inside the bar. "Won't you get into trouble sitting with me?"

"No," he smiles, beckoning one of the other waiters over. "I'm only helping out. It's my cousin Daryl's bar."

"Oh, that's right, I forgot. You've been helping him set this place up." I look all around me, it's very stylish and obviously very new, all the furnishings are gleaming and fresh. "It's nice."

He smirks, puffing his cheeks out on an exaggerated sigh. "It is now. A lot of hard work though." Studying me for a moment, a frown slips into his brow and his expression becomes more serious. "I've been calling you, Viv. I was worried about you." Concern softens his voice, and he does look genuinely sad. "I would have come to see you earlier, but I wasn't sure you'd want to see me. Besides, I thought you would have gone back to London by now."

His concerned eyes trail over my face as tears begin to prick my eyes. Any amount of sympathy seems to set me off.

"Lucy and Dan came to see me before they went home," he adds, realising I need another minute. "They told me what happened to Max and his dad, and it's been in all the papers too."

I stare down at my fidgeting hands. "Yes, I'm sorry. I saw that you'd called, but I haven't been able to talk to anyone since…" I don't feel confident finishing that sentence without bursting into tears. He smiles sympathetically, which only serves to make me feel even more tearful.

Reaching across the table, he rubs my hand. "I understand. I was just calling to let you know I was thinking of you."

"It was William's funeral yesterday."

"Yeah, I heard," he says, softly. "I can't imagine how difficult this must be for you."

A cheery waiter interrupts, giving me time to compose myself.

"Bonjour! Que voulez-vous?"

My appetite has vanished, so I just order a glass of iced water. Once we are alone again, Mike leans forward and takes my hand.

"I'm so sorry, Viv. If there's anything I can do."

I look away, trying not to cry but failing miserably. I know he's only trying to help but I can't cope with all this sympathy.

He offers me a napkin to dry my tears, his soft eyes searching mine. "Does anyone know what happened to him yet?"

"No." I give myself a moment to deal with my emotions, everything feels so raw. "The police haven't come up with anything yet, and Vinnie's been doing his best to trace the missing waiters but so far, we've got nothing." I can't help it, the tears flow unbidden. Everything feels so hopeless.

Mike squeezes my hand. "Viv. I'm so sorry."

As the waiter returns with our drinks, I hastily pull my hand out of Mike's and dry my tears, people are starting to stare.

"It must have been Monica though, right?" Mike asks, sipping his beer. "I mean, that crazy cow has had it in for you from the start."

Even with no physical proof that she had taken Max, I know she was behind this. It had to be her. "Yes, she has been the proverbial thorn in my side. And I'm sorry, Mike. I should have listened to you when you tried to warn me."

He blushes, lowering his head. "So, what happens now? Why are you back here, haven't you got a new business to run?"

"I can't go home yet. I need to know where he is. I need to find him."

Mike's concerned eyes level on mine. "Look, I'm only out here for a few more days, and Daryl doesn't really need me here anymore, so if there's anything I can do to help, you only have to ask. I told you, Viv. I want to stay friends and I'd like to help you in any way I can."

I stare up at him with tearful eyes. I'm speechless at his kindness. He's changed. Grown up all of a sudden. It wasn't that long ago he was cursing Max's very existence, but here he is offering to help me find him. His kindness brings on more tears.

Leaning over, he gently blots them away. "Come on, dry those pretty eyes."

I take a moment to compose myself, then take a long sip of my iced water.

"Where are you staying?"

"On the yacht."

"Oh, right." He seems lost in his thoughts for a moment, absently running his fingers up and down the beer glass, removing the condensation. "What can I do to help?"

I sit back in my seat to give it some thought. "Well, John is helping me distribute some 'missing' posters all over town and the neighbouring villages but neither of us speak French, and some of the business owners are hard to talk to. Maybe if you could talk to them in French, it might help."

He shrugs and nods in agreement.

"We think Max was taken away in a car, there was a trail of blood on the pier, but we haven't been able to find any c.c.t.v. footage in the marina or—"

"Maybe he was taken away in a boat?"

We both look up at the young waitress cleaning the table next to us. Mike is scowling at her for eavesdropping on our conversation, and she dips her head in embarrassment before scuttling off to clean another table.

"A boat?" I whisper to myself. Staring down at my glass, I contemplate that thought. The girl is right, but I hadn't even considered that Max may have been taken away by boat that night. It's pretty obvious considering there are tons of them around here.

Still irritated with the girl, Mike drags his eyes back to mine. "Erm, you mentioned Vinnie was checking on some waiters…what did you mean?"

"There were two new waiters hired at short notice for Lucy's wedding. Locals I think. They approached Sasha looking for work, but they both disappeared when Max did and their phones have been disconnected. They must have been involved in his abduction. We need to find them. I've put out a reward, hopefully that will help."

Mike's eyes widen as they flip up to mine then he quickly glances over his shoulder. "Is that wise?"

"What do you mean?"

"Well, think about it, Viv. Every gold digging nut-job will be trying to claim the reward."

I sigh in frustration knowing he's got a point. "But it could also lead us to Max. I have to try everything I possibly can to find him."

His cautious eyes narrow on me. "Do you really think he's still alive?"

Mike's pessimism stabs me in the heart. Anger forces my shoulders back and my hand starts to clench into a fist on the table. "Yes. Of course I do. He has to be."

I can see the scepticism in his eyes. I've seen it before, many times in the eyes of the police. They haven't said it to my face in so many words, but I know they think that because there haven't been any demands for ransom, Max is already dead. Their negative attitude stinks.

Mike looks away as I continue to glare at him in disbelief. Why doesn't anybody share my optimism?

Gazing down at the table cloth, he seems deep in thought. Over his shoulder, I see a dark haired, very tanned man striding toward our table.

"Mike! Are you going to do any work? Or are you just going to sit on your arse all day chatting up the pretty girls?"

Mike smirks up at the guy, who's now standing beside our table with his heavily tattooed arms folded across his chest. There's barely any skin showing on his sleeves of green, red, and black ink.

Mike laughs. "Daryl, you really should think about asking for your money back. That charm school was a complete waste of time. Vivienne, this is Daryl, my cousin."

Uncrossing his arms, he reaches down for my hand. His dark, glossy eyes drinking me in, trailing lazily all over my face. It makes me very uncomfortable.

"Ah, so you're Vivienne." He bends and kisses the back of my hand making me blush. "Mike's told me all about you. In fact, you're all he talks about. It's very nice to meet you, Vivienne." His smarmy grin exposes all his absurdly white teeth.

Mike looks embarrassed, so that makes two of us!

I smile up at him politely, but there's something about Daryl that puts me on edge. His stare is cocky, arrogant, and way too intense for my liking. I'm sure it charms the knickers off the tourists, but for me, it's just annoying.

I remember Dan saying he didn't get on with Daryl. Maybe he's just one of those people you can't warm to straight away. I know I haven't.

"I'd better get back to work," Mike says, rising to his feet. "How about we meet up later for a drink, or dinner?"

I stand up and grab my bag. I'm not really in the mood for socialising. "Not tonight, I'm tired. But what are your plans for tomorrow?"

He looks up at Daryl expectantly. Daryl stares back at him for a moment like they're having a wordless conversation, then he throws his hands in the air. "Fine! Take the day off. But you can work tonight to make up for it."

Mike grins at him, then at me. "I'm free all day. I'll pick you up from the yacht at ten tomorrow morning."

"Okay. See you then." I start to walk away, then I stop and turn back. "Oh, do you know where it is?"

"Yeah," he smirks. "You can't miss it. It's the biggest one in the marina."

As I walk away from the bar, I get the feeling both of them are watching me. I'm glad I bumped into Mike, he could be useful to me out here. His French is very good, and now I can go back to all those people I had struggled to communicate with and ask them if they know anything.

My stomach grumbles as I make my way back to the yacht. I'd lost my appetite at the bar so hadn't bothered to order any food, but once I'm back on board, I head down to the galley to ask Sean, the chef, if I could have a sandwich and some tea. I was going to make it myself but he insisted I let him do it.

Heading up to the office, I begin printing some more posters and flyers for our next trip out, then my phone rings.

"Hey, Viv. It's me."

I smile when I hear Lucy's voice.

"So, how was the funeral?" Lucy asks softly.

"Painful, but William had a nice send off."

I wish I had something to tell her, some news about Max, but every call has been the same since she went back to London, so I decide to try and lighten the conversation.

"How's married life?"

"Pff, it seems to have given Dan the idea that it's perfectly okay for him to leave his pants and socks on the bedroom floor, and to avoid the dishwasher at all costs. And for him to even consider doing his own ironing? Pff, I'd have more luck picking up a turd at the clean end. Other than that, great!"

I smile, Lucy always has a way of cheering me up, even when I'm at my lowest.

"I miss you," she sighs, "I wish there was something I could do to help."

My throat tightens, I miss her too. "I know. And you are helping, you're always there when I need you."

We both go silent for a moment, our emotions getting the better of us.

"I met Mike today. He's still out here at his cousin's bar."

"Yes, me and Dan went to see him before we came home. We wanted to thank him for his wedding gift. I told him what happened, he seemed genuinely upset for you."

"Yes, he's offered to help me look for Max. I'm meeting him tomorrow morning."

"Are you?...That's good. He can help you with the lingo. I take it the police haven't found Monica or those two waiters yet?"

"No, not yet. And someone came up with the idea that maybe Max had been taken away by boat instead of a car. The police never mentioned that possibility."

"Oh, shit. It's so obvious! But I'd never thought of that... Hey, I know you said the police checked the marina, but there must be cameras all over that place, what with all those posh boats moored up. I'm sure some of them would have their own security cameras on board. Maybe you should find out if the police have checked them out. You never know, one of them might have filmed something without knowing it."

"That's a great idea. I'll do that first thing tomorrow."

Lucy and I say our goodbyes, then I eat my sandwich, waiting for the printer to dish out the last batch of copies. Once I've organised my plan of action for tomorrow, I head off to the cabin. I'm exhausted.

As I enter my cabin a shiver spirals up my spine. I always feel it when I enter this room. Sasha wanted to move me to another suite but I wanted to stay here. This was our room. Where Max had held me in his arms. I feel close to him here.

His scent still lingers and it gives me comfort.

Tired and miserable, I sit on the edge of the bed. Staring at the scan of our babies held together with tape, I wipe away the tears pooling in my eyes. I don't want them to grow up never having known their father.

"Oh, Max. Please don't make me live without you."

TEA WITH HARRY

Sasha wakes me with a nice hot cup of tea.

I sit myself up and rub the sleep from my eyes, resting back against the headboard. "Any news from the police?" I ask, ever hopeful of some good news for a change.

She shakes her head, smiling sympathetically.

I didn't get much sleep last night and I can't focus on my watch. "What time is it?"

"It's eight o'clock. John's had his breakfast and he's already left." Looking thoughtful she moves toward the bed, sitting on the edge. "I've been racking my brain to remember anything about the two waiters I hired at short notice, and I suddenly remembered something this morning. They both had a small tattoo on the inside of their wrists. It was just a shape, like a symbol of some kind. But I remember they both had the same tattoo. I don't know what it was, or why I hadn't remembered it before, but I mentioned it to John, and he's going to see if he can find out if it means anything. He said he'd call you when he's finished, but it could be a few hours."

"That's good. Well done." New hope springs to life.

I take a sip of my tea as Sasha rises from the bed and walks over to the door hesitating for a moment. She looks like she has something else to say but doesn't know how to say it.

"What's the matter?"

Her eyes lower to the floor as she nervously wrings her hands in front of her. "Vivienne, I feel so responsible for what happened. I should have done a thorough background check on those guys. I just wanted the night to go well for Lucy and Dan and I didn't—"

"Sasha," I interrupt, forcing a small smile. "It's nobody's fault. God knows Monica's cunning and ingenuity has out-foxed us all at one time or another. We just have to hope and pray that we find Max and bring him home safe."

She offers me a weak smile, bowing her head as she leaves.

My belly churns as I watch her go. I feel ashamed. I had blamed Sasha when I knew the waiters were involved. And I was angry as hell that she'd brought them into our lives. But it wasn't really her fault, none of us were prepared for what happened that night.

My eyes are drawn to the photograph of me and Max on my bedside table. It was taken on the night he proposed. Tears well in my eyes as the images of that perfect moment dance through my mind. *You promised me forever. You promised.*

Once I've allowed myself a good cry, I get dressed and head up to the office.

Stuffing as many copies of the 'missing' posters into the rucksacks as I can, I grab the list I had prepared last night. I feel positive about today. While Mike is busy going to all the places on the list, I'm going to take Lucy's advice and try to speak to all the yacht owners about their security cameras. With renewed enthusiasm, I head down to the pier to wait for Mike.

At exactly ten o'clock, Mike comes strolling along looking cool and casual in his cut offs and faded t-shirt. Pushing his sunglasses up on top of his head, he leans in to kiss me on the cheek.

"Where's your bodyguard?" he asks, looking over my shoulder.

"John? Oh, Sasha remembered something about the missing waiters having the same tattoo, he's looking into it."

A frown slips into his brow. "Really?… What kind of tattoo?"

"I don't know. I didn't see it."

He nods absently, like he's deep in thought, then he snaps out of it. Clapping his hands, he rubs them together. "So, where are we heading this morning?"

I hand him the list. "These are the places in and around the marina that I've already visited, but because I don't speak French, I don't think they understood a word I had said. I would like you to go and speak to them and maybe put some posters up in their establishments if they'll let you."

Pulling his sunglasses down from the top of his head, he glances down at the list. "Okay, let's go." He links his arm through mine and starts to turn away but I pull him to a stop.

"Actually, Mike. I thought we should split up. I'm going to visit each yacht in the marina and ask if they can check their security cameras. That girl at your bar gave me an idea when she said he could have been taken away by boat. One of the boats might have filmed it without knowing."

"Oh. Yeah. Good thinking… Hey, you know what? I could do that after I've done this list if you like."

"No, it's okay. I need to keep myself busy." I hand Mike one of the rucksacks and we arrange to meet up at his cousin's bar at three o'clock, then we go our separate ways.

~

Many of the yachts I called at didn't appear to have anyone home, so I left one of the posters with a message on the back. I can only hope whoever finds the poster won't ignore it and chuck it straight in the bin. Some of the people who I did manage to speak to were very friendly, and kindly agreed to contact me if anything helpful showed up on their cameras.

After a couple of hours, John calls. "Ma'am? Everything okay?"

"Yes, I'm fine."

"I called Sasha, she said you left at ten this morning. I wish you had waited for me to come back, it's not safe for you to be out on your own."

"I'm fine, really. I'm just wandering around the marina handing out posters and talking to people. Any luck?"

He sighs, sounding deflated. "No, not really, but I've still got a few more places to try. I'll be another couple of hours at least. My phone signal keeps crapping out, so if you're trying to reach me, leave a message and I'll call you back."

"Okay, don't worry. I'll be staying in the marina then I'm meeting up with Mike at three o'clock."

"Mike?"

I forgot, John hasn't met Mike yet. "Yes, he's a friend of mine from home."

"Okay, take care of yourself, Ma'am."

"You too."

Once I've called at every boat, yacht, and anything that floats, I finally reach the end of the marina, so I wander over to the small concrete wall and take a seat. Carrying the heavy rucksack with all those posters has made my back ache.

As I sit hunched over resting my chin in my hands, staring out at the water, my phone rings. I don't recognise the number but it could be someone with news about Max.

"Hello?"

"Vivienne. How are you?"

Cole's velvety voice catches me by surprise, it's like Max is talking to me. My heart flutters and my mouth has become dry as a Martini.

"I'm okay. Still searching… So, to what do I owe the honour? Is everything alright at home?"

"Everything is fine here, don't worry… Listen, I've been thinking. Monica's still on the run, so she must be hiding out somewhere, and it occurred to me that she knows about the chateau, she's been there many times. She would know it's been closed up for months. Mom always keeps the freezers in the cellar well stocked with food so it could be a perfect hiding place for her. She may even have a key. Maybe you should get John to check it out."

I sit up in a rush as adrenaline courses through my veins. *Oh my god, of course!*

"Vivienne? Are you there?"

"Thanks Cole, I really appreciate the call. Can you text me the address?"

"Sure… But Vivienne, you can't go there on your own, it's too dangerous. If she's there, you'll need John with you at the very least. I tried calling him but I can't get through."

"Yes, he's in a bad signal area. Don't worry. And thanks for letting me know."

Ending the call, I stand up and start pacing back and forth, eagerly waiting for Cole to text me the address. I'm literally buzzing with adrenaline.

He's right about the chateau, it would definitely give her a safe place to hide out until the heat dies down. I just hope we're not too late to catch her.

My heart races in my chest as the anticipation of finding Max fills me with renewed hope. With trembling fingers, I dial John but it goes straight to answer-phone, so I leave him a message to meet me at 'Coeur Du Mer' in the marina at three o'clock, and then I start walking.

I know I should wait for John but I can't, he'll take too long to get back. I have to know if Monica's there because if she is, then so is Max. I'll just go and check it out from a distance and if I see any evidence of her, I'll wait for John and call the police.

Cole's text arrives. Eagerly opening up my Sat-Nav app, I quickly enter the details. It's only twenty-six kilometres away, so I hastily head back toward the main boulevard to find a taxi.

The taxi rank is empty, so I start walking in the direction I'm headed. After a few minutes, I spot a moped hire shop. *Perfect!*

As I'm handing over the cash, the salesman asks me to sign a waiver, stating that I can't sue the company if I'm horribly maimed, injured, or die. Once that's completed the eager salesman shows me to my vehicle. It's got to be the crappiest looking moped in the history of automotive vehicles, but it's got a full tank of gas and moves like shit off a shovel, or that's what the over-zealous salesman implied in his broken English.

Besides, it's the last one so it'll have to do.

The salesman points me in the right direction and off I go… on the wrong side of the road. I forgot that in Europe everyone drives on the right. I can just about hear the salesman screaming at me to change lanes above the high pitched whine of the spluttering, mosquito sounding engine.

After a near miss and some choice words, I finally end up on the correct side of the road and floor it. When I say floor it, I mean poodle along at fifteen miles an hour. It barely blew my hair back! I was being overtaken by joggers for chrissake.

The journey was precarious to say the least. I had to negotiate the moped while trying to follow my hand held Sat-Nav without crashing. And when I finally arrive at my destination, I park the wheezing pile of junk behind some bushes at the main gate.

I've watched enough thrillers and cop shows to remember to check if the entry gate has cameras but I don't see any. Just to be safe, I decide to walk around the perimeter fence to try and find a point of entry other than the main gate. If Monica is here, the last thing I want to do is give her any warning that she's been found.

The chateau is huge, lying within acres of landscaped gardens surrounded by a high stone and railing boundary wall. I walk for ages around the perimeter until I finally find a break in the bushes and a convenient tree to climb.

Carefully climbing over the pointed railing fence and down the other side, I drop down a few feet to the soft grass below. But now my next problem is trying to make it across the sprawling open lawns to the house without being seen.

I take a couple of deep breaths, then leg it across the immaculate open space, hiding behind small bushes, pergolas, and water features conveniently dotted along the way. When I reach the house, my lungs and muscles are burning from exertion in the afternoon heat.

The chateau is an impressive stone and flint building with rusticated masonry, ornate conical turrets, crenellated battlements, large arched lead-light windows, and high Gothic style doorways. The imposing structure sits several storeys high with thick, stone, ivy covered walls, and ornate chimney pots protruding from a grey slate roof. On a dark stormy night this place could scare the crap out of you, but bathed in sunshine it's really quite charming.

I creep along the west side of the house poking my head up at every window to peek inside. Every room looks the same in as much as all the furniture, chandeliers, and wall paintings are covered in dust sheets.

As I reach the back of the house, I gingerly poke my head around the corner to check the coast is clear before I continue.

When I reach a large glass conservatory, I have to crouch down and literally crawl along on my hands and knees. The windows are vast and the low brick wall is all that hides me from the view of anyone inside.

Once I've crawled past the conservatory jutting out from the building, I come face to face with a pair of dark green lace-up boots. Men's boots, at what looks like the back door, which is open a few inches. The boots are very large and the soles are encrusted with dried mud and grass. My nerves kick up a notch. Someone's here.

Scrambling to my feet, I lean my back against the cool stone wall, listening intently. My heart is pounding in my chest, all my nerves are jangling, and in my head the voice of reason is telling me to leave, to run as fast as I can, but I feel compelled to stay. If Monica's here then so is Max, and I'm desperate to find him.

As I can't hear anything, I poke my head around the open doorway. The door leads into a kitchen. An old fashioned kitchen with a huge farmhouse range, copper bottomed pots and pans hanging from an overhead rack, and a long, worn, wooden table in the centre. There is a kettle sitting on the stove, and on the other side of the kitchen, there's a red mug with a spoon in it sitting on the worktop.

Hesitantly, I enter the kitchen and tiptoe my way through toward another open door on the far side. As I reach the door, the kettle begins to whistle its high pitched alarm as steam shoots out of the spout, making me freeze on the spot.

A cold sweat trickles down my back and my stomach churns anxiously when I hear a man's voice approaching.

"Alright, alright, I'm coming. Keep your hair on."

I panic. My eyes darting all around me for somewhere to hide but it's too late, he's already seen me. The wide eyes of the tall, grey haired man stare at me in shock as he stumbles to a halt right in front of me.

"Jesus!" he says, clamping his hand over his heart. "Who the hell are you?"

The kettle screeches out its high pitched whistle behind me, ramping up the tension in my nerves.

"I'm sorry. Um, I'm Vivienne. I know the owner of this house. I was just, ah, I was just looking for him."

The man's angry eyes narrow on me as he studies me from head to toe. He's an old man with a weathered face, but he looks like he can still handle himself. Straightening his back and clenching his strong fists, he looks past me to see if there is anyone else with me.

"Mr. Foxx isn't here," he says, in a low, threatening voice. "Nobody's here." Lowering his bushy eyebrows he levels his steely grey eyes on mine.

"Look, I'm sorry, I shouldn't have just barged in. I'm Max's fiancé. Sylvie knows who I am. Call her if you don't believe me."

His frown deepens as he studies me closely. "If you're his fiancé you'd know Mr. Foxx was kidnapped two weeks ago."

I take an anxious step forward. "That's why I'm here. I came to see if Monica was hiding him here. Cole thinks she might have a key to this place."

The man looks thoughtful for a moment then his eyes slide over to the screeching kettle. His threatening demeanour evaporates and his eyebrows spring upward as he walks past me toward the stove.

"Fancy a cuppa?" he asks, removing the kettle from the heat, then he walks it over to the other side of the kitchen and pours the boiling water into the red mug.

I stare at the back of his head totally bemused. Turning to face me, he raises his eyebrows in anticipation of my answer.

"Um, yes. Thanks. No sugar."

As he finishes stirring both mugs of tea, he walks them over to the kitchen table and nods at me to join him. "I'm afraid I ate all the biscuits," he smirks, looking down at a plate of crumbs in the centre of the table. "I'm partial to a hobnob or two."

I hesitantly sit opposite him.

He slides my mug over to me then offers me a sympathetic smile as his eyes wander over my face. "I'm Harry, the gardener. Well, I'm retired now, but I've known the family for many years. I come here once a month to check on the place, keep the lawns tidy, turf out the weeds, that sort of thing. I've been here for the last two days and I haven't seen hide nor hair of anyone."

My heart sinks as I sag with disappointment.

Harry's eyes glaze over as he stares into his mug of tea. "It's such a shame about William. He and I go way back, but I couldn't make the journey to London for his funeral. My wife... she hasn't been well." Emotion clips his last word, it's clear his wife's illness has been hard for them both.

"I'm sorry to hear that."

"I've never liked the woman."

His comment throws me a little. "Pardon me?"

"Monica," he clarifies. "I always knew she was trouble. My wife can't stand her and she's always been a good judge of character."

It's only now, I realise Max and Cole were the only ones who hadn't felt that way about her, at least, not until she'd ruined their lives.

I'm disappointed Monica's not here, but then I remember something Cole had said. "Harry...Cole mentioned a cellar. Have you been down there since you've been here?"

"No." He looks thoughtful for a moment then he reaches into one of his pockets. "But I've got the keys if you want to have a look?" He jangles a large bunch of keys in the air.

"Yes, please."

Harry rises from his seat, taking one last slurp of his tea before moving toward a long, thin, metal cupboard by the stove. Unlocking it, he pulls out a double barrelled shotgun. My eyes widen as I watch him pop two red cartridges into the chambers, then he snaps it closed.

"This way," he says, over his shoulder, already on the move.

I follow him out to the hallway then he turns down a long narrow corridor toward a large, gnarly wooden door with a black wrought iron handle. Picking through the large bunch of keys, he selects a long brass one.

The heavy wooden door groans and creaks its way open. A waft of damp, stale air seeps into my nose as I follow him inside. He reaches up to a pull cord just inside the door. The overhead lighting flickers alive, illuminating the worn stone steps leading down to the cellar.

"Mind your head," he says, ducking under an overhead beam.

The cellar has a medieval feel to it. The walls are rough flint and stone with vertical, aged, timber beams. The floor is smooth cobble stones with well-worn pathways. It comprises various compartments housing wine racks, oak casks, various tea chests and freezers.

Harry and I wander around its vastness, but no one's here. It's clear to see no one's been down here for a long time. And as Harry leads me back to the steps, my heart sinks with each footfall. I had pinned all my hopes on finding Max here today.

As we ascend the steps, a clonking noise makes me jump. Harry doesn't flinch.

"What's that?" I ask freezing on the spot.

He turns to face me with a smirk on his weathered face. "That'll be the plumbing. It's just the pipes."

"Have you checked all the rooms since you've been here, Harry?"

"Yes, I always have a look around in case there's been a leak or someone's broken in. I checked all the rooms yesterday, but you're welcome to look for yourself," he shrugs, heading back to the kitchen.

"What about the attic? Does this place have an attic? Or a garage, or garden sheds?" I know I'm grasping at straws now, but I can't leave without knowing I've checked every possible place.

Harry stops in his tracks, breaks the gun open and turns to face me. His rugged face frowning down at me like he has something on his mind. "Do you know what? I did check the outbuildings and the boathouse but I must admit, I haven't been up in the attic for years. As far as I know it's empty." He doesn't wait for me to comment, walking past me, he marches off. I quickly follow him through to the main hallway and up the grand sweeping staircase.

Even though everything is shrouded in dust sheets, it's clearly a very beautiful home, authentically decorated to reflect the period in which it was built, but modern enough to make it feel homely. Although, I wouldn't want the job of dusting or hoovering it.

We walk up several flights of stairs, along a parquet floored corridor, and then Harry comes to an abrupt stop right in front of me, I almost bump into him. Looking around me, it appears he's stopped for no reason, the corridor has no doors at this end other than a dumb waiter set into the wall on our left.

Grumbling under his breath, he searches through the bunch of keys, finally picking out a long silver one. There are so many, I marvel at how he knows which one to choose.

Turning to face the wall beside him, he slides a section of the dado rail upward, revealing a hidden lock. It's a secret door disguised by the wall covering, dado rail, and fake skirting board.

With a hefty tug, he opens the door outward and I follow him up the dusty wooden stairs to a vaulted attic. The floor is bare boards, apart from a ton of cobwebs and an inch of dust covering the floor and window sills, the whole space is empty. Disturbed dust motes dance in the sunlight blazing in through the lead-light windows.

As I stand in the middle of the empty attic, I feel a strong pull in the pit of my stomach, like the feeling Max evokes whenever he's near. I can't understand why, but there's something odd about this space. Maybe it's just the angle of the aged and misshapen timber beams sprawling across the vaulted ceiling. Or maybe it's just the crashing disappointment that Max isn't here that is skewing my perspective.

"I'm sorry, Vivienne," Harry says, making me jump. I'd almost forgotten he was with me. "I don't know where else to look."

My heart sinks, my body sagging with disappointment at my miscalculation. I'd had such a good feeling about this, but now all I feel is despair. As I turn to face him, his sad eyes lower to the floor.

"Thanks Harry. I appreciate your time."

"I hope that young man is returned to you safe and sound, dear. Poor Sylvie," he sighs, "she must be going out of her mind."

Locking the room again, Harry walks me downstairs to the main hallway. I give him my phone number just in case, then he lets me out through the front door.

"Safe journey, dear," he says, warmly. "I'll open the gates for you."

With a heavy heart I begin my long walk back to the moped. As I trudge down the driveway, Harry calls out to me. "Keep your eye out for Percy!" I turn to face him but he just waves and smiles. "No, it's okay, don't worry. I think he's out the back."

I assume he's referring to his dog, so I smile and wave as he closes the door.

Once I've retrieved the moped from the bushes, I start up 'wheezy-Joe.' It splutters to life in a cloud of grey smoke as I take one last look back at the chateau. I really thought today was the day I'd find Max and bring him home. I could almost feel him in the house, but now, I realise it was just my irrepressible hope deceiving me. My heart aches for him, and as each day passes, the pain grows deeper and deeper.

Where are you?

INFINITE BLACK

Once I've delivered the wheezing heap of scrap metal back to the moped hire shop, the salesman has the cheek to inspect it for damages. Naffed off and fed up, I wearily make my way back to the marina. It's a little before three o'clock so I head straight for Mike's cousin's bar.

I'm a little early, and as I take a seat and order a coffee, my phone rings.

"Hello?"

"Vivienne, what the hell do you think you're doing?"

Cole? He may look and sound like Max, but he has absolutely no right to tell me off like him. And I'm not in the mood for Cole right now.

"What's your problem?" I snap.

"I've just had a call from Harry. He said you went to the chateau all on your own looking for Max and Monica. What did I tell you about going there on your own? What are you, nuts? What's wrong with you? And don't even *think* about hiring out one of those mopeds again."

"How the hell do you know about the moped?"

"Harry told me you rode off on some clapped out piece of junk. You could have got yourself killed, Vivienne. Jesus! I can't believe you did that."

Rolling my eyes, I impatiently tap my fingers on the table while he finishes his lecture. "Oh, wait..." I start, with sarcastic indifference. "Let me check my give-a-shit-what-you-think pocket. Nope! I got nothing."

"Vivienne, you of all people know how dangerous Monica is." He pauses to let out an exasperated sigh. "I'm just worried about you, that's all."

His tone has softened considerably and now I feel bad for being so moody with him. Leaning forward, I rest my elbows on the table huffing a deflated sigh. "She wasn't there anyway."

"I know...and I'm sorry," he says, softly. "We'll find him, Vivienne. I promise."

I close my eyes as tears well up in them. Nobody can make promises like that.

As I end the call to Cole, Mike walks out from behind the bar with two coffees in his hands. I hadn't realised he was already here.

"Here's a coffee on the house, how did you get on?" A frown forms on his face when he notices my teary eyes. "What's the matter?" Taking the seat next to mine he curls his arm around my shoulders.

"Nothing. Just more dead ends." I can't be bothered to tell him all the details, it's depressing enough, and I don't want another lecture about me hiring the moped. Mike will flip.

"How did you get on?" I ask, drying my eyes and taking a sip of my coffee, wishing it was tea.

"Well, I spoke to as many people as I could, and I gave out all the posters—"

"What, all of them? That's great! Did anyone know anything?"

"No," he shrugs, shaking his head. "No one remembers seeing anything out of the ordinary that night."

I wince at the disappointing news, releasing a tired sigh. Today's getting worse and worse.

With a sympathetic smile, he nudges my shoulder. "Hey, why don't you let me take you out to dinner tonight. You look like you need cheering up."

"Yes, that would be nice." I don't really want to go out, and I'm not in the mood for socialising, but I owe Mike for helping me today, he's been a good friend.

John arrives looking fairly pleased with himself until he notices Mike's arm curled around my shoulders. His confused expression makes me uncomfortable, then I remember John hasn't met Mike yet, so I make the introductions, telling John that we're old friends, which seems to assuage his worrisome brow.

"Ma'am, I've been doing a little research and I found something interesting about the tattoo and what it means."

Glad of something positive for a change, I lean forward to hear his news, unwittingly dislodging Mike's arm from my shoulders. John takes a seat opposite, reaching into his back pocket, he produces a crumpled photograph of a tattooed arm which he lays out in front of us.

"I found this on a wall in a tattoo parlour. It's similar to the symbol Sasha had seen tattooed on the waiters wrists."

Mike and I stare down at it, but it means nothing to me. It's just a solid black figure eight with two black dots, one at each end.

"What does it mean?"

"It's a gang marking," Mike answers softly, still staring down at the photograph. I turn to face him, surprised he would know. Mike's eyes flick up to John's then to mine. "At least I think it is?" he adds on a shrug.

John's eyes linger on Mike's face. "It is," he says, thoughtfully. Then his eyes travel over to me. "It's an infinity symbol used by a gang affiliated to the Romanian mafia. They're known as 'Infinite Black.' They have a deep rooted network all over Europe. They're into everything from arms, drugs, and money laundering, to gambling, human trafficking, and prostitution."

My mouth drops open as I blink up at John.

"But the guys Sasha hired, they're just minions," he adds, resting back in his chair. "Sasha said the tattoos they had were just empty infinity symbols with no dots. That means they have no rank or power. They're just foot soldiers, cannon fodder. The symbol means they've taken the oath, but they're new. Only the top guys have a completely solid figure of eight, and the dots outside the symbol signify first or second in command within the clan. It's just hierarchy bullshit."

My head begins to feel hot and fuzzy. My watery eyes blinking up at John as I stare at him in disbelief. I'm confused, and even more worried knowing Monica has joined forces with such dangerous people.

But why would she do that? She's a control freak, and they don't sound like the sort of people she could control. Surely she wouldn't want Max dead, or harmed. She's in love with him.

Mike puts his arm around my shoulders, giving me a reassuring squeeze. I realise my hands are trembling when I put my cup down on the table, almost spilling it.

"Hey, come on," Mike soothes. "Don't upset yourself. I'm sure Max is fine. We'll find him, okay? I promise."

Why does everyone keep making me promises they can't keep? I feel anxious, like I'm suffocating. The fact that we've heard nothing from Monica, or anyone else for that matter, has left everything up in the air. If Max is being held by these people what chance does he have of surviving?

A frightening thought enters my scrambled brain. "I don't understand… These people Monica's using must know Max is wealthy. Surely people like that would be looking for ransom, for money, but we've heard nothing."

John's cheeks puff out on a sigh. "I know, but maybe that's a good thing. Vinnie's sure it was Monica who took him, and the fact that no ransom demand has yet been made just confirms that it was her."

Everything he's saying sounds plausible, but his expression puts me on edge.

Noticing my concern, he offers me a reassuring but harried smile. "Maybe they were just hired to get him off the yacht and to hide him somewhere. From what Vinnie told me, she had plenty of money to pay for their services."

John's reasoning calms me slightly. He's right, she'd never have been able to move him on her own. She could have hired these people to do it for her. Maybe their affiliation with this gang is just a coincidence.

"But…what if they realise there's more money to be had. What then?"

John's brow furrows as our eyes meet. I can tell by his expression that this worrying thought has also crossed his mind. "Then Monica may have a fight on her hands. But either way, it's been two weeks and there have been no demands made yet, so there's every reason to think Monica has him hidden away somewhere, and that he's still alive. We just have to hope that the people she's colluding with don't get greedy."

My belly churns into an anxious knot. Nothing about that woman is ever cut and dried, or easy.

Oh, Max, where are you? Oh!… Oh no!

"Ma'am? Are you okay?"

"I'm going to be sick." Rising to my feet in a rush, I clamp my napkin over my mouth. Mike grabs my arm and rushes me through the bar to the ladies toilets.

Barging in, I make it just in time before the contents of my stomach make an appearance. Mike stands behind me holding my hair away from my face, rubbing my back as my body convulses over the toilet bowl.

When I'm finished, I grab some tissue paper to wipe my mouth, then I splash my face at the sink. My hands are shaking and I feel like I've been wrung out and put through the mangle.

"I'm sorry, Mike. I don't know what came over me."

He stands behind me, our eyes connecting through the mirror. "Don't apologise, Viv. You've been through hell."

I can't stop the tears as they well up and spill over my lashes. "Oh, Mike." Turning toward him, I bury my face in his shoulder and sob.

"It's okay. Just let it all out," he soothes, rubbing my back as he lets me vent my emotions.

I feel so foolish crying on his shoulder. I've tried to stay strong, only allowing myself to cry when I'm alone. But the pain of losing Max and never knowing if I'll ever see him again is unbearable, it's twisting me up inside.

I pull away, hastily wiping the tears from my cheeks as the toilet door opens and the young woman I had seen cleaning the tables, walks in. She seems surprised to see Mike in here, then she smiles at me sympathetically. "Are you okay?"

I nod shyly, feeling foolish and embarrassed. "Yeah."

"Come on," Mike says, looking down at my top, "come with me, I'll lend you one of my t-shirts to go home in."

I look down at my top, now stained with splashes of vomit.

The young woman smiles at me, moving aside to let us pass, then Mike leads me up a narrow staircase behind the bar to the upper floor. Opening a door, he leads me into a large bright living room.

"Is this where you've been staying while you're out here?"

"Yes, Daryl lets me crash here whenever I come over."

"It's nice."

The room is tidy and fairly sparse with just a large, saggy cushioned couch, a small coffee table, a TV on the wall, and a music system on a cabinet by the window. An archway leads through to a small kitchen, and Mike disappears into another room through a heavy brown curtain.

"I've got black or white or Arsenal red," he shouts out.

"The black one will be fine." I take a seat on the arm of the couch. My stomach still feels queasy and my legs are shaking.

Mike reappears offering me a black t-shirt. Holding it against my body, I chuckle. The slogan on the front in bold white letters says; 'Instant human being: Just add coffee'. "You never were a morning person."

He smiles and shrugs then nods toward another door. "The bathroom is through there."

I head for the bathroom and change out of my stained and stinky top. I look pale and drawn as I stare at myself in the mirror, and my eyes are puffy, red, and watery. Once I'm dressed, I ball up my dirty top and head back out to the living room. Mike is standing at the open window gazing out, I walk up beside him to take a look.

"Wow, you have a great view from here." I notice a pair of binoculars resting on the window sill, so I pick them up. "Don't tell me you've become a peeping Tom!" I smirk, pulling them up to my eyes. "Hey! I can see the yacht from here."

La Raposa stands out amongst the other smaller yachts in the marina. She's more like a small cruise ship. Her sleek navy blue hull with three white upper decks, stands much taller than the others too.

Mike turns to face me and if I'm not mistaken, he's blushing. "They're Daryl's," he smirks, "he likes to watch the girls sunbathing topless." Taking them out of my hands, he gives me the now empty rucksack that I'd given him this morning.

"Thanks for the shirt, I'll clean it and get it back to you as soon as possible."

"Keep it," he smiles. "I've got plenty."

He steps closer, too close, then he runs his hand up and down my bare arm, his big brown eyes gazing down at me like they used to when we were together. I begin to feel very uncomfortable and when he starts to lean in for a kiss, I step back in shock.

"No! Mike, please I… I don't want that."

The air is charged with tension. I step away from him, shocked that he would even consider trying to kiss me. My skin is boiling hot and freezing cold all at the same time. He's totally flabbergasted me.

"Viv..." He reaches out for my arm but I pull away, staring at him in disbelief.

"Why would you do that? I thought you said you'd be my friend, Mike. I thought you understood."

Dragging both hands through his hair, he looks at me with genuine regret. "I'm sorry. You're right. I just hate to see you so upset and I… I still have feelings for you."

My heart sinks at his pained expression, he looks thoroughly embarrassed, but the last thing I need is this.

"Mike... I don't—"

"I know," he interrupts softly, holding both hands up. "It was a stupid thing to do and I'm sorry."

After an awkward pause and an unspoken agreement that it will never happen again, we head back down to the bar.

John is anxiously waiting for me. "Everything okay?" he asks, rising to his feet, warily eyeing my new t-shirt.

I cringe, rolling my eyes. "I had a little accident." Holding up my soiled top proves the point, then I shove it in the rucksack. John gives Mike a disapproving glare before turning his anxious eyes back to mine.

"I'm okay, John. Really."

I turn to give Mike a kiss on the cheek, but then I decide against it. I don't want to encourage him, so I offer an awkward smile instead. "Thanks for all your help today, Mike. I really appreciate it."

"No worries. What time shall I pick you up for dinner?"

I'm beginning to think that may not be a good idea, especially after what just happened. "Ah, I'm sorry Mike, can we do that another time, my stomach's still not feeling great."

"Yeah, of course. I understand."

I can see the disappointment in his eyes. I feel bad, despite his coming on to me, he's been very helpful today. My conscience gets the better of me, overriding my common sense.

"Why don't you come down to the yacht later on for a drink, say eight o'clock?"

His frown disappears. "Okay, great! I'll see you then."

John and I leave the bar and head back to the yacht.

"Isn't he an old boyfriend?" John asks, obviously aware that he is, but having to ask anyway. I look up at him but don't respond, I'm interested to know where he's going with this.

He slips me a sideways glance. "It's just that Vinnie said he could be a bit volatile. He told me to keep an eye on him."

I chuckle to myself, but I suppose Vinnie did see Mike's darker side when he and I first broke up. "Yes, Mike can be hot headed, but he's okay. We've made our peace and we've managed to stay friends." At least I hope that's all it is.

John doesn't seem impressed. "Do you really think you can trust that guy?"

I can tell by his tone that he's less than enamoured with Mike, but then John doesn't trust anyone when he's in bodyguard mode.

"Yes. I do. Why wouldn't I? He's been very helpful to me today and he's always offered to be there for me when things have hit the crapper."

He doesn't comment any further, choosing instead to walk back to the yacht in silence.

As we board the yacht, Sasha comes striding up to us, looking stressed out and angry. "I'm glad you're back," she sighs. "The police came here to see you, they've only just left. Apparently, the phones have been ringing off the hook down at the police station since you advertised a reward." Sasha's expression and tone of voice confuses me. It totally conflicts with the good news she's just given me.

"That's great though, isn't it? Did they get any new information?"

She shakes her head, arching her brow. "No! And they're furious with you. They're angry that you've wasted their time with hundreds of crackpot calls from every money grabbing idiot in France. They said you should have told them you were offering a reward so that a designated number could have been set up. Apparently, the local police station has been overrun with calls since your appeal went out this afternoon." She huffs and tuts, folding her arms across her chest. "If you ask me? Their attitude stinks."

I'd never given it a thought. I assumed they'd handle it. "Well, it's too late now."

Sasha wanders away muttering under her breath about how useless the local police are, and John excuses himself to go and call Vinnie. He wants to tell him about the tattoo he'd investigated today.

I check my phone, but I still have no calls or messages from the people I had visited in the marina this morning.

Another day with no news, it's so depressing.

Dragging my weary body down to my cabin, I lay on the bed miserable and totally deflated.

DOPPELGANGER

"You drive me crazy, you know that?"

"Crazy-good?"

"Yeah, crazy-good. I love you, baby"

"I love you, too."

"Vivienne?"

"Yes."

"Vivienne?"

"I'm here, Max."

"Vivienne?"

"Vivienne?… Vivienne, I'm sorry to wake you, but you have a visitor."

"Huh?" Peeling open my tired eyes, I see Sasha's smiling face poking around the door. That awful pang of disappointment hits me head on now that I'm back in the real world.

"What time is it?" I mumble, stretching then staring down at my fully dressed body. I must have dozed off.

"It's seven o'clock. Sean's made a cold buffet for you up on deck. Oh, and Sylvie called earlier, but she said not to wake you."

"Okay, thanks." My mouth is so dry and my stomach is hungry. "Any news?"

She shakes her head with a stiff smile and a resigned shrug.

As Sasha leaves, I rub the sleep from my eyes and pull myself upright. I'm exhausted, but I haven't slept well for weeks. Not since…

Something fragrant wafts into my nose. The smell is very familiar, instantly transporting me back to the serene comfort of our bed in the penthouse.

My eyes seek out the fragrance, finally landing on the white rose in the narrow glass vase next to Max's photograph on my bedside table. It triggers a sharp intake of breath and my belly fills with butterflies. "Max?"

Still in a sleepy daze, I look all around me for any sign that he's been returned to me while I was sleeping. Only he would give me a single white rose.

I rush into the bathroom, but its emptiness hollows my stomach, and then I start to question whether I'd seen the rose at all. *Christ, Viv. Pull yourself together.*

I walk back into the bedroom. Unless I've gone completely bonkers, my eyes confirm the rose is definitely there. Reaching out, I gently brush my fingers along its delicate velvety petals. Then I remember Sasha had said I had a visitor.

"Mike! Shit, he's an hour early! Why can't people be on time. Or late even. I hate early." Muttering under my breath, I stomp into the bathroom.

I have noticed that I've become more snippy and intolerant recently. I know it's just lack of sleep and frustration that there's been no progress in finding Max, but lately, it seems the slightest thing irritates me.

I quickly shower, change, and make my way up to the salon to meet Mike. As I'm halfway up the stairs, I meet Sasha coming down them.

"Sasha, where did the white rose in my cabin come from?"

"They were delivered this evening," she says, brightly, but then her smile disintegrates. "Oh, I'm sorry, Vivienne. Max arranged for them to be delivered today because you were supposed to be staying here on your way home from your honeymoo— Oh, shit. I'm so sorry. I should have cancelled the order."

My heart twists in my chest and plummets to the pit of my stomach as I fight back the tears pricking my eyes. We were supposed to be married by now, husband and wife. A deep yearning ache grows inside me.

"It's okay, Sasha. I just...never mind."

All the ups and downs, the hopes and disappointments of the last few weeks are playing havoc with my brain. I must learn not to react so eagerly.

As I wander into the salon, casting my eyes along the mouth-watering selection of cold meats, salad, cheeses, and bread, my mouth begins to salivate and my belly grumbles, even though my appetite is waning. I haven't eaten at all today. If Max were here, he would be forcefully reprimanding me for not looking after myself or our babies.

Walking through the glass doors to the outdoor dining area on deck, I stumble to a standstill.

"Good evening, Vivienne. I told Sasha not to wake you."

My heart flutters as I stare up at his beautiful face in stunned silence.

"Cole! Wha…what are you doing here?"

His concerned eyes look me up and down, then he walks toward me in that predatory way he and his brother seem to share. My eyes are fixed on him, looking gorgeous in his white, fitted, open neck shirt and pale jeans. It's ridiculous how alike they are.

Involuntarily, he takes my breath away when he gazes at me with the same crystal blue eyes I'm so used to seeing, and which apparently have the power to melt my bones in exactly the same way. Even though it's just his incredible likeness to Max, and my own stupid mind playing tricks on me, I feel a deep sadness realising how much I've missed those eyes.

"Vivienne, you clearly don't know how to look after yourself." The arrogant curve in his arched brow, is so familiar. "John told me you haven't been eating. You look pale, thin, and exhausted."

Linking his arm through mine, he walks me over to the

table and pulls my chair out. "Sit," he commands softly. I do as I'm told while I try to regulate my erratic breathing and calm my stuttering heart, then I watch him settle into his own seat.

I can't take my eyes off him. As if on cue my butterflies arrive, they've also been deceived by the doppelganger sitting before me. They only usually spring to life when Max is near, but for all intents and purposes I'm looking straight at him.

Cole catches me staring at him and tilts his head, making me blush. Unwillingly, I drag my eyes away from his gorgeous face and look down at my hands fidgeting with the cutlery. His warm hand lands on mine, stilling them. The familiar tingle of electricity surges through my skin.

No, Viv! Stop it.

A strange sense of guilt creeps over me. My body's reacting to Cole in the same way it always has to Max.

You idiot. It's not him. It's not real.

"Vivienne? Are you okay?"

I blink up at him, dazed and confused by my own feelings. "Sorry?"

His concerned eyes search mine for a moment, then he removes his hand and pours me a glass of water. I'm thoroughly ashamed of myself for missing the contact of his touch.

"I was just saying, after that stunt you pulled this morning…" He frowns, releasing a sigh. "You're willing to go to such dangerous and extraordinary lengths. I felt it was necessary to come and look after you."

I feel angry that he's here, teasing me, deceiving my heart with his brother's looks, he's not the man I love, just a painful reminder of the man I've lost.

Clenching my jaw, I try to dial down my anger before opening my mouth. "That's very thoughtful of you Cole, but I really don't need, or want you to look after me."

As much as I had tried to keep my voice soft and grateful, it came out in more of a clipped and moody tone while my fingers absently spun the stem of my water glass. I don't look up, but I can tell by the awkward pause that my statement has hurt his feelings.

Without a word, Cole throws his napkin on the table rising from his seat, then he walks off behind me.

I feel awful for chasing him away like that, it was rude of me, but he puts me on edge. He looks so much like Max and I'm way too vulnerable right now.

I had thought Cole had left, but a few moments later he returns with two plates of food. "Eat," he says, placing one of the plates in front of me.

My appetite has vanished but I know I should eat something, so I begin to nibble at the bread.

Cole pours himself some wine. I can feel his eyes on me as I tear off small chunks of bread and pop them in my mouth.

"I'm just trying to help, Vivienne. There's a ton of shit in my past that I'm not proud of, but since Charlie died… I don't know, I guess I just don't want to be a fuck-up for the rest of my life."

I stop chewing, hesitantly glancing up at him. His brow is creased and his sad eyes stare into the wine he hasn't touched. Exhaling a deep sigh, he pushes his uneaten food away from him, then rests his elbows on the table, steepling his fingers, leaning his lips against them.

My eyes trail over his lush lips. The contour of his full mouth is something I'm very familiar with, and Cole's brow even furrows in exactly the same way Max's does. They share the same hands too. Big, strong, manly hands with smooth skin and well maintained cuticles. Everything about him is a dead-ringer. Looking at his gorgeous face both eases the pain and deepens it. It's a contradiction, but I can't stop gazing at him. The paradox of seeing the man I love, but knowing it's not him, is both painful and comforting.

"I miss him too, you know," he says, softly, his voice pulling me out of my head.

"What?"

"The reason we… The reason I hated him so much was because we looked identical and yet he was everything I wanted to be, but wasn't."

I search his saddened face, astounded by his confession.

Lowering his hands, his eyes swing over to mine. I can't look away, so we stare at each other in silence, his sincere blue eyes boring into mine.

"Vivienne, your friend Mike is here, shall I send him through?"

Cole breaks the eye contact first, reaching for his wine. I realise I was holding my breath. "Um, yes. Please do. Thank you, Sasha."

A mild frown slips into Cole's brow. "Mike? Who's he?"

"He's just a friend from London, he's out here helping his cousin in his bar."

I turn to see Mike walking toward us through the salon. His eyes are on Cole and I know he's thinking exactly the same thing I did the first time I saw him. Mike's confused expression, open mouth, and the fact that his walk has slowed considerably, means that he thinks Max has returned.

Cole rises from his seat, extending his hand. "Hi, I'm Cole, Max's brother."

Mike's eyebrows, now released from his confused frown, spring up in surprise as his whole body relaxes. "No way! I mean… Man! You look exactly the same."

After a lengthy, vigorous handshake, Mike leans down to kiss me on the cheek. Cole watches him with a curved eyebrow and quiet curiosity as Mike takes the seat next to me, as opposed to the chair Cole had pulled out for him on the opposite side of the table.

He takes my hand in both of his, which again is something Cole takes note of.

"So, how do you feel? Anymore sickness?" Mike asks, giving my hand a squeeze.

Cole pours him a glass of wine, leaning over to hand it to him, but Mike doesn't release my hand to take it, so Cole places it on the table, throwing me an arched brow.

As a blush warms my cheeks, I pull my hand out of Mike's firm grip. "Much better, thanks."

"Sickness? When were you sick?" Cole asks, obviously

annoyed that I hadn't mentioned it to him, not that it's any of his business.

"It was nothing. I didn't feel so good this afternoon, that's all."

Cole's displeasure is obvious, his furrowed brow deepening as he gives me a look of disapproval. "And that's why you shouldn't be riding around on unlicensed death-traps."

Mike's eyes ping-pong between us. "What do mean?"

"Didn't she tell you?" Cole asks, with an air of smugness. "She hired a moped and drove out to the chateau looking for Max. Alone."

Mike's eyebrows knit together. "Chateau? You didn't tell me."

I'm just about to explain myself when I realise, I don't have to. Mike isn't my boyfriend anymore, and neither is Cole.

"Viv?" Mike prompts me in a tone I recognise from our time together. Both sets of eyes are on me. Mike's are inquisitive, Cole's are amused. Both are starting to piss me off.

"I'm a grown woman. If I want to ride a moped, I'll ride a bloody moped!" It came out with a little more aggression than I had intended, but it did seem to lower the amount of testosterone flying around here.

An awkward silence hangs over us until Mike pipes up, his expression now a little cagey. "So, this Chateau? Where is it? And what made you think Max would be there?"

I sit back in my chair, my hands fidgeting in my lap. "I don't know where it is, I just followed the Sat-Nav. Cole thought Monica may have had a key, and it's been closed up for months. It would have been a perfect hiding place and I just wanted to check it out, that's all." Taking a deep breath, I release a long, weary sigh. "It was worth a look."

"So that's why you looked so upset this afternoon when you turned up at the bar." Mike takes my hand again, rubbing it gently between his.

As Cole's eyes narrow on mine, I begin to feel uncomfortable and another awkward silence falls around the table.

Sitting back in his chair, Cole's eyes bounce between the pair of us. "So, how do you two know each other?"

I open my mouth to respond but Mike beats me to it.

"Viv's my…*was* my girlfriend."

He said it as if saying we were just friends wouldn't have been enough.

Cole's impassive expression remains steady as his eyes flick over to mine. I feel uncomfortable at the way he's sizing me up after Mike's statement. I get the feeling he thinks I'm being disloyal to Max by spending time with an old flame, or maybe that's just my own guilt creeping in for letting Mike hold my hand.

After what happened this afternoon I need to discourage him from thinking there's any possibility we'd ever get back together. Pulling free from Mike's firm grip, I lay both hands in my lap. "We're just friends now."

Cole's eyes remain on mine, studying me for a moment longer before flicking over to Mike where he lets him have the full stare. Both barrels. "And now that my brother is gone, are you thinking you've got a chance, Mike? That you'll just pick up where you left off?"

I blush at his blunt question and look over at Mike. His mouth twitches into a hard line as his brow lowers over angry eyes. "No! Of course not. I'm just here for her as a friend, that's all." His cheeks redden and his body language shifts, becoming more defensive. "Besides, I've got a girlfriend back home."

I'm confused. I thought he and Michelle had split up ages ago. "Did you and Michelle make up?"

"What? Oh, no. She's just a girl I met in Portugal," he stutters, still frowning.

"Well, that's great." I'm genuinely pleased for him. He's the kind of guy who needs to be with someone, and it takes the pressure off me. He's been so touchy-feely lately and after admitting that he still has feelings for me and then trying to kiss me this afternoon, I was beginning to wonder if he was hoping we'd get back together.

As much as I like having Mike as a friend, I could never be with anyone else. Not now. Max is the love of my life and the father of my babies, it's him or no one.

"So, what's the plan for tomorrow?" Mike asks, obviously trying to change the subject.

An involuntary yawn delays my response. "…I was—"

"I'm taking her out for the day," Cole interrupts. Both Mike and I stare at him with mild surprise. "Maybe we'll drop by your cousin's bar for a drink in the evening." Cole rises to his feet, offering his hand to Mike. "It was good of you to drop by, but as you can see, Vivienne is very tired and needs to rest."

Cole's dismissal of Mike is abrupt and compelling. Mike hesitantly stands up and begrudgingly shakes his hand.

"I'll walk you out," Cole says, gesturing for him to go first.

Mike looks down at me with disappointment written all over his face, then he bends to kiss me on the cheek. "I guess I'll see you later."

"Um, yeah. Thanks for coming."

I turn to watch as Cole deftly ushers him from the deck. I'm confused by his behaviour but I'm secretly pleased to be on my own again. With any luck Cole will want to hit the town and party, so I can retreat to my cabin and console my aching heart by surfing through my photographs of Max.

When Cole returns to his seat he nudges my plate of uneaten food closer toward me. "Eat," he commands softly. "You need to nourish yourself, you look too thin and you have the babies to think about now."

Pulling his own plate toward him, he begins to nibble at his food, so I do the same.

He leans an elbow on the table, giving me a sideways glance. "Interesting guy."

"What do you mean?"

He smirks looking down at his plate. "He's so in to you."

I huff out a sarcastic response and shove another piece of bread into my mouth.

"You believe that bullshit about him having a girlfriend?"

he asks, glancing up at me, arching his brow in that cocky, arrogant way of his.

"Yes… Why would he lie?"

"Because he wants you, Vivienne. It's written all over his jealous ex-boyfriend face. Didn't you see the look he gave me when he thought I was Max?"

I scowl at his remark. Cole doesn't even know Mike, and what gives him the right to judge anyone else after the jealous things he's done to his own brother.

Raising his fork to his mouth, Cole pauses for a moment and smiles. With both eyebrows raised in a questioning manner, he tilts his head like a dog. "Come on, Vivienne. Spit it out. I know you have something to say."

He's almost laughing at me which winds me up even more. He's such an arrogant man. "You're right." Crossing my arms across my chest, I defiantly level my eyes on him. "I do have something to say. When we were together, Mike could be a little jealous and hot headed at times, it's part of his nature, but then you'd know all about jealousy wouldn't you."

Cole stops chewing and smirks. "Ouch! Touché, Miss Banks. I guess I had that coming."

Straightening my back, I glare at him. "Yes. You did. And why are you here, Cole? You've never really cared for you brother. From what I've heard, you've stabbed him in the back at every opportunity, why the sudden need to help me find him, there's nothing in it for you. Or am I missing something?"

He carefully lowers his fork, takes a sip of wine, then leans back in his chair. His eyes scan my face then land on mine with narrowed intensity. I find it hard to look away, Max and Cole share the bluest, most intoxicating eyes.

He looks at me thoughtfully for a moment, then his eyes lower to the table. With a deep rise and fall of his chest on a long sigh, his expression saddens. "I was in love with her…" He speaks so softly I can hardly hear him. "I didn't marry Monica to hurt my brother. I married Monica because I was in love with her, and I thought she loved me."

His confession hangs in the silence of the warm night air. I wasn't expecting that response at all.

After flicking me a quick glance, he huffs out a small sarcastic laugh. "We both fell in love with same woman. I guess we're both more alike than either of us would care to admit."

Cole's reminder that Max had once loved Monica, makes me shudder. The ugly head of my green-eyed monster raises above the parapet to poke me with a disapproving glare.

Max and Cole share identical looks, voices, and expressions. They are quite literally carbon copies of each other. Why wouldn't they share the same likes and dislikes?

I had never warmed to Cole because of the way he'd treated his brother, blaming him for their parents' death. That's probably something I'll never truly forgive, and yet, in my heart, I know Max did forgive him. Max had gone out of his way to comfort his brother at Charlie's funeral. He'd reached out to him and they'd begun to communicate again, tentatively beginning to rebuild the bridges they had both burned down over the years. Max was like that. Warm, compassionate, loving. Quite simply the nicest person I've ever known.

Cole lowers his eyes to his wine glass as he absently swirls the contents around the bowl. "I had no idea Monica was manipulating me."

The sadness in his voice grabs my attention.

"I fell in love with her from the very first moment I saw her in high school. But, as expected, she chose Max. I knew I'd never be able to compete with him, so I had to let her walk away. She broke my heart."

Still with his eyes cast down, he takes a deep inhale, releasing a long sigh. Emotion colours his voice, but it's the intensity of it that surprises me.

"When they split up, she came back to me. She told me she'd made a huge mistake, I was the one she really wanted to be with... And I believed her." Shaking his head, he clenches his jaw. "That bitch played us both."

He doesn't look up, but I can see from his deepening frown and the sadness in his eyes that he's speaking from the heart. I had always assumed that Cole had married Monica to hurt his brother. And because of their history, I'd always thought of Cole as a heartless bastard.

But seeing him now and hearing the sadness in his voice, I realise he's just like the rest of us. Vulnerable. I'm surprised, but I feel sorry for him.

A thought suddenly comes into my mind, although I'm unsure whether I should voice it.

"Cole, I don't think Monica's ability to love is the same as you and me, or anyone else for that matter. She was damaged, and so was Max. I think the reason she pursued him over you was purely because she thought she could control him, and up to a point, she controlled you both."

He offers me a weak smile, staring down at his plate of food before sliding it away from him. Reaching for his wine, he finishes his glass then pours another. He looks troubled with a faraway look in his eyes, and I sense he has more to say.

"Max was always the strong, clever, independent one. When we were kids, before our parents died, he would come home from school with his arms full of gadgets that he'd made in class, and the drawings of his space rockets were plastered all over his side of our bedroom. He was so creative and interesting. I was in awe of my brother."

He takes a moment to reflect, still staring down at the table. Taking a drink, he stares vacantly into the glass. I watch his face as his gaze wanders off to some long distant memory, a small smile curling the corners of his lips.

"All the kids in school thought he was a total nerd, but he didn't care. He didn't need their approval like I did. He was an achiever right from the get-go, always top of the class. And if people tried to bully him because he was pretty, he'd either talk them down, or walk away. He was his own man even as a kid."

Shaking his head, he smiles, but then the smile fades. "I was jealous of the freedom he had to be exactly what he wanted to be without worrying about other people. I didn't share his confidence or his drive. I envied that about him."

He pauses to take another deep breath, then his expression darkens. "I was a shit brother. I was jealous of him… I couldn't stand up to the bullies at school like he could. And he'd always defend me, but that just made me feel worse about myself. And you know what? He never once complained when I was mean to him. He'd just shrug it off."

Cole's eyes glance up at me for the briefest of moments, and in that fleeting exchange I can see the glisten of tears in his eyes. I feel sorry for him, but I can't forgive him for dumping his self-loathing inadequacies onto Max in the way that he did. Blaming him for the death of their parents was unforgivable.

"Cole, when your parents died, you should have been supporting each other, comforting each other, but you didn't. You made his life a living hell."

I feel bad for saying it but I feel compelled to. Cole had robbed Max of the right to grieve the death of his parents in a normal way. Guilt should never have been an eight-year-old boy's primary emotion.

"Do you think I don't know that?" His voice is soft and raspy, and the pain in his eyes, and the quiver in his voice surprises me, pulling at my heart.

"I've been a selfish, jealous prick all my life." His voice is tight as he bows his head in shame. "And it's taken the loss of my brother to realise how much he means to me."

Tears pool in my eyes as a lump jumps into my throat. He's shocked me. Even he thinks Max is never coming back. A surge of anger makes my fists clench. He's chosen to let go of any hope that his brother will be found.

"He's still alive!"

Cole looks up at me in confusion.

Lifting my chin defiantly, I glare at him in anger. "I'm not giving up. If you don't think he's coming back then you might as well leave. Max is still alive. He's out there somewhere, I know he is, I can feel it, even if you can't."

I glare up at him unable to curb my tongue. I resent the fact that he's here and Max isn't. "He needs you, now more than ever. But if you're giving up? If you can't help me find him? Then you can fuck off! And take your self-pity with you!"

My bravado retreats with astonishing speed. Overcome with emotion, I sag into a sobbing heap against the table, resting my head on my forearms. I can't think of Max never coming home, it's unthinkable, too painful to contemplate. He has to come home. I need him. We need him.

A warm hand gently rubs my shoulders. Cole crouches down beside my chair resting his other hand on my knee, giving it a gentle, reassuring squeeze.

"I'm sorry, Vivienne," he says, softly. "I do want to help, that's why I'm here."

I'm emotionally and physically drained. These last few weeks have been torture. Without thinking I turn to face him, throwing my arms around his neck, almost knocking him off his feet. "Oh, Cole, I miss him so much." Burying my face in his neck, I sob.

After a beat, he wraps his strong arms around me, and for a moment, I feel like I'm not alone anymore.

We hold each other for a long time, probably too long but I'm reluctant to let go. His strong shoulders and the curve of his neck make me feel safe, like I have Max back in my arms. I want him to be Max, so badly.

After he's stroked my hair and whispered a few soothing tokens of support in my ear, he pulls back, lifting my chin with his finger. I finally release him from my arms, sliding my hands down to rest my palms on his chest. His heart beats wildly through his thin linen shirt. My cheeks flush, I feel foolish for breaking down like that in front of him. "I'm sorry," I murmur, beginning to pull away.

Cole runs his fingers down my cheek, wiping a tear away with his thumb. "Don't be." His soft, familiar voice and the gentle contact of his skin against mine initiates all the long-established responses in my body.

As I gaze at him through tear blurred eyes, the look on his face floors me, igniting my senses, evoking the flutter of butterfly wings in the pit of my stomach. His familiar eyes burn into mine with a curious heat, he has the same expression Max had on his face before he kissed me for the first time. I'll never forget that look.

As I sway under his intoxicating gaze, an automatic response entrenched in my psyche, has me beginning to lean in to him. I feel drawn to him like a moth beguiled by the brilliance of his blazing, hypnotic eyes. Max's eyes. The eyes I've lost myself inside many times. His chest rises and falls deeply under my palms, and his hot breath puffs over my face from his parted lips.

In a jerking movement, he puts me at arm's length then releases me completely. The abrupt manoeuvre snaps me out of my hypnotic daze and back to the real world with laser sharp cognizance. You could hear a pin drop in the awkward silence that follows.

I instantly flush with embarrassment at the realisation that I almost kissed him. I feel ashamed of myself for wanting to kiss him. "Oh my god. Cole, I'm so sorry."

Lowering his eyes, he stands abruptly, dragging his hands through his hair.

"No, it's… I'm… You should…I'm sorry, I…"

Without finishing his disjointed sentence, he reaches over to his wine glass and knocks it back in one go, then he looks down at me with a strange expression. "Goodnight, Vivienne. Sleep well."

I watch him walk away. My feelings baffling the hell out of me.

What the hell was that?

CAN I TRUST YOU?

I lay in bed staring at the ceiling. I'm so tired but my brain won't let me sleep. Whether my eyes are open or closed, all I can see in my mind is Max's face, or rather Cole's face, staring down at me with heat and longing in his eyes. Did I imagine it? Of course I did. I must have. But if I didn't, did I encourage it?

I turn my head to gaze at Max's photo. As much as my eyes crave the masculine contours of his beautiful face, it also evokes the painful emptiness I've felt ever since he was taken from me. I miss him so much that I'm starting to superimpose him in some delusional, mixed up, body swap.

Get a grip, for fuck's sake.

The minutes become hours and yet I still haven't slept. Turning on to my side, I punch the pillow into shape and close my tired eyes trying to settle, but I can't, it's hopeless. Every nerve ending is nudging at me to move, so I get up and make my way up to the deck, hoping the cool night air will clear my head.

I feel foolish and stupid for how I reacted to Cole. I'm extremely vulnerable right now and the fact that he looks, sounds, and feels like Max isn't helping. My body has a will of its own where Max is concerned, but there's no excuse.

The yacht is quiet, everyone is still asleep, and as I take a seat in one of the large sofas out on deck, I stare up at the night sky dotted with twinkling stars and the lustrous glow of a full moon.

The night air is chilly, so I pull the blanket around my shoulders and curl my legs underneath me. The soft tapping noises of the halyards slapping on the masts of countless yachts moored nearby, and the gentle lapping of the water against the hull, lulls me into a semi-doze.

"You can't sleep either?"

Cole's soft voice startles me.

"Oh, um, no."

My eyes trawl over his bare, perfectly toned torso. Hitching up the sweatpants hanging low on his narrow hips, he moves to the edge of the vessel resting his hands on the wooden sill, facing out to the water. I can tell by his body language that he has something on his mind, but I'm the one who should apologise for what happened earlier.

A shiver of embarrassment runs through my body. What must he have thought? He must be feeling very awkward about it because he hasn't been able to face me yet.

His vast back muscles flex as his ribcage expands on a deep intake of breath, followed by an audible sigh. "Vivienne… I need to—"

"No, Cole. Please don't. It's my fault. I'm sorry. I'm just very vulnerable right now and you look so much like Max… But I shouldn't have… Well, I'm sorry. It won't happen again."

Rising from the sofa, I stare at his back waiting for a response but it doesn't come. "Goodnight then."

He bows his head. I can see the muscles flexing in his arms as his hands grip the wooden sill. "…Goodnight, Vivienne."

I wait for him to turn and face me but he doesn't. I don't know what else I can say to smooth things over between us, so I leave and head back to my cabin.

~

When I wake to the piercing shrillness of my alarm clock, my eyes refuse to open. Judging by the way I feel, I could only have managed an hour's sleep last night.

After I had left Cole on deck at god knows what-o'clock, I came back to bed only to toss and turn, agonising over my embarrassingly stupid, almost kiss. I felt disloyal and weak. Guilt and shame made me feel sick. That my body could react to Cole purely because he looks exactly like Max was shameful, but merely proved the point that I miss him. I crave him. I want him back.

Eventually, I peel my eyes open just so I can roll them at myself. "You idiot." I cringe as my stupidity makes me want to throw a pillow over my face and scream.

Once I'm dressed and ready to face the day, my belly churns once more as I leave my cabin. I hope Cole can draw a line under last night's embarrassing episode or today is going to be very uncomfortable.

When I arrive on deck, I take my usual seat at the breakfast table and pour myself a cup of tea. Cole is nowhere to be seen, affording me a little respite from my shame. He's either run back to London glad to see the back of me, or he's still sleeping.

My phone rings, it's Lucy.

"Hey, Viv, how are you?"

"I'm okay."

I don't know whether to mention last night's faux pas. I usually tell Lucy everything but maybe that cringe-worthy moment should be buried and forgotten.

"Any luck with the reward?" Her question just serves to remind me that I'm also on the police's shit list too, which pulls another cringe to my face.

"Not yet, no. I took your advice though, I went around the whole marina yesterday asking people to check their cameras but no one's called me back yet, so I'm going back out today."

I try not to let the despondency creep into my voice but it's almost impossible.

"I know this is hard for you, Viv. Stay strong. If you need me, I'm always here for you; you know that, right?"

Tears pool in my eyes. "I do."

I can hear voices in the background, she's obviously at work. "Sorry, Viv, I've got to go, it's like a friggin' mad house here today."

"Okay, I'll speak to you soon, give my love to Dan."

As I end the call to Lucy, Sasha walks over and hands me a plate of scrambled eggs on toast. "I've been ordered to give you this, and to make sure you eat it."

"John?" I ask, arching a brow.

"Cole," she answers, dryly. "They left early this morning, but Cole said he'd be back for you at eleven-ish to take you out."

"Out where?"

"He didn't say." Sasha starts to walk away then turns back. "Oh, I almost forgot." She pulls an envelope from her pocket. "This came for you this morning." She lays it on the table then continues on her way.

As I finish the last of my eggs, I find myself staring at the plain white envelope with just my name written in blue ink. The penmanship looks familiar but I'm not sure why. The battered envelope looks like it's been handled a lot, it's lost the pristine crispness of new stationery.

Turning it over, I see the back has been sealed, so I pick at it to catch an edge, then use my thumb to tear it open, my hopes rising as I begin to wonder if it could be from one of the boat owners responding to my plea to check their cameras.

Inside the envelope is a single sheet of white paper, I unfold it, staring down at the familiar handwriting.

Meet me at the end of pier 4 at 10am

Tell no one.

Come alone or Max is gone forever.

Oh, my god. Monica!

Now, I remember where I had seen that handwriting before. On my very first date with Max, Monica faked her suicide and left him a note. I had found the note and this one bears the same garish, dramatic swirls and loops as the one I'd seen before.

The paper shakes in my trembling hands. I realise I've been

holding my breath when I gasp in a lungful of air, and my mouth feels so dry as I read and re-read the note over and over again. *Shit! What do I do?*

Regaining my wits, I look around me, thankfully I'm alone. I check my watch, it's nine twenty-four, I haven't got much time.

I sprint down to my cabin and change out of my dress and flips flops, into a pair of shorts, a t-shirt, and converse. If I need to run, I'd better be prepared.

Grabbing my phone, I check the GPS is on. If things go tits-up I want to be traceable and if necessary, I want to be able to record our conversation. I may need proof of our meeting for the police.

Putting my phone to silent, I shove it in my bra.

Before I leave the cabin, I take one last look at Max's photograph. "I'm coming to get you, Max. Please hold on. I love you." I kiss his picture and my babies scan, then leave the cabin.

As nonchalant as possible, I gingerly make my way to the gangway, avoiding the staff and hiding when I hear Sasha's voice. When the coast is clear, I continue at a fast walk. With one foot on the gangway I jump when I hear Sasha calling my name.

"Vivienne! Where are you going? Cole will be here in an hour."

Think, Viv. Think! "I'll be back before then, I'm just going down to the bank."

"If you need cash, I have some on board."

"No, erm. It's just, I need to send some money to my mum."

I can see her brain calculating an alternative option for me to transfer the money but if she doesn't let me leave soon, I'm going to be late.

"And I fancied a walk, it's such a beautiful morning," I add convincingly.

"Okay, see you soon." Sasha seems happy with that and turns away to attend to her duties.

Holding back the urge to run down the gangway, I saunter off until I'm far enough away to change my direction unnoticed. I run to pier four and then all the way down it. By the time I reach the end my lungs and muscles are burning. Sweat moistens my skin, making my lips taste salty as I stand there panting, out of breath.

Looking down at my watch, I relax when I realise I'm not late. As I glance all around me, I notice there are only a few small boats moored at this end and it's very quiet, apart from the low thrum of a diesel engine ticking over nearby. *Where the hell are you?*

"Are you alone?"

I gasp and turn around sharply. Monica's harsh voice is coming from inside the white boat at my right-hand side. The engine splutters out grey clouds of exhaust as it idles in the water.

"Yes." I have to shield my eyes from the sun to see inside the dark, enclosed, navy canopy of the cockpit with its smoked glass windows, but all I can see is a shadowy figure.

"Get in."

I glance around me once more in the hope that I may see someone, but we're very much alone at this end of the pier. Reluctantly, I make the decision to do as she asks.

Adrenaline courses through my veins as I step down into the boat and then my stomach rolls as I see Monica standing in the shadows with a gun in her hand. Deja vu spikes a sickness in the pit of my stomach. She's wearing a blonde wig and dark sunglasses, she looks so different, but I'd recognise her voice anywhere.

"Release the rope," she barks, pointing behind me.

Fumbling with the thick rope, I release it from the cleat and as I turn to face her, she impatiently gestures for me to join her in the cockpit. All my senses are fired up and on red alert. She looks anxious and scared, and I notice her hand trembles as she points the gun at me. This is not the confident, cunning Monica I've come to know. In fact, her demeanour puts me on a knife edge. Something must have happened, or gone terribly wrong.

With jangling nerves, I tentatively move inside the cockpit, even my head is shaking with fear. Although masked behind her dark sunglasses, I sense Monica's cat-like eyes roaming all over me.

"Where's Max?"

"Be quiet!" Her sharp tone makes me jump. Fear clenches my stomach but I can't help myself, I need to know.

"Is he alright, is he alive?"

Pausing for a moment, she slides her sunglasses to the top of her head. That momentary pause fills me with dread, then she levels her contemptuous glare on me.

"Yes… He's alive."

"Thank god!" I almost crumple to the floor with relief.

She stares at me with animosity seeping from every pore, but there's a hint of something else, something I can't quite determine enters her eyes filling them like smoke creeping into a room. For a woman who's normally so confident and controlled, she looks nervous.

"Where is he? I need to see him, please!"

"Shut the fuck up," she hisses, regaining her flinty glare. "I won't tell you again."

Reaching into her back pocket, she throws me a set of silver handcuffs. I instinctively catch them before they hit me in the face.

"Take off your back-pack, put them on, and cuff yourself to the hand rail." Her command is hurried, almost nervous. "Do it!" she adds, with gritted teeth.

Shifting on her feet, she takes a nervous glance around her but no one is near, and now my fear kicks up another notch as I reluctantly do as she says. Once I'm cuffed to the rail, she pushes me down to my knees. Placing the gun in her pocket, she reaches down for my rucksack, throwing it to the back of the boat. Then she takes the wheel and skilfully manoeuvres the boat away from the pier.

Glancing over my shoulder, I spot my rucksack. I had taken a knife from the breakfast table and hidden it in one of the pockets but I've got no chance of getting to it while I'm cuffed to this fucking rail. Panic knots my stomach as I watch the safety of the marina disappearing behind us as Monica takes us out to open water.

The boat doesn't look new or particularly well looked after, but it moves fast in the water. My arse thuds against the hard floor as we bounce over the waves. The cuffs, cutting into my flesh as I'm thrown around like a rag doll, and the wind whips my hair in all directions, slashing violently against my face and eyes.

Monica doesn't look down at me once as she navigates her course, and I'm too afraid to speak. The fear that I've made a huge mistake tackling this on my own, turns the sweat on my body into icy beads, like a frost chilling me to my core. And in my panic, I begin to visualize all kinds of horrific scenarios waiting for me.

After a while, Monica slows the boat, then cuts the engine. The noise from its droning hum is suddenly replaced with the gentle lapping of the sea against the fibreglass hull.

I waggle my head around to try and dislodge the curtain of knotted hair hanging in front of my eyes.

Monica walks to the back of the boat and picks up my rucksack. Checking the pockets, she dumps the contents into the sea and then she finds the knife.

No!

"Stupid bitch." She mutters under her breath, then throws it overboard with the rucksack. I shrink in fear when she turns to face me. I've seen that look in her eyes before, the night she tried to kill me, but she also carries an edginess to her that I've never noticed before. Something's definitely wrong.

"Where is it?"

I shake my head in confusion, I don't know what she means.

"Where's your fucking phone?"

I shake my head again and whimper as she takes an aggressive step toward me, her lips twitching into a snarl of contempt. "I'll ask you again, Vivienne. Where. Is. Your.

Fuc—"

My phone begins to vibrate, stopping her mid-sentence. Casting her eyes down to my chest, she zones in on the light from the screen shining through my top. Lurching forward she snatches it from my bra. "Clever girl, she sneers. "But not clever enough."

I didn't see who was calling, but she rejects the call then throws my phone overboard.

"No!… Fuck!" The blood drains from my head and tears fill my eyes as I watch my only connection to safety go flying through the air, before disappearing into the vastness of the ocean with a subtle splash. I'm completely cut off.

I hastily look around me but we're far from land and I can't see any other boats close enough to be of any help.

Monica begins to pace up and down in front of me. She anxious, violently wringing her hands and muttering words I can't distinguish under her breath. Her eyes are wide and wild. Something is distracting her and whatever it is, has her worried. Her shield of cool, calculating strength seems to have abandoned her.

Fear churns in my stomach. "What do you want?" I sniffle, nervously. "Where's Max?"

Monica stops pacing and frightens the life out of me when she tilts her head back, clenches her fists up by her cheeks, and screams up at the sky. Rage pouring out of her in a blood curdling scream, turning her body rigid and her face bright red. She's like a woman possessed. Then her scream abruptly stops and she begins to sob.

I'm gob-smacked and completely transfixed by her. It's as if she's fighting an inner demon who's much stronger than she is. And now more than ever, I fear for my life.

As abruptly as she began, she stops crying, aggressively wiping the tears from her face, almost as if she's suddenly realised she has an audience.

My heart beats wildly in my chest and my erratic breathing rasps loudly in the now peaceful solitude of the open ocean. My wide, fearful eyes watch her intently, trying to fathom her next move. But I've never seen her like this before. This is a complete one-eighty for her.

Slowly regaining her composure, she turns away from me. When she turns back, it's as if none of what I had just witnessed happened at all. Lowering her wide eyes down to me, she searches my face until a confused frown softens her countenance, throwing me completely off balance. Her expression floors me. What she says next, really fucks with my head.

"Can I trust you?"

"Wh…what?" I blink up at her, not at all convinced I had heard her correctly.

With a quiet ease she moves closer, crouching down in front of me. I shrink back, fearful of what she's going to do. The only thing I'm sure of, is that she's no longer holding the gun.

Her penetrating stare bores into my fearful eyes. "Can I trust you, Vivienne?"

"What the fuck?" I stare at her in shock and utter bewilderment. That was the last thing I expected her to say. "I don't… Why?"

Her lips twitch with disgust, briefly closing her eyes as if I'm trying her patience and pissing her off. What she's asking is obviously going against the grain. When she opens her eyes again, the familiar look of hate and contempt lies beneath her forced composure. "I need to know if I can trust you, Vivienne. If you want to see Max again, you'll have to do exactly what I say."

"Anything!" I blurt. "I'll do anything."

Her piercing green eyes narrow on me, then trail over my face and down my body. With a snarl on her lips she lets out a resigned, exasperated sigh, then stands and begins to pace again.

I nervously watch her, bracing myself for the vicious attack I feel sure she's about to launch. "Please, Monica. Whatever you want, I'll do it. I promise." My voice is anxious and whimpering. I don't understand what she's doing, but right now I'm prepared to do anything to bring Max home.

She seems deep in thought and she hasn't spoken another word.

Wriggling in the confines of my handcuffs, I watch her as she paces up and down the deck. Suddenly she stops, then takes a seat holding her head in her hands. Her stillness bothers me and her body language is freaking me out.

"Monica, please!"

"He's alive," she mutters quietly, begrudgingly. "He's alive, but he's injured." Raising her head from her hands, she looks directly at me. Her eyes are watery and sad, and for once, the hate and bitterness seems to have left her.

"How bad is he hurt? Where is he? Does he need a—"

"He's safe," she interrupts in a quiet voice. Her patience is frayed but she's trying to contain her anger. As measured as she's trying to be, I can see the irritation brewing beneath the surface.

She stands abruptly, continuing to move around the deck, wringing her hands and clenching her jaw. Her body is stiff with anxiety, like a tightly coiled spring.

Panic knots in my stomach. Her mood keeps changing, I can't read her at all. She's volatile, like a firework that's been ignited but failed to go off. Do I step toward it and take a chance? Or leave it well alone in case it blows up in my face.

She sighs with resignation and for a moment, she looks utterly defeated. "I don't know how long I can keep him safe… Or alive."

My stomach rolls as her statement sinks in. "Oh, god! How bad is he injured?"

She ignores me slowly dragging the blonde wig from her head. Before releasing her dishevelled red hair from the confines of the skull cap, I notice she has a large fading bruise on the side of her head, just behind her ear.

"Safe from what?" My voice trembles and I flinch when she faces me head on, the anger and contempt savagely pulling her face into an ugly sneer.

"The men I hired are fucking brutal!"

Fuck! John was right.

Her gaze drifts away from me and for a moment, she looks like a frightened little girl.

The cuffs are cutting into my flesh. Keeping an eye on Monica, I kneel up, then stand to relieve the pressure on my wrists. She doesn't react to my movement, she just stares off in her own little world.

"Monica, who are these people?"

"I just wanted us to be together," she murmurs, ignoring my question and she looks so sad. "I just wanted them to move him… Away from you!" Her eyes swing over to mine with utter contempt, then they slide off my face and down to the wig she's now pulling at nervously in her hands.

"They were only supposed to take him off the yacht. That's all they were supposed to do. I paid them well, but they fucked me over. Greedy fuckers!"

My brain is in overdrive trying to make sense of what she's saying. "But, nobody's made any demands… I don't understand."

Monica stares out in front of her. She looks deeply lost in her thoughts and whatever they are, they're causing a panic in her that I didn't think she was capable of. I've never seen her this unravelled before. Her usually cold, hard, calculating exterior is now crumbling away. She's frightened. And that scares me to death.

"Monica!… Monica look at me! Where have they taken him?" I need her to focus. "Monica!"

She begins to laugh, then she cries, like a crazy person. The hairs on my arms and the back of my neck stand up as a prickle of fear runs over my skin. She's lost the fucking plot!

Her eyes swing over to mine, a hard frown furrowing her brow as her lips curl into a snarl. "You think I'm bad. These people are fucking ruthless! They fucked me over. They were never going to give him back once they'd got the money. They don't give a shit about him or his family. And they certainly weren't going to let me live. Especially not after I stole their ticket to a fortune." A sinister smile creeps across her lips.

"What? ...Monica, what the hell are you talking about?"

She looks irritated at my lack of understanding, but my head is spinning and all I want is for her to get to the fucking point.

Her eyes drift away from me again. Everything about her is freaking me out. Her demeanour keeps flipping from one extreme to another. Clenching her hands into fists, she begins to pace again.

"The night we took him from the yacht, they were supposed to deliver him to my boat. I had everything planned for Max and I to disappear..." Her face becomes sad. "Everything was ready... it was perfect..." Suddenly, she hardens again as she shoots me an angry scowl. "But those assholes fucked me over! They wanted more money! Bastards!"

She doesn't speak for a few moments, then she stops pacing and turns to face me, tilting her head with an eerie, wry smile on her face.

"Hmmf, you should have seen the look on Max's face when he saw me sitting on your bed." Her smile disintegrates and her eyes seem to glaze over as her mind wanders off somewhere else.

I stare up at her utterly transfixed and totally bewildered. She's doing my head in. A shudder spirals up my spine as I watch her, unable to read what comes next.

Her eyelids blink a few times, like she's just re-booted her brain, then she resumes her incessant pacing. "As soon as they got him off the yacht, they knocked me out and dumped us both in a small boat twenty feet away."

The blood drains from my head and I feel physically sick.

"Yeah," she says, smugly, enjoying my reaction. "Galling, isn't it?"

Tears prick my eyes and an overwhelming desire to vomit comes over me as I realise Max had been so close and none of us knew it.

"I woke up and managed to escape while they were sailing us into a private dock a few miles along the coast."

Her eyes begin to glisten, she looks physically moved, but it's the sadness in her voice that really hits me. "They'd beaten the shit out of him." Her hardness returns and as she takes a seat opposite me, her eyes become dark and brooding.

"They hid him in a warehouse. But they underestimated me." Her penetrating eyes flick up to mine with a look of utter contempt. "Everybody does! But we stole him back. We took him from right under their noses too." A small triumphant smile seeps across her face.

Sheer relief courses through me. If Monica has Max, I still have a fighting chance to get him back. She's twisted and fucked-up, but she's in love with him, at least she would keep him alive. I shudder to think what would happen to him at the hands of these other people.

"Monica, if you have him, where is he?"

She takes a long while to answer, staring out to the horizon. "He's safe… I hid him where they'll never find him."

"Where? And who is this 'we' you keep talking about?"

She doesn't answer me. Judging by her glazed expression she's wandered off in her thoughts again.

"Monica please! You're doing my fucking head in! I need to know. Where is he? You said he was injured. How bad is it?" I pull on my restraints, angry that she won't answer me.

My yelling eventually brings her out of her daze and she flicks me a hostile glare. Her confidence and anger have resumed as the hardness returns to her eyes. "You need to help me," she demands in a low grating voice. "I need to disappear before they find me."

I stare at her with my mouth gaping open, completely dumbfounded. What the hell does she expect me to do?

"Don't worry, you'll get what you want," she snarls, begrudgingly. "But you need to help me first. And you need to do it alone. Cole and Vinnie would rather see me burn in hell. I mean it, Vivienne, if you tell *anyone* about this, I'll be gone and you'll never find Max."

I blink at her in confusion. "But…how? …How am I supposed to do that?"

She leans forward resting her forearms on her knees. "I need five million dollars in unmarked hundred dollar bills. You, and only you, will deliver the money to a specified location at exactly midnight tomorrow. Everything is in place, all you have to do is follow my orders exactly. Once I have the money, I'll give you Max. It's very simple, Vivienne. Even you couldn't fuck it up."

She said it like it was an everyday request but I could feel my brain frying under the pressure of trying to break it down into bite-sized pieces, to make sense of it all. But none of this makes any sense. If my hands weren't cuffed to this fucking rail, I would have thrown them up in exasperation.

"But…Wh… How? …I haven't got access to Max's money. How the hell am I supposed to get my hands on five million dollars?"

"The S.R.F. fund. You need to go to—"

"Wait! The what?"

She huffs impatiently, throwing me another flinty glare. "The S.R.F. fund. Safe. Return. of Family. William set it up years ago. There's a vault in their home, which is where they keep the fund for just such an event. It's back up money should any of them be taken by force for ransom."

"But how do I—"

"Sylvie is the *only* person you can talk to about this. She knows how to access the vault and she'll move the money without involving the police. I know her, she'll keep her mouth shut to get her son back. She'll move the money to France, but you, and only you, will deliver it to me."

I stare at her with a bazillion questions flying through my mind.

"Well?"

I'd already made my mind up at the very beginning that I'd do whatever it takes to bring Max home. It's not my money to bargain with but it's a fair trade as far as I'm concerned. I hate Monica with a passion. I've even dreamt about killing her with my own bare hands. But if it will bring Max home safely, she can have it all, every last penny.

Staring up at Monica's face as she waits for me to confirm whether I'm going to help her or not, it suddenly strikes me as funny. All this time she's been my nemesis. The angry, festering boil on the arse of my existence. She's threatened me, tried to kill me twice, she even killed her own son for the love of a man who rejected her completely, and now she's asking me to help save her sorry arse. You couldn't write this stuff!

I lift my chin defiantly. For once in our twisted relationship, and despite the fact that I'm handcuffed to the boat, I feel like I'm holding all the cards for a change. She needs my help. How fucking ironic.

With cool authority, I make my demand. "I'm going to need proof that he's still alive."

After a beat, she reaches into her pocket and pulls out her phone, but a still image isn't what I need. I don't trust her enough for that. I don't trust her at all.

"No! I need to see him for myself, or it's no deal." My quaking knees betray the strong commanding voice I somehow managed to deliver.

Monica narrows her eyes on me before disappearing into the cabin, returning moments later with a small vial of clear fluid. "Open your mouth," she commands harshly, breaking the seal on the glass vial.

I stare at it, then I back up as far as my restraints will allow, clamping my mouth shut. My steely resolve has totally deserted me. "What is it?"

A gloating, smug smile slinks across her face. "Insurance."

"No! I'm pregnant! What is it?"

I see her wince at the reminder that I'm carrying Max's babies. Of all the things I could have said, I'm sure that was the least helpful.

Tilting her head, she hits me with her smug, cat-like smile. "Drink it, and you'll see Max. Don't drink it… I'll tell him you said goodbye."

My whole body sags knowing I haven't got a leg to stand on. Once again Monica has turned the tables, wielding her power over me with a mighty force. I have no choice. As crazy as she is, and against all logic, I'm going to have to put every ounce of faith in this woman.

"Fuck!" I briefly close my eyes, resigning myself to whatever lies ahead, and then I take a deep breath. Tilting my head back, I reluctantly open my mouth. The liquid tastes like shit and slides down my throat with an acrid burn. I cough and splutter but immediately feel every ounce of energy draining from my body. My eyelids and limbs begin to feel like lead weights as my knees buckle underneath me. The last thing I feel is the sharp pain of the handcuffs wrenching at my wrists as I collapse in a heap on the hard floor.

~

"Arrgh." Inhaling a deep breath, I slowly begin to peel my eyes open.

The air smells dusty, leaving a funny taste in my mouth. My eyes struggle to open, they resist so much I have to raise my eyebrows to give them a hand.

I feel groggy and lifeless, my limbs feeling heavy, and a distant unidentifiable noise confuses my brain even further. *What the hell is that?*

Even before I'm fully awake, I'm aware that I'm lying on my side on a hard, cold surface. As my sight focuses on a leg, and then the cute little tattoo of a bumble bee on the ankle, recognition spikes a surge of fear in my belly. *Monica!*

Panic has me sitting up in a rush, banging my head on a hard wooden object. I'm disoriented. As I lift my hands, I'm surprised to see them handcuffed together and then all the pieces start to fit together in my brain.

My wrists are painfully raw and bleeding. I'm on the floor of a tall, narrow, windowless room. The air is dry and dusty, the walls are plain and rough, and the wooden floorboards groan with antiquity.

"Glad you could join us. Get up!" Monica walks toward me, kicking the bottom of my foot. "Get up. I haven't got all day."

Rubbing my head, I scramble to my feet still dizzy from whatever it was she made me drink to knock me out. "Where are we?"

I look around, coughing as the disturbed dust tickles my throat, but there's nothing distinguishing to give me any clue as to where I am. Apart from a dim, free hanging bulb dangling from an old-fashioned cord from the ceiling, a dark brown light switch, which looks like something from the nineteen twenties, and the small, plain, wooden table I had banged my head on, the room is sparse, save for a dark heavy curtain at the far end.

"I like what you've done with the place," I grumble sarcastically, brushing the dirt and dust off my shorts. "Where the hell are we?"

I freeze when a groan coming from behind the dark curtain at the far end of the room triggers my synapses. My heart leaps in my chest. "Max!"

Pushing past Monica, I race to the curtain and pull it back. Max is lying naked on a low metal cot. Tears of relief fill my eyes but my heart breaks at the sight of his battered and bruised body lying helpless before me. Sinking to my knees, I take his hand in both of mine, bringing it to my lips. "Thank God you're alive!"

He looks so vulnerable and weak. He's semi-conscious, half covered under a stained, white sheet, drenched in sweat, and muttering indecipherable words as he jerks and twitches in his sleep.

"Don't leave me," he mumbles, with a deep anxious frown creasing his brow.

Those words chill me to the bone. I don't know whether he knows I'm here, or whether his mind has taken him back to that eight-year-old little boy struggling to save his mother from the wreckage. Either way he's in pain, he needs help.

"Max! I'm here, my love. I'm here. You're going to be okay, I promise. I won't leave you." A pang of guilt creeps over me. I can't promise him anything yet.

Squeezing his hand, I stroke his forehead which seems to calm him. The dark circles under his eyes and the deep hollows in his cheeks frighten me. He's burning up with a fever and he looks under nourished, pale, and very ill. Fear for his safety, curdles my stomach.

"What did you do to him?" I ask, my voice strangled by my tears.

Running my fingers through his hair, they catch on a clump of dried blood matting his hair on the right side of his head. As my eyes scan his body, I see his left eye is swollen shut, his ribs and chest are covered in bruises which should have faded long ago, and his breathing is very laboured and shallow.

I look over my shoulder at Monica. I'm angry she's put him through all this, he doesn't deserve it. "How could you do this?"

She looks at me like it wasn't her fault. "*They* beat the shit out of him, not me! If it wasn't for me he'd be dead."

Anxiously turning back to Max, I survey his cuts and bruises. "Jesus, Monica, he could be bleeding internally, he needs to go to the hospital."

Squeezing his hand in both of mine, I raise it so I can kiss his bloodied knuckles, then I lean down and kiss his M.F. tattoo. I can hear Monica huffing and tutting behind me.

"You can take him to the hospital when I get what I want."

Her cold, selfish response boils my blood. "Monica, look at him! He's in pain! He could have an infection. He could be bleeding internally. We need to get him to the hospital. Right now!"

"And that's just what they're waiting for, you stupid bitch! If they find me, I'm dead. And if you don't help me, so is he!"

She returns to pacing the confines of the narrow room. I study her for a moment. She seems to have zoned out again, probably listening to the little voices in her fucked-up head. I've never met a more complicated individual in all my life. I've spent many hours trying to figure her out, but I don't think I'd ever truly understand what makes her tick. Crazy, delusional psychopath doesn't come close. Even a top Harley Street psychiatrist would struggle to peel her complicated layers back.

I hate her for everything she's done to me, but most of all, I hate her for putting Max in danger just to save her own worthless skin. "Why?..." My voice breaks. These last weeks have been agony not knowing if I'd ever see him again, but seeing him like this kills me. "Why would you do this to him? You must have known this would never work. ...Jesus, Monica, I thought you loved him? How could you put him in danger like this?"

She stops pacing and looks at me with a cold, hard, unyielding glare. But as her eyes move from mine over to Max, they soften. I can see that even she doesn't have an answer for that. This clearly wasn't how she expected this to work out. God knows what she *did* expect, but this obviously wasn't it.

When her eyes return to mine they're cold and threatening. "Well? You've seen him. Are you going to help me or not?"

What choice do I have? "I'll do it. But... You asked me if you could trust me... You can. Despite everything you've done to me, I'm prepared to help you. But how can I trust you?"

Her lips curl into that annoying cat-like smile. "I guess we'll both be wondering if we can trust each other, won't we?"

That wasn't the answer I was hoping for but she's right, only time will tell.

"But how will I get Sylvie to give me the money without her telling anyone or calling the police?"

She shrugs and tilts her head. "That's your problem. But remember, if you fuck this up and the shit hits the fan, and I don't get my money and my freedom, you can kiss goodbye to him. Forever."

The weight of responsibility hangs heavy on my shoulders. My belly churns and the deep breaths I'm taking don't seem to have any oxygen in them. Everything depends on me being able to pull this off. I don't even know where we are, I have no choice but to do as she says and hope that it all goes to plan.

She may be crazy, but she's got it all worked out and so far, she's cleverly managed to evade not only the police, but also these dangerous people she's entangled herself with. She's like a cockroach. Her resilience is astonishing.

With surprising calm, I level my eyes on hers. "I'll do what you want because I want Max home safely. But once this is done, if you come anywhere near my family again, I swear to God, Monica, I'll fucking kill you myself."

She sneers at me like I've said something amusing. I continue to glare at her, sure in the knowledge that I mean every single word. If I thought I could take her wearing these handcuffs, I'd gladly do it now.

My heart leaps in my chest as I feel Max squeezing my hand. I turn to him, wiping my tears against my sleeve, then I lean down to gently kiss his lips. "I'm here, Max. Please hold on. I'm going to bring you home, I promise. I love you so much."

His eyes remain closed under his heavy frown, but he squeezes my hand again, and then I feel the tugging pain of my hair being yanked backwards, forcing my head back and knocking me off my feet.

It all happened so fast, and the liquid slid down my throat before I could even try to expel it.

"No!... Please..."

SHE SAID, 'WE'

I wake with a dry mouth and a throbbing head. My eyes open to something swinging a few inches above my face, it makes me flinch and recoil until I realise it's a small round compass dangling on the end of a lanyard, hanging off the hand rail.

The strong smell of a diesel engine and chemical toilet pervades my nostrils causing my stomach to roll. I'm back on the boat.

I'm lying flat on my back on the floor of the cockpit. My hands are now free of the cuffs. My wrists are painful from the red raw bands of bleeding, broken skin where they had rubbed and pinched relentlessly. A small piece of white paper lies on my chest. I sit up and unfold it.

Take the cell phone.
I'll call you Sunday at 9pm to arrange the exchange.
Be ready. Come ALONE!
If I get my money and leave freely, I'll give you Max's location.
I'll be watching you.
If you involve anyone else you'll never see Max again.
Don't fuck it up!

My belly churns as I process Monica's demands. I feel sick. What if he can't hold on that long? Max looked so weak, what if he can't survive until tomorrow?

What if?... No! Stop it. I have to get back to the yacht and speak to Sylvie, there's no time to lose.

Staggering to my feet, I shove the phone Monica left me into my bra. Unsteadily, I head to the back deck and climb my way up onto the pier. The boat isn't moored in the same place as before and it takes me a minute to gather my bearings.

My legs are shaking and weak, I feel sluggish from whatever it was Monica had drugged me with. Glancing at my watch as I stagger along the pier back to the yacht, the painful, bleeding ring of broken flesh from the handcuffs, stings as my watch rubs against it. It's two in the afternoon, I've been gone for four hours.

"Shit!" Cole and John will be frantic. What the fuck am I going to tell them?

The yacht looms large as I approach but thankfully, I can't see anyone wandering around on deck. Shoving my hands into my pockets, I run up the gangway. If I can get to my cabin unnoticed, I can change into a long sleeved t-shirt. God knows how I'm going to explain the marks on my wrists, I need to cover them up.

Racing through the salon, I head for the stairs.

"Vivienne! Goddammit! Where the hell have you been? We've been looking everywhere for you. And why the hell haven't you answered your phone?"

Cole's agitated voice stops me abruptly in my tracks and I break out in a cold sweat. I'm so close to my cabin but I can feel his eyes burning into my back. *What do I do? Shit!* Taking a deep breath, I arrange a nonchalant expression, then slowly turn to face him.

His angry eyes immediately widen on me. "What the fuck happened to you?" His now anxious eyes search my face. I don't understand why he's looking at me like that, and I don't know what to say. He marches toward me then holds me by the tops of my arms, staring down at me with concern and a certain amount of shock.

"I'm fine! I just… I just wanted to be by myself." Internally, I kick myself for being so useless at lying, I sound like a stuttering fool.

His eyes are trained on my cheek, then he reaches up, softly touching the side of my face. My eyes dubiously follow the movement of his hand and when he pulls it away from my cheek, I see blood on his fingers.

Reflexively, I reach my own hand up to feel it for myself. My cheekbone is wet and painful to touch, and now I have blood on my fingers too. *How did I cut my face?* I can only assume that I hit my face when I passed out from the drug Monica had given me.

Cole's eyes widen even more. "What the fuck?" And then a deep frown invades his brow. Grabbing my raised arm, I see what caused his reaction. The bleeding, broken skin on my wrist.

His angry eyes search mine then he reaches down pulling my other hand from my pocket. I squirm under his scrutiny, knowing I have no feasible excuse for these marks or the wound on my cheek.

Shaking his head in disbelief he surveys both my wrists. "Vivienne. What the fuck happened to you?"

I stare up at him, frantically trying to think of a reasonable answer. "I… Um, I…" Words fail me and I squirm under the intensity of his glare. "Just leave me alone." I try to pull away from him, but he tightens his grip, stopping me from leaving.

His concerned eyes darken and narrow on me. "No, no, no, Vivienne. Uh-uh," he says, with determined anger hardening his jaw. "You don't go missing for four hours and then come back like this, without an explanation. We've been going out of our minds searching for you. Where the hell have you been?"

Cole's angry, anxious eyes search mine waiting for a response. When I don't proffer one, he huffs out a deep sigh, then releases my arms and takes my hand. Without a word, he hastily walks me down to my cabin and through to the bathroom where he lifts me at the waist and sits me up on the side by the sink. "Stay," he says, like he's talking to a dog. I have no choice but to do as I'm told while my mind tries to conjure up a reasonable excuse.

Running the taps, he searches in the cupboards for the first aid kit. Then he dampens some cotton wool, stands between my legs, dabbing gently at the cut on my cheek, cleaning all the blood away. His angry frown deepens casting a shadow over his crystal blue eyes as they focus on my wound. His jaw is clenching like mad, but his touch is soft and gentle.

He's standing so close, I can't help but stare at him. His scent is different to Max's scent, but clean, pleasant, and soothing all the same. His minty breath blows across my face as he huffs out the occasional sigh, shaking his head in disbelief.

Every now and then his eyes flick to mine. He's angry with me but I can also see the concern contained within them. Max would look at me that way when he knew I was trying to hide something from him.

My belly churns into an anxious knot. I don't have much time. I need to speak to Sylvie, but I don't know what to tell Cole.

"This might sting a little," he says, before dabbing some antiseptic over the wound on my cheek. It makes me flinch. "Sorry," he says, softly. "It's not too bad, it won't need stitching."

He lifts my hands to look at my wrists. I resist, trying to pull my arms free, but he glares at me until I relent. Holding my trembling hands, palms up, he looks down at them shaking his head. "Jesus, these look bad." Gently removing my watch, he lays it on the side. "So… Are you going to tell me what's going on, Vivienne?" he asks, arching a brow at me. His expression is stern but his attention to my wrists couldn't be kinder as he gently dabs antiseptic on the chaffed and bleeding wounds. As gentle as he is being, I flinch, stifling a whimper. It stings like hell.

"I'm sorry. I'll need to bandage these."

As he does so, he hits me with another concerned frown.

"Well?" When I don't respond, he takes a deep breath, huffing out an exasperated sigh.

My brain urgently tries to come up with a decent answer that won't provoke a million questions, but so far, nothing convincing has popped into my head.

I want to tell him what happened today. I want to tell him his brother is alive and needs his help. I need his help. I've been in this position before, keeping secrets and telling lies, trying to handle everything on my own. I'm shit at it. I almost got myself killed the last time. I want to tell him, but I couldn't bear it if anything went wrong.

Once he's finished securing the bandages around my wrists, he rests his palms on my thighs, flicking his eyes up to mine and locking me into an intense stare. "Are you going to tell me?"

I look away. I've never been able to resist those eyes.

"Okay," he sighs.... "I'll tell you what I think shall I?"

I squirm and fidget.

"Look at me, Vivienne."

He patiently waits for me to face him again, then he holds both my bandaged wrists up in front of my face and hits me with a hard frown, clenching his jaw. "These are bondage marks. Either you've been getting it on with a Dominant behind Max's back, or you've been restrained by force. Either way, I think you owe me an explanation."

I flinch, but his penetrating eyes searching mine, force me to look at him. I begin to squirm under his intensity as I battle the decision to come clean or remain silent.

His voice is soft, but I can see the deep concern bubbling away under the surface of his cool, hard exterior. "Why didn't you answer your phone?" His grip tightens on my forearms when I try to pull away. "Sasha said you left with a rucksack, where is it?" I blush, then break eye contact and look away as tears pool in my eyes. "Vivienne... I can't help you if you won't tell me what's going on."

"I can't!" It just blurts out of me in frustration. I'm angry with myself for breaking down, I don't want to cry, but today has been an extraordinary day and I can't get the images of Max looking so vulnerable out of my head.

Releasing my arms, he brushes the tears from my cheeks with the pads of his thumbs, then he lifts my chin up, sighing deeply. "It's Monica, isn't it?"

He bends down to try and capture my gaze. I hesitantly look up at him. He knows. Or at least he thinks he does which is just as bad. I'm going to have to tell him. Deep down I really want to, I can't do this alone.

"I need to speak to Sylvie… then we'll talk."

He flinches, narrowing his eyes. I can see he's unsure of why I would need to call Sylvie, but I know he's trying to work it out, and I'm sure it's only a matter of time until he does. He must be aware of the S.R.F fund.

His brow twitches into a low frown then he lifts me down from the side and lets me walk past him out of the bathroom. I feel his eyes on me the whole time.

Standing by the bed with my back toward him, I wait for him to leave.

"I'd better call John, the poor bastard's still out looking for you," he says, walking to the door.

I immediately tense up. "Please! Don't say anything to John."

He stops and turns to face me with a soft, concerned look in his eyes. "It'll be okay, Vivienne. We'll get him back… you and me, together." He doesn't wait for me to respond, closing the door behind him.

My throat shrinks, my belly rolls, and tears flood my eyes. Reaching for Max's photograph, I clutch it to my chest. Seeing him so vulnerable today frightens me. What if he's so badly injured that he doesn't survive? What if we're too late to save him? *You haven't got time for this! Make the bloody call!*

Before leaving my cabin, I quickly change into a long sleeved top, then head to the office on the bridge to make my call to Sylvie. I'm grateful no one is here, I need to speak freely, I don't want to be overheard.

As I dial her number, I'm overcome with nerves.

"Hello? Is that you, Sasha?"

Sylvie's soft, frail voice makes my heart twinge. I've been so absorbed in my own sorrow, and obsessed with finding Max, that I haven't even considered how Sylvie has been coping these last few weeks. I should have been there for her. I should have been more considerate. The poor woman has just buried her husband.

"Sylvie, it's Vivienne. How are you?"

"Oh, sweetheart, how lovely to hear your voice."

Her fragile voice melts my heart.

"I'm fine. Jan and Vinnie have been taking great care of me. And Olivia's coming over next week, she's bringing Mason to stay for a few days. We thought we'd spend some time at the chateau, I'd love for you to join us. William always loved it there at this time of year…"

Her voice trails off as the sadness overwhelms her.

"But, enough about me," she sniffles, "how are you? Have you heard anything from the police?"

Tears bunch against my lashes and an anxious knot builds in my chest. "Sylvie, are you alone at the moment? I need to ask you something."

There's a slight pause before she answers. "Yes dear, I'm alone. But wait a moment while I close the door."

I hear her place the receiver down and then a few seconds later she returns slightly out of breath. "Okay, go ahead."

"Sylvie… I… I saw Max today…"

The sharp intake of air as Sylvie gasps in shock, prickles my skin and her strangled cry chokes me up. "He's alive?" she asks tearfully.

"Yes. He's injured, but he's alive. I saw him, and I talked to him briefly. He squeezed my han..." The lump in my throat cuts my words off as my heightened emotion sends more burning tears to my eyes.

"Oh, thank God!" she says, laughing and crying simultaneously. "When is he coming home?"

I take a moment to compose myself, swallowing to clear my voice. "Sylvie… Monica's got him hidden away somewhere, I don't know where. She drugged me and took me to see him so I'd know that he was still alive, but she wants money… A lot of money. And I need to ask if you—"

"Whatever she wants, give it to her," she says, without hesitation. "I want my son back." Her harsh voice waivers with a mixture of emotion and complete determination. Tears drip down my cheeks and I sigh with relief that it's that simple.

"Thank you, Sylvie."

"I'll get Vinnie to bring the—"

"No!" I interrupt in a panic. "She explicitly warned me not to involve anyone else. Nobody can know, except me and you. She's got herself mixed up with some very dangerous people. They wouldn't think twice about hurting Max."

"But, Vivienne, you can't—"

"Sylvie, our safest option is to give her what she wants and to get him back as quickly as possible. If these other people find him, or her, I don't know what they'll do. But if they scare Monica, then they sure as hell scare me."

The line goes silent for a moment.

"Vivienne… I don't want you to put yourself or the babies in danger. Max wouldn't allow it. I love my son and I want him back, but it's too risky to do this on your own."

I purse my lips and fight the tears that are now burning in my eyes. "I love him, Sylvie. The risk would be not doing as she says."

I choose not to tell her that I'm going to involve Cole, because I haven't entirely made my mind up yet. Involving him may be the biggest mistake I'll ever make, or it could be my best option.

"What do you need me to do? I can transfer the money now but I'll need the details."

"No. She wants cash. Five million in hundred dollar bills in France by midnight tomorrow. She's going to call me tomorrow evening at nine p.m. with the details of the exchange."

There's another long pause. I can hear her moving about and then she speaks with a lowered voice.

"Okay, I can get the money transported by air within a couple of hours. I'll have to call in a few favours, but… leave it with me. The money will be on my personal jet at Renard Airport later on tonight. It's about thirty kilometres from the yacht. I'll email you the address and the pass code for the secure hold, and I'll speak to Bruce at the airfield, he can unload it for you. He has transport vehicles there too, if you need them. Hell, if she wants the jet she can have it. And don't worry, Vivienne, Bruce won't ask you any questions and he reports only to me."

I'm stunned at how efficiently organised she is. The family's contingency for this type of thing bears the hallmark of a well-oiled mission from MI6.

"But Vivienne, how does she plan to make her escape?"

"I… I don't know… All I know is, as long as she gets the money and isn't followed, she'll give me the location to find Max."

"And you trust her?"

My stomach tightens. "…No. I don't. Not one bit. But what choice do we have? The only thing I'm clinging on to with any certainty, is that she's put herself at risk to save Max from those other people. They're vicious. They'll kill her for that if they catch up with her. She's giving us the chance to save him, they wouldn't. And as crazy as it sounds, she reached out to me… this must be killing her."

"Then you give her what she wants and walk away. Once she's gone with the money you call the police and give them Max's location. I wouldn't put it past Monica to be playing both sides. Don't do anything on your own once you've delivered the money. Promise me, Vivienne."

I close my eyes and nod even though she can't see me. The culmination of stress and fear and now finally hope, has left me emotionally exhausted.

"Vivienne?"

"Yes, I promise… Thank you, Sylvie. Thank you for doing this."

"He's my son…"

I hear the pain in her voice. She's tried to maintain her strong demeanour throughout our conversation but she, like me, is struggling to hold it together. I promise to call her as soon as I hear from Monica, and then we say goodbye.

My belly churns as I replace the phone in its cradle. I know I can trust Sylvie to help me without involving anyone else, but now I have the daunting task of having to face Cole.

I'm going to have to make my mind up whether or not I should tell him the truth. Whatever I decide, I need to do it quickly.

When I walk out onto the sun deck, Cole and John are obviously discussing me when their conversation stops abruptly, and they both stare at me with deep frowns on their faces.

Lowering my head, I let my hair fall over the wound on my cheek. I don't want John asking me about it until I know what excuse I'm going to use for having it. Keeping my eyes to the floor, I sheepishly make my way to one of the sofas under a parasol. I'm boiling hot in this long sleeved t-shirt, so sitting in the shade is a necessity.

John leaves with a polite nod in my direction. I feel terrible, I should have apologised to him for worrying him like that, but I haven't got a clue what to tell him. I fidget nervously in my seat as Cole pulls another chair over, handing me a bottle of water.

"Here, you look like you need a drink. I could get you something stronger if you want."

"No, water's fine, thanks." A glass of wine would go down a treat right now, but I won't take a chance with the babies. I'm still worried about that drug Monica forced me to take. I can only hope it hasn't harmed them.

Cole leans forward in his chair, resting his forearms on his knees. I keep my head down waiting for the inquisition to begin. When he doesn't speak, I glance up at him. His eyes are firmly fixed on mine, waiting with a calm patience I wasn't expecting.

"I'm sorry… I didn't mean to worry you, or John." I look

away and fiddle nervously with the hem of my shorts, unsure of what to say. What the hell am I going to tell him?

"Who did this to you, Vivienne?" His voice is soft and raspy.

I flick my eyes up. His eyes are trained on the cut on my cheek, but as they slide over to mine, I quickly cast my gaze down to my fidgeting hands. My wrists throb under the bandages poking out from my sleeves, a vivid reminder of what I've been through today.

His soft voice cuts through the awkward silence. "Whatever you think of me, Vivienne, I'm not an idiot. I know something bad happened to you today, and unless Mike has grown some balls and tried to handcuff you to his bed, I'd say you had the misfortune of meeting Monica today… Am I right?"

Wrestling with my conscience, my brain says, 'Tell him. No, don't tell him. Yeah, tell him. You can't do this on your own.' Puffing out a deep, frustrated sigh, I resign myself to making a decision. One that could change everything.

"You're right… I did see Monica today."

Cole's eyes close, he looks physically pained by my confession. And now I'm frightened I've made the wrong decision. The anger in his eyes when they open is intense, turning his bright blue eyes into dark, stormy pools of burning rage. His hands ball up into tight, white knuckled fists, and the sinews in his arms pull the muscles into hard flexing mounds under his skin. He's riled and angry, but he tries to rein it in, suppressing his anger before he speaks.

"You should have come to me before trying to tackle her on your own, she's dangerous. Jesus, Vivienne, you know that!"

Anxious butterflies hit my stomach. "I know! And you're right, but I couldn't wait for you. She left me a note to meet her at pier four, I had no time. It was then or never, I couldn't take the chance."

I blurt it out as if babbling at high speed would make the stupidity of my actions any less ridiculous. In hindsight,

Monica was on her own and could quite easily have been overpowered had Cole or John been with me as back up. They could have followed us to Monica's hiding place, so yes, it was foolish to have gone on my own.

He drags his hands through his hair, using the same familiar expression Max does when he's trying to control his frustration. I begin to feel sorry for him, he's trying to help me but I'm too scared to ask.

Tears prick my eyes as the images of Max's weak and vulnerable body come flooding into my brain, twisting my heart into a painful knot.

"…I saw Max."

"What? Where?" I now have Cole's full attention.

"I don't know. I got the note from Monica this morning. She told me to meet her at pier four. She had a boat waiting. When I got on board she cuffed me to the handrail. She told me she had Max hidden away somewhere, but she wanted money for his release. I demanded to see him, I needed to know that he was still alive before I agreed to help her."

Cole's brow lowers into an angry frown as his lips twitch into a sneer. "Help her? She doesn't deserve your help! Where the fuck is she? And where's Max?"

I nervously look around as his raised voice rings out. Thankfully, we're still alone.

"I don't know. Please, Cole. Please calm down."

He does, and his posture begins to soften. "But I thought you said you saw him?"

"I did…but I don't know where he is. She sailed us away from the marina. She drugged me and I woke up in this dark, narrow space. Max was there. He's badly injured, but he's alive." Hanging my head, I begin to sob. I'm so scared for him.

"Hey, come on. I've got you." I feel Cole's warmth pressed against my side as he pulls me into a tight hug, rubbing his hand up and down my back. Leaning into his chest, the floodgates open and I burst into tears.

As Cole rocks me in his arms, I gradually stop crying, then I tell him every detail of what happened today, and of the dangerous people Monica has involved herself with. John had already told him about the 'Infinite Black' tattoo, and its meaning. He seemed to know these were very dangerous people.

I feel safe in Cole's arms, but I'm nervous that I've made a huge mistake involving him.

"Do you remember anything at all about where she took you, or how you got there?"

"No. Whatever she gave me made me pass out, and when I woke up we were in this tall, narrow room with no windows. It was fairly warm and dry and old looking. Come to think of it, I don't remember seeing a door."

Pulling away from Cole's chest, I pat my cheeks dry, trying desperately hard to remember anything else about that room.

"There was a draft coming from somewhere, I remember feeling it against my face when I moved to the end of the room where Max was. And there seemed to be some faint natural light coming into the room above Max's bed, but I couldn't see where it was coming from. I know there were no windows, at least none that I could see, and there was only a very dim overhead light bulb."

I look up at Cole in the hope that my feeble description will spark an idea in his brain, but his expression tells me that's not going to happen.

Absently pushing a wayward strand of hair away from my face, his preoccupied eyes follow the movement of his hand, then, as his fingers gently graze my cheek, the intimacy has me locking eyes with him.

My breath catches in my throat. For a moment neither of us speaks and the familiar look in his crystal blue eyes takes me back to a moment Max and I had shared in Rome on our first date. Even the butterflies make an appearance.

I can't get used to how alike they are. Cole shares such identical expressions with his brother. Expressions that evoke exactly the same response, and yet to me, he's still a stranger.

I look away as heat invades my cheeks. I've got to stop reacting to him this way it's embarrassing. When I glance up at him, I see his brow lowering and I feel him leaning away from me. I've made him uncomfortable.

"What about smells or sounds?"

"No, I don't remember anything else. Just the diesel smell of the boat and… Wait! There was a sound. A distinct sound. I remember hearing something, like a bird maybe? It was a brrr sound followed by a cawing sound. But I can't remember if I was on the boat, or in the room when I heard it. Or maybe I'm just confusing myself." I sigh with frustration, I wish I could remember something that would help.

Cole throws his arm over the back of the sofa. He's changed his position, so I turn toward him and cross my legs, resting my elbows on my inner thighs.

"You left the marina at approximately ten a.m. and returned at two p.m. so within those four hours, how long were you at this place?"

Gazing down at my hands, I give it some thought. "I can't be sure how long I was there because she had drugged me, but I would say I was awake there for about half an hour or so."

His frown deepens and I see he's mapping something out in his head. After a few moments he reaches down and takes my hand. The warm softness of his skin against mine is comforting.

"Vivienne, if she's running from these people and she's come to you for help, that means she's on her own, like completely on her own. That's good. We can take her down."

"No! That's not right, she said, 'we.' She said, 'we stole him back.' She must have someone helping her."

"Then why did she come to you? That's totally out of character for her. I still think we can take her."

I reach out and squeeze his hand looking up at him with pleading eyes. "Cole, I've told you because I had to, but I don't want to jeopardize Max's safety. Sylvie doesn't care about the money and I don't care about Monica. I just want Max home safely. Please don't do anything that will put him at risk. Please! I beg you!"

His concerned eyes search mine, it's clear he's in conflict.

He wants to take his revenge for Charlie, but I can't let him do that if it means Max could be lost to me forever. I don't trust Monica, if she gets a whiff of Cole, Vinnie, or John she'll bail, and I can't take that chance. I can't let that happen.

His troubled gaze lingers on my face. Squeezing his hand a little tighter, I wait for the uncertainty to leave his eyes. He takes a long, deep breath then offers me a reassuring smile.

"Okay."

I sag, as the anxious breath I was holding sighs out of me.

"What about John? Did you tell him anything?"

He shakes his head. "No. Only that you tripped and fell." He pulls the sleeve of my t-shirt down to cover my bandage. "I don't know how we're going to explain these."

My belly churns. He's right, they're so obvious. Slipping my hand out of Cole's, I miss the warmth and the feel of his strong hand wrapped around mine, but I've got to stop using him as a substitute for Max. The loss I feel inside draws me toward him, but it's not fair, or appropriate. "So, what do we do now?"

He starts to rise. "We should go down and take a look at that boat, if it's still there we may be able to find some clues."

"No!" Panic grips my chest. "If she sees you there, she'll know I've told you. We can't take that chance."

His brow furrows, I can tell he's itching to go and have a look, but that could spoil everything. I know how frustrating it is to sit and wait, but that's all we can do.

"Please, Cole. Please don't do anything that will hurt Max. I beg you."

Dragging a hand through his hair, he hits me with a pair of frustrated eyes. "Well then, I guess we just wait for her to contact you and see where it takes us."

His expression hardens as a deep frown darkens his eyes.

"But know this, Vivienne. Max would never allow you to put yourself in harm's way, and I feel the same. Whatever she has planned, and wherever she arranges to meet up with you, I *will* be there. I promise you, I'm not going to let you down, but I will be there to protect you. You can't trust her."

I nod, realising that now he knows, it would be impossible for me to go it alone. But inside I'm relieved. I've tried to be strong but Monica always manages to catch me off guard.

She's smart, and despite her insanity she's always been one step ahead. I couldn't bear it if all this is just an elaborate plan to fleece the family for five million without any intention of giving Max back to us. That's unthinkable.

"Hey. You okay?"

"What? Sorry, I was just, I'm fine."

"Listen, how about you go and get some rest, then we'll go out for dinner tonight and just blow this off for a little while. You look like you could use the distraction."

I sigh deeply. "Yes, I think you're right." Unfolding my legs, I rise from my seat but then I pause and turn to face him. "You promise you won't do anything while I'm asleep?"

His sad eyes search mine as a small smile twists into his mouth. "I promise. I won't do anything to hurt Max. Get some rest, you look exhausted."

Cole's right, I feel exhausted and weary and way over my head with Monica. Why is my life always so intense and dangerous?

Life before Max had been challenging enough. Greg Taylor had all but ruined my childhood. My mother's addictions and reluctance to do anything about them had made growing up a dark and unhappy affair, and the death of my father on my sixteenth birthday just solidified the feelings of solitude and hopelessness.

The way my luck had been going up to that point, the light at the end of the tunnel would be an oncoming train!

But despite events that would break the will of most people, I had somehow managed to forge ahead and plough through the darkness. I met Lucy and Mike, both of whom gave me strength, love, and the ability to become hopeful again. Something inside me never really wanted to give up, so I didn't.

And then I met Max. The love of my life, the man of my dreams. The man of any woman's dreams. He loved me with such a mighty force that it completely eradicated every hurtful thing that had ever happened in my life. Freeing me from the pain of my past and dazzling me with a bright and hopeful future.

But with his love, came Monica. And because he'd chosen me over her, Monica's rage and jealousy was unleashed. A tenacious woman with an axe to grind, she became my nemesis.

I've somehow survived both her attempts to snuff me out, but now, in the most absurd of twists, if I have opened the gates of hell by involving Cole and anything happens to Max because I haven't done as she asked, I'll die anyway from a broken heart, and it will be all my own doing.

INTERLUDE

"I've done all my thinking, Vivienne. I know what I want. You're my once in a lifetime love and I want you, exactly as you are... What do you want, baby?"

"You... I want you, Max. I need you."

I wake to the sound of my own voice and the dull thud of arousal in my sex. My dreams are so vivid, so real. My skin is alive with a buzz of anticipation. The smell of him taunts me, I can still taste him.

The crashing disappointment when I realise it was only another dream, depresses me. Turning to my side and curling myself around Max's pillow, I succumb to the tears that I have no control over, and no desire to stop.

Anxiety and hunger vie for attention in my stomach. I haven't eaten since breakfast and I hate myself for not keeping my nourishment up for the sake of our babies. Cole had suggested going out to dinner. I don't really feel like it, but I know I should eat, and I need to keep an eye on Cole. I don't want him doing anything that could affect Max's safety before Monica calls.

Looking down at my watch, I see the bandage around my wrist. I'd almost forgotten about those.

Hauling myself upright, I wander through to the bathroom

to get ready. The cut on my cheek is easily covered with makeup, but apart from a long sleeved t-shirt, which I wore earlier today, I only have strappy dresses and tops in my wardrobe, in this heat that's all you need.

To disguise the red cuff marks around my wrists, I remove the bandages, apply some antiseptic cream, and cover them with bangles and bracelets. It's not the most comfortable form of disguise but it does the job.

Folding Mike's washed and ironed t-shirt, I place it in my bag so I can return it to him should we end up at his bar tonight.

Cole is waiting patiently up on deck. Looking very casual and sexy in his fitted, black, open necked shirt hanging loosely outside his well-cut pale grey jeans. He looks gorgeous. His wavy, collar length, black hair surrounds his tanned and chiselled face and the sight of him makes my heart flutter with want that it should be Max sitting there.

As I approach him, his dazzling blue eyes look up at me with that familiar heart-melting smile. I almost stop just to be able to gaze at it in its fullness.

"Vivienne? Everything okay?" he asks, oblivious to the pain he causes me every time I look at him.

"Yes, everything's fine." My forced smile seems to have been sufficient.

Striding toward me, his eyes trawl over my plain, but pretty summer dress, taking a while to return to my face. "You look beautiful," he smiles, leaning in to kiss me on the cheek. I blush and smile back, his lips are soft, and he smells amazing.

Reaching down, he takes both my hands in his. "And I like what you've done with your bangles, very resourceful."

I blush and jangle them, regretting it instantly. "Ow!"

He shakes his head at me still smiling, while I burst out laughing at my own stupidity.

"Well, that's better," he grins, "it's good to hear you laugh. Shall we?" He sticks out his elbow for me to link arms with him, then we head off to dinner.

As we walk in the warm night air, the smells and sounds

from the busy bars and restaurants bring the promenade to life. My empty stomach grumbles loudly with hunger.

"Was that you?" Cole asks, smirking down at me.

I blush and curse my stomach for being so un-ladylike. "I'm afraid so."

He grins, patting my hand and squeezing my arm into his side. "Well then, it's just as well I'm taking you out for something to eat."

We walk to the main street where John is waiting in a black Range Rover. I feel a bit nervous as I haven't spoken to him since Cole arrived, but he puts me at ease with a warm smile as he opens my door. "Evening, Ma'am."

Once we're settled in, John glides away from the kerb, heading out of the hustle and bustle of town. We appear to be driving along the coast road, so I gaze out at the calm waters of the ocean, enjoying the last crest of orange sunlight shimmering across the horizon before it sets for the evening.

"Where are you taking me?"

"Somewhere nice," he replies, without elaborating further.

After a while, John pulls into a car park behind a quaint little restaurant on the beach. The fragrant smell of hibiscus surrounds us as we walk up to the entrance.

The Maître d' shows us to our table on the open terrace covered in twinkly lights, and a stone's throw from the white sandy beach. I can't help but be moved by the amazing view.

"It's beautiful."

"Not even close," Cole murmurs softly. When I look up at him, he's staring down at me with a serious expression that throws me for a moment. With a small shake of his head he then gestures for me to sit down at the candle lit table.

The Maître d' snaps his fingers and a waiter appears with two large menus.

"We'll just have some iced water please, no alcohol," Cole says to the young man.

"Certainly, Sir. I'll be back in a moment to take your order." Smiling politely, he disappears.

"Are you not drinking?" I ask, unfurling my napkin.

He shrugs, unfurling his own. "Ah, no. I figured it wouldn't be fair to drink if you can't."

I raise my eyebrows at his gallant gesture. "Well, I'll be honest with you, there was a time I could probably drink you under the table, but I haven't had any alcohol since I found out I was pregnant, and I think I've become a bit of a lightweight. One drink and I'm anybody's."

Cole pretends to snap his fingers at the waiter. "Could we get a bottle of wine over here?"

I laugh, realising that's the second time I've laughed today. I haven't been able to laugh in such a long time. I don't know why, but I'm surprised that Cole is so much fun. He has a similar sense of humour to Max so it shouldn't really surprise me, but I'd always had him down as a bit of a self-centred shit.

I start to read the menu and then realise it's all fish and seafood. Peering over the top of my menu, I catch his eye with a smirk. "Um, Houston? We have a problem."

Cole's eyebrows raise and he does a double take at my cringing face. "We do? What is it?"

"I can't eat fish. I'm allergic. I'll end up looking like Mick Jagger, or a Puffer fish."

He blinks at me for a moment with a concerned frown. "I'm sorry, I never thought to ask. Come on, we'll eat somewhere else." He begins to rise from his seat so I reach out to stop him.

"No, don't be silly, I'll just have a salad or something."

Slipping me a sideways frown, he continues to rise from his seat, then he walks away from the table toward the Maître d'. They have a short conversation and I notice Cole slipping some cash into the guys hand in one of those secret handshakes, then he saunters back followed by the Maître d'.

"Would Madam care for steak or chicken? The Poulet de Provencal c'est magnifique!" he says, kissing the tips of his fingers as he reaches over to take the menu from my hands.

"The chicken sounds great. Thank you."

Once Cole has ordered our starters and his sea bass, the Maître d' walks away and talks to a waiter who then briskly disappears.

"Cole, I hope you haven't gone to any trouble. I would have been perfectly happy with a salad."

"Nonsense," he scowls, laying his napkin over his lap. "You need some protein. You're too thin and rabbit food will hardly nourish the babies."

I marvel at his thoughtfulness then smile up at him and take a sip of my water. He doesn't know that normally I can eat for England.

"So, tell me about yourself, Cole. I'm afraid my only point of reference for you is what Max has told me, which wasn't a lot, and that night you groped me at the Velvet Lounge."

He stops drinking his water, staring at me wide-eyed and open mouthed. "Pardon me?"

I pinch my lips together to stifle a smirk. He obviously doesn't remember that night, so I decide to have some fun and make him squirm a little.

"Yes, you were a little worse for wear. You groped me at the bar when you rudely barged in front of me to order your drinks. We had words, or rather I had words, you just looked down your nose at me, and then you rather rudely turned your back."

His brow scrunches into a confused frown. "I did?"

"Yes, you did," I giggle. "Then later on that night, when you were completely shit-faced, you barged into me a second time nearly knocking me off my feet. That's when you groped me again and called me sugar-buns."

His frown deepens and I can tell by his expression that he doesn't recall any of it.

"I apologise… You must think I'm a complete asshole." His cheeks flush with embarrassment which makes me smile.

"Well, I don't know you well enough to know if you're a complete arsehole, and at the time I thought you were Max, so I guess that lets you off the hook."

"I'm sorry," he says, shaking his head. "I must have been totally wasted." He looks upset with himself.

A flashback to the night I puked up over some random

guy's shoes makes me smile. "Don't worry, we've all been there."

Our starters arrive, melon for me, crab cakes for Cole. And we eat in silence for a while listening to the melodic tunes of a steel band playing on the beach.

When Cole strikes up a conversation, he surprises me. "Vinnie told me what you did for Max, how you stopped him from hurting himself. It took a lot of guts."

I'm surprised, I didn't realise Cole knew about Max's self-harming. Or his room of guilt. I don't know what to say and I'm confused as to why he brought it up, considering he was the one who instigated Max's self-harming by blaming him for the death of their parents.

Looking down at my plate, I can feel him looking at me but I can't bring myself to acknowledge that memory, not yet.

"You're a strong woman, Vivienne. That's to be admired. Monica is a strong woman, but in all the wrong ways. Her heart is black, yours is quite the opposite."

I blush and push the last piece of melon around on my plate for something to busy myself with. When I finally glance up at him, he looks away, reaching for his water.

"What about you?" I ask hesitantly. "When Monica broke your heart for the second time, what happened to you, I mean, did you ever really get over her?"

His laugh is bitter and sarcastic. "Yeah! Real quick! The day I found out that she'd killed Charlie, was the day any love I still had for her was completely gone."

His jaw clenches as an angry crease invades his brow. "Then she took my brother, which killed my father… Believe me, the feelings I have for that bitch are as far removed from love as you could get."

I feel sorry for him. I know how devastating it is to lose a parent. Cole has lost his son, his father, his adoptive father, and his natural mother. I can't imagine how that feels. But even though he refutes his love for Monica, she was his first love, and I get the feeling he still carries a torch for her somewhere deep inside.

A waiter arrives to take our plates. I find myself staring at Cole's profile. Whether he's the image of Max or not, his masculine beauty can't be denied, nor should it. His handsomeness is a treat for the eyes and should be admired and gazed upon. Besides, mine aren't the only pair of eyes drinking in his handsome face. Every woman in this restaurant has had a sip.

He smirks, slipping me a sideways glance. "Anyone ever tell you it's rude to stare?"

"Huh?" I suddenly realise I am staring. "Sorry. Force of habit I'm afraid. You have his face."

He throws me an indignant frown. "Well, damn. I always thought he had my face."

"What's it like?" I ask, still gazing at him.

"What's what like?"

"Being a twin. What's it like knowing you're not unique?"

He arches an eyebrow with an affronted expression. "Are you trying to hurt my feelings?"

I blush, realising that was a terrible thing to say. "Oh, no. Not at all. It's just, well, you're both separate people, but I know every inch of Max's face and body, and you are exactly the same to look at, you even sound the same. I find that amazing. It's kind of cool if you think about it."

His eyebrow remains arched but his lips tip up in a smile. The smile soon fades and his expression becomes concerned. After a moment our eyes meet, his searching deeply into mine.

"I remind you of him, don't I?"

My smile withers. "Of course," I whisper, looking down at the table. Picking up my fork, I start fidgeting with it in my hands. Cole reaches over and stills them. The heat and softness of his hand on mine is immediately comforting. My skin aches for Max's touch.

"The look on your face when you saw me in the shower, you looked like you'd seen a ghost… I know how deeply you love my brother, and I know how hard it is for you to look at me and see him. I don't want to hurt you like that, Vivienne. I was worried about coming here, I knew you were fragile. I wasn't sure you'd be able to cope."

Looking up at his concerned eyes, I realise I've made a bad call about his character, he really is very kind and very thoughtful.

"It's okay, and I'm sorry I stare at you all the time. It's just, I miss him so much. I don't know, sometimes looking at you helps."

Our eyes lock for a long moment, then I look away. Remembering how I almost kissed him the other night causes my cheeks to heat with embarrassment and I'm grateful to see the waiter returning with our food.

The Maître d' was correct about the chicken, it tasted divine and I ate everything on my plate. After that I ploughed my way through a crème brûlée enjoying every mouthful. I'm aware of Cole staring at me as I scrape every last morsel from the dish.

"You know, I won't tell anyone if you want to lick the bowl."

"Nah, it's okay. I'm full up," I giggle, licking the back of my spoon.

"A woman with a healthy appetite sure is unusual. Most of the women I know are all on a diet."

"Not me, I love my grub."

That reminds me of the night Max had taken me to Rome. He too had been surprised at my willingness to eat, especially as we were on our first date.

An overwhelming sadness weighs heavy in my chest. I've enjoyed my evening, but I feel guilty. This interlude has been just what I needed, but the reality that Max is still lying injured at an unknown location chills me to the bone.

The clock is ticking, and in just over twenty-four hours I hope with all my heart to have Max back where he belongs. But knowing Monica as I do, I fear things may not run as smoothly as I'd like. She's volatile and dangerous, and history proves she can't be trusted.

Tears begin to moisten my eyes but I fight them back. "Cole? Do you think she'll keep her word?"

His expression darkens as he reaches out to take my hand,

rubbing his thumb over the back of it. He takes a long time to answer which worries me. He doesn't trust her, neither do I. But I have to believe somewhere deep inside her, she has some shred of humanity left.

"Vivienne, I'd be lying if I said I understand that woman. Once upon a time she was the sweetest girl with nothing but kindness in her heart. But then, somewhere along the line, she became this dark version of herself. Now she's sick and twisted and for all we know she'll take the money and run. But she went to a lot of trouble to hide Max from those thugs. And to come to you for help? That's not like her… Unless…"

Panic churns my stomach. "Unless what?"

Taking a long breath, he expels a deep sigh. "As much as I hate to admit it, Max was the love of her life." His jaw is clenching madly, his brow lowering over his troubled eyes. Those words have the same effect on me, I feel myself physically wince. I hate remembering that Max and Monica were once a couple, once in love.

"After they split up, I think the only reason she came to me was because, like you, I reminded her of him. That's why she married me. She wanted to make him jealous. I think I always knew it, but I was so fucking in love with her, I chose to ignore it. I think she realises now that she can't keep him, but she can't let anything bad happen to him either. That's love for you. Loving the one you can never have…" Huffing out a bitter laugh, he releases my hand to reach for his water. "It's a killer."

As I witness the pain in his eyes, I realise that even though he'd said he doesn't love her anymore, he's clearly never stopped loving her. And he's still deeply scarred by the fact that Monica had only ever truly loved Max.

"I bet you wish that was a glass of whiskey right now, huh?" As a waiter walks past, I catch his eye. "Could we have a Jack Daniels on the rocks, and a cup of tea, thank you."

"Certainly, Madam." The waiter clears our empty plates then disappears.

Cole narrows his eyes on me. "How do you know what I

drink?"

I smile at him, raising an eyebrow. "It's what Max drinks. You're too alike for it to be anything else."

His lips curl up into a warm smile as he shakes his head. "I hate being that predictable."

He's joking, but underneath his carefree facade, I see the unmistakable hurt of being judged by the standards of his brother. The brother who'd stolen the heart of the woman he'd loved.

I feel sorry for Cole. Growing up as an identical twin but not having the strong character Max had, meant that he'd grown up in his brother's shadow. Losing his parents must have affected him just as deeply as it had affected Max. Cole had blamed Max for their deaths, but maybe the fact that he wasn't there when they died, maybe that had spurned the jealousy and resentment he'd wielded against his brother. Without warning and without being able to say goodbye, his parents had died, he needed someone to blame.

Because of Max's innate fortitude, he'd accepted the blame and dealt with it in his own way. Even after their death, Max wanted to please his parents, so he continued to strive for, and reach, much greater goals than Cole had even bothered to aspire to.

Choosing the path of least resistance seems to have been Cole's modus operandi. He should have been inspired by his brother's strength, but his weakness of character rebelled against it, creating the rift they both perpetuated for far too long.

In a way, Cole was his own worst enemy. And when Monica played them against each other, what chance did he have? She manipulated Cole to get what she wanted. It couldn't have been easy loving a woman whose heart belonged to the brother you wished you were.

Reaching for his hand, I smooth the back of it. "Cole... Monica hurt you, I can see that. But someday a woman who is worthy of you will come along and show you what true love really feels like. And when that happens, none of what Monica did to you will matter anymore."

The look on his face almost brings me to tears. His sad eyes linger on mine then retreat to the table as he slips his hand out from mine in a hurried movement.

I feel like I've over stepped a boundary of some kind. I didn't mean to offend him, but his body language makes me think that's exactly what I've done.

The waiter arrives with my tea, a short crystal tumbler, a bucket of ice, and a bottle of Jack Daniels. Cole makes quick work of icing his glass and pouring himself a large shot, then he throws it back in one go.

I stare at him a little confused. "I'm sorry… I didn't mean to—"

"You didn't," he says, abruptly, pouring another shot.

Before throwing back his second drink, he lowers his glass and looks at me, clenching his jaw. His eyes gaze longingly into mine, locking me into an intensely heated stare that burns right through to my soul. I know I should, but I can't look away. I've missed those eyes and the affect they have on me. Even the v-shaped indentation between his brows creases in exactly the same way. Everything about him is intoxicating. Everything about him is Max. I should know, I'm fully acquainted with every curve and plane of his handsome face.

Disturbed by my own feelings, I shift uncomfortably in my seat and force myself to look away before I begin to lean into him.

"Vivienne… The way you look at me, because I look like Max… He's a lucky guy." He swallows the contents of his glass in one gulp.

After throwing some cash on the table, he rises from his seat. "Come on, let's go and find your friend's bar and have a drink there. I should apologise to him for being such an asshole last night."

His tone of voice and the smile he offers me betrays what I see in his eyes, but I sense he's not prepared to discuss his feelings any further and I need to respect that.

YOU LIED TO ME

Cole's mood in the car is very quiet, almost introvert. I can see his preoccupation with something ticking over in his mind but he doesn't voice his thoughts, he just gazes out of the window. Maybe his feelings for Monica will never go away and I shouldn't keep opening that wound.

John drives us back to the Marina. Cole invites him to join us for a drink. John declines at first but Cole practically forces him to stay. I start to wonder whether Cole invited him so he wouldn't be stuck on his own with me, I still feel like I've upset him in some way.

We walk to the 'Coeur du Mer' for a nightcap. As we enter the bar, the boys take a seat at one of the tables out on the terrace.

"Okay, my treat, what do you boys want?" I ask, removing Mike's t-shirt from my bag and rummaging around for my purse.

"Beer for me please, Ma'am," John answers, taking a seat.

I look over at Cole trying not to smirk. "Jack Daniels?"

He raises an accusatory eyebrow with a cheeky smile. "Actually, no. I'll have a beer. I'm feeling unpredictable tonight."

I smile and shake my head then wander inside toward the

bar.

As I wait to be served, the girl I had seen cleaning the tables here the other day, and who had been very sympathetic toward me when I had thrown up, gives me a beaming smile.

"How are you? Better now I hope." Her warm greeting and smiling eyes remind me of Lucy.

"Yes. Much better thanks. Actually, I wanted to return this to Mike." I hold up Mike's t-shirt.

"Okay, he's on a break, go on up. If it stays down here someone will pinch it."

"Can I order two beers and a lemon tea, it's that table over there." I turn and point to the boys sitting on the terrace. Cole and John are engrossed in a conversation. "I'll be right down." I leave some money on the bar then make my way upstairs.

As I reach Mike's door I can see it's open slightly but I knock and wait. When he doesn't answer I knock again then poke my head around the door. The lights are on but the living room is empty. "Mike? Mike, it's me, Viv. I've brought your t-shirt back."

When I realise he's not here, I decide to pop it on his coffee table and leave him a note. I search in my bag for some paper and a pen, I have a pen but I haven't got anything to write on, so I walk over to the cabinet and open one of the drawers to look for some. The drawer is empty, so I open the cupboard beneath it and see a large cardboard box. I pull it toward me to look inside. My eyes search the contents for a moment while my brain organises the visual messages into something I can comprehend.

Slowly reaching into the box, I pull out one of the many photographs of me, all taken without my knowledge. I grab a few more. Most of them are just me on my own, walking into the Foxx-Tech building, sitting in Java's having a coffee in the window seat, or walking alone in the high street browsing in the windows.

But as I dig down underneath those, I see there are lots more photographs of me on the yacht and some close-ups of Max.

My heart starts to beat a little faster as I sift through hundreds of photographs. Clearing a space underneath, my eyes zone in on a printed sheet of paper lying below the pictures. I tilt my head to process the upside down text. 'Missing - Have you seen this man?' My stomach slides and I collapse to my knees. It's one of my posters.

I quickly pull out all the photographs lying on top and throw them on the floor beside me, then I lift the poster only to find another one behind it, then another. As I dig down, I see the whole batch of posters I had given to Mike to distribute are all here, stacked in the box.

"You lied to me!"

Anger and disbelief course through me as I pull the box from the cupboard and tip it upside down splaying the contents all over the floor. Suddenly, the air in my lungs feels toxic. I can't breathe.

The contents of the cardboard box lay strewn across the floor. My eyes are immediately drawn to the sheets of yellow paper which had been buried beneath the photographs and posters. That shade of yellow is permanently ingrained in my memory. The threatening letters delivered to our home, the last of which, found in our cabin the night Max was abducted, are not something to be easily forgotten.

Tears of anger flood my eyes as my stomach rolls violently. Clamping my hand over my mouth to stop the surge of bile from being ejected as I wretch and gag, I stagger to my feet, suddenly aware that I'm no longer alone.

"Vivienne?" Mike's nervous voice puts a shudder down my spine. I spin around to face him. His eyes are wide and scared as they slide down from my face to the scattered items on the floor. His body fills the door frame blocking my exit, but for some unknown, illogical reason, I don't want to run. I want answers. I need answers.

"I… I can explain…" He begins to walk toward me but I back up, holding both hands up to stop him.

"Don't!" I spit out angrily. "How could you do this to me? How could you lie to me, after everything you said? And how could you send me those disgusting letters?"

The shame and fear in him pulls his brows together into a nervous frown, his lips twitching with unspoken words as they catch in his throat. I can see him trying to formulate an excuse but he remains silent, just staring at me with nervous eyes.

My anger builds to breaking point, then incredulity takes over when I realise his deception goes far deeper than I had originally thought. "All this time you've been acting like the concerned friend, telling me you want to help, making yourself useful. Jesus! I fell for it hook line and sinker."

Panic strangles my stomach causing the bile to rise again in my throat. "It was you! You helped Monica! Oh my god! What have you done?"

Mike takes another tentative step toward me but I quickly move to stand behind the couch so I have a physical barrier between us. "Tell me, Mike! What the fuck did you do?"

He drags both hands through his hair, wrestling with his guilt and shame at being caught out.

"Mike. If you don't tell me what the fuck you've done, I'm going to call the police. Right now!"

My whole body is shaking with adrenaline and fear and utter fury. I know Mike, at least I thought I did, but now I don't know what to think. Would he harm me? Is he capable of that?

"Viv, please. Let me explain." He nervously edges further into the room but he keeps his distance. "I love you, Viv. I just—"

"Don't you *fucking* dare!" Every muscle in my body contracts and hardens. I'm incensed by his betrayal. I can't believe he'd do this to me.

Quickly bending down, I grab handfuls of the sheets from the floor. "These!" I yell, holding up the now crumpled 'missing' posters in my right hand. "You told me these had been delivered. You told me you wanted to help me find Max. You fucking lied!... And these!" I hold up the yellow sheets in my left hand. "These disgusting, malicious threats... How could you do that to me?"

His shoulders sag as his eyes lower to the floor. His body language answering loud and clear.

I begin to sway as a wave of nausea hits me head on.

Slowly raising his eyes back to mine, his bottom lip begins to quiver and he speaks in a small, pathetic voice. "I couldn't bear you being with him. I love you, Viv. I've always loved you."

Angry tears burn in my eyes. Clenching my fists against my thighs, I crumple the papers in my hands. His deception and betrayal brings a churning sickness to my stomach. My chest heaves with short erratic breaths making me feel lightheaded and queasy. I want to fucking scream!

"What have you done? …Tell me!" Grinding my teeth, I force myself to listen to his treacherous excuses.

He looks nervously over his shoulder toward the open door. "Please, Viv. Please keep your voice down. I'll tell you everything. I promise."

I stare at him incredulously. How dare he tell me to keep my voice down. But something about his nervous expression and the fact that he keeps looking toward the door stops me from yelling back at him.

He scrubs at his face with shaking hands, taking a deep breath. "Viv, the day Monica kidnapped Lucy, you called me for help. You wanted me to trace a phone number, remember?"

I don't respond. On the verge of a melt-down I just stand my ground, glaring at him to continue.

"You and Max had split up after you got out of the hospital, you even told the press that you didn't remember him, and I thought… I hoped, that maybe in time, you'd come back to me."

He sheepishly looks down when he realises I'm not going to give him an inch. Even his pathetic attempt to make me feel sorry for him is just winding me up even more.

Clearing his throat, he continues. "That day you called me for help, I had done as you asked, I traced the phone to your building. I couldn't reach you on your phone, so I came over. I was just pulling up to your building when I got a call from Max, he was already there looking for you, and I knew… I knew I didn't stand a chance."

Mike shuffles over to the couch and slumps down with his head in his hands. I watch him carefully, any trust I had in him has been totally erased.

"I parked around the back of your building and I just sat in my car and wept. You'd broken my heart all over again… I wanted you back, Viv, but I knew… I knew you'd choose him."

He takes a moment to wipe the tears from his cheeks. His tears just deepen my anger.

"I was just about to leave when Monica staggered out of the building. Her eyes were streaming, it was obvious she couldn't see properly. I instantly knew who she was, and I knew she'd been trying to hurt you because of Max so at first, I was going to hand her in to the police, but then… then I started to think that maybe if I helped her, we could both get what we wanted."

"You helped her escape? After everything she did to me? To Lucy? You fucking helped her!?" Bile burns in my throat as my stomach shrinks and rolls. I can't believe he would do that to me.

His eyes flick up to mine looking for forgiveness, but a violent anger builds inside me. Mike was someone I had once loved and trusted above all others. It's unbelievable that he would deceive and manipulate me like this. For months he'd filled my head with empty gestures of friendship, and I had fallen for every single lie.

"Go on!" I snap, straightening my back.

Lowering his watery eyes, he bows his head. "We sent the letters to try and scare you off, but when that didn't work we decided to take Max." In a sudden movement, he spins around to face me, making me jump. "I swear, Viv. I didn't mean for anything bad to happen to him. She wanted Max, and I just wanted Monica to get rid of him, to get him out of your life long enough that I could get you back."

My wide, angry eyes stare down at him in shock and revulsion. I'm utterly speechless.

Mike stands and walks to the door, closing it quietly. My heart sprints as renewed fear flows through me.

"What are you doing?" I don't feel safe and as he starts toward me, I immediately back up and hit the wall in a panic. "Don't come near me!"

He stops in his tracks, holding his hands up defensively. "I'm not going to hurt you." His sad eyes and soft voice seem genuine but I don't trust him. "Vivienne, I won't hurt you, I just want to explain."

Mike begins to pace, then he stops and faces me again with fear and sadness in his eyes. This time he keeps his distance. Taking a deep breath, he releases a resigned sigh. "Viv, I swear. I didn't mean for any of this to happen, not really. I just wanted you to see me again. To love me. I wanted you to forget about him and come back to me. You have to believe me."

I glare at him in disbelief and a growing, gnawing hatred. "Go on!"

He flinches. I can see how much this hurts him to confess, but I need to know everything.

"I said, go on!"

"...We decided to wait until Lucy's wedding because we knew there would be hardly any security, and it was easier to take him from the yacht. Monica said she had a plan to kidnap him and then they'd disappear for good. She had money, lots of it. And she'd already managed to get herself several new identities back in the U.K. I didn't care what she did, I just wanted him gone. And I knew if Monica had what she wanted, she'd leave you alone."

I stare at him trying to absorb his skewed reasoning, but he's put my brain in a tail spin.

"This is all my fault," he mumbles, stating the friggin' obvious, looking at me like that excuses everything. "My cousin Daryl knows people who organise this sort of thing, so I asked him to help us. I should never have got him involved."

Mike starts to sweat. Dragging his trembling hand through his hair, he looks nervously toward the door.

I suddenly realise why Mike looks so scared. If Daryl comes upstairs and hears us, things could get very ugly.

"I didn't know what I was getting into, Viv. I swear! I made a huge mistake. I didn't know Daryl was going to take over and fuck it all up."

His expression twists into a frightened scowl.

"He wanted more money than Monica could give him. He threatened her, and the people Daryl knows are fucking hard core. I tried to talk him out of it, I swear to you, Viv. On my life! …But Daryl got greedy. He cut Monica out completely… Fuck! I didn't want this, Viv. I tried to stop it but Daryl threatened me to keep quiet. He told me he'd hurt you if I said anything, and I couldn't let that happen."

I feel frightened and sick to my stomach. "Who are these people? Is Daryl part of this gang, this Infinity gang?"

"No. But the people he knows are, and he owes them money. That's why he double crossed Monica. He wanted more money and she wouldn't pay him, so he was going to use Max as leverage…Jesus! It's all fucked-up."

I feel like I haven't taken a breath since he started talking. Gasping for air, I feel the blood draining from my head, every muscle in my body trembling. Tears stream down my cheeks as horror grips my heart with a steel stranglehold. All the strength flows out of my leg muscles and I can't stop myself from sliding down the wall to the floor.

"Viv!" Mike rushes over crouching down in front of me, but I hold out my hands to stop him.

"Don't touch me!"

"Viv, we got him out! Monica escaped! And I knew where Daryl had taken Max, so I helped her to get him away from there. He's still alive, Viv! She won't hurt him, I promise you… But I'm a dead man if Daryl finds out I went behind his back. We're both in danger if he finds out I've told you."

The panic in his eyes instils a terror deep inside me. Mike's clearly frightened of Daryl, and now I know why I had felt that instinctive feeling about him the first time I'd met him.

A shudder rattles down my spine. Remembering the look in Daryl's eyes when Mike had introduced us, makes me think I could also be a target if money is what he's after.

"Fuck!"

Mike has totally knocked me off balance and shocked me to my core. With my mind in turmoil, a haze of red mist descends over my eyes as a percolating rage bubbles up to the surface. Lurching forward, I grab the front of Mike's shirt in both fists. "Where is he? Where the fuck has she taken him?"

He shakes his head with a pathetic shrug.

"Tell me!" I yell, shaking him violently.

"I don't know! I swear!" he stutters. "She had a boat. I helped her to get him out of the warehouse, away from Daryl, but she made me wear a blindfold and earphones. When we came to a stop, she made me carry Max into a building."

"Where?"

"I have no idea! I'm telling you the truth, Viv. I couldn't see fuck all! I almost broke my fucking back carrying him, he was so fucking heavy." Mike looks down shaking his head, releasing a deep, pathetic sigh.

"You must remember something! A noise? A smell? Anything!"

"Viv, I told you, she made me wear a fucking blindfold and earphones. I'm not making this up!"

Tightening my grip on his shirt, I push my face into his. I'm so angry with him, I could kill him. "Don't fucking lie to me, tell me where he is!"

His watery eyes look squarely into mine. "I don't know. I swear to you, Viv. I don't fucking know."

I push him back, knocking him off his feet, then I scramble up to a standing position and begin to pace. Adrenaline racks my body with the shakes and I need to calm my breathing down before I have a fucking seizure! My mind is in chaos trying to think.

Mike has betrayed me in the worst possible way, but even in my confused state, I know him well enough to know that he's telling me the truth. He doesn't know where Max is, only Monica does. And maybe that's a good thing. Daryl could break Mike like a twig.

Mike sits there crying, hunched over on the floor. "I'm so sorry." His voice is meek and pathetic, fuelling my anger.

"Save it for someone who gives a fuck!"

A thought suddenly occurs to me.

"How do you communicate?"

He hangs his head refusing to give me eye contact. "She calls me… And I know what you're going to ask me, but I've tried to trace her phone, and I can't," he mumbles pathetically.

"Fuck!" I tilt my face to the ceiling and close my eyes, daring myself not to cry and scream my fucking head off.

Grabbing my bag from the floor, I quickly head to the bathroom to sort my face out. I look a mess! My eyes are puffy and red, and all this drama has left a permanent crease in my forehead.

Propping my hands on the edge of the sink, I lean over it and take a couple of calming breaths. The swirling sickness is getting worse. I don't even know how long I've been up here but if I don't make an appearance downstairs soon, Cole or John will come looking for me. What the fuck am I going to tell them?

Once I've fixed my makeup and smoothed my dress, I walk out of the bathroom and stop to look at the pathetic figure sitting on the floor. I can barely bring myself to look at him.

Mike's teary eyes look up at me with a pleading that would normally tug on my heart strings, but all I feel for him is pity, contempt, and a deep seated loathing.

Lifting my chin, I defiantly look him straight in the eyes. "We're done! Unless you find out where Max is, I never want to see or hear from you again." My voice is cold and hard, because that's exactly how I feel toward him.

"Viv, please."

I turn and walk out the door. With shaking legs and a tight chest, I make my way down to the bar. Knowing Daryl was involved in Max's abduction strikes fear in my heart and I can't wait to get out of here.

As I walk past her, the barmaid gives me a cursory glance then a look of concern. I offer a tight smile in return then head to the table where the boys are sitting.

Cole is on his own with an empty glass in front of him and my cold tea sitting beside it. He stands as I approach, his anxious frown deepening. "Is everything okay? The bartender said you'd gone up to speak to Mike, I didn't want to interrupt."

"Yes, I'm… Where's John?"

"He's gone back to the yacht to get some sleep." His wary eyes search my face. "You don't look okay, what happened?"

Tears begin to seep into my eyes and all the pressure of tonight has left me weak and fragile. I need to leave. I need to get away from here.

"Let's go, I'll tell you when we get back."

Cole's face hardens, his eyes becoming dark as he narrows them on me. "What did he do to you?"

"No, nothing. Come on, let's go."

Our walk back to the yacht is silent and steeped in tension. Cole sits me in one of the sofas on deck and brings a blanket, throwing it over my legs. The cool sea breeze has brought a chill to the night air. Once he's settled in the seat next to me, he leans his knee up on the cushion and drapes an arm over the back.

I glance up at him. The worried look on his face and his constantly ticking jaw puts me on edge. I need to tell him what happened but I'm frightened that he'll do something rash.

"What happened, you looked white as a sheet when you came down to the bar… Did he touch you?" His voice is curt and to the point.

"No. No, he didn't touch me." I pause to swallow the hardening lump in my throat. I still can't get my head around Mike's involvement. How could he do that to me? Cole's face softens as he waits for me to speak. I take a breath, trying to prepare what I want to say to him in my head.

"Cole… Mike was the 'we' Monica was talking about. He

helped Monica move Max, and apparently, Mike's cousin Daryl, the bar owner, is the one who had helped Monica abduct him in the first place. Him and his thugs are the ones Monica's frightened of."

"Well, fuck me!" I flinch when he rises abruptly from his seat. Every muscle is pronounced and hard as steel. "I'm going to go and kick his fucking ass!"

"No!" I reach out and grab his arm, halting him in his stride. "No, you can't do that!"

"Yes! I fucking can!" he spits out, the vein in his neck now pulsing.

I tighten my grip and pull on his arm but he almost drags me out of my seat.

"No! Please! Daryl will hurt him, and me! He can't know that Mike's told me any of this. You beating him to a pulp will only make things worse!"

Cole stares down at me with disbelief and anger alternating in his face. "You can't let him get away with this, Vivienne. Jesus! Both those pricks need to be taught a lesson. I'll take John with me. We'll make him tell us where Max is." He starts to walk off but I pull him back.

"Cole, please!... You're right... But I need to get Max home safely before you go charging in like a bull in a china shop. Max is my priority. Nothing matters except bringing Max home safely. Nothing!"

I'm relieved to feel the tension releasing from his arm and the anger slowly dissipating in his eyes. Begrudgingly, he takes his seat, leaning forward to rest his forearms on his knees.

After a few moments his phone rings, when he takes it out, he gives me a sideways glance as he answers it. "Mom, hi. How are you?... Good... Okay, I'll tell her... No, nothing yet... You too. Bye."

He slides his phone onto the coffee table, then sits back in his seat draping his arm over the back of the sofa. "Mom said the money's at the airfield. Bruce is on standby and she's sending the code for the secure hold to my phone."

I sit up in a rush. "You two have discussed this? But I

hadn't told your mum that I had involved you."

He sheepishly looks away for a moment. "I called her and told her you'd spoken to me."

My eyebrows shoot up in alarm as my stomach tilts. "But I'm not supposed to be involving anyone else, what if Monica finds out?"

"Vivienne, I couldn't let my mom sit there worrying about you, she feels better knowing we've got your back."

"Wait, we?"

His lips twist into a wry smile and his expression becomes shifty. "I told John and Vinnie everything."

In a rush, I sit forward with my head in my hands as my stomach knots into a tight ball and my chest constricts. "How could you be so stupid as to involve more people! If Monica finds out, God knows what she'll do!" Panic and dread overwhelms me. "She'll find out. She'll know, she always does."

"Hey, it's okay," he says, reaching for my hand, "they're professionals, they know how to keep a low profile. I won't let anything jeopardize Max's safety, I promise."

I relax my scowl but inside I'm still panicking. His promise is well meant and offered with the greatest of intention, but how can he promise an outcome that none of us can predict.

Fear lurks deep in my belly. I feel like I can't breathe, so I throw back the blanket and move toward the side of the yacht. Nothing ever seems to go right for long, and now that Mike has scrambled my brain with his involvement, I feel like my whole world is slowly caving in around me, suffocating me.

My emotions are precariously teetering on the edge of the precipice. How long I can bear the strain of Max's loss and the events that conspire against me? When will this pain ever stop? And who will be left standing when it does?

Resting my forearms against the wooden sill, I stare out with tear blurred eyes at the pale moon casting shimmering reflections across the undulating surface of the black ocean.

A warm pair of hands gently land on my shoulders. As Cole moves close enough that I can feel the heat from his body against my back, his warm minty breath blows softly against my cheek as he speaks in a low, husky voice. "I'd never do anything to hurt you, Vivienne. I promise."

The sincerity in his voice makes my heart and my shoulders sag. My spirit is broken and without the will to stop them, the floodgates open.

As I begin to sob loudly and without control, Cole wraps his arms around my shoulders and across my chest, nuzzling his face in my hair. "It's okay," he whispers. "I've got you." Resting my chin on his forearm, I let it all go and cry my heart out.

Gently rocking me in his arms, he whispers soothing words until the worst is over. I'm thankful of his understanding, I hate to cry in public. When I blink away the last of my tears, I tilt my head back to look up at him, the engagement of our eyes makes my breath catch in my throat. The sight of his devastatingly handsome face gazing down at me with the same scorching look I've seen so many times in Max's eyes, makes my heart stutter.

Am I imagining it? Or am I simply willing it to be so.

My eyes slide down to his mouth. His full, lush lips slightly parted, releasing short, hot breaths against my face. His arms are still taught around my shoulders as his warm, hard chest rises and falls against my back.

My eyes trace the contours of his lips. I feel a pull deep in my belly, an irresistible need to connect, to touch, to kiss. My skin is tingling with fiery sparks and every nerve ending in my sex is alive with arousal. I drag my eyes away from his lips and as our eyes reconnect, that familiar connection draws me toward him. Without breaking eye contact he begins to lower as I begin to rise.

As his mouth gently brushes over mine, my tongue slips between his lips eager for a taste of him, but as our tongues meet I recoil sharply.

Cole's arms release me immediately as he rocks back on his heels.

"Vivienne—"

"No! Oh, Cole, I'm so sorry. I shouldn't have… I'm sorry. Please forgive me."

We stand apart both looking down. I'm mortified that I responded to him that way and even more so that he reciprocated. I don't know what to say, so I turn to leave.

"Vivienne! Please don't go."

I stop in my tracks, more because of the emotion in his voice than the words he had spoken. But I can't look at him.

"I'm sorry, Vivienne. But you have to know that I—"

"No! …Please don't. I'm sorry, Cole. I'm very vulnerable right now. We're both very vulnerable. Let's just forget it."

I walk away on shaky legs without looking back. I'm scared to look him in the eye. I'm scared to see his expression. My resolve is weak and I'm scared of what I may do.

OBJECT OF HIS AFFECTION

I wake as I have so many times during the night, with an ache in my heart and a head full of worries. We're on the homeward stretch. One more day to survive before Max comes home. One more day to agonise over his health and wellbeing. One more day to pray that Monica will keep to her word.

Hold on, Max. Please, hold on.

I'd come down to my cabin last night and just flopped on the bed fully dressed. I had walked away from Cole because I didn't want to hear it, and he didn't have to say it; it was written all over his face.

Looking back, I'd seen it many times before. But each time I had seen it in his eyes, I thought it was just my misinterpretation, because ultimately, I was longing for him to be Max.

Floods of tears had followed, and at some point in the night I heard Cole outside my cabin door. I prayed he wouldn't act on his need to confess his feelings for me. I wasn't ready to hear, or deal with that devastating news.

We're both in a heightened emotional state, clinging on to each other because the one's we really love are lost to us. I can't blame him, and I won't. It's my weakness for Max that has brought us here. My love for Max won't let it go any further.

Hauling myself upright, I shuffle into the bathroom. Still dressed in last night's clothes, I peel them off and painfully remove all the bangles and bracelets before my shower.

Standing under the spray, I sob quietly as I have every morning. But today I feel especially sad, and worry gnaws at my insides like a ravenous creature nibbling away at my mettle. We've come to the penultimate hurdle. The money's in place. Cole has promised he won't intervene in Monica's escape, provided she keeps her bargain, and I'm ready to face any challenge in order to bring Max home. But something dark lurks in my mind.

An unsettling feeling pushes at my acutely cautious brain, forcing away any feelings of optimism. Caution has always been my standpoint, garnering me the title 'Cautious Viv' from all who know me. But today, it feels like it's been ramped up to the highest level, which only serves to put more feelings of doubt and fear in my head and heart.

The red cuff marks on my wrists have settled into a more pinkish hue. They're less obvious and not nearly as painful. As Cole seems to have told John everything, there's no need to hide them away anymore either.

I dress in shorts and a strapless top, leaving my feet bare. I'm not intending to leave the yacht until I get the call from Monica. Tying my hair up in a loose ponytail, I take one last look at Max's photograph. I trail my fingers over his gorgeous face then I kiss it and my babies scan, then I make my way upstairs.

When I arrive on deck, I realise I'm a little early for breakfast. The rising sun is only just beginning to warm the air, so I wander up to the highest deck to find a sun spot.

As I reach the top deck, I hesitate when I see Cole sitting on one of the sun loungers. His tanned muscular legs are spread either side of it as he plays a card game by himself. His torso is bare, the sun is bouncing off his oiled biceps and strong shoulders. His wavy black hair, framing his handsome face, gently floats in the soft sea breeze.

I bite my lower lip, deciding whether to stay or leave. I'm not sure I can handle anymore confessions or awkwardness between us. Cole hasn't looked up, there's a good chance he hasn't noticed me yet, so I begin to turn away.

"I'm not going to make any excuses for the feelings I have for you, Vivienne. But I promise not to make you feel uncomfortable about it." His eyes are still cast down to the cards. "Join me. I could use the company," he says, looking up at me with his dazzling smile.

I can't hide from him all day, so I take a deep breath and wander over.

"Sit," he commands softly, pointing at the end of his sun lounger.

I stand up on the lounger and fold into a cross legged position, pulling my sunglasses down from the top of my head. I need a barrier of some kind, the sunglasses afford me a little space to watch him without it being obvious.

"What are you playing?"

"It's called 'Beehive Solitaire'. It's a game Max and I used to play as kids. Do you play chess?" he asks, collecting the cards together.

"Yes."

"Are you good at it?"

"Average," I shrug.

"Great. Let's play chess." He scoops up the cards and hands them to me to put back in the box, then he jumps up and grabs the chess set from a nearby cupboard.

I feel an arse-whoopin' coming on. His arse, not mine. I was chess champion at school, I even beat my dad a few times, and he was an excellent player.

~

It didn't take me long to reach checkmate and achieve the arse-whoopin' I had planned. Judging by his disgruntled expression, our game of chess wasn't going the way he had hoped. Eyeing me with a squint and pursed lips he conceded to a defeat and declined when I asked him to play again.

"Hmmf. Something tells me you lied about your chess skills, Miss Banks."

I shrug, leaning back on my hands, unable to hide my smug smile. "I may have left out the bit about me being chess champion at school."

Shaking his head, he carries the chess set back to the cupboard, muttering something under his breath about me denting his ego, then he returns with two bottles of water from the small fridge.

"Here. Don't choke on it." Handing me the water with an arched brow, he takes a swig from his bottle. "Wanna shoot some hoops?"

"Shoot some what?"

"Basketball, do you play basketball?"

"You mean netball?"

His brow lowers then he smirks, his facial expression amusing me. "What's that? Code for, I'm an NBA champion? My best friends are Shaquille O'Neal and Kareem Abdul Jabbar?"

"No," I giggle, "I promise, I've never played."

"Perfect! Let's shoot some hoops before you completely ruin my masculine dignity."

We wander over to the recreation area on the top deck, where a basketball hoop, a golf tee, and skeet shooting are available. Cole explains the rules of basketball which fly straight in one ear and out the other.

After several attempts to win the ball from him, I decide to give up and watch him expertly slam dunk every ball. His strong, muscular body is quick and agile, and like Max, he has a fluidity and gracefulness about his movements. He can even throw the ball from the furthest point, facing the wrong way, and still hit the target. Obviously one of his strong points and a well-practised trick.

We hit a few golf balls off the deck, none of mine going very far and a couple of them were still sitting on the tee after I had swung my club relentlessly and missed them completely.

Cole was being very charming and funny, making me laugh

and showing great patience at my ineptitude for the sports he seemed to excel in. I knew exactly what he was doing. He was trying to smooth over the awkwardness of last night, and I was grateful for that. I'm sure he was also trying to keep me occupied, knowing the tension was building as we drew nearer to the exchange.

After I nearly took his head off with my golf club on a particularly bad swing that knocked me off balance, we decide to call it a day and head to the salon for breakfast.

John, looking unusually casual in shorts and a t-shirt, joins us as Sasha is taking our order. I marvel at the amount of food that man can eat in one sitting, and yet he's not got an ounce of fat on his body.

Pouring my tea, I offer some to the boys but they're sticking with their coffee. I catch John eyeing my pink banded wrists but he doesn't comment.

"So, what's our P.O.A. for today?" John's question is directed at Cole, but I haven't got a clue what he's talking about.

"P.O.A.?" I ask, adding the milk to my tea.

"Plan of action," Cole answers, clearing that up. "I thought we'd stay close to the yacht. Monica's not supposed to call until tonight but I want to be ready in case she calls earlier."

John nods thoughtfully. "Vinnie's managed to identify the last known coordinates of Vivienne's phone on the day Monica took her out on the boat. He's mapping the variables for where she could have sailed to within the time frame. It's a long shot, and it could take a while, but he's working on it."

I flick my gaze between the two of them. They're talking like I'm not even here. But at least they're investigating every avenue.

When my plate of food arrives, my appetite seems to have disappeared. I stare down at it despondently.

"Eat, Vivienne. Please."

Cole's soft voice is almost drowned out by John's cutlery clacking away against his plate loaded with food. I know he's right, I should eat, so I begin to nibble at the bacon, I no longer have the stomach for the eggs.

Once I've eaten as much as I can, I lay my knife and fork against the sides of my plate, leaning my elbows on the table. There's something bothering me and I need to get it off my chest.

"John, I know you're a professional, and I know you're good at your job, but I need to know that we're all on the same page. I don't want anyone to do anything that may cause Monica to run without giving us Max's location."

John stops chewing. The big clump of food resting in the side of his mouth bulges his cheek out like a hamster. Flicking his eyes to Cole for silent approval, Cole nods ever so slightly then turns to face me as John continues chewing.

"Vivienne, John knows what's at stake. No one is going to do anything to harm Max's release. You have my word."

The sincerity in Cole's eyes and the fact that John is nodding in agreement, continuing to work his way through his enormous plate of food, tells me he's telling me the truth. I should trust him. I'm just nervous that we're so close and yet, I feel a sense of dread building in my stomach that something will go wrong. What if Monica knows I've involved Cole and John? What if I've made a huge mistake?

Noticing my unrest, Cole gives me a reassuring smile then he reaches into his pocket and hands me a new phone fully loaded with all my old contacts, photos, music, and apps. "It's the same number you had before. Did you charge the phone Monica gave you?"

"Yes, I've got it in my pocket." I take it out and place it on the table.

"Good. John and I are on your speed dial and we'll be a safe distance behind you wherever she tells you to go, so don't worry."

I nod, unable to push any words through. I'm nervous and edgy. I just want today to be over and to have Max home safe and sound.

"Right!" John says, wiping his mouth and rising from his seat. "I'll see you both later." Grabbing his keys from the table, he marches off.

After breakfast, I sit in the shade reading my book while Cole heads down to the gym for a workout. I have to give it to him, he's been very attentive and has kept his word about not making me feel uncomfortable about our kiss last night.

I've read the same page of my book over and over again. I can't concentrate, so I fold the corner of the page and set it down. The constant churning in my stomach has almost sent me down to the cabin several times thinking I may throw up, but thankfully, that hasn't happened.

As I gaze down at my engagement ring, tears pool in my eyes as my mind fills with images of Max laying battered and bruised on the cot in that small, dark space. Running my hand over my tiny bump, over our nuggets, I feel so lost without him. My heart yearns for him. I want him back. I want him in my arms, inside me, all over me. I've missed him so much it hurts. And as the time slowly ticks by, I long for the moment Monica calls to put an end to my misery and suffering.

At breakfast, we had discussed how and where we would take Max for medical attention. Vinnie wants him to be airlifted back to London straight away. It seems a sensible option and security would be easier to organise back in London.

Benny is due to arrive this afternoon at Renard Airport with a small medical team from The Limberton, so everything is in place. Now, we just wait.

Cole wanders up on deck with a towel draped around his neck and sweat beading and dripping down his impressive chest and carved abdominals. His arms are pumped and the thick veins threading down his muscles, protrude under the skin. He's a sight for sore eyes in his low slung shorts and bare feet, his wavy mane of black hair, slicked back with sweat.

He takes a bottle of water from the small fridge offering one to me, then he saunters away in that predatory swagger he and his brother share. "I'm going for a quick shower, I won't be long," he says, over his shoulder. I watch him walk away, absorbing both the pleasure and the pain that he evokes.

As he leaves my sight, tears threaten my eyes. I feel so sorry for Cole. If he does have feelings for me, then that means he's invested his heart in the wrong woman twice. As much as I thought him to be a selfish, arrogant man, he's proved himself to be quite the opposite. He's more like Max than even he would give himself credit for.

Sometimes I forget that he's suffering too. Max is his blood, his brother. The only reason he'd been jealous of Max in the first place was because he'd admired him so much, even as a child.

Max was a force of nature, inherently driven to succeed. Cole had to work at it. Maybe that was the biggest difference between them.

And Monica? Well, she burrowed right under Cole's skin. He'd fallen in love with her only to be rejected. She'd chosen Max, breaking Cole's heart and increasing the jealous rift between them. But when she came back to Cole and then married him, it was just a cruel ruse to manipulate the brothers, but Cole loved her, he'd never stopped loving her. He didn't stand a chance.

I'm sure his feelings for me are just the misplaced feelings he still holds for the woman who broke his heart. Or could it be that as twins, their genetics govern their emotions in the same way they govern their looks. Maybe falling in love with the same woman is unavoidable.

I'm drawn to Cole because of the striking and undeniable similarities to Max, but I know with all certainty, as identical as they are, my heart will only ever belong to Max.

"Ma'am."

John's voice pulls me from my reverie. He's walking toward me, but my eyes are drawn to the attractive, dark haired woman standing behind him talking to Sasha. I've never seen her before.

"Ma'am. Mike's left town. He's gone back to London."

As I stare at John, panic sets in giving me the shakes. "John, I told you not to go to the bar! Daryl will—"

"No, it's okay. I didn't go. Julie did."

"Oh." I look over John's shoulder at the woman talking to Sasha realising she must be Julie, Johns wife. "Well, if he's gone, maybe that's for the best. One less thing to worry about." Mike is weak and stupid. Involving himself with the likes of Daryl was going to get him killed. I could never forgive Mike for what he'd done, but I didn't want him harmed.

"What about Daryl?" I ask. "Do you think he knows Mike has told me everything?"

"Don't worry about Daryl, Ma'am. Julie's had him under surveillance. I didn't trust Mike when I first met him, and when you went missing, I brought Julie in to follow him."

I gape up at him in surprise.

"She overheard an argument between Mike and Daryl early this morning. She followed Daryl to a warehouse about twelve miles away. The guy is dealing drugs, he's got a large shipment stashed away in his warehouse. She's given the police all her surveillance data, they'll be arresting him any time now."

Relief surges through me. I stand and walk over to John to give him a hug. "Thank you."

His cheeks flush then he turns to his wife. "Julie! Come on over honey. Come and meet Vivienne."

The girls quickly end their conversation and Julie comes bounding over.

"Hi," she says, extending her hand. "I'm Julie, you must be the feisty brunette John talks very highly of. It's nice to finally meet you, Ma'am."

Her liquid brown eyes smile at me affectionately. She's very striking with a short, sleek, black bob and strong athletic physique.

"Please, call me Vivienne. And you must be the ass-kicker. I've heard great things about you too."

Julie laughs and John smirks, looking equally proud and bashful.

"Please, have a seat." I gesture to the sofas and Sean arrives with a timely tray of drinks and sandwiches, followed by Cole, fresh from his shower and looking very handsome in his shorts and fitted t-shirt.

I falter slightly as I lower myself into the sofa. Although they are both dressed in summer clothes, John and Julie are removing their concealed weapons in order to sit down comfortably. I marvel at the arsenal piling up on the coffee table, trying to figure out where the hell they could have hidden them.

Cole takes a seat next to me. As I'm about to tell him what John and Julie have been up to, John confirms that he'd already relayed the information to Cole via phone a few minutes ago.

"So, here's the plan," John says, reaching for a sandwich, then looking over at his wife. "Honey?"

"Oh, I almost forgot," she chuckles, pulling off the black wig. Removing the pins and clips, she runs her fingers through her long auburn hair shaking it loose.

"From a distance, Julie could be mistaken for you, Ma'am, so she'll go with the money and—"

"No!" Panic swirls in my stomach and a surge of adrenaline races my heartbeat. "No, I'm sorry, I can't take that chance. If Monica sees it's not me this whole thing could blow up in our faces."

"But—"

"No!"

I say it with complete authority, wringing my hands in my lap. No one speaks for a moment and I'm angry they're not listening to me about this. Why am I the only one who wants to get this right?

Julie places her hand on her husband's knee giving it a squeeze. "She's right, John. If it were you, I wouldn't want to risk it." Her soft, brown eyes gaze lovingly into his. She knows how I feel, she understands why I can't mess this up, there's too much at stake.

"Monica's never met me before, I should be the one closest to Vivienne. I can follow at a safe distance and be her back up. Monica wouldn't know that I was connected to you, so I could stay closer to Vivienne than either of you could."

All of us nod in agreement, even John, although it's

reluctant. I wait until John's eyes swing back to mine. "I'm happy with that."

Julie disappears for a moment, returning with a metal briefcase. Opening the lid, she begins to take out various items, explaining how we'll be using the earpieces and microphones to communicate. It's all a bit Secret Service and bewildering to me, but I feel safe in Julie's hands.

Cole's phone rings. After answering it, he hands it to me. "It's Mom," he says, softly.

"Hello, Sylvie. How are you?"

"Oh, sweetheart, I'll be better when all this is over. How are you holding up?"

I close my teary eyes, trying not to sound upset when I answer. "I'm fine… Has Olivia arrived yet?"

"No, she'll be here tomorrow, it'll be good to see her." The emotion in her voice weakens my resolve. Fighting the tears, I take a short pause to control the aching lump in my throat.

"I'll call you as soon as we hear anything, Sylvie."

"Okay, sweetheart. Take care."

I hand the phone back to Cole who stands and walks away from us to talk to his mother.

Julie leans forward, offering a reassuring smile. "Vivienne, please don't worry. We'll get him back. I promise."

My heart sinks as yet another well-meaning person promises me something none of us can be sure of.

Slightly overwhelmed by it all, I decide to take myself down to the cabin for a lie down. With another five hours to wait, the anxiety is causing havoc with my stomach. I feel teary and nervous. I just wish the time would come for Monica's call.

While I lay on the bed, I send Lucy a text from my new phone. Just a brief outline of what's happened so far, and a warning about Mike. I promise to fill her in on the Mike scenario when I next speak to her, but I let her know that I've cut all ties with him, forever.

Just thinking about Mike's betrayal makes me feel sick to my stomach. I had once loved him, trusted him. I'd even forgiven him for fucking Michelle behind my back. But this?…

No. There was no forgiveness for his involvement in taking the one thing I treasured the most.

And yet, I had still protected him from Daryl's brutality, from Cole's pulverising blows to seek revenge for me, and from prosecution by the police for aiding a fugitive. Be it a weakness or a strength, I'd come to realise I didn't care enough about Mike to seek revenge. Mike was dead to me now, and I knew that in itself would be enough.

Taking one of Max's dress shirts from the wardrobe, I strip down to my bra and knickers and put it on. As I wrap myself in it, breathing in the scent of him embedded in the fabric, the feel of the luxurious silk against my skin, and knowing this was the shirt he had worn when he'd asked me to marry him, brings a sentimental ache to my heart. If only it was enough to be sheathed in the materialistic accoutrements that had once adorned his magnificent body.

Tears fill my eyes as I lie on the bed and curl around Max's pillow, inhaling his lingering scent that I crave so much.

As the time for Monica's call draws near, butterflies and panic intermingle inside me. With the phone she gave me gripped tightly in my hand, I lay there staring at the darkened screen willing it to ring.

Soon, Max. I'll see you soon. Please hold on. I love you.

THE KEY

Jerking out of sleep, I'm suddenly aware of anxious, whispering voices outside my cabin door. A little disoriented, I sit up in a rush and hold the phone still gripped in my fingers, up to my face. The time display reads seven forty-three p.m. My heart skips a beat. Only another hour and a quarter to wait.

A light knocking at my door makes me jump and has me sitting up swinging my legs over the side of the bed. I quickly check to see I'm covered in Max's shirt.

"Come in." My voice is soft and croaky, so I clear my throat and repeat my invitation.

The door opens slowly and Cole walks in with a pained expression on his face. As he comes further into the room, I see John and Julie standing behind him. They too have a worried expression on their faces. All my nerves vibrate as a tight knot in my chest makes it hard for me to breathe.

Leaning forward, I bring my hand up to my mouth as a wave of nausea heats my skin causing an ice cold sweat to form all over me. "Something's wrong." The words in my head make it out in a whisper.

Looking up at Cole with panic in my eyes, I feel a deep sense of dread in my heart. His eyes confirm my fears. Glistening tears cling to his dark lower lashes, then drip down his cheek in a rush, only to be caught in the contour of his top lip.

"What is it? What's happened?" I flick my eyes between them but none of them speak. "Tell me. What is it?"

Cole's eyes briefly close, forcing another tear to escape, his jaw clenching repeatedly. When he opens his eyes he seems to be holding his breath. Straightening his shoulders, he steps toward me, sinking to his knees right in front of me so we're eye to eye.

He takes the phone out of my hand and sets it on the bed beside me, then he gently brings my other trembling hand down from my mouth, holding both of them in his, staring into my eyes with the saddest expression.

I can't bear it. I know he has bad news, it's written all over his face. Whatever he's about to tell me is devastating him, and I fear it will completely destroy me.

"No...Cole... Please don't." My voice is broken, barely a whisper.

"Vivienne..." A kaleidoscope of emotions colour his face until his brow lowers heavily over darkened, watery blue eyes. "...Monica's dead."

A white noise fills my head and everything suddenly feels off balance. "Wha...what did you say?"

His words don't make any sense. Shaking my head, I search his grief-stricken face, watching the tick in his jaw as it clenches repeatedly. I'm waiting for him to take back what he'd said. She can't be dead. That's impossible.

He lowers his eyes briefly but when they return to mine, I see nothing but sorrow within them. His lips quiver and he swallows several times before he finds his voice. "The police are here. They found Monica's body in the water an hour ago. Her throat had been cut and..."

His voice trails off and he tries to compose himself. This is too much for him too. I search his eyes desperately hoping I'll see something other than the truth.

"But... No!... No, she can't be dead? They must have made a mistake... She can't be dead. She's the only one who knows where— No!"

As I absorb the enormity of his statement, knowing Max is now lost to me forever, I feel its powerful truth plunge the jagged dagger of realisation into my heart. The pain in Cole's eyes driving the blade to the hilt. Only Monica knew where he was. Only she could save him. But now she's gone. There's no coming back from this.

"NO!"

I pull against his hold but he won't release my hands. And as the blood drains from my head, my body convulses with pitiful, racking sobs, tearing my heart into a million pieces. I'm suffocating, drowning in my own tears. I can't get any air into my lungs and the ache in my chest is unbearable.

Releasing my hands, Cole bands his arms around my shoulders pulling me in and pinning me to his chest. "Vivienne. I'm so sorry." His voice breaks as he holds me in a crushing hug while I sob into his neck feeling his body jerking with tears of his own.

My head is spinning and suddenly, my whole world seems to be on mute. I can't even hear my own wails of disbelief anymore. As if I've just stepped out of my own body, I feel numb, cold, and empty. Like a Vivienne shaped vessel without any innards.

Turning my head, I rest my cheek on Cole's dampened shoulder as the tears continue to flow. His strong arms still encase my body but I can't feel them, I can't feel anything.

My blurry eyes land on the photograph of Max. His stunning face gazing back at me hurts my heart. *No me without you…*

In a sudden movement, I pull away from Cole, pushing him back. His grip is strong but he releases me immediately. Scraping the sleeve of Max's shirt across my eyes, I try to clear my vision. "I need to see her!"

"What? Why?" Cole's confused eyes search mine, he looks shocked at my demand.

I stand abruptly and push past him. "I have to know it's her, Cole. I have to be sure!"

"Vivienne." He rises to his feet, staring at me as I walk to the end of the bed to find my clothes. With shaking hands I drag my shorts up my legs and shove my feet into my converse.

He silently watches me, unsure of what to do. "Vivienne…"

"Please, Cole. I have to know. She's faked her death before, I have to be sure."

He stands there gaping at me for a moment, then he nods and reaches out for my hand. "…Okay."

I take his hand, grateful that he understands my need to see her. Without speaking, he leads me upstairs to talk to the police.

The detectives stand as we approach. A female police officer with excellent English, explains that Monica's body was found floating face down in the sea. She was found a mile out from shore and twelve miles up the coast. She'd been dead for a number of hours. There was nothing on her except for two items stuffed inside her bra. A mobile phone and a set of keys.

"Where exactly was she found?" John asks.

The officer checks her notepad. "Twelve miles west of here, near the Plage D'Amber area."

John and Julie exchange a look. "You said she had a phone. Do you have it?"

"Oui, but it doesn't work. The sea water has broken it."

Julie and John share another knowing look, and I pray they know a way of fixing it.

"Can I see her?" My voice breaks.

"Oui. Of course. We need someone to identify the body. Can you come now?"

Cole reaches out and squeezes my arm. "Vivienne, you don't have to do this. I can identify her body."

I rest my hand over his, swallowing back the tears. "I have to see for myself. But…would you come with me?"

Wrapping his arm around my shoulders, he kisses the top of my head. "Of course I will."

John and Julie drive us to the morgue following the police

car in front. Cole sits with me in the back seat of the Range Rover, gripping my hand to the point of pain.

I know for Cole, this must be a double whammy. His brother, and the crazy woman he had loved. But for me, the overwhelming knowledge that Max is still out there somewhere, now totally vulnerable and alone, kills me. How long can he survive on his own? Where is he?

Closing my teary eyes, I run my hand over my belly picturing the night he'd asked me to marry him. *You promised me forever, Max. Don't make me live without you.*

We follow the detective into a modern looking building. She hands us over to the chief coroner and another man who informs us that he's been liaising with D.I. Langford from the Met police.

Once it was clear Monica had faked her death in Portsmouth and had subsequently disappeared, the U.K. police had reached out to all the law enforcement agencies across Europe to cast a wider net for her capture.

After asking us a ton of questions, we're finally taken through to a chamber for viewing. Several anxious hours have passed in the meantime, and I thought that I had prepared myself enough to see her, but as we are met at the door by the morgue attendant, the acrid smell seeping into my nose triggers the bile to rise in my throat. My legs begin to shake and the sickness in my stomach threatens to break free at any moment.

Cole holds my hand as we walk in, but I can feel the tension flowing through him. We both tense up as we near the open drawer where Monica's body lies covered in a white sheet. Dropping my hand, he wraps his arm around my shoulders and we brace ourselves for the moment of truth.

The attendant hesitantly nods at us before pulling the sheet back and when he does, we both recoil letting out an audible gasp as her bloated, grey-skinned body is revealed.

Cole's grip tightens to a band of steel around my shoulders and I feel him trembling against my side. Resisting the urge to look away, I force myself to look at her, trying not to gag at the horrific sight before me.

Her neck has been slashed from one side to the other. Temporary staples hold the skin closed across her throat and down her chest in a Y-shaped formation. The crude closure from the post-mortem examination.

Seeing her this way is surreal. Even in this appalling condition, I can see immediately that this is Monica, but I can't stop myself from checking to see if she still has the bruise on the side of her head, the one I'd seen that day on the boat.

Her skin is so discoloured that the bruise is barely visible, so I pull away from Cole's arm and walk to her feet to check if the little bumble bee tattoo is there.

"It's her." My voice is small and barely audible. The realisation that Monica is indeed dead, makes my sense of loss even greater as my heart cracks wide open.

I never thought it possible to be devastated by her death, but in a perverse, twisted way, she had become my lifeline. She was my only link to Max. She was the only person who knew where he was. But now she's dead, and all hope of finding him has died with her. Something inside me breaks, leaving me more empty and lost than I've ever felt before.

Looking up from her lifeless body, the strangling lump in my throat constricts even more when I see Cole's devastated face. His eyes are full of tears, his face contorting with pain and heartache, etching its path across his brow like a dark shadow. This woman had once beguiled him and he had loved her with a passion. As crazy and fucked-up as Monica was, she was his first true love, and I know from my own experience, a love like that leaves an indelible mark on your soul.

Our eyes meet as I walk over to him with open arms. Staring down at me for a long painful moment, he lets me wrap him in my arms. Sinking his face into my neck, he releases all his pent up emotions in silent, jerking sobs.

Tears burn in my eyes as I try to comfort him. I'm an emotional, empty wreck, I have nothing to give, but I hold on to him regardless, afraid to let go.

Maybe now, Cole can move on. Maybe now, he has the

chance to start a new life, to find a new love. One that is clean and pure, one that will save him.

I wish I had the same possibilities waiting on the horizon. But then, I wouldn't choose them even if I did. For me, Max is the only man I will ever love. His brilliant light will never shine from another's eyes. No one will ever make me feel the way he did. He's unique. A one off. My once in a lifetime love. And life without Max will be the hardest challenge I will ever have to face.

Once we've had time to compose ourselves, we head back to the main desk to collect Monica's belongings. Their tech and forensic departments have tried to power up Monica's phone but it won't work. After a bit of haggling, John persuades them to let him take it, promising to share any information should he be able to get it to work.

They take impressions and photographs of the keys found on her body, and hand them over too. Her clothes are destroyed. That's all there was.

Cole leaves his details, so they can contact him when her body is ready to be repatriated back to the U.S. for burial.

I understand Cole's need to do right by her, even though she had made his life a living hell. And maybe that was just another thing about the brothers that makes them special. Their hearts are kind and compassionate, and even in the extremes of adversity they always end up doing the right thing.

We sit mostly in silence all the way back to the yacht.

Cole calls his mother to tell her about Monica. It's a painful conversation ending in tears on both sides. Sylvie knows the significance of Monica's death. She knows we have no way of finding Max without her. I hope she isn't on her own. No one should receive news like that without the support of family or friends.

My mind is raw with worry and thinking.

When we get out of the car and walk the short distance to the yacht, John and Julie walk ahead deep in conversation. They're arguing over the different methods they should use to get Monica's phone to work. They each have skills way beyond my comprehension, and I pray with all my heart they will find a solution. I pray that somehow there's still a chance to find Max, even though that possibility is rapidly ebbing away.

I walk up the gangway behind them. Cole is last on board, deeply lost in his own thoughts.

As he heads straight to the bar to pour himself a large Jack Daniels, I walk over to the side of the yacht and lean on the edge, staring blindly across the expanse of black ocean wondering how has it come to this? Tears spill down my cheeks as the pain crushes me from the inside out.

"Here," Cole says, handing me a glass of white wine. "One won't hurt. You need it."

I stare down at it for the longest time. I can almost taste it, my mouth salivating at the prospect of its cool fruitiness sliding down my throat. Temptation and weakness have the advantage as I raise it to my lips. The first sip is heaven. My first alcoholic drink in over three months. But guilt begins to stab at my conscience, wagging its moral finger in my face, telling me what a bad mother I am to my unborn babies. I take a second sip all the same. I need it. I want the alcohol to numb the pain inside. I don't want to feel anymore, feeling is too painful.

How I'd managed to abstain from alcohol throughout this whole ordeal since Max's abduction, I'll never know. Maybe it's because I know exactly what he'd say if he could see me drinking. His brow would be creased with concern, the curve in his eyebrow excessively arched to convey his disapproval, and his beautiful crystal blue eyes would narrow on me with unspoken demands. Oh, God, I miss him so much.

The tears travel their usual path down my cheeks as the ache inside grows deeper and deeper. Leaning over the edge of the yacht, I stare down at the black water. "He's out there somewhere, Cole. But I've failed him. I promised him I'd bring him home. I should have—"

"Vivienne, don't. It's not your fault. I can't bear to see you like this." The catch in his throat chokes me up even more.

Suddenly, everything feels too heavy, too close, too much

to bear. The wine glass slips from my fingers into the sea below and I collapse to the floor, racked with grief, sobbing my broken heart out. "I've lost him, Cole. I'm never going to see him again."

Cole sinks to his knees and holds me as the tears pour out of me. Gently stroking my hair, whispering soothing tokens in my ear, he rocks me gently in his arms.

After a long time has passed, hours for all I know, I gather myself together, pull back, and apologise to him for losing it. I hate to cry in front of someone. Especially someone who's hurting too.

He gives me a look, telling me everything will be alright, even though neither of us really believe that.

Pulling me up from the floor he walks me to the sofa. John and Julie arrive on deck, they sound like they're still arguing but they're just having a heated disagreement about something technological that goes way over my head.

Julie sits next to me giving me a comforting cuddle. John follows Cole to the bar for a drink.

"Any luck with the phone?" I sniffle, scraping my hands across my face. Julie smiles stiffly, shaking her head. I should have known not to pin my hopes on that.

When Cole returns with a bottle of water for me and a large Jack Daniels for him, he pulls something from his pocket, throws it on the table, then sits on the opposite sofa with John. They're deep in conversation. John is explaining what methods they've tried in order to get Monica's phone to work, but his voice seems to become further and further away as my eyes stare down at the bunch of keys Cole had removed from his pocket.

Monica's keys.

"Vivienne?... Vivienne, are you alright?"

I wriggle out of Julie's arm, sitting forward in my seat. My heart beats faster as my eyes become fixed on the keys. On one key in particular.

"Vivienne? What is it? What's the matter?"

Reaching forward, I lift the long brass key from the table.

Its thin shaft looped at one end, with a flag of three indents at the other, triggers a memory. I remember sitting in the kitchen of the chateau with Harry. I had asked him if he'd been down to the cellar, he reached into his pocket and held up a large ring of keys, most of them brass, most of them long, exactly like this one.

I spring to my feet. "We need to go back to the chateau!"

Julie's hand pulls on my arm halting me in my tracks as I try to walk off. "Vivienne, what's the matter?"

I hold the key up in front of her face. "This!"

All eyes stare at me like I've lost the plot. I look at each of their faces wondering why none of them seem to understand.

John clears his throat, placing his glass on the table. Looking straight at me, he rains on my parade with the following sentence, "Ma'am...Julie and I checked it out. We've been all over the chateau. I promise you, he's not there."

Anger makes me snatch my arm from Julie's grip. "I'm going!" I'm annoyed they don't understand my need to see for myself. As I start to walk off, Cole stands up, blocking my path. I look up at him ready to give him a mouthful and push past him if I have to, but he stares down at me with soft, concerned eyes, then he gives me a small nod.

"Dress warm," he says, softy. "And pack an overnight bag. This could take all night."

Tears prick my eyes. I'm so relieved he understands. "Thank you," I mouth, unable to physically voice any words.

WHAT HAVE I DONE?

I quickly shove a few items into a bag and change my clothes. Once I'm ready, I meet the others up on deck. John and Julie ride up front, and Cole and I sit in the back of the Range Rover. He takes my hand, giving it a squeeze but we travel in silence.

It's well after one in the morning when we arrive at the chateau. The moon is blanketed by clouds and there are only a few exterior lights illuminating the long driveway. John activates the gates which slowly begin to swing open.

As we near the high arched doors of the front entrance, Julie pulls her weapon out checking the clip, before doing the same with John's weapon. I sit there with my mouth hanging open, feeling like I've just stepped into a movie. As my wide eyes swing around to Cole, I see him pulling a gun from inside his jacket too, he checks the clip then keeps it in his hand resting it on his thigh.

"Don't worry, it's just a precaution."

I stare at him dumbfounded. As a Brit, we're not used to seeing guns. I forgot that in America, carrying a gun is a constitutional right. I'm not sure if that's a comfort or a worry. I didn't even know he had one.

As soon as the Range Rover comes to a stop, Julie jumps

out and walks to the rear of the car. Pulling a black holdall from the boot, she arms herself with another handgun.

"Okay, wait here while John and I do a recon," she says, sliding the peak of her baseball cap to the back of her head.

Cole and I wait in the back seat, watching them as they slink toward the building like ninjas. I see them checking the windows at the front of the property, then they enter through the front door and disappear inside.

"You okay?" Cole asks softly. I nod, I'm a little lost for words. Reaching for my hand, he gives it a reassuring squeeze.

After a few minutes, the lights go on inside and John appears at the front door beckoning us inside. "It's all clear."

The chateau is a huge, sprawling mansion built over several floors with an east and a west wing. In a methodical sweep, we start at the cellar, checking every door and cupboard we can find before moving up to the next floor. My enthusiasm dwindles after each failed attempt. I was so sure we'd find a lock to match Monica's key.

Julie and John disappear to do a sweep of the exterior, then they're going to try and work out a way of getting Monica's phone to work. If they can, they're hoping to be able to track her movements from it.

After hours of searching, Cole and I eventually end up at the last door on the upper floor. We've checked under every rug, every bed, and behind every wardrobe looking for a door to match Monica's key, but still we've come up with nothing.

"Shit!" I'm shaking with disappointment and frustration. We've come to another dead end. "This key has to fit something. There must be another door somewhere, a secret door, like the one Harry showed me, the one leading up to the attic."

Cole sighs dragging a hand through his hair. "I don't know of any others. I called Mom earlier to ask if there are any more hidden doors in the house, but she said the one to the attic was the only one she knew of, and both John and Julie have already checked up there."

I sag in defeat and exhaustion. My eyes are bugging out

from crying so much and a lack of sleep. They sting as more burning tears begin to well up in them, tears I just can't stop. I wanted so badly to find him here, but again, I've hit a brick wall and the hopelessness is eating away at me.

"Vivienne, we've looked everywhere. I wanted to find him as much as you. I don't know what else to do." Cole's sad eyes glisten and the hopelessness in his voice makes me ache. Stumbling backward, I lean against the wall, defeated and hollowed out with despair.

"Hey, come on," he says, softly. "You need to rest, you look exhausted." With a comforting arm around my shoulders, he walks me to one of the bedrooms.

He pulls the dust sheet off the grand four poster bed, then walks to the wardrobe and grabs two blankets and a pillow from the top shelf. "Here, make yourself comfortable. Try to get some sleep." Gently running his fingers down my cheek, he lifts my chin with his finger. "I'll go and find John to see if they've come up with anything on Monica's phone. I'll wake you if we find anything, okay?"

His gentle eyes and caring smile calm me a little but my insides are churning. How can I sleep knowing Max is still out there somewhere. Injured and alone.

I nod reluctantly but as Cole turns and walks away, my body stiffens with panic. I don't want him to go. I don't want to be alone. I need to see his face. I need to see Max.

"Cole?" My pitiful, whimpering voice stops him in his tracks.

He turns back, the sadness in his eyes tearing my heart to shreds. "Yeah?"

"What do I do?... How do I?..." The barely whispered words get stuck in my throat. I can't cope anymore.

Striding toward me, he wraps me in his arms burying his face in my hair. "Oh, Vivienne, I'm so sorry."

Tears stream down my cheeks as I wail out an incomprehensible string of words while all my emotions explode out of me. His arms and body feel like a protective shield, but the pain is coming from the inside. I've never felt so lost, so completely destroyed. Sobbing into his shoulder, I hold on to him for dear life, needing to touch him, needing the feel of his warm, protective hands on my body. Needing Max.

Pulling my head back, I find his eyes gazing down at me. Surprise and longing blended together in the watery pools of the bluest eyes I've ever known. I need those eyes on me. I crave them. I've missed them so much.

Without thinking, I run my hand up the nape of his neck to feel his silky hair between my fingers. It feels like it should, like it's always felt. As we gaze into each other's eyes, I see Max. Rising up on my toes, he lowers to close the distance between us and after a moment's hesitation, he devours my lips with a passionate kiss.

My fingers urgently grasp and weave through his hair pulling him closer, deeper. The eager pressure of his hands caressing me, holding me against his rock hard body, feels so good, unfurling a deep suppressed longing within me.

I arch my body into him, needing the contact, my body responding automatically without demand. Our mouths possessively taking what we need from each other as our tongues lash and glide in a frenzied kiss. I've waited so long for this kiss. I've waited so long for Max.

No... No... NO!

Breaking the kiss, I push away from him, breathless with both desire and panic. Lifting my trembling hand to my mouth, the feel of his kiss still throbs on my swollen lips. I don't know what came over me. I don't understand how I let that happen.

"Cole, I'm so sorry... I don't know why I did that. Forgive me."

I feel so ashamed. Cole's confused eyes stare down at me, the look on his face shattering my heart. I should never have done that. It's not fair to either of us.

His pained expression cuts right through me. "Vivienne, you know how I feel about you." His voice is raspy, low, and crippled with emotion.

"No. You're upset, we both are. We're both very vulnerable

right now."

I can feel the emotion flowing from him in waves. Dragging his hands through his hair, he takes a step toward me. "Vivienne, please, I—"

"No! Please don't. …I can't do this." Holding my hands up defensively, I quickly step back, my legs banging into the edge of the bed. "This isn't right." Tears breach my lashes. I can't take it back and I'd be lying through my teeth if I said I hadn't enjoyed the kiss. But in my mind, it wasn't Cole I was kissing. *Oh, god! What have I done.*

Keeping his distance, he searches my face as if waiting for me to change my mind.

"Please, Cole, you need to go. I'm sorry. I should never have let that happen. It's all my fault."

I can see him trying to deal with the riot of emotions causing chaos in his mind, and I hate myself for being responsible for the look on his face. I've hurt him, badly. In a moment of complete and utter madness, I've made him my surrogate for Max, screwing with his head, and mine. My selfish need has just made this impossible scenario a million times worse!

~

The awkward tension lingered long after he strode away, closing the door behind him. He hadn't said another word, he just backed away lowering his pained and saddened eyes.

I had hurt him deeply. I knew it, but there was nothing I could do or say to make the situation any better. I wish I could.

How could I not be drawn to him when everything about him reminds me of Max. But wasn't that exactly what Monica had done? I hadn't asked for his love or whatever it is he thinks he feels for me, but I had taken advantage of him for my own selfish need. And now, I'm no better than Monica. He doesn't deserve that.

I collapse down to the edge of the bed with my head in my hands. Shame and regret forcing more tears to flow.

How could I have been so stupid?

SECRET DOOR TO A SECRET DOOR

"I vow to fiercely love you, for every moment of every day, until forever. I promise I'll do whatever it takes to make you always look at me with the love you have in your eyes right now. I'm yours, baby. Heart, mind, body and soul. And you, Vivienne, you are my once in a lifetime love, my crazy-good love. Forever with you will never be long enough. Will you do me the extraordinary honour of being mine forever… Marry me?"

"Yes… With all my heart and forever, yes."

I wake to the sound of my own voice. Tears trickle across the bridge of my nose and soak my cheek as I lay on my side curled around the pillow. As my eyes begin to focus, I sit up with a jolt not knowing where I am. Looking all around me in a panic, I suddenly remember. I'm at the chateau.

The haze of a breaking dawn filters into the room between the gap in the heavy curtains. Checking my watch, I see it's only five o'clock. The birds haven't even risen yet.

The tension in my body, still present from the unfortunate events of last night, makes me feel sick. Throwing the blankets off, I stand to stretch out the kinks of a tortured sleep. I had dreamt of Max all night, tossing and turning but unable to fully wake up. I didn't want to wake up. I wanted to hold on to him for as long as I could.

The all too familiar hollow feeling swirls around inside me.

It's not hunger, it's loss. An ache that grows stronger and deeper every day. I hate it, but I've come to understand it. And the building pressure of my actions last night, dig at my conscience.

Shaking my head, I try to free it of those memories. I owe Cole an apology.

I walk to the window and gaze out at the impeccable gardens. The eerie quietness scares me. *Where is everybody?*

Leaving my room, I stand in the corridor unsure of my bearings. Turning to my right, I eventually find the stairs. As I reach the bottom and walk through the grand hallway, I hear distant voices and the clinking of china. The aroma of coffee hits me as soon as I enter the kitchen, the one I had been in before when I'd met Harry.

Julie and John are sitting at the long wooden table nursing their steaming mugs. They look like they haven't slept at all.

"Would you like some coffee?" Julie asks, rising from her seat.

"No thanks." As neither of them have happy smiles on their faces, I can only assume there's no good news for me this morning. "Where's Cole?"

"He's asleep in the drawing room, he was dead on his feet so we told him to get some shut-eye." John rubs his tired eyes, watching me move to the back door. "Are you okay?" he asks softly.

"Yes, I'm going to get some fresh air."

I feel their eyes on me as I walk out to the gardens.

Destroyed and dejected, I wander blindly across the lawn. Not really caring where I end up, I keep walking as tears build in my eyes and the deep ache of loss grows in my heart.

People often say, 'everything will be better in the morning', but I don't feel it. Every morning so far has brought more and more depression and hopelessness.. Max is gone. Any hope of finding him was destroyed the minute Monica died. And those cold, hard facts bear down on me with searing clarity.

I run my hand over my bump, over our little nuggets. They'll never know the warmth of his hold, they'll never witness the depth of his love shining brightly in his beautiful eyes, or feel the full force of his heart, as I have. I mourn their loss as deeply as I mourn my own.

As the early morning sun begins to rise, glistening off the heavy dew on the grass, I notice a change in the terrain beneath my feet. The crunching stones of a shingle pathway pulls me out of my mindless daze. Looking up, I see the boathouse a few feet in front of me and behind it, a flat calm waterway stretches out beyond.

Looking behind me, the chateau looks much less imposing from this distance.

I'm not ready to go back yet, so I continue walking over to the edge of the wooden bridge running alongside the boathouse. I lean my forearms on the railing staring out at the undisturbed water, its glossy surface reflecting the sunlight like a mirror. It's so peaceful and calm. I can see why William would have loved it here, its tranquillity and beauty is very soothing.

I don't know how long I had stood there, I didn't care. I had finally achieved the numbness I was searching for without a single drop of alcohol. Something inside me had switched off. Resignation had taken hold, utilizing only the necessities required for survival. My body would still function, I'd breathe enough air, and my heart would continue to beat, but I would no longer feel. No. That would be too difficult, feeling hurts too much.

I hear Julie's voice frantically calling my name. I consider ignoring her, and I do for a while, then I turn and head back toward the house. She's standing on the lawn looking anxious until she sees me emerging from the cover of the neatly trimmed willow tree standing between us.

"There you are! I was getting worried about you."

"Sorry, I was just—"

A sound suddenly stops me in my tracks, prickling my skin. I look all around me trying to identify it, but it's stopped. Adrenaline forces my heart to beat faster as I anxiously spin around on the spot looking for whatever it was I had heard.

It's triggered a memory that hasn't fully formed. I need to hear it again.

"Vivienne? Is every—"

"Sshh," I snap, holding my hand up to silence her.

"Vivienne, I—"

"Be quiet!"

I see Julie walking toward me in my peripheral vision as I anxiously wait for it to happen again. It does, and my heart leaps in my chest.

"That's it! Oh, my god! That's the sound. That's what I'd heard!"

I push past Julie and run as fast as my legs will take me toward the other side of the chateau. It sounds closer now, but I don't see it yet and then it stops.

Julie is running behind me. "Vivienne, what's the matter?"

I hear it again. Louder this time. As my eyes eagerly scan the area, the source finally comes into view and the memory becomes complete in my mind.

A beautiful peacock struts around the grounds on the east side of the building with its tail feathers stretched downward behind it. Almost as if on cue, it repeats its distinctive call.

"That's the sound. That's what I heard."

Julie catches up with me, tugging on my arm. "Vivienne, what are you doing?"

Out of breath, I point at the Peacock. "That bird… That sound!…I heard the same sound when Monica took me to see Max."

"What do you mean?"

"He's here! Max is here! I know he is!"

I don't wait for Julie, I start running toward the house calling out his name.. Barging into the kitchen, I frantically begin to search along every wall and floor board, looking for a secret door. Julie catches up with me followed by John and then Cole, who looks utterly exhausted.

"What are you doing?" he asks, rubbing his eyes.

"Remember the sound I told you about? It's a bird. A peacock. I heard it! He's here Cole, I know he is! We just have to find him."

I quickly resume my search, feeling my way along the walls and skirting boards. Without a word, everyone springs to life and joins in.

When we don't find anything on the ground floor we move up to the next one. Adrenaline flows through me like an electric current boosting my synapses and driving me on with a ferocious need to be right. Even as we reach the last floor, our last chance to find him, I keep going. Feeling and picking at every lump, bump, and crevice in the walls and floors.

I reach the hidden door, the one to the attic, the one Harry had shown me. We had tried Monica's key last night. It didn't fit, but we didn't look inside. John and Julie had already checked it. Even I had been up there with Harry and yes, it was empty, but I need to check again. Max is here, I know he is.

"I need the key for this door!" I shout over my shoulder. "It's a long silver one. Harry had it on his keyring."

"Copy that." John runs downstairs to the kitchen to find them, returning a few minutes later. He tries several keys on the big ring before finding the right one.

Once it's open, I barge past him and run up the attic stairs to the attic I had been in before. The others follow and we all stand puffing and panting in the middle of the empty space. The peacock's call cuts through the silence and we all glance at each other confirming we had all heard it.

Running over to Cole, I tug on his sleeve. "That's the sound I heard the day Monica took me to see Max."

In a sudden burst of movement, we spread out and start checking the walls for another hidden door, but after a thorough search we find nothing.

"Fuck!" Angry, frustrated tears spill over my lashes. "Shit! Fuck! Bollocks!" Devastation overwhelms me as my fists ball up at my sides.

Cole moves forward to try and comfort me but I push him away, I don't want his sympathy. I don't want anyone to touch me. I'm too raw. I was so sure I was right about this.

Standing in the middle of the wood panelled room, I stare out of the lead-light windows then crumple to a heap on the floor, sobbing uncontrollably. Everyone else goes quiet.

"Is it just me or does something not feel right about that window?"

I whip my head up to Julie who's studying the window with a deep frown on her face. She angles her head, then turns to face John.

"Yeah, it's off centre… or the wall…" John doesn't finish his sentence. Walking toward the wall he starts tapping it with his knuckles. The heavy thudding sounds the same as he taps his way along it until a lighter, hollow sound happens nearer the window.

"I thought this room felt narrower than it should." John turns to face Julie and Cole, their eyes locked in a wordless conversation until all three of them spring to action. I watch through tear blurred eyes as they try to find a weak spot.

John pulls out a long-bladed hunting knife from a strap around his calf and starts to pry the wood away at a seam. He and Cole tug at the freed corner, eventually stripping it away from the wall with a force that knocks them both off their feet.

I run to the open gap, just a five-inch gap but enough that I can see a dim light coming from the window partially buried behind the wall, and I can feel a light breeze too.

Cole and John push me aside, tugging aggressively at the other panels freeing two more. I poke my head in the gap and look down but I can't see anything.

"I've found it! Bring the key!"

We all whip around to Julie who is standing at the top of the stairs waving at me to follow her. I fumble in my pocket for Monica's long brass key as we race over.

Following her back down the attic steps to the door we had entered by, she stops just short of it pointing to the dark wood panelling at the foot of the stairs on our left. As we bunch up behind her, I look where's she pointing, but I can't see anything except the wall and an old-fashioned light switch sticking out at waist height.

"Here! Look!" she says, lifting the round, brown, light switch attached by a hinge at the top and then I see the keyhole hidden behind it.

John pulls out his phone. "I'll call Benny and get the team here."

I've stopped breathing. My stomach is now knotting with anxiety and a cold sweat mists my skin. This has to be the place. I had seen a light switch like that one before. Fear takes hold when I realise this is when I find out if Max is still alive.

"Oh god, please be alive."

Cole takes the key from my shaking hands and slips it into the lock, then he gives me a tight, sideways glance before turning the key and pushing the door wide open. I recognise the room instantly. Pushing past Cole and Julie, I race to the far end.

"Max!… Max!" In a panic, I drag the curtain aside. "No!" Collapsing down at the side of his cot, I pull the gag down from around his mouth expecting him to gasp for air, but he's deathly still, and when I turn his face toward me, he looks completely lifeless. "No, Max… No!"

Grabbing his hand, I pull it up to my lips. His skin is cool to the touch and I can't tell if he's breathing. "Don't leave me, Max. Please, don't leave me."

Julie crouches down next to me and I feel Cole's hands on my shoulders pulling me away.

"No!" I fight against him but he's too strong.

"Please, Vivienne, let her take care of him, she knows what she's doing."

Reluctantly, I move out of Julie's way, helplessly watching as she calmly checks for a pulse before turning her ear to his mouth. "He's breathing, just. His pulse is very weak but it's there."

My blood chills. He's not responding to anything she's doing. She checks the pupil of the eye that isn't swollen shut. "He's dilated." Checking the wound on the side of his head, she moves on to his chest and abdomen, surveying the dark purple bruises with concern. "He has multiple rib fractures, he could be bleeding internally." She turns to face Cole. "We need to get him to the hospital immediately."

Her voice is calm but her expression scares me to death. I feel like I can't breathe.

Rising to her feet, she reaches for my hand. "He's going to be okay, Vivienne. We just need to get him to the hospital." She smiles, trying to reassure me, but a hint of doubt creeps into her eyes compounding my fear. "John, what's their e.t.a.?"

"Thirteen minutes, I told Benny to land in the front."

"Good." Turning her attention back to me, she smiles. "You saved his life."

I hope with all my heart that she's right. Finding Max alive is a huge relief but I know he isn't out of the woods yet. It scares me to know that until he can receive proper medical attention, something could still go wrong. Something always goes wrong.

"Okay, we need to get him downstairs. The quicker we can e-vac him, the better." John says, organising Cole and I into position. Both thoroughly immersed in their efficient professional mode, John and Julie take the other two corners of the cot and we carry him out of the secret room.

Getting him through the doorway on a tight angle is tricky, but we manage it and carry him down the wide staircase to the main hallway where we anxiously wait for Benny and the paramedics to arrive in the helicopter. Max lies unconscious not responding to my voice, and in the harsh morning light, his injuries look far worse.

The team arrive within minutes. The paramedics take a while to assess and stabilise him before loading him into the helicopter. Everything is happening so fast.

Relief and trepidation battle it out in my brain. Turning to Cole, I throw my arms around his neck, hugging him tightly. As I pull away to look at him, his sad eyes stay lowered from mine. "Thank you," I whisper, unable to speak clearly. Emotion seems to have strangled my vocal chords.

"I'll grab your belongings from the yacht, we'll meet you at the hospital in London." His voice is strained and the look on his face brings me to tears.

I give John and Julie a quick hug, then I board the helicopter, my fear of them greatly outweighed by my fear for Max.

RETURN TO ME MY LOVE

The flight home seems to take forever. I want to hold Max's hand, I need to touch him, but the paramedics are huddled around him so close giving him blood, fluids, and drugs, I don't want to get in their way.

When we finally land at the Limberton Hospital, a young nurse meets me and walks me away from the heli-pad as the crash team rush Max inside the building. I understand they need to work on him, but I'm scared to let him out of my sight.

After pacing up and down the waiting room for what felt like an eternity, the welcome sight of Sylvie, Jan, and Vinnie, brings tears to my eyes. They hug me, all of us in tears, all of us anxious to hear any news.

Sylvie sits beside me gripping my hand for dear life. We've both been put through the wringer. We both need to hold on to each other. She looks exhausted, so frail. I know how I am feeling, but she must be feeling so much worse not having William to comfort her.

After hours of waiting, Doctor Alexander comes to talk to us. His expression when he enters the room frightens me, so much so that my knees start to buckle, but the news is good. Not great! But good.

Max has an infection, he's suffered internal bleeding from a ruptured blood vessel in his abdomen, brought about by the savage beating he'd received at the hands of those thugs. Thankfully, they've managed to repair it, and the strong antibiotics should fight the infection.

Although Max is still in a critical condition, under close observation for the next forty-eight hours, his organs haven't suffered irreparably and the doctor doesn't anticipate any long term complications.

Thankfully, his broken ribs haven't punctured his lungs, and his fractured wrist is a clean break which will heal in time. The wound to his head is superficial which doesn't require stitching. All in all, his prognosis seems positive, but until he is out of critical care, I can't relax.

Once the doctor has left the room, the relief that I finally have him back where he belongs, is overwhelming. He's alive. He's survived his ordeal with impossible odds. I still can't believe it. After fearing that I'd never see him again, I'm practically euphoric.

The trauma of the last few hours, on top of the last two weeks of hell, leave me dizzy and weak. Vinnie catches me before I collapse and sits me down, then he fetches me a cup of water and a chocolate bar to boost my energy. I wolf it down. It's the first time in a long time, that I really want to eat.

"I hear you met Percy," Vinnie says, with a cheeky smirk.

He's caught me with a cube of chocolate wedged in my cheek so I have to mumble around it. "Who?"

"Percy… the peacock."

"Oh, yes. It's frightening. If it wasn't for him, we may have walked away from that place." The thought makes me shudder. We came so close to abandoning Max, it makes me feel sick every time I think about it.

Leaning back in his chair, Vinnie scowls folding his arms across his chest. "Well, it's about time that bird did something useful instead of crapping all over the lawn."

"Hey, don't diss the bird, he's my new BFF."

Vinnie rolls his eyes. "He'll be Christmas dinner if he

chases me round that garden again."

I smile at him, happy to be able to smile without feeling guilty, and without the usual hint of dread in the background.

When the nurse finally arrives to let us know that we can go in to see Max, I stand up in a rush. I've been waiting so long to see him and now the moment has arrived my eyes fill with tears and I fall to pieces. All the built up pressure seems to flow out of me at once and I stand there sobbing like an idiot.

"Come on, sweetheart," Sylvie says, reaching her hand out toward me, "let's go and see our boy, shall we?"

Taking her hand, we follow the nurse to Max's room.

As the nurse opens the door, she offers me a reassuring smile. "We have him sedated and he's on strong pain relief so don't be alarmed if he doesn't respond."

As we walk in, the sight of him makes me draw in an extra breath. He looks so defenceless lying there with tubes and machines attached to his body. Dark bruises stain his chest and ribs in several places, and he has a small dressing on the right side of his abdomen from his surgery.

His left arm is in plaster, and his left eye is still swollen shut. Although his muscular arms and chest still look lethal, he seems so fragile and vulnerable.

Sitting Sylvie down next to his bed, I bring their hands together so she can feel him. Then I walk to the other side and lean down and gently kiss his M.F. tattoo, then his lips. "I'm here, Max. I love you."

"How does he look?" Sylvie asks in a frail voice. I'm glad she can't see him, it's enough to make you weep. If she could see him like this it would break her heart. She deserves to sleep peacefully tonight.

"He looks fine, Sylvie. Just fine."

We sit with him for an hour or so until Vinnie and Jan offer to take her home to rest. Sylvie asks me to go with her, but I want to stay. I don't want to leave him, I've only just got him back.

Without having to ask, Doctor Alexander arranges another

bed to be brought in so I can stay overnight. I don't want to let go of his hand, so I sit at his bedside and hold on to him for hours.

Staring down at his beaten, but still beautiful face, I graze my eyes over every perfect inch of him, I could never tire of looking at him. It hurts me to see him like this, but at least he's alive and back where he belongs.

I never want to feel that kind of pain again. I've missed him so much. I want to crawl into his bed and hold him against me. I've missed our cuddles, being sprawled across his chest with my leg over his hips and his arms around me. But most of all I've missed his eyes, the way they look at me, into me. The way they love me.

~

Something jolts me from my sleep. Lifting my head from the edge of the bed, I stare at our interlocked fingers. He's squeezing me. It's very slight, but I can feel it all the same. Looking up at his face, I see a frown softly forming across his brow.

"Max, I'm here." I squeeze his hand then raise it to my lips to kiss his fingers. "I'm here, my love. You're safe. I love you, Max."

He swallows, then his lips slowly peel apart and I see them move very subtly. He doesn't make a sound but I know that he's trying to say, 'I love you more.'

On a deep sigh, I stare at him through tear blurred eyes as my heart swells in my chest. His eyes remain closed but I feel the pressure from his hand once more. Rising up, I gently kiss him on the forehead, brush my fingers through his dishevelled hair, then I kiss him on the lips. "Until forever, remember?"

Almost imperceptibly he nods his head, his brow relaxing as he drifts back to sleep and I feel the tension in my body evaporate, physically sagging with relief. Resting our hands against my lips I watch him sleep.

~

"Vivienne…"

Peeling them open, I blink my tired eyes. Right in front of

me, lying on the bed, is my babies scan. I lift my head up and see Cole walking toward the door.

"Cole. It's okay, I'm awake," I say, taking a deep inhale as I stretch out the kinks.

He turns to face me, his concerned, tired eyes sliding over to Max. "How is he?"

I turn to check him, he still looks peacefully asleep. "They said he's going to be okay. You, on the other hand, look awful."

Cole looks exhausted and judging by his clothes he hasn't been home yet either. Shrugging off my remark, he hesitates at the door. "Ah… I had a call from the French police before I left. Daryl's DNA was found on Monica's body, they found the murder weapon in his bar."

"Oh?" I feel terrible. I've been so dedicated to hating Monica that I keep forgetting he was once in love with her, and her brutal death must still be very raw for him. "I'm sorry. I know you loved her. It must be—"

"Save it," he says, abruptly. "She doesn't deserve anyone's pity. She wasn't worth it." His eyes search mine like he has something else on his mind, something he needs to say. I think I know what it is but I hope he doesn't say it.

"Cole… I am sorry… It was wrong of me to…" I can't seem to say it.

His sad eyes linger on mine then slide over to Max. Clenching his jaw he bows his head then leaves the room. I stare at the empty doorway. I never wanted to hurt him but the last few weeks have been painful and extraordinary for all of us.

Picking up our babies' scan, I kiss it, then set it on his bedside table.

"Vivienne?" Max's soft, croaky voice has my head whipping around. "Baby?"

"I'm right here." I lean into him so he can see me through his partially opened eye. My heart flutters in my chest and tears pool in my eyes.

"I told you I'd be back in a minute," he murmurs, with a

croaky rasp.

I smile through my tears. "That was over two weeks ago. I thought I was never going to see you again." The words catch in my throat as a wave of emotion hits me head on.

"Until forever, remember?"

I nod and smile but I can't speak, I'm too emotional. I lean over to kiss him on the lips. "Until forever. It's so good to have you back."

"Go home, baby. Go home and rest." Unable to fight his sedation, he fades back into sleep.

As Max sleeps soundly, I decide to go and check out the restaurant on the ground floor. My appetite seems to have fully recovered now Max is safe. I don't want to leave him, but I'm starving and my stomach has begun to groan loudly. I've been sitting at his bedside for almost ten hours, I need to stretch and take a walk to iron out the kinks.

I wander downstairs to find the empty self-service restaurant. Spooning out a bowl of chicken noodle soup, I pick out one of the crusty rolls from the basket.

"Viv!" Lucy's high-pitched voice startles me.

"Luce! What are you doing here?"

She practically knocks me off my feet with a bear hug, the roll in my hand goes flying.

"Oh, Viv, I'm so glad to see you, and we're so happy that Max is going to be alright. Jan called us an hour ago to say you were here, so we came as soon as we could. Dan's just parking the car."

I hug her back, not wanting to let her go. I've missed her.

She finally releases me and after a few tears and sniffles, she loads up her own tray with food. "Where's the wine?"

"Luce, this is a hospital, they don't have wine."

"Well it's lucky I brought my own then isn't it!" Digging into her bag, she pulls out a miniature bottle of red wine.

I shake my head, staring at her with raised eyebrows. She's so resourceful.

"…What?" she asks in confusion. "They were on sale at the supermarket and they fit perfectly in my handbag."

"Why don't you just chuck a box of wine in a rucksack and get yourself a long straw."

"Hey, that's not a bad idea."

Dan joins us as I'm rolling my eyes at Lucy, she's such a lush. But I couldn't be happier to see them both.

He hands me a bag with some clean clothes and toiletries inside. "Jan thought you might need these," he smiles, giving me a cuddle.

Once we've caught up on all their news, I tell them about Mike. As expected Lucy is furious with him.

"That fucking shit-bag! I knew all that bollocks about you and him being friends was too good to be true. Shifty twat."

Dan sighs, looking upset that he'd put so much faith in him as a friend. "I can't believe he'd be so stupid. I always knew his cousin Daryl was trouble but I didn't realise he was that dodgy."

"Well, I'd prefer to draw a line under it all now. I just want everything to calm down so Max can recover and we can get back to a normal life."

They both nod in agreement then Lucy reaches out to squeeze my hand over the table. "It's been really hard for you hasn't it? I can't believe what's happened, but I have to say, I'm friggin' delighted Monica is finally gone for good." She shudders giving Dan a knowing look.

We've all been at the sharp end of Monica at some time or another and I, more than most, feel relieved that she will never cast a shadow over our lives again.

"Does he know about his dad yet?"

I take a deep inhale. That's one piece of news I really don't want to give him. "No, not yet."

Lucy gives me another squeeze but says nothing. She knows how this news will affect him, he's going to be devastated. It worries me just how deeply it could affect him.

Once we've finished our food, Lucy and Dan give me a hug and head off home. It's almost ten o'clock, it's been a long day and I'm practically dead on my feet.

I head back up to Max's room and after checking him, I

take a quick shower, brush my teeth, and throw on my comfies. My arse can't take the hard chair anymore, so I settle into my bed alongside his laying on my side so I can stare at him. I can never get enough of looking at him, whether he's awake or asleep. And knowing what it feels like to be apart, I'm going to take every opportunity.

The nurse pops in every thirty minutes, checking his fluids and the machines he's attached to. With a smile and a thumbs up, she leaves the room.

BOTTLED UP

"You want to kiss me now, don't you?"

"Yes, I always want to kiss you. And then I want to take you somewhere quiet and strip you naked so I can run my tongue over every perfect inch of your delicious body."

"And what then?"

"Then I'm going to take you in my mouth and suck... hard."

"Erhumm!"

My eyes ping open. The soft sound of chuckling draws my head up off the pillow. Sheila, the nurse I had seen before, is changing a drip in Max's intravenous line. She's a short, round, black woman with a pretty face and a strong, southern, Alabama accent. She smiles a big toothy grin while shaking her head at me, making me blush from head to toe.

"Don't worry, honey, he's hot! If I was sleeping with him, I'd want to do the same thing. Man! He's a fine piece of ass."

I feel mortified that I had obviously been talking in my sleep. The dream was amazing, so real, but I had no idea I was sharing it with Sheila.

Still grinning, she inspects his plaster-cast. "Does he do his own stunts?"

Her dry sense of humour makes me smile, her mannerisms

are comical.

Rubbing my eyes, I sit up in bed. "What time is it?"

"It's a quarter after seven. Can I get you anything?"

"No. I'm fine, thanks."

Once she leaves, I get up and sit at his bedside. He looks comfortable still sound asleep.

Rummaging in my bag, I find my pen. Once I've left a message on his cast, I pop into the en-suite to freshen up.

After a nice hot shower, I pull on my jeans and a t-shirt, then brush out all the knots in my hair. I look like I've been pulled through a hedge backwards.

"Really?"

Max's voice makes me jump as I stroll out of the bathroom, I'm delighted and relieved to see him wide awake. Holding up his plastered arm, he scowls at me until his cheeky smirk takes over. Quickly dumping my stuff on my bed, I skip over to kiss him on the lips. "Good morning!"

The message I had left on his cast reads: 'Leave me again and I'll break your other wrist!' Underneath, in really big letters, I wrote the words; 'I LOVE YOU. X:-))'

"I love you more, baby."

My heart flutters, I've waited a long time to hear that.

His left eye looks better than it did yesterday but it still remains closed. The colour in his cheeks has returned and he doesn't look quite so drawn. I'm so happy to see him awake and smiling.

"God, I've missed you." He sounds dry and croaky so I hand him some water and gently run my fingers through his dishevelled hair. Looking down at my hand holding the water, his good eye widens. "What the hell is that?"

I realise he's seen the pink scar from the cuffs Monica forced me to wear. Grabbing my arm, he takes a closer look, then he hits me with a confused expression. I shrug nonchalantly in an attempt to diffuse his concern.

"It's nothing. I just caught it on something."

I'm relieved my watch is covering my other scarred wrist, I don't want to get into that story yet, it'll freak him out.

Gently soothing his worried frown, I gaze down at him with a distracting smile. He rests his head back to the pillow staring up at me like he's trying to make sure I'm really there.

"I've missed you, too, Max. I can't tell you how good it is to have you back." Tears spring into my eyes. I need to tell him about his father. I know this will kill him, but he has to know.

Reaching up with his good arm, he runs his fingers down my cheek. I lean into it and kiss his palm. I've missed his touch, feeling it again now, I never realised how much I'd missed it.

It's almost overwhelming to see him again. I've waited so long and feared the worst but now he's here, and I'm so happy to have him back. Despite my happiness, my belly churns as I try to organise the best way to tell him about his father. There's certainly no good way.

"Baby? What is it?" he asks, picking up on my mood. He reads me too well.

"Max…" Taking his hand in mine, I hold it against my chest, running my other hand down his cheek, gently rubbing my thumb over his lips. The words seem to be stuck in my throat.

A pained expression puts a deep frown in his brow. "Oh, god! Is it the babies?" The fear in his voice makes my heart clench and I quickly shake my head to get that thought out of his mind.

"No, it's not the babies. They're fine. Max, But… Your father had a heart attack… he passed away three days after you disappeared. I'm so sorry."

Inhaling sharply, he stares at me in disbelief for the longest time, his head falls back to the pillow, his chin quivering as he tries to hold in his tears. There's nothing I can do but hold on to him as the news breaks his heart.

I explain what happened in the kindest way I can, but the devastation of losing his father has crushed him.

I tell him about the service we'd held for William, and all the lovely messages he had received from all those who had loved and respected him. It made me cry too. I miss William.

Max's concern is for his mother, he's always been a good son. But my concern is for him. Max has known far too much pain and loss, it scares me that this could be a loss too great to cope with.

We sit in silence for a while until his tears dry.

He strokes my cheek with his fingers, still looking at me in awe. "It's so good to see you, baby."

"Do you remember anything?"

His good eye slides away from mine, concentrating on his hand as he continues to caress my cheek, his jaw clenching as his expression hardens. "I remember all of it."

Sensing that I'm just about to ask something, he cuts me off. "But I don't want to talk about it. It's in the past now, and I won't waste any more time on that bitch or those assholes. They've taken enough from us already."

He's bitter and angry, and rightly so. His father may still be alive if Monica hadn't abducted Max. But I worry that he's holding it all in, not dealing with it as he should. His ordeal must have been extremely harrowing and he hasn't been able to mourn his father's death. He needs to talk about this.

"I remember hearing your voice," he says, softly.

My eyes widen in surprise. "What?"

"I tried to call out to you, but she gagged me, and I was so spaced out on whatever it was she gave me, I couldn't move."

My blood runs cold. It suddenly dawns on me that the day I had gone to the chateau looking for him, me and Harry had walked right past his room when we had gone up to the attic. He could hear us, but we were oblivious to him.

Dipping my head, I try to hide my tears. I feel awful that he'd suffered so unnecessarily. "Oh, Max. I'm so sorry. I tried so hard to find you. I've been going out of my mind trying to find you." I can't help it, the pent up emotion barges to the surface and takes me over.

"Sshh. Baby please don't cry. You did find me. You saved me, that's all that matters."

Without thinking I lunge at him wrapping my arms around

him, burying my face in his neck. It's been so long since I've held him in my arms.

"Arrggh!"

"Oh, shit, I'm sorry." I pull away laughing and crying and cursing myself for hurting him, the pain is etched all over his face. Taking his face between my palms I lower to gently press my lips to his. "I love you, Max. I've missed you so much. I never want us to be apart again. Never."

"Ah, sorry, I'll come back later."

Cole's voice startles me. I turn to face him, wiping the tears from my eyes. Cole's brow is furrowed and for some stupid reason I feel awkward and shy.

"No, it's okay. I need to get some breakfast anyway. I've just told him about William, you should stay and talk."

Smoothing my hand across Max's forehead, I turn to leave. Cole doesn't give me eye contact and I feel tension oozing from him.

Let it go, Cole. Please.

Before I grab some breakfast, I call Sylvie to let her know Max is awake, and then I call Jan to let her and Vinnie know too. I feel so happy now he's awake, which is reflected in the amount of food I shovel onto my plate for breakfast. The appetite has certainly made a comeback.

I check my emails and make a call to Casper to see how things are going at the office. I've totally abandoned my business since Max disappeared. I know Casper and Ed will have kept things ticking over, and I'm not ready to go back yet, but I need to let them know I appreciate what they're doing for me.

Casper informs me that Ed has held things together very well, however the aerial work has been backing up because, as he recently found out on his first helicopter ride, and much to his annoyance, Ed suffers from air sickness.

It makes me chuckle. I know how much Ed was looking forward to doing his own aerial assignments, I'm sure he's gutted about it.

I leave the restaurant and head back up to Max's room. I'd

been gone for well over an hour, so I'm surprised to see Cole still sitting at his bedside.

"I'll come back," I mumble, turning to leave.

"No, baby, don't go. Come sit beside me, I've missed you." The sad pout on Max's face pulls at my heart. Cole doesn't give me eye contact but he moves out of his seat to let me take his chair, then he pulls another one over for himself.

I had hoped he would leave, especially as I can still feel his tension. I hope he doesn't persist with this awkwardness, it was just a stupid kiss that should never have happened, and one that I've apologised for and sincerely regret. I don't know what else I can do.

The angry expression forming on Max's face sends a streak of fear through me. Surely Cole hasn't told him about the kiss. Why would he do that? He knows I was vulnerable and weak, he knows that I was just—

"Baby? Baby are you okay?"

"What? Oh, sorry I was just… oh, it doesn't matter."

The angry frown returns to Max's brow filling me with dread that he knows about the kiss.

"Cole has just told me what happened."

Oh, no! A nervous sweat moistens my skin.

"I can't believe you'd do that, Vivienne. I can't believe you would put yourself and the babies at risk like that. You know how I feel about you riding motorbikes. And to leave yourself totally unprotected with Monica? Jesus, you could have got yourself killed."

Oh… that!

I lower my eyes then slip a sideways glance at Cole. I could kiss him for not mentioning the kiss, but that would be foolish, opening a can of worms that needs to stay sealed and contained forever.

"I know, but it was necessary at the time and we're fine, I promise."

Max gives me the death stare for a moment longer, then he reaches out and takes my hand, lifting it to his smiling lips. "You really do love me, don't you."

I smile back, with tears in my eyes. "More than you'll ever know."

In my peripheral vision I see Cole shifting in his seat. Rising abruptly, he pushes his chair back with a loud scrape. "I'll leave you two alone."

Max smiles up at him, seemingly oblivious to his frostiness. "Thanks for the visit, and thanks for taking care of my woman. I really appreciate you looking after her while I was gone. It means a lot to me."

Cole returns the smile but it looks forced, and when his eyes swing over to mine, I see the hurt within them.

When Cole leaves, I turn to Max and see a tear slipping down his cheek.

"What is it? What's wrong?"

Shaking his head, he squeezes my hand. "Nothing. It's just…I'm so happy to see you again, baby. I thought I wasn't going to make it, you're all I could think about. Just seeing your beautiful face makes me so happy." His lips curl into a smile but it soon evaporates.

"And Cole… God, it's so good to have my brother back after all these years… But I'm worried about him. He didn't say anything but I can tell, something's bothering him."

My belly churns and a blush heats my cheeks. Max is so perceptive, and Cole's behaviour is going to get us both in trouble. I'm going to have to confront Cole and sort this out once and for all.

"I think Monica's death has hit him hard. I don't think he ever truly got over her."

Max looks confused for a moment then his face hardens. "Well, he should. That bitch was pure evil."

The look on his face jars me. I can tell that his mind is lost in a thought involving her. "What did she do to you?"

His good eye slowly refocuses as his mind comes back to the present.

"Max?"

Squeezing my hand, he brings it up to his lips for a soft kiss. "Nothing for you to worry about."

He's refusing to include me in whatever he's been through and that hurts. But maybe he needs more time. I can't imagine what he's been through. I want to hold him close and show him how much he means to me, how much I've missed him. But for now, until he's healed, all I can do is wait, and be grateful to have him back where he belongs.

Turning his head, he nods up at the bedside table. I know what he wants, so I reach up for the scan of our babies and hold it in front of his face. His teary good eye trawls all over the image, I can see he's confused about the condition of it.

"Monica tore it up and tried to flush it down the toilet."

The torment of her cruel act rides across his face as he exhales a deeply, irritated sigh. "That bitch!"

For a moment, he looks lost in his thoughts again until his eye flicks up to mine. "We'll get another one. And I want you to see the doctor, I'm worried about the drug she gave you, we need to know if it's had any effect on the babies."

"Don't worry. Doctor Alexander ran some tests as soon as we got here, everything's fine and I'm due for another scan soon."

He physically relaxes, but I can see the worry in his face. I don't want him worrying about anything, he needs to rest and recover.

As I gently stroke my fingers through his hair, his eye gazes up at me all soft and loving, I've missed that look. "Max, what happened to you?"

I feel the tension in him immediately I had asked the question. His gaze lowers and he turns away. His reaction confuses me. Lifting my hand from his head, I let it hover. His mood has changed, darkened, all because of my question.

Resuming my gentle stroking of his hair, I wait for him to face me, but he doesn't, he closes his eye letting out a deep sigh.

"Max? Talk to me, please."

He pulls his head away like my gentle strokes are irritating him. "I don't want to talk about it." The clenching in his jaw and the hardness in his voice tells me he's completely closed on the subject. But why? I know him well enough to know that he won't tell me, no matter how much I want him to. I hate it when he shuts me out.

After everything we've been through, we should be closer than we've ever been, but as he's demonstrated before, Max prefers to deal with his pain in a singular, more isolated manner. It kills me, but I know if I press him on it, he'll just become more agitated, so I try to ignore his reticence, even though inside I'm hurt that he's closed himself off to me.

"Baby, would you hand me that bag?" He points to the leather holdall hanging off the back of my chair as he tries to shuffle into a more comfortable position. I pop the bag on the edge of his bed. "Can you open the side pocket and take out the box?"

I open the zipper on the side pocket, instantly noticing the flat, red velvet jewellery box sitting inside. My mouth has gone dry and my heart beats a little faster.

The sight of the box has somehow transported me back to the morning after Max's abduction. Vinnie and I were sitting outside the hospital talking as we waited for news on William. Vinnie had tried to give me this box but I had refused it. I wanted Max to give it to me, even though at the time I was unsure if I'd ever see him again.

"Go ahead," he murmurs. "Open it." His expression is cautious as he watches me remove the box from the bag and hold it in my shaking hands. I don't know why I'm hesitating, I've thought about this box many times, wondering about its contents.

"Max, you know I don't need special gifts to tell me how much you love me. I only need to look in your eyes."

He gazes at me with so much love it almost saddens his face. "That's one of the things I love about you, Vivienne. Your beautiful eyes tell me everything. I've missed the way they look at me." A small smirk curls his lips. "And the way they undress me."

Blushing and smiling, I shake my head, but he's not wrong.

Max lets out a deep sigh and his face becomes sad, his hurt

expression made worse by the eye that's swollen shut. "I had it all planned. Every last detail. I wanted to give this to you on our wedding day, but as that's been postponed…" His eye lowers to the box and I can see how upset he is.

I cup his cheek and stroke it with the pad of my thumb. "I can wait. You can still give it to me on our wedding day."

Leaning into my palm he hits me with a watery-eyed smile. "I want you to have it now. You know how impatient I am."

Butterflies invade my belly and as I slowly open the lid, my breath catches in my throat as tears flood my eyes. "Oh, Max. It's beautiful." The diamond encrusted, heart-shaped locket is the most stunning piece of jewellery I have ever seen.

"It's a symbol of my love. As strong and everlasting as the diamonds. My heart beats only for you, Vivienne. I've loved you since the first moment I saw you. I fall in love with you all over again every single day. My heart is yours, until forever."

His words bring a lump to my throat and a flood of fresh tears. I struggle to speak, I'm overwhelmed, taking his face in my hands, I show him how I feel with a kiss. "I'll cherish this, and you, for the rest of my life. Until forever," I whisper against his lips.

Opening the locket, I expected to see a photograph of us inside, but instead there are two loose diamonds. I look up at him quizzically.

"They're identical diamonds, very rare. They represent our little nuggets. When they're born, we'll put their photographs inside the locket and have the diamonds made into earrings."

I'm speechless and overwhelmed. He always completely floors me with his gestures of love. "Max, I… I'm stunned…It's so beautiful, so thoughtful. I love it. I love you."

The smile on his face when I put it around my neck is just as overwhelming as the gift itself. The weight of it against my skin, a constant reminder that I have the honour of owning his heart.

"Vinnie told me all about your plans for our wedding, it sounded perfect."

Worry lines settle into his brow and then morph into a

scowl. "You should have been Mrs. Foxx by now. In fact, call the priest, let's get married right now. I can't stand all this waiting."

"Well I would," I smirk, "but how am I supposed to get a ring on your finger when your hand is in plaster. Besides, our wedding photos would look horrendous."

He laughs bringing my hand to his lips, planting a soft kiss on my fingers.

"Woman, as soon as I'm out of here, I'm taking you up the aisle."

I raise my eyebrows with a cheeky smirk. "Not without lube, you're not."

He smiles, that bone-melting, radiant smile that lights up his face and sends my butterflies into a frenzy.

"Oh, there you go," he smirks. "You've given me a woody."

I chuckle. "Well, at least the important parts are still working."

As Max's erection lifts the sheet, the nurse walks in as if on cue.

"Oh! Pardon me," she chuckles eyeing the bulge in his sheets. "Don't worry, I have that effect on all my male patients."

Max and I grin at each other like a couple of kids and I notice his erection beginning to wane. Sheila takes a few readings from his machines then elevates the bed a bit more at his head.

"Are you ready for some food, Mr. Foxx? We'd like you to eat something solid today if you feel up to it."

"Yes, okay."

"Good, you need to keep your strength up." On a smirk, she throws me a cheeky wink and then her eyes almost boing out of her head. "Damn, girl. I'm gonna need my shades on with all that bling around your neck."

I smile reaching up to touch my dazzling new heart-shaped locket as a ripple of pride radiates through me. It really is stunning.

After she leaves, muttering under her breath, we burst into laughter, but it's short lived when Max's ribs protest at the movement, they're obviously causing him a lot of pain. His bruises look painful and deep, and a lot worse than the last time he'd broken them when his plane had gone down in Geneva.

When his food arrives, I help him to eat, then as his eye begins to droop with fatigue, I watch him while he sleeps. An hour or so passes quietly so I take the opportunity to rest my eyes.

~

Waking with a jolt, I feel him jerking and pulling on my hand. His brow is beaded in sweat and his lips twitch with inaudible mutterings.

"Max? Max, what's the matter?"

He doesn't respond, but the way he's thrashing around, I'm worried he's going to hurt himself. I press the call button on the side of his bed and try to calm him by stroking his forehead. A nurse walks in and calmly checks his monitors, then his blood pressure, then she changes something on one of the drips.

"Don't worry, he's just dreaming," she says, softly. "I've increased his sedation to help him sleep."

I stare down at him, wide eyed and anxious. I forget that in spite of his lethal body, honed to perfection and strong as steel, his nature is sensitive and his mind is prone to nightmares. He's had them about his parents' death since he was a young boy.

The ordeal of his kidnap must have deeply affected him, regardless of his want to shut it out and never speak of it again. The news of William's death would be hard enough to deal with, but harbouring the memories of his capture, living with their effects, that's not something he should try to deal with on his own. He needs to talk about it, with me. Things like this should never be bottled up. Sooner or later the things we try to bury always rise to the surface.

CLEAR THE AIR, BLUR THE LINES

"Have I got spinach in my teeth?"

Max's lips curl into a smile but his eyes are still firmly closed. I gaze down at him, trawling my eyes over his handsome face. There's something very calming about watching him sleep.

"I can feel you staring at me, Vivienne. I'm not going to disappear. And you should be resting at home, not sitting with me all night. It's not healthy for you or the babies." His sleepy blue eyes peel open and gaze up at me. I love it when his eyes are on me, gazing at me with all that love pouring out of them. Even his left eye, now open but still bloodshot, has the ability to stir my butterflies.

"How do you feel?"

"I'd feel better if you went home and got some rest. You've not been home since I got here. What is it now, ten days?"

"Twelve. But I don't want to leave you. We've been apart for too long. I don't like it when I can't see you."

"Me neither baby, but you have to take care of yourself, and I'll be coming home soon." He reaches up to move a strand of hair away from my face. "You look exhausted, please go home. I'll only worry about you if you don't."

He knows exactly how to push my buttons. I don't want

him worrying about me, but if I leave, I'll be worrying about him. He's had nightmares almost every night. He won't talk about them and it bothers me that he won't confide in me. He's completely closed on the subject, he's shut me out. It's very frustrating and I've had to refrain from pushing him, the last time I did, we had a row, and that's the last thing I want. He doesn't realise I'm just trying to help, and he also doesn't realise how much he's hurting me by closing himself off like this.

His physical condition has improved greatly, although his pain medication makes him very drowsy. His ribs are still painful, they'll take a while to heal as will his wrist, but his bruising has lessened considerably and his left eye is now fully open. But, although he's improving, I still worry about his mental health and the fact that he won't open up to me about what happened to him during his capture.

We've talked, played scrabble, and I've read to him quite a lot too. I even caught him on the phone to Grace trying to organise a conference call with one of his clients, but she's as adamant as I am that he takes the time to heal before going back to work. Besides, Cole seems to be managing things very well so he has nothing to worry about.

Cole's kept him updated about work and he's visited Max regularly, but I get the feeling he's avoiding me.

"What day is it?" Max asks, propping himself up.

"It's Friday, all day." I plump his pillows and elevate the bed to make it easier for him, then I drop a lingering kiss on his very kissable mouth. His tongue glides across my lips which part to accept him. Soon the kiss evolves into the kind of kiss that hits all my erogenous zones at once. I must admit, not being able to have sex with him has been driving me nuts.

He's woken with an erection every morning, I have offered to sort him out, but his room has a large plate glass window to the corridor and the nurses are on a constant watch, so until he's out of this place, a blow job is a no-no.

"Are you going to Mom's this weekend? Olivia and Mason are still there, I know Mom was hoping you'd visit."

I had forgotten about that. Sylvie had invited me over for Sunday lunch and I've only seen her when she's been here to visit Max. I really should make the effort.

"Yes, I'll go. It will be nice to see Olivia again too."

"Good, I know they'll be pleased to see you."

We eat lunch together then we spend the rest of the afternoon playing scrabble and talking. Now that he's much more alert and his brain is fully engaged, he makes me give him a detailed report on everything that happened after he had been abducted.

I'm annoyed that he expects me to give him a blow by blow of all the things that have happened to me while he was away, but he isn't prepared to share the details of his ordeal. He had said that he remembered it all, but he's still unwilling to impart any information. That pisses me off. We're supposed to be a team and yet he won't tell me what he's been through.

My mind has already conjured up several theories, all of which chill me to the bone, and yet, when I push him on it, he just changes the subject or tells me that he doesn't want me to keep asking him because he's never going to put those thoughts in my head.

We've come to an impasse, and I know we'll only end up having another row if I continue my line of questioning, so I give up. For now, at least.

For all the things I had been through, I decided tell him everything, even about Mike's involvement. It doesn't go down very well but I figure there's no point in lying, he'll hear about it sooner or later. We talked a lot about his father too. William's death is hard for me, I can't imagine how hard it must be for Max. William and Sylvie had invested so much in his life, and for Max not to have been there when his father died, and to have missed his funeral, I know that's hit him hard.

~

Cole has brought Sylvie for an evening visit so I wander down to the restaurant for a cup of tea and to call Lucy. We chat for ages and when I finally head back up to Max's room,

I'm shocked to see my bag has been packed and my bed has been removed.

"What's going on?" I'm a little irked at being forced to go home.

"Baby, please, just humour me. Go home, I'm worried about you. You need to sleep in your own bed. You need to get some proper rest. Besides, Doctor Alexander has just been round and it looks like I'll be coming home on Monday."

I feel better knowing he's coming home. Only another three days, I can handle that. "Okay, I'll go. But I'll see you in the morning. Promise me you'll call me if you need me." I walk over and kiss him on the lips, the forehead, and his M.F. tattoo. "I love you."

"Love you more, baby. Sleep well."

I linger at the doorway not wanting to leave him, but as his eyelids grow heavy and then close, I blow him a kiss and close the door quietly to let him rest.

"Where's John?" I ask, as Cole slips into the driver's seat of the Range Rover.

"Max has given him a few days off, to spend some time with Julie before she goes back to work. And Vinnie and Jan have gone up to Scotland to sell her mother's house.

"Oh." I feel so out of the loop. I've been so focused on Max that I've pretty much ignored everything else.

Cole drops Sylvie back to her house, we arrange a time for Sunday lunch and then I see Olivia opening the door for her, welcoming her home. I'm glad Sylvie has company, it must be very lonely for her now.

Cole drives me back to the penthouse. I feel awkward around him. I noticed him looking at my new necklace which pulled a frown into his brow. I haven't taken it off since Max gave it to me but Cole hasn't mentioned it once. His body language is frosty and he's hardly spoken on the journey home.

The ride up in the lift is painful. Neither of us knowing what to say leaves an awkward silence hanging between us. He's obviously still angry with me for what happened at the chateau. He probably thinks I was leading him on, but I'd never do that. I don't even know why I let it happen in the first place.

But actually, I do. I was weak, destroyed at the thought of never seeing Max again. Cole looked like him, sounded like him, he even felt like him. I just couldn't help myself.

I had forgotten he was staying at F1, but it's big enough not to be too much of a problem. I'm sure we can stay out of each other's way.

Once we arrive at the penthouse, I thank him for bringing me home and then I make my way upstairs to take a shower. A tremor of excitement courses through me when I walk into our bedroom. Thinking about Max coming home, and for us to finally be able to lie in bed together, sends my butterflies into overdrive. I've missed our cuddles, and the sex.

After a lovely hot shower, I wrap a towel around me with one on my head and pad into the bedroom to find my robe. A light tapping on my door makes me backtrack out of the dressing room.

"Yes?"

"Ah, it's me," Cole says through the door. "I was just going to order a curry, would you like me to order something for you?"

I had planned to pop down to the kitchen and make a sandwich but hearing the word curry makes my mouth water. I haven't had one of those in ages and I'm starving. As if on cue, my belly rumbles loudly.

"Ah, yes, sounds great. Can I have Chicken tikka masala, a peshwari naan, some poppadoms and some rice, please. I'll be down in a minute." I cringe at the amount of food I've just ordered, but I do love my food.

After drying my hair, I throw on my comfies. I hate to be constricted when I'm eating. Cole is sitting in the kitchen with a glass of red wine, reading the paper. He looks up when I walk in, so I lower my gaze and take the seat on the opposite side of the island. He makes me feel awkward and something about the look on his face tells me we're about to have a discussion to clear the air.

"Vivienne…"

Here it comes.

"I want to clear the air…"

Bingo.

"I'm in love with you."

Wait! What!?

A slap in the face with a wet kipper would have been less of a shock. Absently reaching up to fondle my locket, I run it along the chain in a nervous fidget. "No, Cole. You're still in love with Monica, you just don't have anywhere to put those feelings. It's not me you love, it's her."

His eyes burn into mine, I find it hard to disengage.

"You're wrong. I've had feelings for you since Charlie died. I've been in love with you since that night you passed out in the bathroom."

I stare at him open mouthed, completely lost for words.

"Vivienne, you look at me the way you look at Max, your eyes are so expressive, and I like that feeling very much."

The sad sincerity in his eyes floors me. "But, Cole, I was just—"

"I know. You wanted Max, not me. I get that. And I can't do anything about your feelings for him, or my feelings for you. I just wanted you to know."

Suddenly Cole's glass of wine looks really inviting. Anxiously rubbing at my temples, I have no idea what to say but I know I have to say something, anything to stop this in its tracks. Cole and Max have been in a love triangle all their adult lives, it can't happen again, for all our sanities.

"I love Max, with all my heart. I'd never hurt him and I don't want to hurt you, but this has to stop. Max needs you as a brother, now more than ever now that William has gone, and I can't let you waste your time or your feelings on me. What I did at the chateau—"

"You kissed me. It felt like you meant it." His sorrowful eyes crush me inside.

"I did… I did mean it… but not with you. I'm sorry, Cole. I was foolish and selfish. I thought I'd lost him and I couldn't bear it. You look like him, you sound like him, my god you even taste like him. I really am sorry. Someday you'll find someone who really deserves you, who'll really show you what it is to be loved. But that won't be me."

You could hear a pin drop in the silence that follows. Both of us eye to eye until he looks down at his wine.

"Well then, I guess that told me," he sighs, spinning the stem of his glass.

"Cole… If you're half the man I think you are, you'll understand."

His eyes flip up to mine. The sadness lingers in his eyes, but a crooked smile creeps across his lips. "I do understand. You're an incredible woman, Vivienne. And Max?… Well, he's a lucky guy."

I feel awful and still a little shocked. I know I hadn't helped matters by being so drawn to him as surrogate for Max, but I was sure that he'd responded to me purely because Monica had fucked him up, and he just needed someone to cling to. But if his feelings for me are real, where the hell does that leave us now?

My stomach churns into an anxious knot and the curry doesn't seem like such a good idea anymore.

"Hey, are you okay there? You look a little pale." Rising from his seat, he walks to the fridge. "I'll get you some water."

Fuck the water! Reaching across the island, I slide his glass of wine toward me, then I take a long, deep draw on the delicious aromatic liquid.

"Hey!" He takes it out of my hand exchanging it for a bottle of water. "Are you trying to get me in trouble? Look, Vivienne. I needed to tell you how I feel. But that's it. I can't change the way you feel any more than you can change how I feel, so let's just agree to move on, okay?… Friends? And I don't mean like 'Mike' friends, I mean like real friends… I'll get over you, you're not that special."

I find myself smiling at him, it's hard not to. He's going out of his way to smooth things over between us and I have to help him. I don't want another bust up between the brothers, especially not over me, I couldn't live with that.

The curry arrives minutes later and once the smell hits my nose my appetite returns with a vengeance. Plus, Cole is making an effort to put me at ease and lighten the mood, so I try to do the same.

After he dishes up my food he hits me with a curious smirk. "You eat all that in one sitting? What have you got, hollow legs?"

I load up another forkful. "I am eating for three now."

"Oh, yeah. And they're like this big, right?" He pinches his thumb and forefinger together making a tiny measurement. "I don't get it, for the last two weeks you've been living on air, and now I find you can eat more than John."

He makes me laugh. He's right, when I'm on form I love my food. I can't help it.

"So, how's things going at Foxx-Tech, everything running smoothly?" I ask, shovelling another forkful in.

"Well, I haven't bankrupted the company yet, or lost any clients if that's what you're asking? In fact, Greg Taylor has just signed a very substantial deal."

Oh, god, I'd forgotten about him.

My hand stops midway to my mouth. As the food slides off my fork, Cole stops chewing, staring at me in confusion.

"What? What did I say?"

"Nothing." I quickly retrieve the piece of chicken and pop it into my mouth. My appetite has vanished at the mention of Greg's name but I don't want to let Cole know I'm flustered by him. Nobody can know why I hate that man so much.

After our meal, which I couldn't finish, I clear the dishes and get rid of all the empty cartons. "My treat tomorrow."

"Great. Unless you're cooking, of course. But it's okay, I'll wear my fire-retardant suit."

I throw him a disgruntled scowl. "Max has a big mouth."

"And an asbestos stomach from what he's told me." He smirks walking out of the kitchen throwing me a cheeky wink over his shoulder. If he keeps this up, we have a very good chance of getting along just fine.

When I've finished in the kitchen, I wander out to the living room and open up my laptop to check my emails. Casper has sent me some updates on my work schedule, which I really must sort out before next week. I'm going to have to get back to work for the aerial assignments as soon as possible, but until Max is home and settled in, I don't want to confirm anything yet.

Cole is in the study, I can hear him on the phone so I take my laptop, call out 'goodnight' then head upstairs to bed.

Settling into the comfort of our huge bed, I curl around Max's pillow and immerse myself in the many photographs of him on my laptop.

Goodnight Max, sleep well. I love you.

~

I wake to the sound of a crash, bang, wallop, followed by a slurred voice hissing out a string of expletives. It jolts me upright and I'm so disoriented in the darkness, it takes me a moment to realise I'm back at the penthouse.

My eyes widen, trying to see as I fumble for the light switch. Swinging my legs over the side of the bed, I spring to my feet. All my nerves are on edge and I strain to listen, but it's all gone quiet.

I quickly make my way to the door and gingerly open it a couple of inches. I can't see anything, but the light from downstairs is hitting the ceiling of the upstairs landing so I edge out of my room to take a look.

Cole is lying on his back with his legs draped up the stairs and his head on the living room floor.

"Jesus! What the hell happened?" I race down to him. His eyes are closed. I can't see any blood but I'm frightened to touch him, he could have broken his neck or his back.

"Cole! Oh, my god. Cole! Are you alright?"

His eyes flicker open and he moves his head to look at me with blurry eyes and a stupid smile on his face. "I think I might have slipped," he smirks. The smell of alcohol hits me in the face.

"Oh, for fuck's sake, I thought you'd killed yourself. You're drunk!"

He giggles then sighs deeply. "I am," he slurs defiantly. "You broke my heart Vivninen, Viven, Viniv,... Lady!. You broke my heart and I nearly broke my fucking neck."

Angry and relieved, I shake my head at him. I thought we'd agreed to move on, but clearly he's decided to drink himself stupid, almost killing himself in the process. "Cole, you're an idiot!" I grab him under the arms and pull him away from the stairs. The marble floor makes it easier to slide him along but his weight is still straining my muscles.

Grabbing a cushion from the sofa, I tilt his head up to slide it underneath. Years of practise with my mother's alcoholism means I know how to position him to reduce the risk of him choking on his own vomit.

I kneel down beside him and check for any bumps or cuts, but he seems uninjured. "Do you need to go to the hospital?" I ask, gently slapping his face to rouse him from his drunken stupor.

He blinks up at me a few times trying to focus. "You're so beautiful."

I sigh with aggravation, but I feel so sorry for him. I don't want him to have to get drunk to cope with his feelings, I want him to be happy and content, the way I am with Max.

"So beautiful..." His eyes close and he settles into a deep slumber almost immediately.

Worried that he'll throw up, I grab a bowl and some towels, before making myself comfortable on the sofa so I can keep an eye on him.

SWEET DREAMS

A deep, low growl wakes me from a light sleep. I've woken up every time Cole has moved, fearful that he'd throw up and choke on his own vomit. The morning sun almost blinds me as I raise my head off the sofa cushion to look at him.

"Oh, god," he groans, his screwed up face and deep set frown turns toward me. "Wha…why am I on the floor?"

"You fell."

"Did you push me?"

"Pff, don't tempt me."

"What happened?"

He drags himself into a sitting position. The sunlight blinds him too so he shields his eyes with his hand.

"You tell me. I woke up in the middle of the night and found you lying at the bottom of the stairs. Drunk."

He flicks me a sheepish glance. "Oh, yeah... Sorry."

"You could have killed yourself. God knows how you didn't." Dragging my weary body up off the sofa, I head toward the kitchen to make some coffee. The clock on the oven says seven a.m.

I set Cole's coffee mug on the island as he wanders in a little unsteady on his feet. "Here. Drink this."

"What is it, poison?"

Launching the death stare, I sit opposite to drink my tea.

"Okay, okay. I'm sorry. I had a few too many last night and judging by your expression I pissed you off, right?"

My heart sinks. I don't want him to feel bad, he's had a lot to deal with lately, but I can't encourage him with this reckless behaviour. He has to realise, getting pissed won't solve a thing. Matters of the heart and alcohol are a lethal combination always resulting in a shitty finale.

"How's your head?"

His cringe says it all. "It's been better. Nothing a lobotomy wouldn't cure."

"You'd need a brain for one of those."

"Ooh, that was below the belt, Miss Banks. I see we're fighting dirty."

"We're not fighting at all, you're just behaving like an idiot. Your headache is your own fault. Own it, and deal with it."

I find some Advil and slide them along the counter toward him.

"Thanks." He pops a couple out of the blister pack, wincing. "Why do they have to make these packets so noisy."

I smile at him shaking my head. I've suffered the after effects of a bender many times. It's always more fun to see it played out on someone else. "Right! I'm going to get showered and dressed then I'm going to the hospital." I say, popping my cup in the dishwasher.

"I'll drive you, just give me a minute to shower," he mumbles, nursing his coffee.

"No. I don't think so. You're still going to be over the limit. I'll drive myself, you should go back to bed and sleep it off."

He winces. He knows I'm right.

I start to move away.

"Look, Vivienne… I'm sorry about last night."

I don't turn around and I don't respond. I'm sure he is sorry, maybe not as sorry as I am considering I hardly slept at all last night. But we've both laid our cards on the table, he's going to have to take responsibility for how he handles it from now on.

After my shower, I get dressed and grab the keys for the DB9. I've always wanted to drive it and now is my chance. The thrill of driving a DB9 is, to put it in American terminology, awesome. I loved every exhilarating minute of the journey to the hospital.

I park up, and I'm just getting out of the car when I spot nemesis number two exiting the doors at the main entrance. "Fiona," I huff under my breath. "Great!" I wondered when I would see her again. She's obviously been in to see Max, she's got a great big smile on her face.

Standing at the car, I watch her walk to her Audi, fluffing her curls and tottering along in her high heels and expensive outfit. I feel self-conscious in my faded jeans and converse. I didn't bother with any makeup this morning either, I just wanted to get to the hospital as quickly as possible.

I watch her drive off before making my way inside. When I reach Max's room, Sheila is removing some of his IV lines.

"Good morning," she says, in a cheery voice. "Hot stuff here, has just had his breakfast and is doing very well, although, I caught him on his feet last night and had to tell him off."

Max cringes then lifts his arm beckoning me over to him. "Baby, I've missed you."

I walk to his bed then lean over to kiss him on the lips. The faint glisten of lip gloss on his upper lip stops me before I make contact. Pulling back, I brush my thumb across his lips to remove any trace of her.

"Did Fiona visit by any chance?" That woman really chaps my arse. I don't know why I even asked the question, I already know she did. I hate feeling so jealous and possessive, but his lips are mine. Nobody else has the right to kiss them. Nobody.

He looks at me with concern wrinkling his brow. He's waiting for me to kiss him, so I close the distance and give him my best shot.

"I'll leave you two alone," Sheila says, chuckling to herself.

I'm sure the depth and passion of our kiss has made her

feel uncomfortable but he's mine, and I want him to remember that. When I break the kiss, he takes a deep breath. I think I may have starved him of oxygen with that kiss.

"Wow," he smirks, out of breath and looking down at his erect penis under the sheet, his eyes sparkling with a cheeky smile. "I take it you missed me last night?"

My heart melts. "Of course I missed you." I really did miss him. Until I can finally wrap myself around him and feel every inch of him pressed against me, I'll always ache for him. I hate that we're still apart, it's been too long.

I decide not to let all my jealous thoughts of Fiona disrupt my time with him so I pull a chair over and reach for his hand. Entwining our fingers together, I stroke the back of his hand, one of his many beautiful features. His hands are big and strong and his skin is soft and always warm. They can rip your knickers off in a heartbeat, and caress you in such a way as to leave you breathless and needy. I love the way my hand disappears inside it, safely cocooned in his protective grip.

"So, what did she want?" I hadn't intended to talk about Fiona, but as usual my mouth totally ignored my brain and it just slipped out.

"Fiona? Nothing. She just wanted to see how I was."

Nothing in his face tells me anything to the contrary, but when he's feeling better we need to put down some ground rules about his lips. They belong to me and me alone. Fiona can go and find somebody else's lips to tarnish, Max's lips are taken.

"Where's Cole?"

I don't want to explain his drunken behaviour last night. "He's busy this morning."

Max tenses up, his abdominals tightly bunching together. The pain of his sudden movement makes him groan and wince. "You came on your own? Goddammit! I told him to look after you while John and Vinnie are away." He's angry, the vein in his neck is starting to pound. "Monica may be dead, but there are still too many fuck-ups out there for you to be unprotected. I don't want you going anywhere on your own."

"Max, I'm perfectly capable of driving myself from one door to another, besides, I've always wanted to drive the Aston Martin."

"I know baby, but I just… The Aston?"

A flurry of turbulent butterflies invade my belly. I shouldn't have driven his car without asking him first. I know how mega expensive it is and I don't even know if I'm insured to drive it.

"You drove here in the DB9?"

I nod sheepishly, bracing myself for a telling off.

"Well, damn!" he smirks. "My two favourite models together. That's kind of sexy."

His comment makes me laugh. "I wasn't draped over the bonnet in a bikini."

A salacious grin spreads across his face. "There you go, putting thoughts in my head." His grin evaporates and a serious longing replaces the sparkle in his eyes. Untangling our fingers, he pats the side of the bed. "Come here." His voice is low and raspy. I hesitate for a nano-second then kick off my converse and gingerly scoot up onto the bed beside him.

The groan and tightening in his face worries me as he slowly lifts his arm to wrap it around me so I can rest my head on his shoulder. I'm frightened to lean on his body, his ribs are still painful, so I delicately trace my fingers up and down his chest and stomach.

Closing his eyes, he releases a long sigh of contentment. "I've waited a long time for this, Vivienne. A long time. I've missed you so much." His voice trails off, all his muscles relaxing as he drifts off to sleep with me snuggled as close as his injuries will allow.

I lay with him for ages just watching him breath, and happy to be closer to him than I've been in a long time. His scent soothes me and the silky softness of his warm skin beneath my fingertips feels so good. I know every inch of his face and body, but the feelings I get every time my eyes gaze at his handsomeness never diminishes. In fact, they seem to grow stronger.

He's an opiate, an anodyne. Spellbinding and hypnotic. His

masculine beauty only eclipsed by the tenderness of his heart. He's possessed me from day one and I revel in the rapture and serenity of his love. I can never get enough of him. This man is my everything.

~

Max slept for such a long time I was starting to worry. When the nurse arrives to check on him, she explains that they had upped his sedation this morning because he'd had a rather aggressive nightmare last night. They had found him sleep walking still attached to his machines.

He had pulled out one of his lines, so they decided it would be safer to sedate him so he could rest, and to stop him from getting out of bed again.

This news frightens me. He won't talk about his ordeal, but this just proves that he's struggling to cope with what he's been through.

The nurse is very sympathetic, she explains that many patients suffering from this type of trauma have nightmares, it's fairly common and mostly treatable with therapy. That puts my mind at rest, but the fact that he won't talk about it with me makes me doubt that he'll want to talk about it with anyone.

Max had woken up several times but only for brief periods. He'd opened his sleepy blue eyes and smiled each time I had kissed him on the lips, then he would squeeze me until he dozed off again.

This time, he seems much more alert when he wakes, and he delights in informing me about Cole's recent achievement while acting as CEO in Max's stead.

I know Cole has been keeping Max informed on any new developments at the office. One development in particular has struck a nerve with me, although, I'm not able to voice my concerns.

Max had previously negotiated a deal with Greg Taylor, the man I despise with a passion. Cole finalised the deal yesterday. Just the mention of his name turns me rigid as all the memories come flooding back to haunt me.

I hate the fact that Max is dealing with such a loathsome creature. I can't tell him, and I won't, but the man who had crept into my bedroom and so viciously robbed me of my innocence, is now held in high esteem, intrinsically woven back into the fabric of my life. I hate that. I hate knowing Max will shake his hand and greet him as an equal.

As he explains all the details of their deal, I try to hide my feelings about Greg, although it isn't easy. Every time Max mentions his name I fidget with my new locket, something I've found myself doing a lot when I'm deep in thought or anxious.

But I'm becoming proficient at swerving Max's concern at my sudden mood changes, and I make up an excuse to steer him away from what I'm really thinking.

Eventually, he drifts back into a deep sleep, so I decide to head home. I'm exhausted from the lack of sleep after Cole's shenanigans last night and I really need a solid, undisturbed rest. Although, now Greg's face is firmly stuck in my mind, I don't expect that will happen.

Leaving the hospital, I feel hungry and I had promised to feed Cole, so I stop at the store on my way home to buy some ingredients for dinner. I can't go wrong with a couple of Lasagne ready meals.

When I return to the penthouse I'm glad to find a note from Cole apologising for, in his own words, 'being such a prick,' and telling me that he's going to eat out tonight. We're going to Sunday lunch at Sylvie's tomorrow, so he reminds me to be ready for noon.

While the Lasagne is heating up in the stab and ding machine, I check my phone for messages. Lucy has left me a text telling me she's freaking out about having to cook dinner for Dan's parents, which makes me giggle. She's as bad as I am at cooking, so I text her back with my favourite recipe...the phone number for 'Barney's', who deliver a pretty amazing roast with all the trimmings. They even provide starters and desserts.

Once I've eaten, I head upstairs to take a long soak before an early night.

~

"No! Stop it! Don't touch me!"

"Be quiet."

"Mum! Mum, help me!"

"She's not coming, no one is coming. Except me."

"Get off me! Please… Don't!"

"Stop! STOP!"

My body springs forward in a frenzied attack, legs and arms flying in all directions. My senses are in chaos, the room is dark and I can't catch my breath, but I can hear myself screaming.

"Ow!"

Movement beside the bed has me scurrying backward, flattening my back against the headboard. Wide-eyed and fumbling for the light switch, I find it and turn it on.

"Jesus Christ, Vivienne. You almost knocked my goddamn teeth out."

"Cole?.. Wha…what the fuck are you doing in my room?"

My heart is pounding in my chest which is heaving as my lungs try to drag in as much air as possible. My body is racked with adrenaline and the tremors that come with it.

He holds his bottom jaw between his thumb and fingers, moving it from side to side with a pained expression on his face. "I came in to find out what all the shouting and screaming was about."

"What?" *Shit!*

I realise now that I had been dreaming and talking in my sleep.

"I know you're mad at me, Vivienne, but you didn't have to slug me like that. I think you've cracked a tooth." Staggering up to his feet, he perches on the edge of the bed. He looks like he's just woken up, he's only dressed in a pair of pyjama bottoms and his wavy black mane is all over the place.

"I'm sorry… I…" I'm lost for words. I was dreaming. I was fighting Greg Taylor, trying to push him off me. He had me pinned underneath his heavy, sweaty body as he tried to kiss me. I can still smell the stale beer and cigarettes on his breath. I shudder, and sickness takes hold in my stomach as the bile rises in my throat.

Cole eyes me warily. "Are you okay?"

I reach up to fondle my new locket, it always seems to bring me comfort. "Yes."

My less than convincing answer has him studying me for a moment. As he searches my face, I lower my eyes, pulling the sheet up to my chin.

"What were you dreaming about?"

I don't respond. I don't want to talk about it. Ever.

"Alright… Have it your way, but I think I can guess."

My eyes dart up to his in sheer panic. I don't want him to know. I don't want anyone to know, especially not Max. "It was just a dream, a bad dream, that's all."

His eyes continue to search mine, then he moves his hand away from his bottom jaw. There's a cut on his cheek oozing blood. I must have caught him with my engagement ring. "Oh, I'm sorry. I've cut your face."

Swinging my legs out of bed, I race into the bathroom, returning a few moments later with the first aid kit and a towel. Kneeling down in front of him, I use the antiseptic wipes to clean the wound. It's only shallow, just a graze really, so I clean it up and then blot the blood away with some tissue.

I can feel his eyes on me, but I don't give him eye contact. It's like deja-vu in reverse when he'd cleaned the wound on my cheek after Monica had drugged me.

"If you want to talk about it, Vivienne, I'm a good listener."

I pause what I'm doing for a moment, but still don't look him in the eye. "I told you, it was just a dream. I should cut back on the horror films." I smile, but even I can feel how fake it must have looked.

Once I've finished, I busy myself with putting the stuff back in the first aid kit. Cole rises to his feet and heads to the door. "I hope you haven't ruined my good looks." He pauses in the doorway. "Sweet dreams, Vivienne."

"Yeah. You too."

Once he's left the room my shoulders sag and I can finally relax. What a pair we are. With Max's sleep walking and now my sleep talking, bed time is going to be a whole new ball game. And as much as it hurts me that Max won't talk about the horrors of his kidnap and the constant dreams that are troubling him, I'm doing the same thing to him with Greg Taylor and the horrors he had bestowed upon me as a child.

Max had once asked me why I thought I would never be able to have children, I couldn't tell him the truth. Max is so protective, I knew he would have gone out and sought his revenge over the wrong Greg had done me. I couldn't let that happen.

When I had sidestepped the question, he knew I was holding back, and I knew it hurt him, but I was trying to protect him from the devastation it would have brought, I couldn't live with that. Was that what Max was doing? Trying to protect me from something?

I haven't dreamt of Greg Taylor for such a long time. Crazy-pants Monica and then Max's disappearance had taken priority in that department. I thought I had dealt with the horrors of my childhood, especially since I'd become pregnant. But something had triggered tonight's nightmare and I wanted to know what it was so I could avoid it like the plague in future.

If talking in my sleep is going to become a regularity, I need to find a way to stop it, or at least guard against it. Max will be home soon, we'll be sharing a bed together. I can't be divulging my hidden truths. And if I name my attacker all hell will break loose.

No, I only have one secret, but that secret must remain buried for all our sakes.

An amusing image pops into my head as I snuggle under the covers leaving the light on. The image is of Max and I lying in bed together as I secure his restraints to keep him from sleep walking, then buckle up my own gag to keep me from blurting out the secrets of my past. *Jeez, what a pair!*

TREAT? OR TORTURE?

I didn't get up until late this morning, I needed to catch up on my sleep so I hit the snooze several times before finally hauling myself out of bed.

As I finish getting dressed for lunch with Sylvie, I make a quick call to Max. Hopefully, he'll be awake to take my call but if not, I'll leave him a message.

"Hey, beautiful." His velvety voice caresses my ear putting a flutter of butterflies in my belly.

"Good morning, how did you sleep?"

"Like a log," he sighs. "I enjoyed our snuggle yesterday. I miss you."

"Yeah, me too. I'll come and visit after lunch, and if you're a good boy, I may have a little treat for you."

"I'll be whatever you want me to be, baby. You know I can't deny you anything."

I sense the smile in his voice. "That's good to know. Now get some rest, your treat requires your full attention."

"Yes, Ma'am… Uh-oh. I'd better go, baby. Nurse Ratched has arrived."

"Oh no you di'int! I heard that, Mr. Hot Stuff! Don't think you can sweet talk me just 'cuz you're pretty!"

I can hear Max and Sheila enjoying a moment of banter,

which means he's feeling much better.

"I'll see you soon, Mr. Hot Stuff. I love you."

"Love you more, baby."

Cole is in the study talking on the phone, it sounds like he's arranging a meeting with a client, so I wander through to the kitchen to have some orange juice before we leave.

Cole walks in trawling his eyes all over me. "Wow. You look gorgeous."

I blush at his comment. I had made an effort when I got ready this morning. I was sick of seeing myself looking so drab in washed out jeans and no makeup, so I decided to style my hair and wear a pretty dress with some killer heels to match.

Cole looks amazing. Like Max, he looks good in anything. He's wearing a marl grey open neck shirt with dark charcoal trousers and a matching suede Harrington jacket. His highly polished Mantellassi shoes, morning stubble, and wayward mane of wavy black hair just completes his stunning look. He smells good too.

It's strange but the minute Max came back to me, everything changed. Now, when I look at Cole, I just see Cole. Yes, he's the spitting image of Max, gorgeous to the bone, that's undeniable, but now I see Cole as himself. An individual in his own right. It makes living with him so much easier.

He gives me a knowing look. "Did you sleep okay, after…"

I smile and nod, trying to convey a nonchalance about last night's little episode. I'd rather he didn't keep bringing it up. "You?"

He arches an eyebrow, waggling his bottom jaw with his hand. "I slept like I'd been knocked out."

I sigh and shake my head, smirking. "You big baby." I feel bad about that, but I'm sure it wasn't as bad as he's making out.

On the drive over to Sylvie's, Cole tells me he had gone out to dinner with a client last night and hadn't drunk a drop of alcohol. I'm impressed, he seems to be trying to make an effort to sort himself out.

Sylvie greets us with a warm welcome, ushering us into the

living room. Olivia is sitting on the sofa cradling Mason in her arms.

"Hi, Vivienne. Oh, wow. *That* is stunning," she says, eyeing my new heart-shaped locket. I can't help the beaming smile as I reach up to touch it.

"Max gave it to me."

From the corner of my eye, I notice Cole scowling but I choose to ignore him.

Olivia lets me have a cuddle of Mason, he's grown so much since the last time I had seen him. We chat about Max and William for a while, then the conversation inevitably arrives at pregnancy, babies, and all things maternal.

It's great to see Olivia and Sylvie again, but the house feels so different without William. I'll never forget how he and Sylvie welcomed me into their family. I miss him, like my own father.

Jimmy, the housekeeper, kindly brings in some refreshments and then leaves to answer the doorbell.

"That will be Fiona," Sylvie says, with a beaming smile.

Hmmf. If I had known she was coming…

As I'm in company, I have to fight the urge to lower my brow and pout like a teenager. I knew she'd crop up every now and then being a friend of the family, but I hadn't expected to see her today. And I'm still miffed about her kissing Max on the lips when she visited him in hospital. Maybe today's the day I tell her exactly how it is.

Fiona wafts into the living room in a diaphanous cream and beige ensemble, like a floating angel with her flowing locks of pale blonde hair bouncing around her shoulders.

Really?

Her eyes lock on to Cole immediately. "Cole, how lovely to see you again."

He rises from his seat and kisses her on the cheek. I try to control a smirk noticing her disappointment when he immediately turns away from her and sits down again. I get the feeling she was expecting him to make more of a fuss over her.

Quickly composing herself, she wafts over to me. Her eyes

immediately land on my dazzling diamond encrusted, heart-shaped locket, but strangely enough, she makes no comment.

I stay seated. "Fi." I can't even be arsed to finish her name or add the pleasantries 'nice to see you', and she seems to get the hint by rapidly seeking out Sylvie so she can fawn over her with empty sympathetic noises about William.

Ugh, I've seen more sincerity at an awards ceremony. Something about that woman rubs me up the wrong way.

As we walk into the dining room, Fiona takes the seat next to Cole. I start to wonder if she's given up on Max and has now set her sights on his brother. It irks me a bit. He could do worse, but he could do a whole lot better too.

She's a pretty young woman and I'm sure she has some nice qualities, if you dig deep enough. But I just can't warm to her. It's probably my possessive streak disabling my ability to like her. Maybe if she hadn't been so obvious in her affections toward Max, I might have found her more appealing, but I'm afraid that ship has sailed.

Cole's heart has already been trampled, I wouldn't want that to happen to him again. I'd like him to know true love, like I do. I want him to find the kind of woman who will love him for the man he is inside, not just his outside appearance and insane wealth. We're all programmed to seek out perfection and beauty, but the beauty will eventually wane, it's the heart inside that really counts.

When Fiona's beauty fades, I doubt there will be little more than the dusty remains of a vapid clothes horse.

Much to my disgust, Cole finally succumbs to Fiona's constant attempts to engage him in conversation. Up to that point, he had been the perfect gentleman, but he'd spent most of the meal talking with his mother, which I was pleased to see. She needed the connection with her children. God knows, losing her husband must have left an aching chasm in her life.

As I listen to Olivia and Sylvie discussing the joys of motherhood, I keep one ear on Fiona and Cole's conversation. I'm good at bi-listening. Unless I've zoned out completely in my own head, which happens a lot, I can listen to two conversations and read a book at the same time with great success. It's not going to garner me any awards for paying attention, but it does come in handy when you're trying to eavesdrop.

Fiona is definitely on the prowl. Hanging on his every word, she engages her most coy and seductive smile fluttering her eyelashes at every opportunity, which we all know is pretty girl code for: 'Take the hint and ask me out, sucker!'

He's toast!

Once we've stuffed our faces with a very hearty meal, I take some photographs of everyone so I can show them to Max. Fiona does her best to drape herself over Cole, but I'm a professional photographer, cutting her out is easy. You just need to know how to set your focus.

Cole and I say our goodbye's, then we head off to the hospital.

"So, did you get her number?" I ask, with a grin.

He grins back. "Why? Would it bother you if I did?"

Oh, shit! That's not what I meant. "No! Don't start that again. I just don't want to see you get hurt."

"That's rich coming from the woman who breaks my heart every single day."

I feel awful, and his words leave an awkward silence between us.

"Sorry," he sighs. "That was out of line. I can't help it, Vivienne, I can't just switch off my feelings to make you feel better."

"Cole I… I'm really flattered. I do care about you, but, it's just not in the way you want me to. I'm sorry." I reach up to my locket anxiously fidgeting with it.

"Hey, it's no biggie. Like I said, I'll get over it."

I know he's smiling at me, I can hear it in his voice, but I don't want to see the hurt in his eyes. This situation isn't going to resolve itself any time soon, but maybe when I go back to work, and when John and Vinnie return and Max is home again, maybe then he'll be able to move out and move on. I hope so.

Cole drops me at the hospital, telling me he'll wait for me down in the café. I'm glad to be visiting on my own, it's essential for my little plan, but I feel sad knowing Cole and I haven't resolved anything.

Before I enter Max's room I have a quick word with the nurse on duty then I check my makeup and hair before entering his room. As I quietly walk in, I see his eyes are closed. *Perfect!*

Grabbing the drawing pins and sheet from my handbag, I cover the plate glass window to the corridor outside. Once we are shielded from prying eyes, I remove my wrap dress and drape it over the back of the chair. My legs are shaking, I feel self-conscious, but I can't wait to see the look in his eyes when he wakes up.

I take a few minutes trying out various positions in the chair, I want him to open his eyes and see me looking sexy and seductive in my red lace underwear and stockings. They're his favourite, and the treat I had promised him earlier. Once I find a sexy position, which isn't the most comfortable, I wait for him to wake up.

After a while, I try to hurry him up by coughing. Still nothing. Then I get the idea to lay back in the chair with my stilettoed feet crossed at the ankles up on his bed.

I get up and bend over with my arse in the air to lift the heavy chair so it doesn't scrape on the floor.

"I know that face."

His voice makes me jump and his grinning smile makes me blush as I turn and look over my shoulder. "Max! I wasn't ready." Turning fully to face him, I pout, placing my hands on my hips.

He reaches out and beckons me to him. The look on his face was the one I had wanted to see, his eyes burn with lust, almost knocking me off my Manolo's.

"Come here, you hot, sexy temptress. Is this my treat? I've been a good boy, I promise." He runs his fingers over my bump, the look on his face is a mixture of raging desire and complete awe.

I lower down to kiss him fully on the lips. Our tongues stroke gently at first then he wraps his hand behind my neck, pulling me closer, deepening the kiss to a toe curling, groin throbbing affair that even makes my nipples ache.

When he breaks the kiss, I rest my forehead against his and close my eyes. He takes every scrap of oxygen when he kisses me like that.

"I love my treat." His hooded, lust filled eyes scorch me with desire as his hand skims my neck and shoulders, caressing, griping, stroking, then it slides down my back to my behind.. He squeezes the curve of my bum cheek, then skims his hand downward to the delicate lace of my stocking tops. His chest rising and falling in short urgent breaths, blowing hot across my parted lips.

"I want to rip your panties off and bury myself inside you right now. You're making me so fucking hard."

I kiss him again. The hunger and desire in his voice is turning me on, making me wet, the look in his eyes filling me with need. My pulse quickens and the familiar throb of arousal hits me right between my thighs.

He slides his fingers across my exposed skin and into my knickers. With his expert fingers, he skillfully strokes my throbbing clit. Need and want flow through me as I feel the quickening wave of desire pulsing and rippling out all over my body.

His soft groan makes my nipples tighten as my skin moistens with sweat. I'm so close, and the building sensation drives a moan of ecstasy from my throat. My hand curls into his wavy hair, gripping it tightly as the feelings deepen inside. My legs shake from the muscle spasms and the tightening of my body around his skillful and generous fingers. Every stroke makes my hips roll.

As he takes my mouth with his passionate kiss, he brings me to orgasm with his touch. My moans of pleasure devoured by his kiss.

Bringing me down from my heady cloud, he slows, patiently drawing out the very last pulse of my orgasm until I relax and pull away, dragging his bottom lip through my teeth.

I rest my forehead against his, utterly spent and thoroughly satisfied. "That was well worth the wait," I whisper, trying to catch my breath.

"I love to watch you come." His low, raspy voice gets my eyes open. As I pull my head back, his fingers gently slide out of me. Bringing his hand up to his lips he licks the wetness of my arousal from his fingers.

I lick my tongue across his lips then kiss his eyes, nose, and cheeks, before continuing down his throat, shoulder, and chest. Running my fingers gently over his bruises, I kiss each one then slowly move down to his hips, nipping and lapping his gorgeous skin. His scent is driving me wild.

Pulling the sheet back, I reveal his twitching cock as it rigidly bounces against his lower belly. His hand fondles and caresses my behind as I bend down to lick the bead of arousal from the tip of his penis. The soft groan escaping his lips, turning me on even more.

Wrapping my fingers around the thick base of his pulsing cock, I lift it up, then lower my mouth and take him in as far as I can. The fullness of his erection filling my mouth, is so erotic. His silken skin gliding over the hard muscle beneath my firm grip sends tingles all through me, and it shows me he's primed, ready and as turned on as I am.

As I begin to pump him, it brings me closer to another orgasm, I can feel it building in my core. Heat and desire coursing through me as the head of his cock expands in my mouth.

Driven by desire, I increase the pressure and speed needing to feel the spurt of his hot ejaculate on my tongue. But suddenly his hand grips my arm with such a force that the pain makes me yelp. I pull my head back still holding his penis in my hand.

"Stop! Stop!"

His voice is urgent and final and his erection dies in my hand.

I look over my shoulder to see his face. I don't understand.

His plastered arm is slung over his eyes and the sounds he's making bring a lump to my throat.

"Oh, my god I've hurt you! Max, I'm sorry, I didn't mean to…" I try to pull his arm away from his eyes but he won't let me. His muscles flex and harden the more I try. "Max, please! I'm so sorry."

I try again but he's resisting. He's much too strong for me, even in his injured state. His teeth are bared in a pained grimace, and I can see the tears rolling down his cheek. His chest is panting with heavy ragged breaths, but I have no idea how I've hurt him. I'd never want to do that intentionally, he must know that.

"Max, please talk to me. What did I do?"

"Nothing. You did nothing." His voice is low and strained.

"Then why won't you look at me."

He doesn't answer and I can see he's still tortured by whatever it is I did wrong. I feel like shit! I'd never have instigated this if I thought it would cause him pain.

"Max—"

"Go home, Vivienne."

It's not an appeal for me to leave, it's an abrupt and final command.

"Max I—"

"Go!"

I'm stunned, completely bewildered, and utterly hurt. He's shutting me out.

Standing here in my underwear, I wrap my arms around my stomach as all my confidence drains away and my insecurities inevitably begin to take hold. I stare down at him with tears in my eyes as the flush of humiliation heats my cheeks, sending my butterflies into a frenzy. "What did I do?"

He still hasn't removed his arm from his eyes, and I long for him to look at me, just once, so I can see that he still loves me. "Why won't you look at me? Max, please."

The pain in my voice should have brought him running, but he remains closed off and shielded.

"Vivienne. Go home. Please."

The finality in his voice kills me. I reach out to gently graze my fingers over his chest but when he flinches like I've just burned him, I die inside. Tears flood my eyes and I bite my lip to stifle the sobs building in my throat.

"You can't treat me like this. You can't keep shutting me out!"

With fumbling fingers, I wrap my dress around myself tying the belt to secure it, then I run from his room sobbing.

"Vivienne, what's wrong?" Cole reaches out catching my arm as I run through the lobby toward the exit. "Vivienne. What is it? Has something happened to Max?"

I shake my head but I can't speak, I'm too upset.

"Are you sure?" He continues to probe, unable to understand why I'm so distraught. I nod my head as another wave of sobs spill out of me. I need to leave.

Studying me for a moment with confused eyes, he then leads me out of the hospital and drives me home in silence.

Once we're inside the penthouse, I walk toward the stairs with my head down, I need to be on my own. I need to lock myself in my room and cry.

"Vivienne, whatever it is… If you want to talk—"

"No. I'm fine, I just… I'll see you in the morning." The last thing I want to do is discuss my love life with Cole. I don't know what happened with Max, I don't understand it. All I know is how much I'm hurting right now.

EPIC FAIL

The shrill, persistent noise from my alarm clock stirs me from another night of tossing and turning. It's hard to sleep when worries are constantly bouncing around in your brain. Throwing my arm out of the covers, I hit the snooze, cursing its repetitive ear-piercing trill.

Before I open my eyes, the sun blazes into the bedroom forcing me to bury my head back under the covers. But I can't stay here for long, I had already made a decision to go back to work this morning, so I'd better get up.

Max is coming home this afternoon. I should be ecstatic, but apprehension seems to have crept in. After yesterday's disastrous attempt to make him feel better I had somehow managed to make us both feel like shit!

We're supposed to be a team, a partnership. The pain I had felt losing Max for those nineteen days was unbearable. I'd never felt pain like it.

Now he's back, but if he closes himself off to me like he did yesterday, I haven't got him back at all. I don't know what I did wrong or how to deal with it, but I know I'll go crazy if I sit around crying. I need to immerse myself in my work so I can focus on something else for a while.

I take the lift down to the twelfth floor. When I arrive at

the front desk, I'm greeted warmly by Casper who is a sight for sore eyes. I'd forgotten how beautiful his pale hazel eyes looked set against his caramel skin.

"Vivienne, it's good to have you back. We're all so happy to hear Mr. Foxx has been returned safely. You must be so relieved. Please give him my very best wishes."

His genuine concern is very touching.

"Oh, and wow!" he smirks, eyeing my new locket. "That is gorgeous. But don't let my girlfriend see it, it'll give her ideas."

He walks with me to my office then disappears to bring me some tea and a bacon sandwich. Ed strolls out of his studio. "Viv! It's great to have you back, babe." He wraps me in a big bear hug. "How's the old man?"

"He's recovering nicely, thanks. He's coming home this afternoon." My belly churns a little at the thought which upsets me. I want him home.

"That's great. So why are you here? Shouldn't you be at home warming his slippers and plumping his pillow?"

I pull out of his hold and walk to my desk. "I'm only staying until lunchtime. I just wanted to catch up on my schedule."

I can tell Ed is sensing my edginess. I am edgy, I wish I wasn't. I've been so full of angst and fear since Max's abduction, but even though he's back it still feels like I've lost him, or part of him anyway.

"Viv?"

"Sorry... How's thing's? Casper tells me you've been holding it together, thanks for that. I owe you one."

"No you don't, I was glad to help." His voice is soft and sincere. "You've had much more pressing things to worry about. Anyway, apart from the fact that I can't handle air travel, everything's been ticking along nicely. We've got a few new clients too."

"What about Nova? Are you two still…?"

His cheeky smile and reddening cheeks tell me their relationship is blooming. I'm surprised, Ed has always had the relationship capacity of a Mayfly. But maybe it needed someone like Nova to tame him.

I spend most of the morning making calls to the clients who want our aerial service, and then Casper and I tie up the dates with Grace so we can confirm the use of the Foxx-Tech helicopter. As Monday mornings go, this one felt very productive and I was glad of the distraction. With all the chaos of the last few weeks it's been nice to ground myself with some normality again.

"Vivienne? Sorry to disturb you but it's two o'clock. Mr. Foxx will be arriving home soon you should go, I can clear your desk for you."

I look up and see Casper's smiling face poking around my door. He's right, I need to go. I hadn't realised the time.

"Okay, thanks." Gathering my stuff together, I flip the lid down on my laptop. "Just call me if you need me. I'll be in tomorrow."

"Okay," he shrugs, "but if you don't make it tomorrow don't worry we'll manage, and I'll send everything to your app."

I leave Casper and head up to the penthouse.

As I exit the lift and walk toward the penthouse doors I feel mild anxiety setting in. Max is due home anytime now. I'm looking forward to having him home, of course I am, and I'm sure he's looking forward to coming home too. But I'm apprehensive of how we left things yesterday. I don't understand what triggered him to behave that way.

I've changed the bed sheets, ordered his favourite foods, and laid out his silk pyjama bottoms. I'm feeling nervous, it's like a proper homecoming. We've both been under so much pressure lately, but hopefully, getting back to a normal routine will ease both our troubled minds.

I miss Lucy, Vinnie and Jan. They've always been a shoulder to cry on and a great support to me. Since Max came back, I haven't left his side and I've hardly spoken to anyone about how it's affected me. Maybe I should?

My heart leaps and nervous butterflies invade my belly as the doorbell chimes. I take a deep breath before opening the door but it's not Max. As if the huge bouquet of white roses wasn't speaking for itself, a young guy staggering under its weight makes his announcement. "Flowers for Miss Banks."

"Come in." I open the door wider, but he still has to turn sideways to get the flowers through the door. The fragrance is amazing, filling the whole room.

"Where do you want them?" he asks, slightly out of breath. I haven't seen his face yet, he's still buried behind the bouquet.

"Over here will be fine." I direct him to the grand piano where he deposits them, blowing out a tired sigh.

The roses are absolutely stunning, the smell is a heady, familiar fragrance, and there's a white card nestled in amongst them.

You own my heart completely, and I'm honoured that you do. But if for any reason you doubt it, just look into my eyes.

My heart beats only for you. I don't deserve your love, but I will always cherish it.

Love you more, until forever.

Max

X;-)

His words are beautiful, bringing tears to my eyes and a lump to my throat. Breaking down and running away was a selfish act on my part. I was shocked and hurt by his reaction and I overreacted badly. I should have been more sympathetic toward him.

As usual I had taken his rejection personally, thinking only of myself and not of his feelings. I should have known he wasn't ready. He's been under so much pressure and medication, and I'm moving too fast. He needs time to adjust, to heal. My impatience to get back to a normal existence has only set us both backward.

As I dry my tears staring down at the card, I hear the penthouse door opening. I run to the door so excited I almost fall over my own feet.

Max walks in aided by Sheila, and Cole follows with his

bag. He's in pain, I can see it in his face.

"Max! What are you doing on your feet, shouldn't you be in a wheelchair?"

Sheila, the same nurse I had seen many times at the hospital and who was never short of a dry, witty comment, rolls her eyes and tuts loudly.

"Pretty-boy wanted to walk," she says, in her dry southern drawl. "And I'm fed up arguing with him, he's your problem now, girlfriend." Her exaggerated hissy-fit expression, cracks me up.

Once we have him settled in on the sofa, Sheila gives me all his medication then pats him on the top of his head. "Now, don't forget what Doctor Alexander said, take it easy. You can bathe and shower but no work, no gym, and no swinging from the chandeliers. Finish your course of pills and call us if you have any problems, okay?"

He gives her one of his mega-watt smiles.

"And you can stop that right now, Pretty-boy," she smirks. "Lord knows, I should be used to it by now but that smile should be illegal." She fans her face and turns to leave, bumping into Cole. "Oh, my!" she sighs, turning to face me. "You have two of these beautiful creatures living with you? Man, I'm never that lucky." With that, she waddles out of the penthouse muttering under her breath.

Cole turns and follows her. "I'm going to head back down to the office. I'll see you both later."

I sense he feels uncomfortable now Max is home, but I'm glad he's leaving. He needs to realise his misplaced feelings for me have no place here, especially now Max is home.

Max calls out to him. "Thanks bro."

Cole just raises a hand and carries on walking.

Something inside me relaxes, like an elastic band holding all my emotions together in one nervous lump has just been removed, letting everything spread out and find a space to breathe.

He lifts his head off the back of the sofa, opens his eyes, and hits me with the bluest, sparkliest gaze of appreciation. I melt, as I always do.

Holding out his arms with a wince, he waits for me to join him, so I gingerly sit in his lap, leaning my back against the armrest. His arms slowly curl around me and even though I can see it hurts, he leans forward to kiss me tenderly on the lips. "I'm sorry."

The sadness in his eyes melts my heart and I gently pushing him back to rest his abdominals, then I take his face in my hands. "Me too. I rushed things. You need time to recover, and I'm going to take care of you." I tenderly press my lips to his. The soft connection of our mouths gently brushing against each other, and the fact that he's here right in front of me, takes away all the angst that I had allowed to build up.

Before he was returned to me, I had spent so much time contemplating a life without him knowing that I'd never survive it, not emotionally anyway. And he was right, his eyes really do tell me how much he loves me.

"The flowers are beautiful, Max. Thank you."

We sit for a while just gazing into each other's eyes, a silent trade of unspoken pledges. I'd missed these moments in the days he was gone. No one ever looks at me the way he does. *Except for Cole.* That thought suddenly causes a flash of heat to break out across my skin.

"What is it?" Max asks, reading every nuance of my body language with perfect accuracy.

"Nothing…You should go to bed and rest, you look tired."

"I'm fine, I want to be with you. I've missed you, baby." The sadness in his voice pulls at my heart.

"Okay. Come on, Pretty-boy." I peck him on the tip of his nose, then swing my legs off and stand up. His confused eyes stare up at me. "I'm going to help you upstairs and then we're going to have a nice long soak in the tub."

His eyes shine and that beautiful smile of his spreads all over his handsome face.

Getting him upstairs is a slow process. He's a little unsteady on his feet and every movement hurts his ribs. On my last visit to the hospital, the nurse had told me that his ribs were taking longer to heal because his nightmares had caused him to thrash around and twist in his sleep. The bones were trying to knit back together but he was slowing the process down.

They had given him some pretty strong medication which should knock him out so hopefully, he won't suffer from anymore nightmares for a while.

I sit him down on the chaise in the bathroom, then I run the bath. While the water fills the tub, I leisurely drag my eyes over his bruised but gorgeous body while I strip him naked.

His bruises are fading, but still lurking underneath the skin. The small scar on his abdomen has healed very well, and his left eye is almost back to normal. I notice he has a few more quotes on his cast too:

'Tough break!'

'I do my own stunts... badly!'

'I went all the way to France and all I got was this stupid cast!'

His greedy eyes are all over me as I step out of my dress revealing my sexy underwear. A ripple of heat runs through me, his eyes caress my skin just as easily as his hands do. It isn't easy to ignore the automatic responses my body has to his scorching gaze but I ignore it as best I can. He isn't helping. His breathing has deepened and his erection is a dead giveaway to how I'm turning him on.

I feel nervous about what happened yesterday, so I try not to focus on his growing erection or the fact that his pupils are dilating as his eyes become more hooded with desire. God! How I've missed those eyes.

Helping him to his feet, I walk him over to the tub. This is the first time I've been able to hold his naked body in my arms. A flicker of excitement shoots through me and I love how it feels to have his warmth against me.

I step in first so I can sit behind him, there's no way he can take the weight of my body against his ribs. Carefully, he steps in then slowly sinks into the water. His painful groans as his body twists into position makes me cringe, I can almost feel his pain. Maybe this isn't such a good idea after all!

Eventually, he settles. With his plastered arm hanging over the edge of the tub to keep dry, I take his weight against my chest and slowly lower us back against the tub.

"Man, that was painful," he groans, clearly suffering.

He feels heavy against my chest, but I love the feel of him between my thighs, and his broad shoulders, taking up most of the width of the bath, feel powerful and yet silky soft beneath my hands.

I lather up a sponge and begin to drag it lazily over his skin, being careful not to put too much pressure over his ribs and bruises. Moaning a soft noise of pleasure, he rolls his head back against my shoulder with his eyes closed.

"This is perfect," he sighs, a soft smile curling his lips. "Skin on skin. I've missed this, baby."

"Yes. Me too."

His penis is now in a state of semi-lob, bobbing in the water. His body feels totally relaxed and his breathing is calm and even. As we lay relaxed in the warm water, I internally debate whether I can ask him about what happened between us yesterday. I hate that he doesn't open up to me about the things that worry him.

I thought we'd conquered all that after his room of guilt, Monica, and the threatening letters. I don't like it when he shuts me out. But why would he do that? Especially now when there's nothing left to hurt us.

"Max?"

"Mmm-hmm?"

"Why did you react like that yesterday?"

I feel his breathing pause for a moment, and I can feel the tension oozing out of him.

"I don't know… Maybe I'm still strung out… I said I was sorry."

"I know, and I don't mean to push you, it's just… What about the nightmares you've been having, what are they about?"

"Nothing for you to—"

"Worry about?" I finish his sentence with a certain amount

of sarcasm. "I've heard that line before, Max. It means there is something for me to worry about but you're not going to tell me what it is." I didn't mean to be so direct but I'm worried about him. I've been in a state of anxiety for weeks.

He swallows, his jaw clenching repeatedly. "Baby, it's just the medication, it makes me hallucinate."

Neither of us speaks for a few minutes as I digest that remark. I don't believe him about the medication, but we've been at this impasse before, and no amount of prodding on my part will budge him until he's ready, so I decide to drop the conversation all together.

Once I finish bathing him, I carefully wash his hair then band my arms around his shoulders and we sit in a perfect silence, enjoying the warmth of the water and the closeness of each other's bodies.

This is what I've missed. The contact. Skin on skin. Our chests rising and falling at the same steady rate. Our hearts beating at the same steady rhythm. We belong together, we love each other. Being apart has crippled us both.

As I gaze down at his gorgeously handsome face, I remember the note he had sent me with the beautiful white roses this afternoon. I don't doubt his love. He's right, just one look in his eyes tells me how much he loves me. It's something we both express through our eyes. Something he'd seen in mine long before I had known it myself. But yesterday, when he'd shielded his eyes from me, what was he hiding? What would I have seen?

Getting out of the tub is a lot harder than getting in it! I don't have the strength to lift him so he has to manoeuvre himself upright, causing him great pain in the process. Once he's up, he looks tired and pale, so I make him perch on the edge of the tub while I dry him off, then I dress him in his black silk pyjama bottoms and walk him through to the chaise.

I like his stubble, which is really a beard now. It's manly and sexy, but he wants to get rid of it, so I stand between his legs and shave it all off. His constant interruptions as his hand caresses and fondles me, makes it very difficult to concentrate, but I'm proud to see I haven't nicked him, and underneath all that fuzz, he's even more handsome.

The sight of his gorgeous face takes hold of all my senses. He really is effortlessly and breath-taking.

He won't let me brush his teeth, that's an emasculating step too far and he wants to do it on his own, so I walk him over to the sink and watch him wincing and flinching through the whole sorry episode.

After that, I get him into bed, then I finish my own ablutions before slipping on my shorts and a sloppy Joe t-shirt. It's still early, I'm not ready to fall asleep yet, but Max is struggling to keep his eyes open so I snuggle into his shoulder, carefully avoiding his torso, and I tell him all about my morning at the office.

After a while, his heavy breathing alerts me to the fact he's drifted off. I have to pinch myself that he's really here, home and safe, and all mine.

After gazing at him for a few more selfish moments, I quietly remove myself from his side, kiss his M.F. tattoo, and leave him to sleep.

~

I spend the rest of the afternoon organising my schedule for the next few days, which keeps me busy, then I call Lucy. Staying with Max in the hospital, and Lucy being a new bride, has left us with little time to meet up for a chat. I miss her.

"Hey, Viv! How's Max?"

"He's home now and doing really well, but he's still in a lot of pain."

"Oh, I know, ribs can be a bastard to heal. I broke one when I went snowboarding once."

"Yes, I've heard snowboarding's really difficult."

"Oh, it wasn't that. I was shit-faced on Glühwein and I fell off the chair lift."

"Why doesn't that surprise me," I laugh. "Luce, you're a monster. How did your meal go? Did you poison the in-laws?"

"Actually, it went very well. I burned the soup and my pineapple upside down cake looked more like pineapple right side up cake, but other than that it was a success." We burst into giggles, neither of us can cook to save our lives.

"Have you heard from your mum since you've been home?"

"No, but I'll give her a call when things get back to normal." I feel bad, I haven't even attempted to call my mother since we went to France for Lucy and Dan's wedding.

"We should have a girlie night in soon, it feels like we've got loads to catch up on, and I miss you."

"Yeah, me too. I'll call you soon, Luce, I promise."

Talking to Lucy always puts a smile on my face.

I've been up to check on Max several times, but each time he's been fast asleep.

Before she went to Scotland, Jan had left me a basic, easy to follow dinner making guide with easy recipes and instructions that even a numpty could follow.. Of course, it would still be a challenge for me, but I thought I should at least attempt to make my man some dinner.

Once the stew is in the oven, and the potatoes have been peeled ready to boil, I text Cole to let him know there'll be enough for him if he wants to join us, or I'll leave some in the fridge if he has other plans. He hasn't replied, so I assume he has other plans.

Getting Max up and down the stairs is a challenge and I'm worried he'll fall, so when dinner is ready, I plate it up and pop it on a tray to take upstairs.

"Well hello, Mr. Sleepy-head."

His sleepy blues land on mine causing the usual tingle deep in my belly, and his big smile puts a glint in his eyes. God, I've missed those eyes.

"What time is it?" he croaks, trying to push himself up.

"It's seven thirty. Just stay there, I'll help you." Setting the tray down, I help him to sit up, shoving some pillows behind him. "Better?"

"Much better." He traces his palm up and down the back of my thigh. Before I get side-tracked by his touch, I rest the tray across his lap then I go back to the kitchen for my tray so we can eat together.

"Did you make this?" he asks, eagerly forking in another mouthful.

"I did." I cringe, awaiting his verdict. "You can be honest if you don't like it, I won't be offended. We both know what a rubbish cook I am."

He smirks at me with bulging cheeks. "Tastes pretty good, that's why I had to ask."

"Less of your cheek, Pretty-boy."

"Why do I get the feeling that name's going to stick?" he says, giving me the eyebrow.

Max polishes off his meal then takes his meds. I help him get into a comfortable position before I clear the dishes and run them down to the kitchen.

When I return, his head is resting back on the plumped pillows and his eyes are closed. My breath hitches as I hesitate in the doorway. I can't help but stare. His gorgeous physique is strong and perfectly proportioned. Every slab of muscle is pronounced and defined beneath his golden skin. His freshly washed hair is laying in a perfect halo of dark silken strands around his chiselled, perfectly constructed face. Mine.

I sometimes can't believe he is mine. Heart, mind, body and soul, all mine.

"Are you coming in, or are you going to stand in the doorway staring at me all night?" His velvety voice stirs my passion but the fact that he's aware that I'm acting like a love sick fool makes me blush.

I giggle releasing a contented sigh. "I can't help it, Pretty-boy. You dazzle me, and I've missed you."

His eyes open landing on mine with hooded, blazing intensity. "I've missed you more," he rasps, softly. My heart swells, my butterflies making their usual appearance. They too are seduced by his sexy voice.

Walking over, I crawl up the bed so I can nestle into his less injured side. He looks rested and comfortable, but I know he's still in a lot of pain.

"How do you feel?" I ask, tracing my fingers lightly over

his chest. I feel his breathing pause for a moment and his arm tightens around me.

"I never want to be apart from you again, Vivienne. Never." The desperation in his voice has me looking up at him. His eyes stay locked onto mine, scorching me with so much love, it almost burns me. Lifting his plastered arm, he traces my lips with his fingers.

"Vivienne, I know what it feels like to be without you. I couldn't survive that again... I thought I wasn't going to make it back, and all I could think about was you. You and the babies. I can't live without you, Vivienne. I can't. There is no me without you."

Tears pool in my eyes and his sincerity melts my heart because his words reflect my feelings exactly. I brush my fingers down his cheek, smiling through my tears. "You promised me forever, Mr. Foxx. I intend to hold you to that."

For a fleeting moment, something I can't quite determine enters his eyes, is it doubt? Whatever it is, makes me feel sad.

He places his finger under my chin, tilting my head back, his scorching eyes still locked onto mine as he lowers to kiss me. The grazing brush strokes of his tender lips send tingles all over my body. His tongue gently teasing my lips apart before gliding over mine with soft reverent strokes. His kiss is luxurious and sensual, provoking a heightened awareness from all my senses.

As always, our kiss evolves into a hot, passionate trade of tongues and lips. Taking and giving as the potency unfurls our innermost desires. I'm lost in his kiss, and completely overwhelmed by his passion. A deep thud of arousal pounds in my core and the air around us is charged and alive with the crackle of sexual need.

The weight of his cast rests on the back of my neck as he draws me closer to him deepening the kiss. His other arm tightening around my shoulders. My fingers greedily fist in his hair, pulling him closer, deeper.

In a swift move, he rolls on to his side pushing me onto my back. But his body tenses up immediately with the shock of his pain as he abruptly breaks the kiss with an urgent gasp for air.

"Max! Take it easy." I gently ease him back to the mattress. I really feel for him, the pain must be excruciating.

His eyes are tightly screwed shut, his face portraying his discomfort as he exhales a painful groan through his bared teeth until the stabbing pains in his ribs ebb away.

"Max, you have to be careful. You'll never heal if you keep re-breaking your ribs." Propping myself up on one elbow, I gently soothe his furrowed brow and tenderly kiss his lips, then softly stroke his hair away from his face. "All in good time, Pretty-boy. Let me take care of you."

My body is still in hyper mode. He'd turned me on so much with his kiss that if he'd carried on for a few more minutes, I would have come for sure. Despite his pain, his erection is still solid and straining against his pyjama bottoms, the little patch of wetness shows me he's in hyper mode too.

I run my hand lightly down his side, across his lower abdominals, then I slide it under the loose waistband. The silkiness of his pyjamas and the silkiness of his skin caress my hand both front and back. His cock pulses as my fingertips trace around the slick head, my thumb smoothing away a bead of his arousal at the tip.

I continue to trail my fingers down his thick shaft to the solid base, where his balls lie full, heavy, and aching for release.

My tongue slides out to lick his lips as my breathing deepens. I want to grab hold of his cock and play with it the way I know he likes, but I check his reaction, to seek his approval before I continue. I don't want to make the same mistake I made yesterday. His eyes are hooded and glazed with desire. He wants this, he needs this as much as I do.

Removing my hand, I kneel up and pull my t-shirt over my head, flinging it to the floor. His darkened eyes rake all over me with heat and longing burning within them. "So fucking beautiful," he whispers. The look in his eyes is exactly the look I needed to see.

My breasts are free and heavy, my nipples hard and aching for his touch. His lips part to let out his ragged, heavy breaths.

Without removing my eyes from his, I stand dragging my shorts and knickers down my legs, kicking them off the bed. His eyes survey me so intensely with need and want pouring out of them, they're like soft fingertips caressing every inch of my bare flesh.

I loosen the tie cord on his pyjamas and slide them down his thighs, freeing his thick, pulsing cock lying heavy on his stomach. My eyes lazily drag all over his fine, mouth-watering body. Every slab of muscle carved and perfectly formed.

The soft moan of pleasure from deep within his chest as I straddle and lower myself down to sit on top of his thighs, fills me with desire, empowering me to continue. I love the sounds he makes, the special carnal sounds that only we share, the ones that only I am responsible for. We've both been so deprived of our need for intimacy and connection. It's been way too long.

As I take him in my firm grip, I check his expression once again, but he's blissfully lost in the moment. His arms lay softly at his sides. His mouth is relaxed with his lips slightly parted, and his eyes are now closed with only a faint twitch of his eyebrow. I've got him in the palm of my hand, quite literally, and it feels amazing.

I begin to move at a leisurely pace, my hips rocking forward and back to each stroke of my hand up and down his shaft, allowing his balls to graze the sensitive, swollen bud of my sex. When I look down at myself with his huge cock in my hand at the apex of my groin, it looks like my own appendage, like I'm masturbating myself. It feels amazing, the more I rub against the base of his cock, the faster I want to move, the friction is perfect.

"Oh, baby that feels so fucking good." His head pushes back into the pillow, his lips forming a small circle as the pleasure takes hold of him. As I build the pressure and speed, I can't keep my eyes open. The wicked sensations building and rippling out from my core make it impossible not to roll my eyes into my head and moan as they take over my body.

Deep groans of pleasure rumble out of his chest and hiss

through his teeth. His thighs flexing and stiffening beneath me. His cock hardening in my hand even more, the head swelling to the point where I know he's as close as I am.

Soft whimpers fall out of my mouth as I climb to the peak, I'm so close. Increasing my grip, I pump him harder, faster, arching my back, absorbing the deliciousness of my impending, earth shattering orgasm.

"Stop it! Stop it! Stop it, you bitch!"

TRUST, GUILT, PUNISH

It all happened so fast. I don't even know what happened but I'm lying on the floor beside the bed in a shaking, dazed heap. My cheek feels like it's on fire.

It takes me a moment to pull my head together. I'm naked and trembling, with heavy tears blurring my eyes. I don't understand.

"Vivienne! Jesus! I'm so sorry. I… Oh, Jesus! I'm so sorry." Max's panicked voice pulls my head around to face him and I look up at the bed in total confusion. He would never hit me? He wouldn't do that. My mind is all over the place, steeped in conflict. But he did. He did hit me. Even in my confused state I know he did.

Max cries out in pain as he struggles to sit forward. With great difficulty, he leans over and tries to reach for my arm but instinctively, I pull away from him. I think I'm in shock. I know I'm confused.

With tortured eyes, he stares down at me repeating the same words over and over again. "I'm so sorry. Please, baby. Please forgive me."

Scrambling to my feet like a frightened puppy, my limbs uncoordinated, I rush to the bathroom.

"Vivienne! Please, I'm so sorry."

I don't want to hear it. Closing and locking the door behind me, I rest my back against it, completely addled and shaking like a leaf. An overwhelming desire to throw up has me rushing to the toilet bowl where I lean over and let it all go.

What the fuck just happened?

Once my stomach has evacuated all of its contents, I splash my face and rinse my mouth out at the sink. My reflection in the mirror is a shock to the system. The deep red smudge across my cheekbone is painful, beginning to form a lump under the skin. Proof enough that whether he meant to or not, he hit me.

My eyes travel down to my heart-shaped locket, its brilliant diamonds sparkling under the halogens. What a paradox. The gift of his love nestled eight inches below the bruise of his brutal actions.

I take a few moments to calm myself down. All my nerves are jangling, my teeth chattering together as I begin to shiver with the shock. I can't believe he would do that.

With my teeth sawing away at my thumbnail, and my mind a car crash of thoughts, I pace the bathroom trying to think, understand. Trying to decide my next step. But only one thing is clear. I can't stay in the sodding bathroom for the rest of my life.

I pull my robe from the back of the door and wrap it around me tight, feeling fragile and vulnerable. Although my heart is still beating a million miles an hour, I take a deep breath and quietly open the door.

Max is lying on the bed with his arm over his face, shielding his eyes. He's still racked with guilt muttering his apologies. And now I've had time to absorb what he did, shock, anger, and frustration course through me like hot molten lava rising to the surface. If I was hurting him, why didn't he say something? Why would he lash out like that? And why did he call me a bitch?

"Max?..."

"Oh, god, Vivienne. I'm sorry, baby. I can't tell you how sorry I am." His strangled voice pulls at my heart. Of course he's sorry, he loves me, he'd never hurt me intentionally. He'd never strike out like that if I hadn't done something to cause his reaction.

I nervously edge closer toward him. "What did I do?"

"Nothing. Oh, god, you did nothing." His voice is strained and his eyes are still hidden from me.

I tentatively make my way to the bed. With trembling fingers, I reach out for his arm to pull it away from his face, but he flinches at my touch and won't let me move his arm away. He's resisting me with a force I can't break.

"No! Please don't look at me, I'm so fucking ashamed. I didn't mean to hurt you, baby, I would *never* hurt you. Jesus! I'm so sorry."

"Max, please… Why won't you look at me? What did I do?"

"No, baby. You did nothing."

"Then why won't you—"

"Just!… Just leave me alone. Please."

His harsh tone makes me balk, and I instantly lift my hand from his arm and leave it hovering just above his skin, like I'm unsure if touching him again would burn me.

My brain is fried trying to understand. I stare down at him with wide tear-blurred eyes and a sick feeling knotting inside me. The air around us is charged with his guilt and frustration, and my disbelief wrapped in a painful silence.

"Why are you doing this?" I ask, in a whispered croak.

This is exactly what he did yesterday at the hospital. I had thought it was just a one off, maybe his medication had something to do with his behaviour, but this definitely isn't normal. And for him to strike me like that? Whether he meant to or not, whether he's sorry or not, it's totally unacceptable.

"Max, if you won't tell me what's going on, how can I help you?" My voice is broken and small. I feel broken and small, and my cheek is throbbing from the crack it received from his plaster cast. The solid blow to the side of my face has left a mark along with a headache that's starting to pound. But the fact that he's shutting me out hurts more than anything.

He won't talk about his capture, he made that clear the last time I tried to ask him about it. He admitted that he remembers everything, but he still refuses point blank to discuss it with me. I hate that. I hate being excluded from something so important in his life, something that's affecting us both.

But something must have triggered this behaviour and I need to know what it was. How can I deal with this if I don't know what I'm dealing with?

"Max… What did she do to you?"

His hand hardens into a tight fist, and the muscles flexing in his arm across his eyes confirm that this has everything to do with Monica.

Goosebumps creep across my flesh and the familiar knot of dread sits heavy in my chest. "I need to know what she—"

"No! No you fucking don't!" His jaw is clenched so tight it could possibly crack. And his fists are white at the knuckles. Every muscle in his body, hardening and shaking. And all his anguish speaks a thousand words. Without telling me anything he's just confirmed Monica clearly did something terrible to him to make him react this way.

My heart plummets as the rest of me sags inside with despair and revulsion. Even after her death, Monica is still torturing us, wielding her sadistic power from beyond the grave. It sickens me that the joy of having Max back where he belongs is tainted with her lingering presence. But until he chooses to include me in this, until he stops shutting me out, what am I supposed to do?

Anger builds inside me like a slow boil of emotions. I can't stand to see him hurting, but he can't lash out like that without an explanation. It's not normal.

"Vivienne."

I look up and see him slowly removing his arm from his face, the look in his eyes breaks my heart. He's struggling to come to terms with what he's done, his face is racked with guilt, but when his eyes land on my bruised cheek they close, forcing tears out at the corners. "I could cut my fucking arm off for hurting you like that. You're the last person in the fucking world I would ever want to hurt. I love you, Vivienne. I'm so, so, sorry."

His watery eyes stare up at me with so much anguish and regret, it makes my throat close as fresh tears blur my vision. Without removing his watery eyes from mine, his trembling hand slowly reaches out for me. I look down at it, willing myself to take his hand in mine, but I hold back for just a moment. My eyes dart up to his, as if needing his assurance that I'm safe. Those eyes, the eyes of the man I fell in love with, the eyes that tell me everything he's feeling, give me that assurance and I reach out to meet him halfway.

His fingers tenderly wrap around my trembling hand, his thumb gently tracing my palm, then he squeezes my hand in his, interlocking our fingers. Sad blue eyes survey the red mark he left on my cheek. Guilt and regret etched all over his face.

"Max, I know you're sorry, and I know something painful drove you to do this, but I can't let you shut me out anymore. I need to know what happened to you."

Two watery pools of shame and sadness gaze back at me. "Baby, I know this is hard for you to understand right now, but I can't. I won't put those thoughts in your head. I'll deal with it, I promise." His eyes darken with determination. "And I swear on my life, Vivienne. This will never happen again. I love you, baby. Hurting you fucking kills me."

The quiver in his voice and the pain in his eyes, breaks me. Leaning forward with a deep wince and a painful groan, he gently tugs me closer. As painful as it must be for him, he wraps both arms around me, leaning his forehead against mine. "Please, baby. Please forgive me."

We sit in silence for a few moments. I don't respond to his request, I'm not sure why because I do forgive him. I know he would never willingly want to hurt me. What he doesn't seem to realise, is that by him keeping his secrets and closing himself off to me, he's hurting me far more than any physical pain ever could. I've only just got him back, but now I feel like I'm losing him all over again.

He kisses my cheek ever so softly, still whispering his apologies, but the sweat beading on his forehead and his sharp intake of breath as his pain becomes unbearable, forces him to rest back against the pillows.

"You should get some rest. And I need to put some ice on this."

The look on his face haunts me a little. I know how I would feel if I were the one who had lashed out.

Offering him a reassuring smile, I pull the sheet up to his waist and stroke his hair back from his face. "It's okay, Max. Get some sleep."

As I begin to turn away, he reaches up for my hand and catches my wrist. "Baby, I really am—"

"I know," I whisper softly. I stroke his cheek with gentle fingers, reassuring him with my smile. He leans into my hand and kisses my palm. His uncertain, questioning eyes lingering on mine.

"I'll be up soon. Get some rest."

He closes his eyes in relief as much as tiredness and I back away from the bed.

The icepack on my cheek makes it burn even more, until the increasing numbness begins to take the heat away. The hard shiny lump on my cheekbone feels tight and tender, throwing my symmetrical face out of shape. "Why is it always my friggin' head?"

As I sit alone in the kitchen hunched over the island, wishing I had a glass of wine but nursing a hot cup of tea instead, my imagination runs riot imagining all sorts of horrendous scenarios.

Max's physical injuries were bad, but all of them were consistent with a beating given by Daryl and his henchmen. This aggressive behaviour is born from something else, something far more sinister.

Monica hadn't physically tortured Max, not with anything obvious anyway. Her torture appears to be psychological, primarily linked with… "Oh, Max. What did she do to you?"

"Hi."

The familiar voice and its cheery delivery startles me and has me looking toward the kitchen door. Cole strides in looking suave and businesslike in his work attire. He dresses well, just like his brother and there's something about a good looking man in an expensive suit that becomes a feast for the eyes.

I feel remarkably under dressed sitting here in my short silky robe. His eyes rake up and down the length of me as I self-consciously pull at the hem, trying to hide the amount of bare flesh on display.

"There's some stew left over if you're hungry," I say, nodding toward the fridge.

He stops walking, his eyes widening on me. "What the hell? Jesus! Are you alright? What the hell happened to your face?"

Shit! I blush, lowering my head to let my hair cover it. "I tripped." My big fat lie brings on another blush.

He shakes his head at me, with a get-the-fuck-out-of-here look on his face.. "You tripped?... What was it? A bit of fluff? A shadow? What are you a danger magnet or something? You know, there's a yellow hard hat in the study, maybe you should wear it. Like, always."

I roll my eyes and smirk back, but he's got a point. The hard hat was a gift from Vinnie after Monica had beaten me around the head with my own baseball bat.

Cole walks over to the fridge and opens it up, reaching inside for the stew I'd left him. "Did you cook this?" he asks giving it a hesitant sniff.

"Yes."

"Will I need a shot? Or a stomach pump?"

I give him a moody scowl. "Well, me and your brother seem to have survived it."

He walks over to the microwave and pops the stew inside to heat it up, then he grabs a beer from the fridge. "So, how's big brother doing today?"

"Big brother? I thought you two were twins?"

"We are, but he came out first so he's older." He flips off the top of his bottle then takes a long draw, letting out a contented sigh after swallowing the cool beer. "Man, that's good."

"He's… fine." I lower my eyes, knowing that's an outright lie. Even I can hear the despondency in my voice. I quickly try to add some nonchalance. "He's still in a lot of pain, but he's happy to be home."

Cole studies me for a moment like he's seen right through me, then he takes another sip of his beer. "Hmm, it's funny, you don't look so happy that he's home."

I shift in my seat as the heat in my cheeks flares up again. "I am happy… I'm just tired, that's all."

He studies me a little longer, then the microwave dings breaking the awkward silence.

I quickly scoot off the stool and put my cup in the dishwasher. "Enjoy your meal, I'm going to bed. Don't forget to lock up and turn the lights out. Goodnight."

"Goodnight, Vivienne. Sweet dreams." I don't look back, but I can feel his eyes on me as I leave.

When I enter our bedroom, Max is lying on his back clutching my pillow to his chest, he's fast asleep. I notice he hasn't taken his night time medication yet, but I don't want to wake him up just for that. As I walk over, I take a selfish moment to look at him, drinking him in. His handsomeness is beguiling even in sleep. It's quite an art that he can stir my passion as well as my butterflies without moving a muscle.

I gently finger a silky strand of hair hanging over his brow and brush it back. He's so handsome that sometimes I don't even want even the smallest obstacle between my eyes and his gorgeous face.

A small contented smile hits my lips. We've been through so much together but we've survived it all. Despite what happened earlier, this man fills me with a longing so great, and a need so deep, that the only thing that could really hurt me, is if he ever stopped loving me.

His bedside drawer is slightly open, so I push it closed and gently lift his hand to pull my pillow out from under. Little smudges of red catch my eye and it takes me a moment to process what it could be. The sheets were clean on this morning for Max's return, I'm sure I would have noticed a lipstick mark when I had made the bed up.

Suddenly, my skin prickles when I realise what it is. Blood!

I quickly check the small scar on his abdomen, but it looks fine, it's still a little pink but it's not bleeding, and I can't find any open wounds on his torso.

I check his head, but that wound had healed long ago. As I frantically search his exposed skin, I finally see them. Three perfectly straight cuts sliced into the skin just above his plaster cast on the underside of his forearm. My blood runs cold, my heart breaking. "Oh, Max, no." Tears prick my eyes and a sadness that he's chosen this path again, brings me down to a depressing low.

The cuts are thin and straight. I open his bedside drawer, looking for a razor blade or a small knife. His phone, his wallet, and a folded monogrammed handkerchief are all that are in there. I lift the handkerchief to reach the wallet underneath but something slides out from the folds, glinting up at me from the bottom of the drawer. I freeze for a moment, staring down at the thin sliver of stainless steel. It's then that I notice the mottled blood spots staining the underside of the handkerchief. His guilt at hurting me has made him revert to the mechanism he's always used. Self-punishment.

If he caused harm, or couldn't protect someone he loved, he'd have to punish himself. A crazy notion to the rest of us, but perfectly reasonable in his mind.

Max is a complicated soul with a difficult and painful past. His forearms bear hundreds of tiny white scars, and his back is latticed with whip marks, each one a badge of atonement for the misplaced guilt he had felt when his parents died.

When we first got together he'd hidden this side of himself from me because he feared I wouldn't understand. He'd hidden it right up until Charlie died and then Vinnie, knowing how badly Charlie's death would affect him, was forced to show me Max's room of guilt.

Max thought I wouldn't understand, but I did.

I had come close to hurting myself many times after Greg Taylor had turned my innocent life upside down. I had wanted to feel the pain of a sharp blade biting into my skin, or the burn of a flame searing my flesh. Anything, so that I didn't have to feel the shame and guilt that I had somehow brought this on myself. But after one failed attempt, I realised I couldn't do it, I was too afraid.

We had talked about it many times and I had helped him overcome the need to self-harm. I thought it was all behind him now. Clearly, it was only lying dormant, waiting for the trigger to unleash his need to punish himself. Hurting me was the trigger.

When Monica had tried to kill me, he admitted coming close to cutting himself again, but he'd made me a promise not to do it, and he fought hard to resist the temptation, winning that particular battle.

But history proves that he prefers to bottle things up and keep them inside, trying to deal with them in his own way. I don't want him shutting me out. I want him to tell me everything, so we can get through it together. We're a team, a partnership. If we're going to be man and wife and raise a family, we need to be able to trust each other with anything.

Maybe that's it? Maybe he doesn't trust me enough? That awful thought snags me and guilty feelings of my own begin to come to the fore in a conflict of conscience. I want Max to be open with me about what he endured during his capture, especially as the consequences seem to be affecting us both. But I haven't been open with him.

I had purposely held back some of the details of Monica's first attack. I didn't know if he could deal with it. I didn't want those images floating through his mind because I was afraid it would trigger his guilt at not being there to protect me. I hadn't trusted him to be strong enough.

I hold another secret too. Greg Taylor. A pang of guilt churns my stomach. Who am I to demand full access when I hold secrets of my own.

Once I've brushed my teeth and taken a shower, I inspect the lump on my cheek, it's pretty bad and the redness is now turning into a bruise. Great! Another bump on the head. My skull must be made of Kevlar.

I flip Max's bedside light off, leaving mine on so I can read my book, but I can't concentrate on the text, my mind is still grappling with the mind blowing events of today, so I close it and lay it on the side table.

As I snuggle under the covers, Max's scent hits me like a soothing balm. Looking over at him sleeping, I switch off the light, plump my pillow, and settle onto my side clutching my locket in my hand. As my eyes adjust to the moonlight shimmering in through the windows, I let my eyes drag lazily over his handsome profile before slipping down to his sculpted chest. His broken arm is resting at his side, the hand of his other arm is resting on his lower belly. His fingers twitch slightly, but he's relaxed and out for the count, sleeping soundly.

"Goodnight, Pretty-boy," I whisper kissing the end of my finger and very softly placing it on his lips. With my hand resting over our nuggets, I drift off to sleep.

VIOLENT HEART

Something draws me from my deep sleep. I'm awoken by a strange scraping noise that I don't recognise. Unwillingly, I open my eyes, but Max's side of the bed is empty which instantly puts me on alert, making my heart beat out of my chest.

I sit up and rub the sleep from my eyes. They take a while to adjust to the ambient light of the cloud speckled moon throwing deep shadows across the room.

Max is on the other side of the bedroom, standing naked with his back to me. The sound I had heard is coming from him. "Max? Are you alright?" My voice is hoarse, and a prickle of goosebumps run over my skin when he doesn't respond. "Max?"

I watch him for a moment. Both of his hands are raised to the wall, he's feeling his way along it very slowly like he's looking for the door. The sound which had woken me was his cast scraping along the wallpaper.

"Max?... Baby?"

He still doesn't hear me, so I throw the covers back, swing my legs out of bed, and stand there for a moment, watching him the whole time. He continues to feel along the wall, reaching up above his head, then down low in a slow precise movement, meticulously feeling every inch of the wall beneath his fingers.

Although his ribs are broken, his bending and stretching doesn't appear to be hurting him in the slightest, and he still hasn't acknowledged me which is freaking me out. It's then I realise, he's sleep walking.

I have no idea how to tackle this, so I slowly move toward him. "Max? Sweetheart? It's me, Vivienne. I'm right here."

His hands stop moving and he straightens his body, still facing the wall. It's the eeriest thing to see. He's standing completely still, like his batteries have run out.

I edge closer, gently placing my hand on his shoulder, moving closer to his side so he can see me. "Max, why don't you come back to bed, I'll help you. We can find what you're looking for in the morning." My voice seems to be resonating this time as he slowly turns his head to face me. His eyes are open, shaded by his heavy frown, but it's as if he can't see through them.

Taking his arm, I gently lead him away from the wall, over to the bed. Even as he lowers and sits on the edge of the bed, he doesn't show any signs of pain. I softly brush my fingers through his hair and kiss him on the forehead. His eyes soften and begin to droop, so I encourage him to lie back, which he does without resistance.

In a matter of seconds his breathing is deep and he looks peaceful and relaxed. After covering him with the sheet, I walk around to the other side of the bed and slide in. He's still out like a light, so I snuggle into his side and watch him for a while until my eyes begin to droop.

~

"No!... Stop!... You're hurting me!"

"Don't fight me bitch! You want this? You want me to come? Is this what you want? You want me to fuck you?"

"Stop! Please!... I can't breathe. I can't—"

"Shut up! Shut up and fucking take it, bitch!"

My lungs are starved of oxygen as I frantically gasp for air, but it's no use, my airway is blocked by the heavy, suffocating weight across my throat, pinning me down to the mattress. I will myself to wake up from the horrors of my nightmare. I'm almost there, almost at the stage where I'll jolt out of rem sleep and realise everything is fine, but my brain won't let go.

My eyes are closed and I can hear my muffled, gurgling screams pleading for release as my arms struggle against the heavy restraint pinning them above my head. I feel the weight of something hard and unyielding pressing down against my throat bearing down even harder as I fight against it. The whole bed is moving. My legs are spread painfully wide, my right leg hooked over Greg's broad shoulder, slipping and sliding on the sweat as he aggressively thrusts forward and back, pounding into me over and over again.

"No! Stop! Please!"

My eyes spring open in a wide panicked rush. The sound of my own garbled voice is ringing in my ears. This was the jolt I was subconsciously waiting for, but it doesn't bring the traditional feelings of relief and calm, quite the opposite.

I thought I had been dreaming. The same dream I've always had. Greg's sweaty, grimacing face leering down at me as he violently prods at my innocent ten-year-old body. The pungent vapour of his sweat and sex filling my nostrils, churning my stomach as it always did, but this isn't a nightmare.

I'm awake. Fully awake.

Confused and panicking, I still can't breathe, and now I realise the weight across my windpipe is very real and very frightening. Max has my arms pinned above my head with one hand. He's leaning the plaster cast of his broken arm across my throat, and he's fucking me with wide, glazed, hostile eyes, a horrible sneer on his lips.

Max?... Panic and fear ripples through me as I gasp for air. "Max! Stop!" But there's no volume to my strangled voice. I try to wriggle out of his clutches but I'm practically crushed beneath his powerful body, weighing me down and pushing me into the mattress. I desperately need air. His glazed eyes are open, looking down at me with venom and hate pouring out of them, but he can't see me. He can only see what's in his tortured mind.

With anger burning in his wild eyes, he grits his teeth ramming into me over and over again, hissing out his spiteful torrent. "You. Fucking. Want. This. Bitch?"

Max! Stop!...Please stop!

Suddenly, I hear the bedroom door bursting open and Cole's angry voice shouting at Max as he violently wrenches him off me.

Once the pressure of his arm is gone, the air rushes into my lungs on a series of long desperate gasps, burning and course against the raw tissues of my throat. I cough and splutter as the oxygen fills my lungs. Raking at the bed, I pull the sheet over my naked form as my body convulses with sobs and gulping breaths.

"What the fuck are you doing?" Cole yells, staring down at his brother. Max is sprawled out motionless on the floor staring up at him with confused blinking eyes.

I had heard the break of bone as Cole grabbed him around the chest, hauling him off the bed. Max cried out in a blood curdling yelp, and that's what finally woke him up, bringing him out of his nightmare.

Max looks up at me from the floor with utter bewilderment. He has no idea why I'm crying, or why he's on the floor with Cole bearing down on him.

I'm shaking like a leaf with tears streaming down my face. It's obvious by his expression, he has no idea what just happened.

"Vivienne?..." Max tries to move but his freshly broken ribs make him cry out, and then he passes out from the pain.

I stare at him in complete shock, trembling from head to toe. He had been so violent, so savage and unrestrained. Even his injuries hadn't stopped him from his brutal attack. It was as if he couldn't feel anything. Only what was inside his head.

As disturbed as I feel about what he did, I know it wasn't me he was choking and fucking. It was more than a fuck. It was a brutal, heartless, mindless debasement aimed at Monica, who had somehow pushed him to breaking point.

While he was buried inside me, I could see in his eyes that his mind was buried in a nightmare of his own, revisiting some dark and painful moment from his capture. A moment Monica had controlled then, and still controls now.

The cruelty of life's twists and turns seem to mock me tonight.

The nightmares of Greg Taylor raping me as a child still haunt me with disturbing regularity. He was a stranger who took advantage by violating and defiling my innocence in the worst way possible. I've hated him with a passion for the last fourteen years, and although he's a client of Foxx-Tech, I would go out of my way to avoid ever having to see him again.

Avoiding him was something I could control. The nightmares were still a reminder, but they were something I had long since learnt to cope with and bury the next morning.

But Max. Max is a different story. He's the man I love. He's my protector. Being violated by him brings a whole host of new problems to our door. Least of all, how Max will react to what he's done. This will kill him.

I'm in no doubt that his actions were in some way controlled by Monica and whatever cruel things she had done to him. But I'm fearful that the emotional damage could be catastrophic.

Hurting and being hurt by the one you love, leaves an indelible mark embedded deep inside. Because of my past, I need to be able to trust my sexual partner, not fear that he would do the very thing I had nightmares about.

And Max, how will he ever be able to reconcile this?

"He's out cold! What the hell happened here? I mean, fucking hell, Vivienne, if I hadn't been here, he could have fucking killed you!"

Cole drags his hands through his hair clearly worried and agitated.

Shaking and sobbing, I pull the sheet right up to my chin and lean my back against the headboard clutching at my locket. I'm guessing it was pretty obvious what Max was doing to me, but I don't know what to say.

Cole walks over and sits on the edge of the bed. His wide eyes are wary, surveying me with concern. "Well?" he prompts.

"He was having a nightmare." My voice is frail and quivering, I can't seem to control it.

Cole's disbelieving eyes search my face then he looks down at his brother. "I think he should go back to the hospital, he's going to need another x-ray. Did you hear the bones crack?"

I nod. That sound will live with me forever.

Cole reaches forward and takes my hand, holding it in both of his. His expression flipping between anger, concern, and disbelief. "He had no right to do that to you, Vivienne. Jesus! What the fuck's wrong with him?" Cole's fuming, and the contempt on his face as he stares down at his brother, makes my heart twist.

"It's not his fault. He's suffering."

His face hardens as his eyes whip back up to mine, silently asking me to qualify that remark. "Suffering? I'll make him fucking suffer! I'll break every bone in his fucking body if he ever does that to you again."

Releasing a deep sigh, I pull my hand out of Cole's. "It's Monica," I whisper, bringing my knees up to my chin. I band my arms around them, it's a reflex to the dull pain building in my belly and groin from the battering I just received. "She did something to him, Cole. Something bad… But he won't tell me what it is."

"It's no excuse! Vivienne. Jesus!" Recognition enters his eyes as they trail over my face. "He did that to you too, didn't he?" His eyes darken as he points at my swollen cheek. I nod, sheepishly. "Fuck! He's hit you and tried to—"

"Cole, please," I interrupt, not wishing to hear him say the words. "He didn't know what he was doing. The medication and whatever is going on in his head is causing these outbursts."

"Really?" he huffs sarcastically.

"Yes. The nurse caught him sleep walking before he left the hospital, and he did it again tonight. He's never done that before, not since we've been together. He needs help!"

Cole's angry eyes slide off my face as he shakes his head at me, pulling his phone out to dial the hospital.

As we wait for the paramedics to arrive, I leave Cole with Max who is still unconscious on the floor. I grab some clothes and head to the bathroom to take a quick shower. I want to go with him to the hospital. He's going to be so upset with himself when he wakes up, I don't want to leave him on his own.

Maybe now he'll talk to me. Maybe now he'll see how important it is to include me in this. He can't shut me out now.

I wear a turtle neck sweater to cover the red marks on my neck, but the swollen bruise on my cheek still shows even with concealer. There's a dull pain building in my groin and lower belly from Max's brutal lunges and I feel uncomfortable inside, so I take a couple of painkillers.

My eyes are still teary and red-rimmed, but I try to engage a less traumatised expression before I leave the bathroom. As I walk into the bedroom, Max is semi-conscious on a stretcher, groaning with pain. The paramedics are just about to move him out.

"Where are you going?" Cole asks, eyeing my change of clothes.

"I'm going with him to the hospital."

He stares at me for a moment, like I've gone mad, then he sighs and shakes his head. "I'll drive you."

I walk over to Max taking his hand in mine. A new bruise is forming on his side where an old bruise had begun to fade. His eyes are glazed from the pain relief medication, they land on mine, drifting in and out of focus as his heavy eyelids resist the temptation to close.

"Max, I'm right here."

Tears fill his eyes. They're tears of sadness, not pain, and his hand squeezes mine so tight it almost crushes my knuckles together. "Vivienne, I didn't mean to hurt you. Fuck! I'm so sorry." His voice quivers and his face is racked with guilt and sorrow.

"I know," I whisper, bending down to kiss him softly on his lips.

"No!" He turns his head sharply away from me before I reach his lips and his hand immediately releases mine. His rejection hurts me deeply, but I try not to show it. And without looking at me again, Max is stretchered out and down to the waiting ambulance.

LOOKING FOR A WAY OUT

Cole and I sit in the empty waiting room while Max is taken for an x-ray. The bright, fluorescent, overhead light hurts my tired eyes as I anxiously pace the carpeted floor.

My throat is still tender from the pressure of Max constricting my airway with his heavy cast. And my mind is beset with flashbacks of his savage attack, each one making me shudder. As I bring my hand up to my chest, I feel the heart-shaped locket beneath my fingertips. His token of love. His heart on a chain. Tears pool in my eyes and a dull, relentless ache throbs inside me.

Visits to this hospital have been a regular occurrence over the last few months. I know all the staff by name, and I could probably tell you their favourite colours too. But knowing Max is in safe hands doesn't make it any easier when the person you love is suffering.

The hurt I felt when he turned away from me, went deep and still lingers. It was obvious he felt ashamed about what he'd done, and yes, I admit it, when I realised it was him on top of me, and that it wasn't a dream, it scared me to death. I don't think I could survive another night like this.

It's taken me fourteen years to come to terms with the horrific events of my childhood. The memories will always be there, lurking in the shadows. But I've always managed to deal with them, to bury them away in a dark corner of my mind so that I could function without them clouding my brain every time I had sex. It was a survival mechanism. I wasn't going to allow Greg Taylor to take everything from me. What he'd taken was enough.

Of all people, Mike had been the one who had patiently helped me learn to deal with my deep-seated anxieties. He waited a whole year for me to be comfortable enough to venture into anything remotely sexual. By the time Mike had ruined our relationship, I had become much more confident with my own sexual needs.

But it wasn't until I met Max that I truly understood my own desire. He took away all my inhibitions, I wanted to share my body with him, completely and without barriers. The way he looked at me, the way he loved me, and the way he made me feel about myself set me free.

I love Max with all my heart. I've always trusted him and felt safe with him. How could I not, his love is pure, powerful, and deep. But as much as I hate myself for allowing it to affect me like this, Max's actions tonight have triggered something deep inside me, bringing all the suppressed and buried memories and fears back to the surface. Opening an old wound that clearly has never truly healed.

Max's physical injuries, although significant, are thankfully not life threatening. But his mental trauma worries me a lot. And the fact that he resorted to self-harming again tells me he's not coping with whatever troubles him.

What a pair we make. Two fucked-up souls, hopelessly drawn to each other, deeply in love, and bound with emotional ties that should withstand anything. At least I hope they can.

I can deal with him cutting himself, I'm strong enough for that. And I hope and pray that I'm strong enough to deal with what happened tonight.

I know he would never hurt me intentionally. I know he's struggling to cope with something he won't share with me. But I need to be able to trust him. Trust is everything to me. I couldn't bear it to happen again.

I know I can help him overcome his urge to self-harm, but he has to meet me halfway. If he doesn't trust me enough to let me in, what chance do we have?

As I pace the floor, I gradually begin to piece together all the elements that have brought us to this point, and then it all starts to make sense.

"Vivienne? Are you okay?"

I'd almost forgotten he was here. "Cole… I think I know what's troubling him." I continue to pace the eleven steps back to the window. I had stopped counting them when my brain had begun to organise the facts into some sort of order. "I know Monica definitely screwed with his head during his capture, and I've got a horrible feeling… Well, never mind." I shudder at the thought of her laying her hands on him.

"Tonight, when I caught him sleep walking, he looked like he was searching the wall with his hands, like he was looking for something." I stop pacing to face Cole. He's staring up at me with a confused frown, waiting for me to go on.

Turning on my heel, I begin pacing again, I'm too agitated to stand still. My belly is churning, and all of a sudden a surge of adrenaline hits me when I realise something I had overlooked. I stop abruptly, dragging my hand up to my mouth with a gasp. "Oh, my god! That poor man. He must have been dreaming about his incarceration in that secret room at the chateau! It's obvious she must have left him alone in there several times, like the day she came to find me. But when he was left on his own he must have freaked out. There were no doors or windows…"

Cole and I stare at each other. He's not quite understanding me yet, but at least he's listening.

"It must have been so frustrating for him. He knew there was a door, but he couldn't find it. He couldn't get out. It was there all the time, cloaked by an optical illusion, but he couldn't see it. And even now, in his dreams, he's still looking for it. Looking for a way out."

Cole stands, shoving his hands in his pockets, giving me a

look that tells me he's unimpressed with my theory. "That doesn't explain him trying to rape you," he grates, bitterly.

A deep sigh wafts out of me as my shoulders sag. "…No."

My stomach rolls as that particular memory rears its ugly head. I know it wasn't me he was thinking about in that moment, only Monica could instil that amount of hate. And even though it was a brutal act, meant to cause pain, and executed with venom, the fact that Monica was in his mind at all, has left me wondering if she will haunt us forever.

"Miss Banks."

Doctor Alexander's soft voice filters through my thoughts, pulling me out of them. As he walks toward me, I can see him looking at the bruised lump on my cheekbone with concerned curiosity. I don't look away but if he asks, I don't want to talk about it. He seems to sense that, casting his eyes over to Cole, releasing me from his inquisitive stare.

"You'll be pleased to know he's okay, apart from re-breaking two of his ribs. I'd like to keep him in overnight and maybe for a few days, just to monitor him, but he should be fine."

I blow out a sigh of relief. "Can I see him?"

"Yes, of course, but I'm afraid you won't get much out of him." He frowns then raises a brow. "We've had to sedate him to keep him in bed. He was adamant that he wanted to find you, and it took three of us to hold him down. I think a good night's sleep will do wonders… for you both."

A fleeting sense of relief comes and then disappears just as quickly. Doctor Alexander hasn't mentioned the new, self-administered cuts to his forearm, but I get the feeling he's more than aware of Max's history with self-harming, and will want to assess him mentally when he's had a decent night's sleep.

On a reflex to the uncomfortable feeling in my lower belly, I curl forward slightly, placing my hands on my stomach. Both the doctor, and Cole take an anxious step toward me, hesitating to move in all the way.

"Miss Banks, I'd like to examine you. In fact, Mr. Foxx

insisted that I do."

I feel awkward. Max has obviously told Doctor Alexander what he did to me. How many of the staff know too? I don't want people to think badly of him, but I'd be lying if I said I wasn't worried about the babies. The dull ache in my lower belly is getting stronger.

Nodding sheepishly, I let him escort me to his examination room.

~

"Everything seems to be fine," he says, in a cheery voice from the other side of the pale blue curtain.

I sit up, swing my legs over the side of the examination table, and stand up. After I've pulled my knickers up, and my skirt down, I swish the curtain back and walk over to him.

"Please, take a seat," he says, gesturing at the chair alongside his desk. "You're a little bruised and tender, which is to be expected, but there's nothing to worry about, the babies are fine."

His kind eyes skim over my bruised cheek, and he leans an elbow on his desk facing me head on with a look on his face like that of a concerned parent. "Vivienne, I've known Mr. Foxx for many years. He's not a violent man, far from it." Offering me a sympathetic smile, his eyes linger on mine. "And I know I wouldn't be breaking a confidence, or going against my ethics as a doctor, by telling you that I'm fully aware of his tendency to self-harm."

I lower my eyes for a moment, staring down at my fidgeting hands.

"We'll need to address the issues which have caused his behaviour tonight, so I'd like to refer him to a therapist, maybe you could go together. It's important to understand why he's reacting in a way which is completely unrelated to his normal behaviour."

I nod, still staring down at my hands.

"Good, I'll arrange an appointment with Doctor Fielding for next week. In the meantime, Vivienne, try not to worry, and try to get some rest." He gently pats the back of my hand

and I see his eyes revisiting my bruised cheekbone, but he says nothing more.

I leave the examination room and find Cole waiting patiently for me where I had left him. His anxious expression relaxes a little when he sees me, and then he closes the distance wrapping his arms around my shoulders to give me a comforting hug. "Everything okay?" he asks, kissing the top of my head.

"Yes. Everything's fine." My eyes begin to tear up as the built up pressures of tonight find their way out. Cole tightens his arms around me as I sniffle into his shoulder, but he lets me get it all out, rocking me from side to side.

"Doctor Alexander thinks he should see a therapist."

Cole hugs me a little tighter. "Yeah, well, somebody needs to find out what the hell is going on in that man's head."

I don't know whether his feelings for me are playing any part in his attitude, but the tension in his body and the contempt in his voice, means he hasn't forgiven Max for hurting me, even though I already have.

We walk down to Max's room. Sheila, the nurse I had met before, is just leaving his bedside, marking some notes on a chart. She dims the lighting to a soft ambient tone by a switch at the doorway, then she offers me a toothy smile.

"Hi." Her big brown eyes sparkle in her round chubby face. "Pretty-boy just couldn't stay away, huh! I know what it is, they can't resist me. I'm a babe magnet." Her eyes swing up to Cole as he enters the room behind me. "Oh, my!" she says, feigning a mild seizure, "I need to go lie down for a bit. There's just too much eye candy in this room." Fanning her face, she squeezes between us muttering a string of comical quotes as she wanders away.

"She's interesting," Cole grins, watching her leave.

"Yeah," I chuckle, "she's a hoot."

I take a seat beside Max's bed and Cole moves to stand behind me. Resting his hands on my shoulders, he gives them a gentle squeeze. As if he can feel the tension in my body, he removes his hands and walks over to the window.

I reach out for Max's hand bringing it to my lips, gently kissing his fingers. He looks so peaceful and relaxed. The cuts on his arm have a small dressing over them now, and as he lays naked from the waist up, I can see the fresh bruises staining his golden skin like blotches of ink.

His eyes are still, and his breathing is even. All I can wish for is that he's sleeping soundly, not being tormented by any more nightmares.

Knowing Cole has an important meeting in the morning, I tell him to go home and get some rest after the first hour has passed. He argues, of course, but I finally convince him to go. I too have work in the morning, but I know Max will only torture himself with guilt and regret at what he did to me if I'm not here to reassure him.

I don't want to leave him, he's been through so much, he needs me. And I need him to know I forgive him, and that I understand. I know we can get through this, he just needs to open up to me.

After a couple of hours, Doctor Alexander enters the room and stops in the doorway. "Vivienne. I'm sorry, I didn't realise you were still here. You look exhausted why don't you go home and get some rest."

I am exhausted but I don't want to leave. "I want to be here when he wakes up," I say, stifling a yawn.

"I'm afraid Max is heavily sedated, he won't wake up until we lower the dosage. Go home, Vivienne. Go home and get some rest, I'll call you in the morning."

I look at Max, who's sleeping soundly. I do feel extremely tired. "Okay, but please, call me before you wake him. I want to be here before he opens his eyes."

"Yes, of course," he says, giving me a stiff smile. "I'll get one of the nurses to call you a cab."

I kiss Max on the forehead and squeeze his hand before lowering it to the bed. "Sleep well, my love. And dream only of me."

Even though it's the middle of the night, the cab ride home through the busy streets of London is hampered by Taxi cabs, night buses, and throngs of people pouring out of the many bars and clubs in the city. I gaze out of the window as some of the finest architecture and buildings of significant historical value stream past me unnoticed. In my mind, all I can see is Max shuffling along the bedroom wall, searching for a way out.

It breaks my heart that during his capture he must have heard my voice so many times, and been too weak to make his presence known. If he had managed to struggle out of bed, searching for the door he knew was there but couldn't find, it would have been so frustrating.

Monica's words suddenly hit me. She told me that at the beginning of his capture he had been held in a small boat not twenty feet away from our yacht. Could he have seen us? Had he heard us talking? Had he tried to escape?

Nineteen days is a long time to be incarcerated not knowing your fate. A shudder rattles through my spine and tears prick my eyes. No wonder he's traumatised.

The cab delivers me to the Foxx-Tech building. James, the night security officer, buzzes me in and calls the lift down from the penthouse. On my way up, I send a quick text to Max. I know I'll probably see him before he reads it but I want to let him know I'm thinking of him. Always.

```
Sleep well, my love.
Don't think too much,
and dream only of me.
I love you.
V
X:-)
```

Entering F1 I feel shattered. I take off my shoes so as not to make any noise on the marble floor and wearily drag myself upstairs to bed.

The sheets are in disarray from the chaos of earlier, and I have to force the memories of tonight out of my mind. Luckily, I have exhaustion on my side and my eyes are struggling to stay open. Stripping naked, I leave my clothes where they fall and dive into bed curling around Max's pillow.

LEAVING

"Don't fight me bitch! You want this? You want me to come? Is this what you want? You want me to fuck you?"

"Stop! Please!… I can't breathe. I can't—"

"Shut up and fucking take it, bitch!"

"No! NO!"

I jolt upright in a flailing panic gasping for air. My skin and hair is drenched in sweat and the sheets are all over the place. Bile burns in my throat as the image of Max's malevolent grimace bearing down on me, begins to fade away as I wake more and more from my nightmare.

An icy shudder spirals down my spine as I try to catch my breath and shake off the terrible feeling of dread lying heavy in my chest. I'm nauseous and lightheaded. I've hardly slept a wink all night. Every time I closed my eyes I would dream, but my lucid dreams had taken on a frightening edge.

Usually the dreams which woke me this way were of Greg Taylor pinning me down with his brute force as he savagely violated my ten-year-old body. But this time my dream had been different. Much more terrifying. This time it was Max.

I'm exhausted, but the thought of going back to sleep only to relive those nightmares forces me to get up.

Doctor Alexander should be calling soon to tell me Max

will be woken up, and I'd like to visit him before I go to work. Remembering why Max is back in the hospital makes my belly churn and last night comes flooding back into my brain with sickening clarity, making me tense.

My neck feels stiff, my throat is still scratchy and sore, and my groin aches from his brutal attack, but the ache in my heart that Max may not know how to deal with what he's done, kills me.

Now, fully awake, I'm aware of the sub bass reverberating through the walls and floor of my bedroom. Sia's 'Alive' is blaring out nearby. It's a great track but not first thing in the morning. The alarm clock hasn't even gone off yet, and as I squint at the digital display I realise it's only six o'clock.

After a quick shower, I put on my grey shift dress with leather piping and black heels. A matching silk scarf covers the red marks around my throat and concealer does its best to hide the bruise on my cheek.

Staring into the mirror, I run my fingers over my locket. A pang of sadness takes me over as I recall his words when he gave it to me. It always seems our moments of happiness never last very long. When will our luck ever change?

Once I'm ready, I head downstairs for some tea. I can't think about functioning without a cup of Yorkshire tea.

Bruno Mars is now blaring from the living room speakers, making the crystal chandeliers chink to the beat. As I walk into the kitchen, I'm confronted by Cole in just his Calvin's as he drinks his coffee at the island reading a newspaper. His tall, lean, muscular frame and exquisitely handsome profile get my eyes open, chasing away the remnants of insufficient sleep. He certainly is a sight for sore eyes.

"Sorry. I didn't realise you had come home last night." He quickly grabs the remote, pointing it at the panel on the kitchen wall which instantly lowers the volume by a few ear-splitting decibels. His confused eyes rake over me. "I thought you were staying at the hospital?"

I look away when I realise I'm still hovering in the doorway staring at him. I walk over to the kettle and check it has enough water before switching it on. "I was, but they had to sedate him heavily last night, so I came home. I'm going back there in a minute."

Folding his paper, he throws it on the counter. "How do you feel?"

"Fine." I'm not in the least bit fine, but I'm not prepared to discuss my nightmares with Cole.

"Really?" he says, with a condescending sigh. "You're going with fine?"

His sarcasm doesn't go unnoticed. "Yes. Of course." I shrug, then turn to face him, his concerned eyes linger on mine for a few moments then he stands up. I notice he has a small bruise on his right side. "What happened?"

Twisting his body, he looks down at himself, his tightly packed abdominals bunching under his tanned skin. My eyes rake over him. It makes me smile, the brothers really are two perfect specimens of gorgeousness. I make sure to look away before he catches me checking him out. Nurse Sheila was right, Max and Cole really are eye candy.

"Oh, yeah, Max elbowed me when I was hauling him off you last night."

My smile disintegrates as that awful moment flashes through my mind.

With a silly grin, he holds his lower jaw. "It's nothing. He doesn't pack as much of a punch as you do!"

I shake my head. "You big baby."

Abandoning my tea when I realise the time, I grab a bottle of water from the fridge and head out. I need to get a wiggle on.

When I arrive in the lobby, James rises from his post at the security desk. "Do you need a cab, Miss Banks?"

"Please."

Within a minute, the familiar sight of a black London Taxi pulls up to the kerb.

The cab driver delivers me to the Limberton Hospital, skillfully avoiding all the hot spots of traffic that seem to permanently clog the city. By the time we arrive at the hospital,

I know the driver's name is Luis, and he kindly gave me a brief outline of the many celebrity guests who had also graced the seat I was occupying. He's a pleasant man with a cheeky wit and he made the journey much less mundane than expected. I ask him to wait for me, then I run inside.

Taking the lift, I head straight for Max's room but when I arrive, his bed is empty. Panic brings a cold sweat to the back of my neck. Has something happened to him during the night? Turning on my heel, I run to the nurse's station.

A nurse I haven't met before sits behind the desk. I wait for her to finish her telephone call but I can't stop fidgeting. Her reluctance to acknowledge that I'm standing right in front of her, is beginning to irritate me too.

"Can I help you?" she asks, finally dragging her eyes up to mine.

"Yes. Where's Max, Mr. Foxx, he was in room six last night but he's not there." My words spill out in a rush.

"Are you a relative?" Her tone is efficient, but condescending.

"Yes. No. Erm, I'm his fiancé."

She checks her screen then removes her glasses before speaking. The woman clearly doesn't feel the need to rush. If she moved any slower I'd have to check her pulse!

"He's been discharged."

"Discharged? What do you mean?"

She looks up at my confused face, then past me over my shoulder, and I hear footsteps approaching behind me, so I turn around to follow her gaze.

"Doctor Alexander! Where's Max? She said he's been discharged… I don't understand."

He stops right in front of me, reaching forward to take my arm but something in his expression puts me on edge.

"Please, come with me," he says, softly, leading the way.

We arrive at his office and he closes the door, then he takes his seat behind his desk. His expression is unreadable but I notice he hasn't given me eye contact yet and a worrisome frown is beginning to settle in his brow.

"Doctor, what's going on?"

"Vivienne… We gave Max enough sedation to knock a horse out, but he fought against it and he woke up just after you left last night."

"What? Why didn't you call me?"

He rises from his seat and perches on the edge of his desk right in front of me. His frown deepens and he takes a few moments before continuing.

"He asked me not to, Vivienne." He says it quite plainly while removing his glasses, sliding them into his top pocket, his wary eyes on me the whole time like he's expecting me to react in a specific way. I don't know how to react. I don't understand what he's saying.

"I'm sorry, Vivienne, but I must respect his wishes."

"But… I'm sorry, I… Where is he?"

Interlacing his fingers, he rests them on his thigh, rolling his thumbs over and over in a fidget I've done many times myself, usually when I'm anxious.

"We had a long chat last night. He told me that he had struck you, and that he had physically attacked you while you slept… He's worried he may try to harm you again so—"

"He wouldn't!" I blurt it out, anxiously clutching at my locket. "It wasn't his fault."

"I know," he says, softly. He smiles, though it barely makes an impression on his face. "Believe me, he was full of remorse. He cares for you very deeply, Vivienne. Hurting you has distressed him greatly. I must say, it was very uncharacteristic of him."

"But…why did you discharge him? You said you wanted to keep him here for a few days."

"I didn't discharge him."

I tilt my head like a dog. Not sure I had heard him correctly.

"He discharged himself, Vivienne." His eyes express a sadness which increases my anxiousness.

"But… I left home half an hour ago and he wasn't there, so, where is he?"

His frown deepens as his eyes leave mine and lower to the floor. Taking a deep breath, he rises from the edge of his desk and walks back to his chair.

"Vivienne, believe me, I don't like doing this, but he asked me, in fact, he *ordered* me not to tell you."

My mouth gapes open as my wide eyes stare at him in disbelief. A burst of sarcastic laughter spills out of me in a rush. "What the hell does that mean?"

"Max wants you to stay away from him until he can get to grips with his problems. He's being well looked after and he's agreed to have counselling. He wants you to carry on with your life as normal, and when he's ready, I'm sure everything will resolve itself.... He gave me this to give to you."

Pulling out a white envelope from his top drawer, he reaches over the desk to hand it to me. I stare at him open mouthed, trembling with anxiety. A fair amount of anger is also beginning to build inside me too. This isn't Max shutting me out. This is him cutting me off completely.

I take the envelope, staring down at my name handwritten with Max's unmistakable flair.

Doctor Alexander rises from his seat and walks to the door. "I'll give you a moment."

I hear the door close behind me but I can't seem to move. My mind is a riot of emotions and questions, my heart is beating wildly in my chest, and my shallow breaths don't seem to contain any oxygen.

Opening the envelope, I pull out the handwritten note with shaking hands and a deep knot in my chest.

Vivienne,

Your beautiful eyes tell me everything I need to know, especially what's inside your heart. They've always shone so brightly with love for me, and I cherish that, more than you'll ever know.

But tonight, I changed the look in your eyes. Tonight, I put fear inside them, and I can't live with that.

You need to be able to trust me, but right now, you

can't. I can't trust myself.

You, and you alone are my reason for living, but I'd rather die than hurt you again.

I don't ask for your forgiveness, I don't deserve it. But I will always protect you, even if it's from me.

My heart beats only for you, Vivienne. Always remember that.

I love you more.

Max X

The tears rolling down my cheeks drip off my chin and splash down to the letter shaking in my trembling hands. "No! You can't leave me... I won't let you."

"Ma'am?"

His voice startles me. Swiping the back of my hand across my cheek to dry my tears, I turn to face the familiar voice behind me. John is standing in the open door, filling the space with his broad, well-muscled frame. His eyes are hidden behind dark aviator sunglasses, his tanned face giving nothing away, but I can tell by the set of his jaw that his eyes are watching me with concern.

"Ma'am, I've come to take you home."

Folding the note, I place it in my bag and rise from the chair, smoothing the front of my dress. I'm speechless and numb. Max has crushed my heart with a single sheet of paper, completely knocking me off balance.

"Ma'am?"

My tear filled eyes look up at John, wondering how he came to be standing there. He's supposed to be on holiday with his wife. How did he know I was here?

Of course...Max.

As a flurry of anger surges through me, my shoulders lower and settle backwards and my back straightens. Setting my jaw, I look him straight in the eyes behind his aviators, then I walk toward him. "Take me to him. Now!" I briskly walk past him, jostling his shoulder when he doesn't move quick enough, and I keep walking until I'm outside in the car park.

I had forgotten the cab driver was waiting for me so I quickly hand him some cash then I continue over to John at the Range Rover. He hurries to open my door.

"Ma'am?"

John seems uncharacteristically nervous. With a straight face and absolute determination, I turn to face him. "Please, John, let's not make this difficult. I know that you know where he is, so let's cut the faff. Please take me to him."

The flush in his cheeks and the slight lowering of his head tells me I'm right. It makes sense. Max must have arranged for John to be here knowing how upset I would be reading his letter. I'm more than upset. I'm broken. He thinks he's protecting me, but he's hurting me more than anyone else could. Doesn't he realise I've been through enough already? I've only just got him back, but now, he's not only shutting me out, he's cutting me off. A dagger to the heart would have hurt far less.

"Ma'am I—"

Pinching my fingertips together to emphasise the severity of my impending melt down, I give it to him straight. "John. I'm *this* close to losing it right now. Either take me to him, or brace yourself for the fall out. But I'm warning you, it's going to be ugly."

I don't wait for him to respond. Sliding into the rear seat, I stare straight ahead. He hesitates for a moment, then closes my door and makes his way to the driver's seat. Swiping a glance up at the mirror to gain eye contact, he nods very softly.

I release a deep sigh and relax into my seat, gazing out the window. I'm curious to see where John will take me.

After I've managed to calm myself down, I realise I've been mean to John. It hurts me to have been so rude and short with him. None of this is his fault. "I'm sorry you've been pulled away from your holiday with Julie, please give her my apologies."

His smiling eyes swing up to mine in the rear-view mirror. "It's fine, Ma'am. We actually got back last night so there's no problem."

I still feel bad. Nothing ever seems to run smoothly for long.

I notice his eyes checking out my bruised cheek in the mirror, then his brow creases before he looks away again.

"I assume you're up to speed on our latest dilemma?" I ask sarcastically.

He offers me a stiff smile with a tilt of his head. "It's such a shame, you two never seem to catch a break."

"Pff, you can say that again."

As John swings the car around a corner, and up a familiar tree lined road, I realise where we are. This is the road to Max's parents' house. I should have guessed, but I'm relieved he's somewhere safe, where he's loved, and where he will be cared for in any way he needs.

Anxious butterflies fill my belly at the prospect of seeing him. I'm desperate to see him.

John swings the car into the gateway looking up at the security camera with a small shrug, the gates swing open and John continues up the long gravel driveway.

Grabbing the letter from my bag, and before the car has even come to a stop, I open my door and jump out, almost twisting my heel in the loose stones. I run up to the door and hammer on it like a bailiff. Tears pricking my eyes, but I hold them off as best I can. I don't want to fall apart, there's so much I need to say.

"Max!... Please, let me in."

After a few moments, the door slowly opens a few inches and Jimmy's cautious face peers out at me.

"Jimmy! Please, let me in. I need to see him."

His sad eyes lower as he shakes his head. "I'm sorry, Ma'am. I've had my orders. And the Master's sleeping."

I try to push the door open but Jimmy holds it fast.

"Sylvie? Sylvie, please let me in. I need to see—"

"Mrs. Foxx isn't here," Jimmy interrupts softly. "She's at the chateau with Miss Olivia and baby Mason," he adds, offering me a stiff smile.

"So, who's taking care of Max?" Surely Sylvie wouldn't

leave him here on his own. Unless… Unless she doesn't know he's here? "Max!… Max! Let me in!" I yell, pushing against the door but Jimmy's stronger than he looks.

A faint voice in the background shuts me up.

"Now who the hell is doing all that yellin'? I've just got Pretty-boy off to sleep." Sheila, the nurse I had met at the Limberton, arrives at the door with a face on.

"Oh! Vivienne. Hi." She taps Jimmy on the shoulder, moving him aside, but she doesn't open the door any further. "What can I do for you?"

I stare at her in bewilderment. "Well you can let me in for a start."

"Nope. No can do I'm afraid. I'm on the payroll and Pretty-boy has made it very clear not to let anyone in."

I'm shocked at her stubbornness to keep me out. "But, I'm not anyone. I'm his fiancé."

"I know sweetie, but…hang on a sec." She nods to Jimmy then squeezes her plump body through the door which closes behind her. Taking my elbow, she walks me back down the steps toward the car.

"Look, I know you want to see him, but I can't let you in. I'd lose my job. You understand, right?"

I sag. I don't want her to lose her job, but I don't understand why he's being so ridiculous. I need to see him. We need to talk.

"Sheila, he left me this." Tears fill my eyes as I hand her the letter he'd written me. "It's like… It's like he's saying goodbye. I don't understand, I need to see him."

Sheila's eyes scan the letter and a frown pulls her heavily pencilled brows down low. "Damn, girl, that man really loves you. Ain't nobody ever said stuff like that to me." Her expression softens, and she offers me a genuine smile as she hands the letter back.

"Then why won't he see me? Why is he shutting me out? I can't bear it. I've only just got him back." Tears trickle down my cheeks as my chest tightens with anxiety.

"Listen… I'm just a nurse being paid to do a job I'd like to keep. I don't know all the ins and outs, but I know he's been through some pretty crazy-ass'd stuff lately. Maybe he just needs a little time to get his head around it, you know?"

I stare into her kind, smiling face. But his rejection is crushing me.

"Doctor Fielding is coming by later, from what I've heard he's the best therapist there is for this type of thing. I'm sure he'll be able to help him get over whatever it is that's troubling him. Just give him some more time."

I realise she's walked me back to the car when I look up and see John standing by my open door.

"Sheila …Please tell him I love him… and I miss him. I want him home where he belongs."

She smiles and nods as she rubs my arm in a gesture of sympathy.

Reluctantly, I climb into the car and watch her walk back to the house as John closes my door then slides into the driver's seat. Before he pulls away, I glance up at the upper floor windows when something catches my eye. Whatever it was moving in the window has gone, but I continue to stare in the hope that I might still catch a glimpse of him.

VANQUISHED
~MAX~

"If you ask me, you're one dumb-ass fool for letting that girl go."

"I didn't ask you."

"No, you sure didn't, 'cuz I'd have said let her in. Y'all gotta talk about your problems, share things. You can't hide away like a goddamn hermit. You need to talk about what ails you. That's what women need. Communication. Words. Connection. Not a goddamn door slammed in your face. And that letter? Oh, no you di'int. Yeah, she showed me that damn letter. Seriously? The poor girl's in tears and you write her a goddamn letter. Man! If you were my fiancé, I'd whoop yo' ass."

"Are you finished?"

"Uh-huh. I'm just sayin' that's all. It's good advice, you can take or leave it, Pretty-boy …Come on now, scooch on over, I need to give y'all another shot."

"Does it have to be in the ass?"

"No, but you're getting it there anyway. Besides, you've got such a fine ass. I need some perks to make this job worthwhile. And quit your grumblin', Pretty-boy. I got a suppository wit' yo' name on it, and I ain't afraid to use it."

I can't help the smile seeping across my face. Sheila's turn of phrase and the looks that go with her dry sense of humour, tickle my funny bone.

"And I hired you because....?"

"Because I'm a two hundred twenty-five-pound goddess, with a fine black ass and a smart mouth. Admit it, you're crazy about me. Now quit yo' blabbin' and take your pills, Pretty-boy."

Sheila finally leaves me, grumbling as she goes. She's a breath of fresh air in my world of doom and remorse. The temporary lift she brings with her constant chattering quips in her lazy southern drawl, gives me momentary respite from the agonising pain in my heart.

I feel so ashamed.

I've relived what I did to Vivienne over and over again since I woke up in the hospital last night. I had hurt her so badly, not just physically, but emotionally too. I'll never forget the look on her face or the fear in her eyes. The fear I had put there. And even though I never intended to hurt her, I had done just that, in the worst possible way.

She trusted me. She loved me. I was supposed to protect her, but I didn't. I almost killed her.

Catching a glimpse of her from my window just now, fed the overwhelming ache in my heart. Her tears and the anguish in her voice cut me deep, tearing into me like a rusty blade.

I know she doesn't understand why I'm shutting her out, but I know that if I take her in my arms, I'd never let her go. I'm too selfish about her.

Her beautiful face is permanently emblazoned in my mind. The feel of her delicate silky skin taunts me. Every curve and plane of her sexy, voluptuous body provokes a need so deep to touch and possess every inch of her.

The spell she holds me under with just a look, or a smile, evokes a carnal desire raging so strong within me, I just can't trust myself to stay in control. And oh, those amazing eyes. She's everything I would ever need or want. Being apart kills me, but I can't, and I won't hurt her again.

My phone vibrates on the bedside table. It's another text from Vivienne. Closing my eyes to absorb the tears, I steel myself to read it.

Please don't do this.
You're breaking my heart.
I need to see you.
Call me. Please!
I love you.
V X:-(

"I love you more, baby." I drag my fingers over her beautiful face before my tears blur the screen and the screen fades to black.

Leaning back against the pillows in the soft, earthy tones of my mother's guest suite, I stare up at the ceiling. Concentrating on the ornate overhead light hanging central to the room, my vision closes in to a dark pin spot as the memories of last night prowl through my consciousness.

Vivienne had become wary of me since I pushed her away in the hospital that night she had tried to give me a blow job. I couldn't blame her, it had shocked me too. It felt so good, her touch was like an electric shock swathed in velvet. I needed her so badly, not for the sex, although I could see in her eyes she had missed that as much as I had, but for the connection we had lost. We'd been forced apart for far too long.

In the hours, days, and weeks away from her, I was never completely sure I'd ever see her again, and that brought a pain like no other, crushing my very soul. I couldn't breathe without her. I couldn't live without her. I wouldn't want to.

I needed to feel her in my arms. I'd missed the intimacy of her legs tangled around mine, our fingers weaved together as she lay on my chest with her chocolate brown waves fanned out across my shoulder. I had missed the sound of her breathing, her low sultry voice, her husky raucous laugh, and her scent that could soothe and arouse me in equal measure.

The look in her beautiful eyes when she'd rake them over me with lust and desire burning within them was something I craved deeply. I couldn't survive never seeing her eyes again.

Her kisses left me breathless, wanting more, always more. I

had missed everything about her because she was, and is, my everything.

She had come to the hospital that night to give me a treat. She looked effortlessly gorgeous, as she always does. The curves of her sexy body drive me insane, but to see her standing there in the red lingerie, lace top stockings, and fuck-me shoes, just blew my fucking mind and made me so hard for her.

I've known many beautiful women, but none like Vivienne. She's rare and unique. She can blow me away with her smile, and with just a look across a crowded room she can take my breath away and bring me to my knees.

She walks with a sensual sway I could watch for hours. Everything about her is feminine and beguiling, everything about her draws me in. Gazing at her insanely hot body, I felt privileged to be the focus of her desire.

During my capture, I had longed for the moment I would see her again. I had heard her distant voice many times as I lay in the room Monica had brought me to. She seemed so close. I tried to call out to her, but I was so weak. The pain was excruciating, and Monica would muffle my cries with a pillow, or gag me before she would leave me by myself.

I don't know if it was a dream, it felt so real, but I swear I could feel Vivienne's hand in mine. I could smell her scent and hear her voice. That brief moment had given me hope, and then she was gone.

When she finally came to my rescue, I had almost given up. I was ready to die. Anything would be better than the personal hell I was existing in. But Vivienne found me, and I was grateful to be alive. The woman I loved with all my heart had saved me, I had everything to live for.

As Vivienne, the temptress that she is, stood by my hospital bed in her skimpy, sexy underwear, I felt a rush of pride and longing. She bent down to kiss me. Her kiss overloaded my senses with desire and a deep need to bury myself inside her. I wanted to make her body writhe beneath me as I brought her to orgasm in the many ways I knew I could. I wanted to satisfy her in every way I knew she craved, but my injuries were a straitjacket, robbing me of movement and the freedom to take her in my arms and make love to her.

My heavy muscles had been pulverised in the brutal beating I had taken at the hands of my captors. My ribs reminding me of the painful breaks every time I moved or breathed deeply. I was useless to her. All I could move was the arm that hadn't been broken. It wasn't enough.

I stroked her skin and slipped my hand into her satin and lace panties. The feel of her hot, wet, and ready for me, sent a pulse through my blood. I could smell her need intermingled with my own.

Her body swayed and her hips rolled as my fingers found and caressed the bundle of erotic nerves nestled inside her. Her seductive eyes, heavy and hooded, gazed into mine with so much love and desire pouring out of them, I could feel it like a tangible weight.

The pleasure I was giving her rebounded on me through her beautiful eyes. I ached for that look every moment we were apart.

As her body rolled and shuddered, she griped my hair tightly in her fingers as her orgasm drew closer. The soft erotic moans sighing from her parted lips floated over me like diaphanous silk. As she held her breath and bit down on her bottom lip, I knew she was right where I wanted her. I took her mouth in a greedy, passionate kiss, devouring her cries as her climax burst onto my fingers, shuddering and rippling out all over her body.

I lived only to please her. She was my world, my life, the mother of my babies. I couldn't wait to marry her, to make her mine.

Once we had both caught our breath, she began a slow erotic path down my body until her firm grip took hold of my dick sending shock waves right through me. It felt amazing, she felt amazing. It took every ounce of control not to come straight away. I needed to savour every single moment, even though she was blowing my fucking mind.

Hearing my name from her lips and watching her come had been enough, but now the sensation of her gentle touch and her skin against mine, triggered sparks all over my body, heating my blood and misting my skin with sweat.

Her scent was driving me fucking wild. Her soft tongue and the warm caress as her mouth enveloped my rock hard dick, threw me into oblivion as she stroked, lapped, and sucked every inch of me. She had such an amazing mouth, and a willingness to take me deep. Her soft moans only elevating my arousal.

Vivienne had skills I truly admired, but her heart and the way she loved me was the force pulling me toward her. She held my heart and soul in the palm of her hand, and I was hers, completely.

Lost in the moment, I felt swathed in the luxurious pleasure so intense I couldn't see straight. As Vivienne took a firmer grip, increasing the pressure and speed, something inside me tilted off balance. My gut churned and suddenly I couldn't breathe. I was slowly suffocating as the walls were closing in around me.

My eyes were screwed shut, but Monica's face was right in front of me. I could smell her sickly, sweet, French perfume. I could feel her weight as she straddled my hips. I was too weak to fight her off, too injured to move, the intense pain dulling my reflexes, taking me dangerously close to the edge of a blackout.

The pressure of her slight, pale, naked body balanced on my thighs, pinned my weakened frame to the hard metal cot I'd been lying in for days. A sheen of sweat glinted off her breasts in the dull light of the darkened room of my door-less, window-less prison cell.

She moaned and licked her lips, flicking her long red hair over one shoulder as her bony fingers wrapped around my dick, pulling and tugging till it hurt.

'Make love to me, Max. I need you inside me. Come on, that's right… Come on, Max… You know you want me. I'm the one you need. She can't love you like I do."

With every ounce of will power, I fought against her pathetic attempts to make me hard, but as I felt my dick stiffen in her firm, relentless grip, bile began to rise in my throat. My dick hardened and pulsed. I didn't want her to control me like this, I couldn't stand it. I felt sick, digging deep to find the inner strength to fight her off.

"Stop it! Stop it! Stop it, you bitch!"

Lunging forward, I grabbed her arm to stop her from pumping me, and to stop the uncontrollable tightening and throbbing in my balls as the blood rushed into my groin. My body was reacting to Monica's touch and it sickened me. I couldn't bear to have her hands on me, stroking and touching. The sight of the red-haired woman I had once loved, now repulsed me.

Revulsion churned my stomach, her constant irrational demands for sex and affection stretched my resolve to breaking point. The woman was mad. Delusional. But I had no power, no strength to fight back. I felt utterly alone and completely defenceless to her skewed and perverted perspective of reality. She had brought me to this hell on earth. Saving me from the brutality of the men who had taken me by force, only to enslave me for her own sick and twisted needs.

The sharp stabbing pains in my ribs as I lunged toward her, brought me out of my hell and back to the hospital. Monica disappeared as I blinked my eyes open, driven back to the dark recesses of my tortured mind. The sound of Vivienne's startled yelp and her stunned expression was now suddenly in sharp focus.

In a heartbeat, I realised that I had been reliving a tormented moment from my capture. The vivid memories of Monica's depravity merging seamlessly into the present with laser sharp reality. Shame and humiliation soaked through me, right to the bone. I had lost control of my own mind.

Vivienne's stunned and beautiful face, staring at me with confused, frightened eyes, was too much to take. I didn't want to look at her with images of Monica still seared into my brain. They were as different as night and day. Vivienne was loving, kind, and innocent. Monica was twisted, hostile, and driven by something dark and malevolent.

I pushed Vivienne away, shielding my eyes. I couldn't deal with the look I knew I would see on her face, so I took the coward's way out. I avoided it.

I fought against it, but I couldn't control the way Monica had made me feel, and I hated that. I was angry that even after her death, I allowed her to invade a private and deeply personal moment between Vivienne and I. She'd managed to tear us apart all over again.

Vivienne thought it was her fault. She thought she had hurt me. I could have laughed out loud if it wasn't so tragic.

After Vivienne had left in tears, because I had refused to explain myself, I felt the cold, hard weight of depression looming toward me. I had fucked up big style.. Pushing Vivienne away was a stupid, selfish mistake. She wanted to help, to understand what I was going through, but I couldn't bear to tell her, so I pushed her away. I made her leave. But I needed her, now more than ever.

The urge to feel the sharp sting of a wafer thin blade slicing through my skin, grew stronger and deeper. I knew it would take the pain away, for a while at least, but I was trapped in a hospital bed. I had nothing at my disposal except the pain of my own injuries, so I used them, twisting my body around until the pain was too great and I passed out. The nightmares and sleep walking that followed, had been manifested by the torment lingering in my subconscious.

When I woke the next morning, I remembered them vividly. I'd spent too many nights on my own in that hell. Searching. Trying to seek out the door that I knew was there but couldn't find. It had to be there, how else was Monica coming and going? There had to be a way out. There just had to be.

Every time Monica had left me alone, I would struggle to get up and move along the walls. The pain would sometimes force me back to the cot, but I had to try. I was suffocating in that room. I was desperate to get out, desperate to find

Vivienne.

When Monica left me alone, she'd leave me in pitch darkness with nothing but the sound of my own ragged, frightened breath. I'd stumble along the walls, feeling my way along every inch searching for a door, an opening, anything to get out. I had to get out.

I thought my reaction to Vivienne in the hospital was a one off. I put it down to the drugs I was on and my fragile condition. I still needed to heal from the traumatic events of the last nineteen days. I had been a hostage, beaten to within an inch of my life, and at the mercy of a woman I detested.

I could handle a few nightmares, a few cold sweats, a few memories that would send a shiver down my spine. But when I was finally sent home from the hospital, I realised too late that the conditions of my captivity had instilled consequences that would change everything.

My reactions had gravely threatened Vivienne's life. I knew then, that I had to take control.

That night, before the paramedics had taken me back to the hospital, Vivienne had already forgiven me, I could see it in her eyes and feel it in her touch. She seemed to understand that I was being controlled by something dark and overwhelming, but I couldn't forgive myself for hurting her like that.

Despite her forgiveness, doubt and fear were written all over her face. It crushed me to know I had caused it. She was the one person I could never hurt. Not intentionally. And it killed me to know that I had. She was my life, my love, I couldn't bear to lose her, but I couldn't bear to hurt her.

I didn't ever want Vivienne to know what Monica had done to me, she'd suffered enough at her hands already. Why would I ever burden her purity, her innocence, with such lurid and graphic images. They were a curse that only I should bear, and even now they make me feel sick to my stomach.

Guilt, shame, and loss crowd in on me with oppressive force. I'm trying to protect the woman I love, but I'm hurting her more by pushing her away, the lesser of two evils in my reckoning.

I was lucky Cole had been on hand to intervene. What I had done was bad enough, but what I could have done still scares the shit out of me.

WHEN IT RAINS, IT POURS ~VIVIENNE~

"Ma'am, your phone has been ringing in your bag."

I drag my teary eyes away from the upper window as John drives down the long gravel driveway toward the opening gates. Swiping the back of my hand across my cheeks to dry my tears, I shove the letter in my bag and remove my phone. There are four missed calls, one from an unknown number, the rest are from Lucy:

"Viv! I've been trying to call you for ages."

"Sorry I—"

"Viv…your mum's been rushed into hospital. Mavis, her neighbour, called me when she couldn't reach you. Where are you?"

The shock of her news and the urgency in her voice, addles my brain for a moment. "When it rains, it fucking pours." I knew at some point Mum would have to face the consequences of her self-destructive lifestyle, but her timing couldn't have been worse. "What happened?"

"Overdose maybe? I don't know."

"Where is she?" I flick my eyes up to the rear-view mirror. John has sensed my angst and slows the car to a halt as the gates swing closed behind us.

"She's been taken to St. Thomas' Hospital. Mavis said she's on Albert Ward. Do you want me to come with you? I can cancel my clients."

"No, it's okay, I've got John with me. I'm on my way. Thanks, Luce, I'll call you later."

John swings around to face me, waiting for his instructions.

"I need to get to St. Thomas' Hospital. It's my mum."

"Yes, Ma'am. Copy that."

The glut of London traffic hampers our journey, but when we finally pull up to the drop off point, John tells me he'll wait for my call, then I rush in to find Mum's ward.

Panic settles into my stomach. Mum has been in hospital several times over the years, usually from accidents resulting from her inebriation, but she's also been admitted twice because of a drugs overdose. She seems to have no will to want to change her lifestyle. She's hell bent on pursuing this worthless existence, even after the many warnings she's had.

It makes me sad. She's all I have left, and I know it's only a matter of time before I lose her prematurely to her insane addictions.

As I approach her bedside in the busy ward, tears fill my eyes. She looks so frail and helpless. Mum had been a beauty in her youth, admired by men and women alike. Her striking Sophia Loren eyes and lustrous dark hair were my genetic inheritance. But the ravages of alcohol, drugs, and low self-esteem have slowly but surely eroded her beauty, replacing it with dark shadows and wrinkles far too prematurely. Her skin, once glowing and radiant, now resembles a parchment etched with neglect. For a woman of forty-three she could be mistaken for a woman decades older. I pity her. She could have had so much more but she chose to throw it all away.

I take the chair next to her bed. "Mum… Mum it's me, Viv."

With a flicker of her eyes she pulls a face like there's a foul smell under her nose. Her eyes are glassy and red-rimmed when they finally open searching the space in front of her. When they land on me, she stops moving and I see the instant shame on her face. "What are you doing here? I told them not to call you."

I stare at her, trying to figure out why I really am here. It's not like we've ever had a strong mother-daughter bond, and she's never been willing to accept any of my help, unless it's been a wad of cash to bail her out, or to buy her drugs with.

As much as it galls me to know her hospital visit is self-inflicted, she's still my mother, I can't just abandon her. I won't do what she did to me.

I run my eyes all over her to check for any obvious signs as to why she's here, but there's not a visible mark on her. She's got the shakes, her legs twitch and shift under the sheet. She's confined in a place where the drugs are legal but out of reach, and the prospect of a drink is non-existent. It's written all over her face that being here is a living hell.

"So, what happened this time, did you fall? Or was it another overdose?" The simmering anger that she's never really cared about anyone else but herself, puts a sharp tone in my voice. She's shown no interest in me since my father's death. My engagement, my pregnancy, Max's abduction, it's all been well documented in the press.

I've tried to speak with her many times only to be faced with a drunken, spaced out, garbled response. But she hasn't once called me to congratulate us, or to find out how I am. As far as I know, apart from contacting Max to ask him for money, she's made no attempt to reach out to me at all, her own daughter.

Her eyes lower to the sheet she's nervously pulling at with her fingers. Her twitchy movements, a classic sign she's in withdrawal. She's never allowed herself to go cold turkey before. I don't think I've ever seen my mother this sober. But the clammy sheen of sweat developing on her forehead, and the redness of her skin, tells me she's aching for a drink.

"Well?" My quota for being ignored has been well and truly exhausted today.

Her eyes land back on mine with piercing directness as her body finally stills. "I've got six months, a year at the most."

"Wh…what?" I ask, almost choking. Her voice was strong and clear, but I still had to make her confirm it.

Her eyes swing away from mine. Repositioning the sheet across her legs, she smooths it out with her hands as if she needed to be occupied. "It's cancer, among other things. They can't do anything, it's too late for that."

She said it so matter of fact, like she had expected it. It left me numb and speechless.

"I could really use a drink right now!" she says, using a jovial tone. I suspect she's trying to lighten the devastating news.

My mind is a riot of emotions and questions, but Mum is calm and smiling. It's not something I've seen her do very often. She looks completely resigned and strangely at peace with it.

Tears pool in my eyes and my heart sinks to the pit of my stomach. Our relationship has never been strong, but now there's a limit to the amount of time I'll have with her, I feel the sense of loss already. "Mum…" I'm lost for words, suddenly bursting into tears.

"Don't do that, Vivienne. We both know I'm not worth your tears."

"Oh, Mum." The words lodge in my throat. I lift my head to look at her. The shame in her glistening eyes hurts me. This is the first time she's ever acknowledged the fact that she'd failed me as a mother. Now, when it's too late!

"There must be something they can do," I sniffle, reaching for her hand. "We'll get a second opinion. I'll take you to the Limberton, they have state of the art—"

"No," she says, softly. "I don't want that."

The cold determined look in her eyes angers me. She's giving up without a fight. She's done that all her life and it pisses me off. She has no right to give up, she has a daughter and two grandchildren to live for.

Swallowing the lump in my throat, I study her sunken eyes. She's gazing down at our hands with a far off look in her eye.

"Mum, why won't you let me help you?"

"You can't... Not unless you've got a bottle of Vodka in your handbag."

Her glib remark rankles as a white-hot anger surges through me, but then dissipates just as quickly. I'd always known she'd die young. Nobody could survive the abuse she's levied on her body unscathed.

And what did it matter now? If she wanted to spend her last few months in a drunken stupor, who was I to stop her?

We sit in silence for a few minutes. Mum had been given this news hours ago, I was still trying to come to terms with what it would mean for both of us.

The ward is a bustling hub of groaning patients, bleeping machines, and diligent staff trying to cope with the demand of an overstretched national health service. But as I sit bearing the weight of my mother's news, on top of the morning I had already suffered by being shut out by Max, I begin to feel totally and completely alone.

"I'm glad you got him back, Vivienne. Max is a good man, he'll take care of you."

My eyes fly up to hers. For the first time in years she looks sober and completely in control of her words, thoughts, and actions. An embarrassed smile slinks across her face as she reaches over to pat the back of my hand. "Don't look so surprised. I read the papers."

I'm shocked, I hadn't expected her to be aware or care about anything that happened in my life. This is a first.

She narrows her eyes on me, like that of a concerned parent. Also a first. "The stories are true?" she asks. "About your pregnancy, I mean?"

"Yes. I've called you many times to tell you about it, but..." My throat tightens.

Her eyes become sad, beginning to mist with tears before she lowers her gaze, her grip tightening around my hand. "I'm sorry, Vivienne..."

A forced silence stretches out between us, my emotions are lying too close to the surface to allow me to continue without bursting into tears. I've wanted to talk to my mother so many times, to tell her about the babies, Max, my new job. All the things a mother and daughter should discuss and know about each other.

She should have been my refuge in all the storms of my life, but her selfish choices had taken precedence, leaving little, if any room for communication until now, when we only have a few months left to make things right.

Today is the first time in a long time that my mother has made an open apology or shown any interest in me. I'm grateful to hear it, but what difference will it make?

Her calloused hands gently rub mine. I can feel the tremble in her fingers as her body fights to control the nerve endings usually dulled and steeped in alcohol, now craving it with an intense need.

"When I read about the babies, I wasn't sure if it was true." Her eyes nervously slide down to our hands. "They said you'd never be able to have children after… I didn't think you'd…" She stumbles over her words, leaving them unsaid.

"Yeah, it was a shock for me too, Mum."

She begins to sob. "I'm so happy they were wrong. Oh, god, Vivienne. I'm so sorry. I completely ruined your life. I should have gone to the police."

I'm stunned, choked up, and fiercely angry that she's chosen now to admit her failings. But I'm also deeply relieved. Knowing she only has a few months left, I need to forgive her, and she needs to know it. It's something I've never been able to do until now because she's never admitted fault before. "Oh, Mum…"

We hug so tightly, I feel like she'll snap. Her frail body convulses with genuine, heartfelt sobs as her guilt and shame is finally released.

~

The strict visiting hours on the ward force me to leave. I stayed right until the last minute, knowing I might never get the chance to communicate with her again without the veil of alcohol between us.

We talked and talked, raking over the past. I was surprised

that her memories hadn't been dulled by the abuse of drugs and alcohol. She had such clarity when she spoke of the past, especially of my father, and of me as a baby.

I was shocked to find out that Mum knew it was Greg Taylor who had raped me. All this time I thought she'd been oblivious.

The night it happened, after he had left, I found Mum passed out in the living room. She had a cut on her cheek and a swollen black eye. At the time, I had assumed she'd fallen over and knocked herself out from too much booze and drugs, but she told me Greg had beaten her, threatening her to keep her mouth shut.

She'd never gone to the police or spoken about it with me, and all this time, I had assumed that she was too drunk to remember him being there that night.

It hurt knowing she had kept that to herself all these years. She had protected him, when she should have been protecting me.

She was surprised when I told her Greg Taylor had resurfaced in my life. She was convinced that he had gone to live in New Zealand years ago. I could see in her eyes, she hated him as much as I did, maybe even more.

She asked me questions about him, wanting to know every little detail. It clearly bothered her that he was still causing me anguish after all these years, especially as he'd never been punished for his crime.

We talked about my new job, my friends, Lucy and Dan, and all the adventures, both good and bad that I had experienced with Max. I decided to leave out recent events, I was hoping they'd be short lived and Max would come to his senses and come home. I wanted to leave Mum thinking everything was rosy in our world.

I was so relieved to have this opportunity to connect with my mother again, it had taken fourteen years but it was worth it. Of course, every silver lining has a cloud, and just before I left, after kissing her on the cheek, she grabbed the sleeve of my coat and whispered, "If you're visiting tomorrow, can you bring a bottle of Vodka?"

I had to steel myself. It hurt so much. After finally connecting with my mother, after all the apologies and words of hope, I suddenly realised nothing would ever be as important as her next drink.

When I leave the ward, I find John reading his Kindle in the main reception area. He jumps to his feet marching toward me. "Everything okay Ma'am?"

I fondle my locket in my fingers, fast becoming a recurring habit when my mind is troubled. "Not really. I'm sorry, I should have let you know I was going to be so long."

"Not a problem, Ma'am. It gave me a chance to catch up on my reading." He smiles warmly then starts to move off. "I'll go get the car and meet you out front."

While I wait for John to bring the car, I call Lucy. She's left a ton of messages. What's more noticeable, is Max hasn't replied to any of mine.

"Hey, Viv, how's your mum?"

A long puff of air hisses out of me, pushing my cheeks out with a weary sigh. "Where do you want me to start? …Oh, god, Luce. She's dying. She's only got a few months, maybe a year." Saying it out loud makes it too real. My heart twists and sinks.

"Oh, Jesus. I'm so sorry, Viv."

"Yes, I know." Tears pool in my eyes, already sore from the tears of earlier. I wished she was here, she gives the best hugs at times like these. "But the good news is, we finally got to talk. About everything."

"Good. That's… Oh, bollocks!"

"What?"

"Dan's parents have just sprung a surprise holiday to Crete on us, to make up for the disastrous honeymoon saga, but we leave tonight for two weeks."

"And?"

"You need me, Viv. I should be here for you."

"Don't be silly. You deserve to have the honeymoon you should have had in the first place. Nothing's going to happen to Mum in the next two weeks. Enjoy yourselves. And call me when you get back. We'll have a catch-up."

"I will. And tell Max to give you a big cuddle from me, if his ribs are up to it."

I don't have the heart or the desire to tell Lucy about what happened last night, or about him shutting me out. She'd never leave, and I don't want her worrying about me when she should be enjoying her honeymoon with Dan.

"Yes, of course. Have fun." My light and airy voice almost chokes me, so I end the call quickly.

John has the good grace not to question me on the way home. He's a solid support with a kind heart, and always seems to know when to leave me to my own devices.

When I enter the penthouse, the smell of something good hits my nose, and Muse are blaring out of the sound system. Cole is singing at the top of his voice, almost in tune.

I try to sneak past the kitchen, but he catches me mid stride and lowers the volume. "Hey, lady! Where do you think you're going?"

Stumbling to a halt, I turn to face him. "I was just going to take a bath and go straight to bed."

"Oh, no you don't." He strides toward me. "I'll bet you haven't eaten all day, and I've been slaving over a hot stove for tonight's meal, so the least you can do is join me for dinner."

Taking my elbow, he marches me over to the island and pulls my bag from my shoulder, then he removes my coat, sits me down, and proceeds to open a bottle of non-alcoholic wine. With an extravagant flourish, he pours us both a glass then clinks them together. "Cheers!"

The wine isn't bad. Not great, but not bad.

After a few clangs, bangs, and muttered expletives when he burns his hand on the hot dish fresh from the oven, he serves us a very respectable beef something or other. When I question him on what it is, he isn't sure, but insists that I eat it.

The beef is succulent and the gravy is something I remember Jan had made once before, it's delicious. I hadn't realised how hungry I was.

"So," he sighs, looking at me cagily. "John tells me Max has pulled a Garbo."

"A what?"

"A Garbo. Greta Garbo… I want to be alone."

A scowl settles onto my face as I stab my fork into a chunk of beef. Max's stubbornness is irritating. "Yes, he has. I don't suppose you could talk some sense into him? He's not exactly talking to me."

Cole sighs raising an eyebrow. "Well, to be perfectly honest, I'm glad he's not here, I'd be sleeping with one eye open if he were."

I shoot him an angry glare. "It wasn't his fault."

"Maybe not, but would you really want to take the risk of him attacking you again?"

On a huff, I take a sip of wine. But he's right. It wouldn't do either of us any good if that happened again. It doesn't mean we can't talk, though. "Why is he being so stubborn? He won't even talk to me. He won't even answer my texts."

Cole shrugs, picking up his wine glass. "The man's an idiot." His angry frown and glib remark makes me think Cole hasn't forgiven him for attacking me last night.

My shoulders sag. Reaching for my bag, I pull out the letter Max had written me. "He gave me this."

Cole reads the letter with a frown which deepens when he's finished reading. His eyes flick up to mine, I can't tell what he's thinking, so I wait for his response. He shrugs again tossing the letter onto the counter. "Okay, so he's a poetic idiot. What do you want me to say?"

Tears begin to fill my eyes. Placing my fork on the side of my plate, I stare down at the letter. "I want you to tell me that he's not saying goodbye. I want you to tell me that he's coming home."

Cole's crystal blue eyes search my face for a long moment. Reaching across the island he takes my hand, giving it a gentle squeeze. The look in his eyes and the fit of my hand in his, reminds me of Max.

"Vivienne, you're asking the wrong guy. You know how I

feel about you."

Anger bursts out of me as I yank my hand out of his. "Oh, for fuck's sake, Cole! How many times do we have to go around the same circle. There will never be a me and you. I love Max!"

His jaw clenches, his soft eyes searching mine with a hurt expression. Reaching across for my hand again, he holds it in his firm grip. "I know you do. I wish you didn't… But if you'd let me finish. What I was trying to say, is that if you were mine, I'd want to protect you as fiercely as he does. I'd do the same thing."

"…Oh."

"Just cut him some slack until he's had a chance to figure this out. As much as I wish it were different, he loves you, he's just trying to protect you, that's all."

My anger fizzles away. Staring down at our hands, I offer Cole an apologetic smile. I feel bad, I always seem to end up rubbing his nose in it, but he takes it with such good grace.

"I'm sorry. I didn't mean to—"

"Apology accepted," he interrupts with a smile, although it doesn't quite make it to his eyes. "Now eat! Or you're really going to hurt my feelings." Dropping my hand, he continues to plough through his dinner.

I have hurt his feelings, not intentionally of course, but while we share the same space, and while I keep looking to him for support, how will he ever move on? I know I'm being selfish, and I've got used to having him around. When Max disappeared and Cole turned up, I had a substitute who was so identical at times it was like the real thing. He's like a 'Max patch.' But it's not fair on Cole, he deserves to be the lead player not the reserve.

"Is your mother alright?" he asks, pulling me out of my thoughts. "John said she's in the hospital."

I stare down at my plate, my appetite has completely vanished. "She's…" The words get stuck in my throat and all I can see in my mind is her frailty.

I had always thought of my mother as a hard woman. Hard

because of her selfish choices and the fact that she could abandon her own flesh and blood for booze and drugs. But in reality, she's just a pathetic, frightened woman who hides her feelings in a bottle, blanking out the real world any way she can.

I hadn't realised I was crying until I feel Cole's arms around me and the weight of his chin on my shoulder. "It's alright, I've got you," he whispers, giving me a squeeze. I can't stop the tears so I let them flow. "Is there anything I can do to help?" he asks softly.

"No. No one can help her now."

Cole holds me until I've cried it all out. He seems to understand that I don't want to talk, I just need to let out all my pent up emotions. As usual, I'm grateful of his support. Knowing how he feels about me makes me guilty that I am once again relying on him. It isn't fair, but without him, I think I'd have a meltdown.

What a day. It feels like the whole world is conspiring against my happiness.

A text alert on my phone makes me jump. "That could be Mum." Pulling out of Cole's arms, I reach for my bag, grabbing my phone.

```
I'm so sorry about your mother.
Whatever she needs, it's hers.
I wish I could be with you right now.
Please understand why I can't.
I will always protect you.
Always.
Max. x
```

Staring down at the message, fresh tears sting my eyes. He should be here with me, comforting me, helping me get through this. Why can't he see that?

I call him straight away, but he declines the call without even letting me leave a voice message.

"Everything okay?" Cole asks warily.

"No! Everything is not okay!" I run out of the kitchen in a flood of tears.

"Vivienne!"

I just keep running until I make it to the bedroom. Throwing myself on the bed, I cry my heart out.

THE FUCK-IT-BUCKET

Standing motionless under the warm cascade of water, I try to wash away the depression I woke with this morning. Trying to get my head around Max's self-imposed isolation and my mother's mortality, has left me emotionally empty. I couldn't cry any more tears if I tried. I feel so useless and redundant.

Max won't talk to me, and as soon as my mother leaves the hospital her addictions will out rank me in the little time we have left. Abandonment has been the theme of my whole life. In one way or another, everyone I love, leaves.

"Where are you going?"

I turn to face Cole as I head to the front door. He's perched on a stool in the kitchen drinking a coffee. His expensive suit and well-groomed appearance affording him a second glance.

"I'm going to the hospital to see my mum."

"Need some company?"

Shaking my head, I start to move off.

"Vivienne."

Begrudgingly, I turn back. He smiles and nods over to the counter just inside the kitchen door. I step forward to see what he's looking at. The fragrance reaches me first, then the sight of the huge bouquet of white roses catches my breath.

"They arrived this morning," he says, finishing his coffee. "There's a note attached."

I see the small white envelope with my name on it nestled in amongst the beautiful roses. I stare at it for a long moment then turn away. "If he has anything to say, he should say it to my face!" Slamming the door behind me, I leave the penthouse.

By the time the lift has brought me down to the lobby, I've regained control of myself. John is waiting for me at the kerb.

When I saw the roses, I felt so angry that Max could think a bunch of flowers and a few words on a piece of stationery would suffice. We're supposed to be a team pulling in the same direction, looking out for each other so we can survive what anyone else throws at us. And we have survived. We've been through more than our fair share of pain and separation at the hands of Monica.

But this time, Max has cut the cord. He's decided to go it alone and leave me to fend for myself. Not in the literal sense, of course. I'm amply protected by muscle and brawn, and cosseted by wealth and status, but the fact that he's abruptly cut me out of his life, effectively leaving me, is too much to bear.

When I enter the hospital ward, I walk straight over to my mother's bed. I have to do a double take as the woman lying in it is not my mother.

"Excuse me." I grab the arm of a passing nurse. "Where's Mrs. Banks? I'm her daughter, she was here last night." I hastily point at the newly occupied bed.

The nurse gives me a look that instantly worries me. "She's gone home. She left last night. We advised her against it, but we can't stop them from leaving if they want to." She hesitates a moment longer, then excuses herself to get on with her duties.

I should have known the call of a bottle of wine or Vodka would be too hard for my mother to resist. The twelve hours she had been here must have been the longest she'd ever gone without alcohol.

When I reach the exit, I call her. It rings out for ages and then she answers. Her slurred and garbled voice brings tears to my eyes and a knot to my chest. What's the point in even trying to have a conversation with her in this state.

On my way to the car, I silently debate my course of action. Should I cave in and let it all get the better of me by running home and wallowing in self-pity with a shit load of chocolate? Or, should I chuck-it-in-the-fuck-it-bucket and give fate the bird?

The fuck-it-bucket wins and I decide to go to work, at least there I'll feel needed, useful, and productive.

~

Casper seems surprised to see me as I enter my office. "Vivienne. I wasn't expecting you today, but I'm very pleased to see you. How are you?"

The genuine concern in his soft hazel eyes is touching, but I've already decided that I am not going to allow myself to get drawn into any negative topics while I'm at work. I need to put all that in the pending tray for a few hours.

"Fine, thanks. I'd like to get up to speed. And we need to organise the aerial work. I'd like to get started on the backlog this afternoon."

"Um, sure."

Casper's surprise at my cheery, albeit fake appearance, tells me he's probably aware of more than I had given him credit for. John has probably prepped everyone who needs to know about the latest dramas in our lives, so I'm sure Casper was expecting me to be much more subdued.

Grabbing his tablet, he follows me into my office.

"Ed is out on a shoot for the Foxx-Glove Foundation. He'll be back this afternoon."

As I tap my laptop to bring the screen to life, I spot the bouquet of white roses a moment after the fragrance hits my nose. The huge bouquet takes up almost the entire glass coffee table. The small white envelope catches my eye, but I return my gaze to the screen and open my schedule. Casper has synced all the details to my app so we proceed to organise a work schedule.

My first assignment for the day will be a flight over The Jenssen Corporation's new skyscraper. If it goes well, I can then move on to the Blackthorne Tower, and if the weather permits, I can squeeze in the new facility at S.M.G.

While I organise my planner, Casper brings me a cup of tea and a sandwich. Once I've eaten, I call John to tell him I'll be in the air all afternoon so I won't need his services, and then I rifle through my capsule closet, picking out an appropriate change of clothes. Tight fitting skirts and high heels make getting in and out of the helicopter hard work.

~

Being in the air above the hustle and bustle of the city below, I feel a sense of calm and freedom. All the pressures I had let build up inside me are still there, but because I have to concentrate on something else it affords me a little respite.

The afternoon races by in a blur of angles, shapes, and spires as we hover above and around some of the city's most inspiring architecture.

By the time I have completed all my assignments for the day, I feel fatigue settling in. I haven't allowed myself to think about Max all day, but I'm missing him desperately. I've checked my phone, but he hasn't made any further contact other than sending me the roses. As beautiful as they are, it annoys me that he thinks of them as a fix-all to everything.

I had removed the note from the bouquet in my office, but I left it unopened. I don't want to read anymore notes. I want him to tell me how he feels in person.

When I touch down on the roof of the Foxx-Tech building and get into the lift to make my way down to my office, it stops at the penthouse. The doors slide open and Cole is standing there looking tall and handsome in his bespoke suit. He looks surprised to see me as he rakes a hand through his hair. His chiselled features break into a mega-watt smile instantly cheering me up.

"You're not getting out?" he asks, pausing for a moment in the open doorway.

"No, I'm heading down to my office."

As he steps forward and enters the lift, he places his hand on my waist, leaning in to kiss me on the cheek. His scent is fresh and clean, the brush of his lips against my skin and the touch of his hand gently squeezing my waist feels intimate, nice, but it's the look in his eyes that holds my gaze.

"How was your mother today?"

His genuine concern feels comforting but I lower my eyes and stare down at my feet as my heart sinks. "I wouldn't know. She discharged herself, and when I called her she was already drunk."

He reaches up to tip my chin up with his finger until we're eye to eye. His soft, kind eyes search mine, then they follow the path of a lonely tear as it rolls down my face before he catches it with his thumb, brushing it away.

The ding of the lift arriving at the Foxx-Tech floor breaks us apart in a jolted movement. Cole walks out but then turns back, stretching his arms outward to hold the doors open. "Hey, are you busy tonight?"

Rolling my eyes, I huff out a sarcastic laugh. "My friends are on honeymoon, my mother's on a suicide mission, and my fiancé is ignoring me. I do have some ironing to do, but other than that, no. I'm not busy."

He laughs, releasing the doors. "Great. Be ready by seven, don't eat, and dress formal."

My mouth drops open as the doors glide shut and the lift begins its decent to my floor.

NEMESES

I place the two unopened notes from the bouquets on the dresser alongside the letter Max had written to me. I've been tempted to read the notes all day, but I've resisted the urge. Max hasn't responded to any of my texts and he still hasn't called, not even to tell me how his appointment with Doctor Fielding went.

I get that he's scared of hurting me, I get that he needs time to understand why he did what he did, but for chrissake, it shouldn't stop him from talking to me on the sodding phone.

Slipping my feet into my heels, I grab my clutch and a wrap for my bare shoulders, and when I check myself out in the long mirror, I'm hit with a pang of sadness. I'm wearing the dress I wore to Lucy and Dan's pre-wedding party. Memories of that wonderful evening come flooding back.

Max had stood behind me curling his arms around my waist and nipping at my earlobe. I was putty in his very skillful hands. He verbally seduced me with his sexy, raspy voice, taunting me with his lush lips as he kissed and nipped his way along the exposed flesh of my throat and shoulders.

He had a way of melting my bones with just a look, his hypnotic eyes speaking volumes, stirring my desire.

He's the sexiest man I've ever met, who can render me

wanton and needy in a heartbeat. His eyes caress my skin as easily as his fingers, stirring a passion so great, and a desire so deep, I can't breathe. I miss him. I miss him so much.

"Vivienne? Hey, babe, we gotta go."

Cole's voice outside the bedroom door pulls me out of my thoughts. My cheeks are flushed, just thinking about Max brings a warm feeling deep in my belly.

"Coming."

I take one final look, then head downstairs.

"Wow." Cole smiles, raking his eyes up and down me. "You look stunning."

I return the smile. I knew to expect he would look amazing. The Foxx men can wear anything and look effortlessly sexy, but in a Tux, they're in a class of their own.

Max in a Tux is one of my guilty pleasures. Stripping him out of it, is another. His urbane, predatory elegance is as much a part of him as the colour of his beautiful blue eyes. Masculine beauty has been bestowed on him without reserve. My friend Clive was right, Max and Cole really are two of the sexiest men on the planet.

"Where are we going?" I ask, as he takes my hand and walks us to the lift.

"It's a fund raising event for the Foxx-Glove Foundation. Max has dropped me in at the deep end. I've got to give a speech and I'm a little nervous."

His cheeky smile doesn't show a glimmer of nerves, and I get the feeling he's just using this opportunity as a distraction for me. He really is a kind and thoughtful man.

I freak out a little as we step out of the limo to the sound of a ton of photographers shouting out Max's name. It's a natural reaction, and it hadn't even occurred to me that they were expecting Max to be here tonight.

"Don't they know you're stepping in for Max tonight?"

"I guess not," Cole shrugs. "It doesn't matter."

Cole doesn't bat an eye, smiling at all the journalists as he leads me along the red carpet, stopping occasionally for a photograph before heading through to the privacy of the main hall of the Cardinal Ballroom.

"Being a twin has its benefits," he says, leading me toward the bar with his hand on the small of my back. His roguish grin makes me smile. "I can do whatever I like and blame it all on Max."

The room quickly fills with ball gowns and Tuxedos. The hum of chatter increasing as they mingle and greet each other. Cole hands me a glass of sparkling water, clinking our glasses together. "You look beautiful tonight."

"Thanks, you're not so bad yourself."

A familiar voice approaches from behind me, wiping the smirk right off my face, my eyes rolling in contempt.

"Cole. How lovely to see you again," Fiona gushes, swooping in and resting her hand on his shoulder, then she leans in to kiss him on both cheeks. "You're a naughty boy, you never called me back," she chides playfully.

Holding his gaze, she scoops her long blonde hair over one shoulder, smiling at him with her 'fuck-me' eyes.

Cole turns to me. "You remember Vivienne?" he says, resting his hand on the small of my back. Fiona's eyes swing down to me with a look of surprise.

"Oh! Vivienne. Yes, of course. I didn't realise you were Cole's plus one." She air kisses both my cheeks in a perfunctory way.

Excusing himself, Cole turns away from us to talk to a couple to his right, leaving Fiona and I to make small talk. Great!

"So, how are you, Vivienne?"

Why don't you just naff off! I can't be arsed to engage her in anything deep. "I'm good."

Her covetous eyes swing down to my heart-shaped locket then sweep back up to mine as a smug smile curls her lips. "Oh. While I remember it, Vivienne. Please tell Max that my uncle said his blueprints will be ready next week. He ordered them ages ago and I meant to tell him this morning, but it went right out of my mind."

A bolt of anger straightens my back, putting a frown on my

face. I know what I heard but my morbid sense of curiosity needs confirmation.

"This morning?" I ask, tilting my head and reaching up for my locket.

"Yes, I went to see him this morning but I left without telling him. Poor Max, he's been through the mill hasn't he? But at least he's still smiling."

Her smug smile lingers on me for a moment, then her focus returns to Cole. Judging by the look on her face, I can only assume that now she knows he's brought me and not some prospective girlfriend, she has a window of opportunity in which to nail him.

I couldn't care less, although, I think Cole could do better. What bothers me is the fact that Fiona has been to see Max, and he's let her in. Why her and not me? Anger simmers behind my fake smile, causing me to fidget. What I wouldn't do for a glass of wine right now.

As Fiona flirts and giggles in front of Cole, I pull away from him and make my way to the ladies' room. Once I'm locked inside one of the cubicles, I pull the lid down and take a seat, then I call Max. The call cuts me off as it always does, so I text him instead.

```
Fiona? Seriously!
Are you trying to piss me off?
Vivienne.
X:-(
The woman who loves you,
in case you've forgotten!
```

I sit there for a few minutes waiting for his reply. I feel sure he won't ignore me this time. But after ten minutes crawl by at a snail's pace, I realise he is. Anger and frustration begin to sizzle. Barging out of the cubicle, I lean on the edge of the hand basin staring at my scowling reflection. "Why her? Why not me?"

Two women enter the bathroom so I pretend to fix my makeup.

Wandering back to the bar, I bump into Grace and her husband Tom.. "Vivienne, how are you?"

I decide to go for the short answer, it'll save a lot of explaining. "I'm good, you?"

"We're fine. How's Max?"

"Oh, he's doing very well. I'm sure he'll be back at work in no time."

Her sympathetic smile is interrupted by her husband trying to introduce her to someone else, so I make my exit and continue toward the bar.

"Where have you been, are you okay?"

Cole's soft voice and the touch of his hand at the small of my back has me turning to face him. "Yes. I thought I'd give you and Fiona some space."

"Please don't," he smirks. "She's pretty and all, but I prefer the chase. There's nothing hotter than a woman playing hard to get. Fiona's a little too keen," he smirks, "she practically strips me naked with her eyes."

I laugh. "Well you do have an exceptionally sexy body under that suit."

His cheeky smile spreads across his face as his eyes narrow on me. "Miss Banks, you sound like you're talking from experience. What would people think?"

Heat rushes into my cheeks. "No! That's not… you and Max, you're the same… I didn't, oh shit."

Cole smirks, kissing me on the forehead. "Awesome! Come on, let's take our seats before you blush yourself into a coma."

~

Dinner was lovely and the conversation at the table flowed with jovial banter and raucous laughter. Fiona had somehow managed to seat herself next to Cole, so at every opportunity she would commandeer him.

I watched him as he engaged her in conversation, her girlie giggles and the way she constantly stroked his arm were a dead giveaway that she was trying to seduce him, but he would turn to me every so often with a curved eyebrow to convey how tiresome she was becoming.

It made me smile, but when he did it again and reached down to squeeze my thigh, it made me blush. No one but Max had ever done that.

When the meal is over, Cole leans into me placing his hand on my thigh again. It brings a heat to my cheeks when I look over and see Fiona has noticed him doing it. I say nothing, not wanting to draw attention to it, but I'm childishly pleased that it seems to have irked Fiona. Anything to piss her off.

"I'm up, wish me luck," Cole whispers, placing his napkin on the table.

I reach up to straighten his bow tie, more to irritate Fiona than to fix an already perfectly positioned tie. "Knock 'em dead."

Rising from his seat, he smooths his jacket and elegantly strides to the podium. Fiona's eyes are on him the whole time.

I turn to face him when he begins with a light-hearted joke, his deep commanding voice amplified by the hidden speakers around the room. The overhead spotlight dances like crystals in his blue eyes, and the smile on his devilishly handsome face warms the room a few degrees. He has everyone fully engaged, listening to his every word. He's just like Max. Powerful, charming, elegantly urbane.

He didn't need luck. He had lead me to believe public speaking wasn't his forte, but as I had guessed, he was a polished, sophisticated orator, commanding the room with ease.

Watching him, I begin to feel sad. I've been in this position before, looking at the doppelganger, wishing he was Max. It should have been Max standing up there tonight giving his speech, and although Cole is a dead ringer and a fine substitute for events like these, he'll never replace the man I love.

Absently fondling my locket, I begin to feel dangerously close to tears as my heart twists in my chest. I can't bear to think of a life without Max. I'll never love anyone the way I love him. But what if I never get him back? What if he can never overcome his demons? What if…?

The applause and whistles drag me out of my dismal thoughts as Cole wanders back to our table. His smiling eyes are on me, but as soon as he reaches our table, Fiona stands up and makes herself the focus of his attention.

"That was wonderful," she gushes, wrapping her arms around his neck, planting a kiss on his cheek. The band strikes up and Fiona drags him off to the dance floor, even though he tries to protest and when he looks to me for help, I just shrug and smirk.

I watch them for a minute, they make a very handsome couple. It's a shame I don't like Fiona, she would be a good distraction for Cole, someone he could have fun with.

I don't feel like dancing so I end up sitting on my own at the table. I don't mind, I like people watching so I'm quite happy.

I feel someone standing behind me so I turn around to face them.

"Vivienne, how nice to see you again."

The blood drains from my head when I see Greg Taylor smiling down at me. His focus moves to Cole, who's still dancing with Fiona.

"It's hard to tell those Foxx brothers apart isn't it?"

I'm lost for words, dying to get up and get away from him, he makes my skin crawl. His eyes swing down to mine, then he lays his big, rough hand on my bare shoulder. His touch makes me flinch and squirm, the fact that's he's touching me tightens every muscle in my body and rolls my stomach.

"I'm good with faces though," he smiles. "I don't always remember a name, but I always remember a face. And you remembered my face, didn't you!" His threatening eyes stare into mine with full recognition. "How's your mum? Still living in that grotty housing estate?"

Bile rises and burns in my throat. Lifting my chin, I grit my teeth. "You stay away from her." Giving him the death stare I push his hand off my shoulder. A shudder rattles up my spine as I touch his skin.

"Well that, my beauty, is up to you." His warning is crystal clear. He smiles like we are old friends, then he turns, his eyes sliding off mine at the last minute before he walks away looking very pleased with himself.

I'm breathless and panting for air. My head feels hot and fuzzy, my stomach is rolling, and a cold sweat chills every inch of my skin. Grabbing my clutch, I race to the exit. If ever I needed a drink it was now.

~

The penthouse feels empty and lonely as I stand in the hallway trying to see the screen of my phone through tear blurred eyes. Max still hasn't responded to my texts.

It hurts like a physical pain for him to cut me off like this. Whatever he's going through, he has to realise this crazy separation is killing me. It's ridiculous. What good are we to each other if we're apart?

Drying my eyes, I kick my shoes off, then wander into the kitchen to get a glass of the non-alcoholic wine Cole had brought in. It's no substitute for the real thing, but it'll do.

My phone rings:

"Vivienne! Where the hell are you?" Cole's worried voice barrels through the phone.

"I'm at home. I wasn't feeling well." It's not a lie. As soon as I saw Greg, I felt sick to my stomach.

"You should have told me. You can't just walk off on your own. I'm on my way."

"No! Please, Cole, I'm fine. I'm going to bed. You stay and have fun." I don't bother to wait for his response, I want to get a drink and head up to bed. I'm tired, fed up, and thoroughly pissed off.

P.O.A.

Something pulls me out of a deep sleep. Feeling the bed move, sets off all my alarm bells. I bat my eyes open and my heart stops when I realise someone is in my room. Scrambling back to the headboard in a panic, I pull the sheets up to my chin and throw the light switch.

"Jesus! What the hell are you doing?"

Cole is perched on the edge of my bed. He's fully dressed in his Tux, but his bow tie is undone, hanging loosely around the open neck of his dress shirt. His hair is all over the place, and he's completely shit-faced.

"I'm sorry," he slurs, spilling the contents of his short tumbler of Scotch as he waves his hand around. "Oh, sorry," he mumbles, apologising for the spillage.

I'm half asleep, my eyes stinging under the glare of the bedside light. It must be very late, or very early, the windows are dark and I feel like I've only just closed my eyes.

"What are you doing here?" I squint at the digital display on the clock. It's four twenty-five in the morning.

"I'm sorry."

"Yeah, you said that already. What do you want?"

"You... I'm in love with you Viniven."

My heart sinks, Charlie used to call me that. I feel sorry for

Cole, but I don't know how many times or how many ways I have to say it. A deep sigh hisses out of me. "Cole—"

"Look, I hear you. I do. I'm not deaf," he slurs, spilling his drink again. His focus is all over the place, how he made it up the stairs I'll never know. "I'm drunk. I'm not deaf. But you've got to admit it, Vivninen, Viniv, Vivin… You've got to admit it, babe, you feel something for me, I can see it in your eyes. You look at me like I'm something special."

My heart slumps and deep inside, I ache a little for him. He's right. I probably do look at him that way. In fact, I know I do. He's the closest thing I have to Max, and if truth be told, he's a very close substitute for the real thing. But he's not the man I love.

"Admit it," he says, taking a sip of his Scotch, then pointing his finger at me. "You ran away because I was with Finona… Fiona. You're jealous."

"Pff."

I suddenly realise I'd been sending out mixed signals all night. My obvious dislike for Fiona wasn't because she was all over Cole, but I could see why he would think that way. And I had selfishly used him to aggravate her tonight. And yes, I do find Cole attractive, why wouldn't I, he's the spitting image of Max.

"Cole, let's talk about this in the morning."

"Monica, please… I need to talk about it now. I love you." His heavy eyes try to focus on me, then he drops his glass to the floor and falls backward on the bed completely passed out.

"Cole?…Shit!"

He had called me Monica. I knew all along he was still in love with her, but knowing I was right doesn't make it any less tragic.

Scooting out of bed, I nip to the bathroom and grab my robe to cover myself up, then I head back to the bedroom to tackle Cole, who is spark out on the bed and snoring like a drain. I swing his legs up onto the bed and pivoting him length ways, then I roll him onto his side, propping him with the pillows. Once I know he can't roll off, I grab some towels and a bowl in case he throws up.

"Men! One I can't get close to, one I can't get rid of."

~

The annoying trill of my phone's alarm clock drills into my brain. Forcing my eyes open, I take a moment to figure out where the hell I am.

Last night slowly comes back to me in small chunks. I'd left Cole to sleep it off in my bed after he'd passed out, and I had come into one of the guest rooms.

I get up and wander across the hall to check on him, but the bed is empty and made. I head to the bathroom, but he's not there either, so I jump in the shower and get ready for work.

As I dress, I see the notes Max had sent me lying on the dresser. Anger prickles through me. I'm not ready to read his words if he can't be bothered to say them to my face. Picking up the notes, I pop them into my bag then head downstairs for breakfast.

"I know, I know," Cole says, pre-empting me. "I fucked up and I'm sorry. I don't know what happened last night but I'm sure I was a complete dick-head and totally out of order, and for that, I'm sorry."

Cole is slouched over the island wearing just his Calvin's with a steaming mug of coffee, and what can only be described as a raging hangover. If it hurts on the inside as bad as it looks on the outside he's in big trouble.

It's not fair. Even in his dishevelled state he's still ridiculously handsome.

I can't help the smirk as I wander over to the kettle to make some tea. "Apology accepted. How's the head?"

"Well, let me put it this way, even my headache has a headache, which I think also has a headache. And could you please lower your voice."

I chuckle as he rubs his temples, looking very fragile.

After I've made him a glass of Andrews Salts so he can replace his electrolytes after last night's drinking binge, I place the fizzing glass in front of him.

"Oh, my god, don't fizz," he groans, wincing at his headache. "Have you got something a little quieter?" he grumbles, pushing the glass away.

Pursing my lips to stifle a giggle, I pour myself a mug of tea and take a seat opposite him at the island. Something has been playing on my mind while I was in the shower. It's probably not the best time to bring it up, but I need to ask.

"Cole, did you know Fiona had gone to see Max yesterday?"

He slowly drags his unfocused gaze up to mine. "No." Straightening in his chair, he suddenly looks a little panicked. "Oh my god! Did I bring her home last night?" he asks in a whispered voice, looking very confused.

"No, I don't think so."

Relaxing a little, he exhales a long sigh. "Good… Um, here's a question. Why did I wake up in your bed this morning?"

I'm not sure whether he doesn't remember barging into my room last night, or if he's just trying to avoid the responsibility of his actions. But it's probably best that we both forget last night.

"You don't remember?" I ask, sipping my tea. He shrugs and shakes his head, but I'm not totally convinced. "You were a bit pickled last night and you passed out, so I left you where you fell."

"In your room?" he asks cagily.

"Well, at least it wasn't the bottom of the stairs this time."

He looks genuinely embarrassed then his brow creases with concern. "Did… Ah, did I do anything stupid last night?"

I smile, finishing my tea. "No. You were a perfect gentleman."

Relief washes over his face.

I stand and place my cup in the dishwasher.

"You look nice, are you going to work?" he asks, watching me slip into my coat.

"Nope! I'm going to see Max. I'm going to find out why Fiona gets to see him and I don't. Your brother has some explaining to do."

~

John drives me to Sylvie's house. I could tell by his face that he thought it was a bad idea, but he didn't voice his thoughts and he delivers me to the front door.

"I'll be right here, Ma'am," he says, holding my door open.

I look up to the windows on the upper floor then stride up to the front door and leave my thumb on the doorbell. After a short wait, Jimmy answers the door with a sheepish look on his face. "I'm sorry, Miss Banks, but I can't let you in. I've had—"

"Yes, I know," I interrupt sharply, refusing to be deterred. "You've had your orders. But I'm not leaving until I see him." With both hands lodged firmly on my hips, I stare at him brimming with bravado while Jimmy and I have a staring contest. But when I realise he's not going to back down and let me in, I'm actually quite shocked.

"Jimmy please. Just let me in. Five minutes, I promise."

He shakes his head then begins to close the door looking down at his shoes. Like a slap in the face, the door closes and I'm left standing there, staring at it.

"What the…?"

I reach up to the doorbell again, my finger hovering over it, but I don't press it. What's the point? Max has clearly made his mind up.

Tears pool in my eyes and bunch against my lashes and a heavy hurt sits like a rock in my chest. I slowly turn and walk down the stone steps dialling Max's phone. As expected, it cuts me off without letting me leave a message.

"Why are you doing this?"

"Psst… Hey!… Vivienne!"

I spin around looking for the whispering voice.

"Psst… No! Over here, Sherlock!"

I spin around again, I can't see anyone, but the voice is coming from the bushes at the edge of the gardens. I look over to John who nods toward the bushes then smiles and returns to reading his paper.

"Quickly! Through here! Come on, and put some stank on it, I haven't got all day."

I see Sheila beckoning me toward an arched gap in the bushes. When I reach her, she starts walking. For a big woman, she's remarkably agile and I struggle to keep up with her in my heels.

"Where are we going?"

"You want to see Pretty-boy, don't you?"

"Yes! Oh, yes, please." Butterflies swirl around in my belly at the prospect of finally seeing him. I can't wait.

"I've just walked him down to the lake. He spends a lot of time down there, thinking I guess, but who would know what goes on in that thick skull of his." She shakes her head, arching a heavily pencilled brow.

"How is he?"

"Physically, he's a lot better, getting stronger every day, but man, what a grouch. He's been a moody son-of-a-gun since he left the hospital, and if you ask me? Which I know you ain't but I'm gonna tell y'all anyway, it's all because he misses you."

I stumble to a halt beside her when she stops to look at me square in the eyes.

"I'm not privy to all the ins and outs of what went on, but I can see a mile off that this dumb-ass'd separation is hurting you both."

She starts walking again.

"It is, and I don't understand why he won't see me and yet he met with Fiona yesterday." The simmering anger Fiona inspires, bubbles beneath the surface.

"Who?... Oh, the skinny blonde with legs up to here and a stick up her ass?" she says, rolling her eyes. "He wouldn't see her either. The only people Pretty-boy has allowed in, is Doctor Fielding and the old guy Miss Fancy-Pants brought along yesterday."

I realise Fiona must have brought her father to see Max yesterday. I'm relieved she hadn't been allowed in herself, and it takes some of the hurt away knowing Fiona hadn't out ranked me. But why did she lie about it?

"What did Doctor Fielding say?" I ask, skipping along to keep up. My heels are hard work in the grass.

"I don't know, that's private. I'm just here for the medical stuff."

We arrive at the paving stone pathway that leads down to the lake.

"I'll leave y'all to it," Sheila says, patting my arm. "If he asks, you snuck in all by your lonesome, y'hear?"

I smile and squeeze her hand. "Thanks, Sheila. I owe you one."

"Hell no. Just put a smile on Pretty-boy's face. I'm gettin' tired of that old sour puss. God knows he should lighten up a smidge. He's got great teeth, he should show 'em off every once in a while."

I watch Sheila muttering her way back up the path toward the house, then I take a deep breath and continue down to the lake.

When the path ends and becomes grass, I stop in my tracks when I see him up ahead. He's sitting on a fallen tree staring out at the lake. A pang of sadness hits me, he looks so lost and alone. Adrift in his thoughts, his chest rises and falls on a deep sigh.

The sight of him makes my heart ache, filling my belly with butterflies. His powerful thighs are spread, with his elbows resting on his knees. The cast on his left arm is no longer there, now replaced with a thick blue wrap. He's dressed casually in jeans, and a t-shirt, showing off his incredible biceps and broad shoulders, and his wavy black hair, caught by the light breeze, dances around his handsome face.

The hard edges of his chiselled jaw, blade straight nose, and a heavy brow create the strong masculine profile of a wickedly handsome man. I pause for a moment to drink him in. I've missed him so much, but now he's right here in front of me, I realise how much I needed to see him again. As I stand here gazing at the love of my life, tears pool in my eyes, my hands begin to tremble, and my heart aches with longing.

As if he senses my presence, he sits up, turning to face me.

His sudden movement and the surprise on his face, makes me gasp. His eyes are glistening with tears as they stare into mine, and I'm already moving toward him when he quickly rises to his feet and turns his back to me.

I stumble to a halt and watch him walk away, toward the water's edge. "N, no!" My emotions are in disarray. This wasn't what I expected. He was supposed to open his arms so I could run into them and smother him with kisses. We've been apart for too long. His first reaction should have been relief, joy, anything but this. I thought he'd be happy to see me. Desperate to hold me. Wanting to run his hands all over me because he needed the feel of my skin, and the softness of my lips against his.

His rejection is all wrong, hurting like nothing else could.

"Why are you here? You shouldn't be here." His harsh voice is low, and although I can't see his face, I hear the emotion he's trying to hide.

I take a tentative step toward him but stop when I see his body turning rigid and his right hand balling into a fist at his side before he shoves it into his pocket.

"Max…" My throat closes, choking my voice, I feel short of breath. I can't bear him rejecting me like this.

"Go home."

Those two little words destroy me.

"Why won't you look at me?" The tears roll down my face, and when he doesn't turn to face me, I begin to sob uncontrollably. "Max, please! Why can't you see how much this hurts?"

His head bows and his shoulders soften, but he doesn't turn around.

"Max, please. Don't make me live without you… I can't… I need you. I love you." I take another step toward him but stop abruptly when he spins around hitting me with the saddest eyes. The sadness is quickly replaced with anger as he drags a hand through his hair. His jaw clenching in frustration before he loses control, yelling at me.

"Do you think I don't know that? Do you think I don't feel

the same? Jesus!"

I'm desperate to run to him but the look in his eyes holds me off. "Then why are you doing this?"

His clenching jaw is at breaking point, and he turns away again planting his feet and stiffening his back. "I don't want you here, Vivienne. Go!"

The finality in his words and the way he delivered them was like a blade to my heart, twisting and shredding.

"No, Max… Please don't do this."

As he continues to shut me out, a whimper sobs out of my chest, tears choking me until a white-hot anger surges through my blood. Opening my bag, I pull out the letter he wrote to me at the hospital, and the notes from the flowers, then I screw them up in my hands and throw them at his back.

"Here! You can keep your fucking words! They're just empty, meaningless promises. You promised me forever, Max. You lied! You fucking lied!"

Turning on my heel in a blur of tears, I stumble toward the path feeling utterly destroyed.

"Vivienne!" His strong arms circle my shoulders bringing me to an abrupt halt. Letting out a groan of pain as his ribs protest to the pressure, he pulls my back firmly into his chest. The scent of him weakens my knees. His hot breath gusts across my cheek as his lips frantically kiss my temple, cheek and neck. Nuzzling my hair, he tightens his hold around me. "I've never lied to you, Vivienne. For God's sake woman, I love you! Don't you know that?"

I can't move, his arms are too tightly banded around me, his forceful, possessive grip full of need.

"I love you too. So much." Tilting my head up, I offer my lips. He takes them, devouring me with a deep, hard kiss, his passion raging in every stroke of his tongue. Tears moisten his cheek and mingle with my own as a soft moan escapes him. My heart is beating out of my chest, my whole body humming and tingling as his love consumes every atom of my being.

Finally releasing me from his arms, I turn to face him. "Oh, Max, I've missed you." My arms fly up and circle his neck, pulling him closer, deeper, and as our mouths smash together, every nuance of our love is brought to the fore in the kiss neither of us wants to end.

Our hands move quickly, eagerly seeking out each other's bare flesh. Our tongues and lips a frenetic coupling, hot and deep with desire, need, and passion. The pain of our separation conveyed without words in the depth of our passionate kiss.

I reach down to pull his t-shirt from his jeans, eagerly searching out the heat of his body. The hard slabs of muscle intricately woven across his stomach and shielded by his soft golden skin, are smooth against my palm. Wrapping my other hand around the nape of his neck, I weave my fingers through his silky hair, pulling him closer. *Mine.* All my senses are alive and the thud of arousal pounds between my thighs. Pushing my hips forward, I feel the hardness of his erection between us.

Max breaks the kiss, his breath ragged and fast as he searches my eyes with longing and regret. "Baby, I'm so sorry." Then he closes his eyes, leaning his forehead against mine. His hot breath wafts over my parted lips. His scent invading my nostrils, calming me, soothing me. This is what I needed. To have him in my arms, to feel his heartbeat and hear his voice. This is what we both needed.

"Max, don't make me live without you. Please come home."

"…No."

That one word destroys me.

"Max, please. I need you. Please! Please come home."

"Baby, I can't. It's too dangerous."

I stare up at him, searching his eyes. The conflict raging within them scares me. Lowering his gaze, he pulls me back into his chest, wrapping me in a tight, desperate hug, his hands gliding up and down my back. One hand settles under my hair at my nape, the connection of skin on skin a necessary element for both of us.

"You have to talk to me, Max. You can't keep shutting me out, I can't bear it. Give me one good reason why this crazy distance will ever be any good for us?"

He kisses the top of my head. "Vivienne… I hurt you…"

His body radiates tension and fear, the quiver in his voice conveying the anguish which still haunts him. I knew he'd struggle to reconcile his actions, but he needs to conquer this for both our sakes.

I pull back, remove my hand from underneath his shirt, then I reach up to cup his face, smoothing away a solitary tear trickling down his cheek. "I know you, Max. You would never hurt me intentionally. It wasn't your fault."

Without warning he pulls away from me, leaving me bereft. I sway on my feet at the sudden loss of his support.

"I'm fucked up, Vivienne. The sleepwalking. The rage. Jesus! I could have fucking killed you!"

He walks down to the water's edge dragging his hand through his hair on a frustrated sigh. I can feel him shutting down. Closing himself off.

Dread sits in my chest like a lead weight. I feel like he's going to let this thing tear us apart, but I can't let him do that. I'm going to fight for us, even if he won't.

"Max I—"

Spinning around he hits me with hard, determined eyes, fiercely clenching his jaw. "It fucking kills me, Vivienne! It fucking tears me apart knowing I've already hurt you twice! Goddammit, I nearly killed you! I can't trust myself. It could happen again!" His flinty glare gradually softens as his steely resolve desserts him. "…What else can I do?"

The pleading in his eyes, and the resignation in his voice, breaks me apart. He's letting this rule him. He's letting this dictate our future.

Slowly walking over to the log, he sits, wincing at the pain in his ribs. Hesitantly, I walk over and sit next to him, taking his hand in mine. I need to hold on to him, I'm so frightened that if I let go, I'll lose him forever.

Swallowing the lump in my throat, I try to settle my breathing before I speak. "What did Doctor Fielding say?"

He stares down at our hands as I lace our fingers together,

then he lets out a frustrated sigh. "He said I have a form of Parasomnia, with somnambulism thrown in for good measure." The sarcasm in his voice is a classic sign of defeat. His strength is being tested and so far, he's losing the fight.

I frown, tilting my head in question. "Som…?"

"Sleep walking," he qualifies. "Apparently, the sleep walking is harmless enough, as long as I'm not near an open window. But the other stuff is…" He pauses, shaking his head. "He's going to prescribe me something to help, but he's not sure if it'll work. He wants me to have regular sessions with him to try and figure out what triggers it."

I wait for his sad eyes to find mine. "Max, you know what triggers it. It's Monica. Whatever she did to you, whatever you're not telling me, we can get through this. Together."

I can tell by the look on his face that I'm right. Monica has been the catalyst for every terrible thing that's ever happened in our relationship.

I rest my hand on his thigh. "Max, why won't you talk to me about this?"

His face hardens and his eyes flare. "I'll never put those thoughts in your head. Never!"

A flash of anger heats my skin. I understand his reticence, but it angers me that even after her death, Monica's still interfering in our relationship. Still controlling him.

I pause to take a calming breath. "You need to talk about what she did to you. I want you to talk about it with me, but if you can't, if you won't, then please tell Doctor Fielding. The sooner you come to terms with this, the sooner we can get back to a normal, happy life."

His eyes search mine, then lower to our hands. His gentle squeeze reassuring me that he'll at least try. "I need time, baby," he says, his voice soft and croaky.

"And I need you, Max. In all your forms." I lift his hand, resting it on my belly. "We need you. Please come home."

His sad eyes search mine and I know the struggle he's going through. "But that's just it, Vivienne. It's bad enough that I've already hurt you. What if I hurt the babies?"

I can feel the resistance in him, which breaks my heart. I don't want us to live apart. After everything we've been through, we need each other now more than ever.

His eyes glisten with tears and his sad expression kills me as he runs his hand over my belly. "I've missed you, baby. So much."

"I've missed you more," I whisper, leaning my head against his shoulder.

We sit in silence for a few moments staring out at the lake. The peaceful tranquillity of our surroundings doesn't dampen the internal battle going on inside my head. I want Max home more than anything, but I'm also afraid. I would never admit it to him, but deep down I'm scared that if I force his hand and he's not ready, the same thing could happen again. I don't think either of us could survive that. A shudder runs through me as I contemplate the risks.

"Are you cold?" he asks, rubbing his hand up and down my arm.

"I'm okay." I don't dare look at him, he reads me too well. "What happened to your cast?" I ask, trying to change the subject.

He pulls back with a wry smirk tipping up the corners of his mouth. "I trashed it during one of my nocturnal walk-abouts."

"Does it hurt?"

"It did when I woke up and the cast was hanging off, but it's okay now. They gave me this new flexi-cast."

I cringe, feeling queasy at the thought of it, realising that he had once again resorted to violence during his sleep. As I try to ignore the worry building inside me, I rest my head back down to his shoulder. "Max?"

He tightens his uninjured arm around me, kissing the top of my head. "Yes, baby?"

"I have a plan, and it's not up for negotiation." I feel him tense slightly. "I'm going to give you one week to try the new medication and to get it all out with Doctor Fielding. After that, if you don't come home, I'm going to move in here. And if you don't let me in, I'm going to camp out on your front lawn."

A soft chuckle escapes him. "Okay."

I lean back to look him in the eyes. "I'm serious, Max. And don't even think about barring my calls. If you don't pick up, I'll come over and get John to beat the door down. Got it?"

His eyes sparkle and a glorious smile spreads over his face. I'm relieved to see it.

"Yes, Ma'am. Got it. Loud and clear."

He pulls me into his lap, groaning as his painful ribs give him a reminder, and then he kisses me softly, tenderly, like we're a pair of lovers without a care in the world.

ONE MORE NIGHT

Ed links arms with me as we hit the lights and leave the office. It's been a long, tiring week, we've both been working our arses off trying to catch up with the backlog from all the time I'd had off, and the demand from the new clients Ed had pulled in while I was away.

"So, are you seeing your Russian Minx this weekend?" I ask, grinning up at him. Ever since my shoot at her fetish club, Ed and Nova, an unlikely pairing, have been inseparable. Ed has always been a love 'em and leave 'em kind of guy, never short of admiration from the ladies, and never seen with the same woman twice, but Nova seems to have tamed him. I've always been too scared to ask how, but he's been a faithful little puppy ever since.

"Yeah," he smiles, cheekily. "And don't give me that look, Viv, it's not like we're getting married. She's just… very…"

"What?… Kinky? Sexy? Good in bed?"

"Yeah," he smirks. "All of the above."

I roll my eyes and nudge his shoulder. "Oh, that reminds me, I need to speak to her."

"What about?"

"Oh, just girl stuff." Ed eyes me suspiciously. "Don't worry, I won't tell her any of your secrets."

"I haven't got any."

"Pff!"

As we round the corner, I stop at the reception desk. "I'm off now, Casper. Have a good weekend."

"You too. And say hi to Mr. Foxx for me."

"I will."

A beaming smile camps out on my face. Max is coming home tomorrow and I can't wait. For the last week, Max and I have been speaking regularly on the phone, and I've visited him every evening after work. I had to push Max to agree to my visits, but he finally realised how important it was for both of us to keep our connection. He refused to let me stay overnight, so I visit him for a couple of hours every evening where we enjoy a meal together and catch up on each other's news.

He's looked better every day, even Sheila has noticed a difference in him.

His sessions with Doctor Fielding seem to have been positive too. I asked if I could sit in on some of them but Max refused and Doctor Fielding couldn't be swayed.

Tonight however, Doctor Fielding has encouraged Max to allow me to join in. Knowing he's coming home tomorrow, he felt it would be wise for us to discuss any concerns we may have about that.

I am concerned, and although he tries to hide it, I know Max is worried too. He's still suffering from his traumatic nightmares, and if he lashes out again, he'd never forgive himself. I dread to think what measures he would take to reconcile that.

After leaving the office I head up to the penthouse to change for our session with Doctor Fielding. The penthouse is empty when I get home, as it has been every evening this week.

Cole knew I had been to see Max last week, and that we'd had a heart to heart. When he asked me how it went, the conversation started out fine, but when I confirmed that Max was coming home soon, he flared up and questioned my judgement. He couldn't understand why I would take the risk of Max harming me again.

Eventually, Cole and I ended up having a heart to heart about his feelings for me, and the feelings he's convinced I have for him. It evolved into a heated discussion lasting two hours, both of us yelling and crying, and him still stubbornly convinced that I was in denial about my feelings for him.

I still believe Cole's feelings were aimed at me because, despite what he had said, he was still in love with Monica and her death had left him bereft.

He denied it of course, but she was Cole's first love. He had loved her for many years, in spite of the way she had treated him. And because I was fragile and needy when he came to my rescue, I was an easy target for his unrequited love.

Looking back, I had even encouraged him. I wasn't proud of the way I used him to pacify my own heart, and I do love Cole, but not in the way he needs.

We bickered and fought until we'd exhausted the topic, neither of us giving an inch, and then he hit me with a string of reasons why I should choose him over his brother. All of them were valid, but none of them would stop me from loving Max.

When I realised we were going round in ever decreasing circles, and as much as I hated the hurt I was causing in his eyes, I turned my back on him and walked upstairs to bed. I couldn't bear to keep arguing with him. We were never going to agree.

That was the last time I've seen him. He still lives here, but he's going out of his way to avoid me which hurts even more.

~

John delivers me to Max just in time for our session with Doctor Fielding. Jimmy greets me at the door, takes my coat, then ushers me through to the living room.

Max rises quickly from his seat and strides toward me. He looks edgy and nervous. Folding me in his arms, he pulls me close, planting a hot kiss against my lips leaving me breathless. I can feel the tension flowing through him and his expression tells me he's very anxious about tonight.

I gently run my fingers down his cheek, then across his lips to remove my lip gloss. "Nice to see you, too."

I feel him relax a little but not completely.

"Ah, Vivienne. I'm so glad you could make it." I glance over to my right and see Doctor Fielding sitting in the leather wingback chair. "Please, take a seat."

Max takes my hand and leads us to the couch. I go to sit at the other end but he pulls me back so I'm sitting right next to him. His hand grasps mine, lacing our fingers together, then he lays our interlocked hands on his thigh, staring down at them with a worry furrow in his brow. Heat radiates through his shirt and jeans, it's like sitting next to a furnace.

As Doctor Fielding regards the notes on his tablet, I look up and give Max a reassuring smile when his eyes flick over to mine. His jaw continues to clench repeatedly.

I feel Doctor Fielding's eyes on me, so I turn to face him. His kind eyes crinkle with a smile as he crosses his legs, laying his tablet on the arm of the chair. Steepling his fingers, he takes a moment, quietly studying our body language, then his assessing eyes stay on mine.

"Just to catch you up to speed, Vivienne, our sessions this week have given me a clear insight into the root cause of Max's sleepwalking and the violence he recently displayed when he attacked you in his sleep. Unfortunately, the aggression he presented when he was awake is a little harder to quantify, but all these manifestations are clearly linked to the traumatic nature of his captivity."

His eyes soften with a kind smile. "Are you alright to proceed, Vivienne?"

Realising I had tensed up, I release the breath I was holding and relax my shoulders. "Um, yes. I'm fine."

"I wanted you to be here tonight, because I think it's very important for Max's progress that he understands how you feel."

I swallow as an anxious knot builds in my chest. "Oh, well, I know Max would never hurt me on purpose."

Max squeezes my hand a little tighter, painfully so.

"Okay, but how did it make you feel when you woke up and found him pinning you to the mattress, choking you, and—"

"I was terrified!" It blurts out of me. I just wanted to stop him from saying any more as the memories of that moment fly through my brain. My cheeks are burning, I feel hot, sick, and shaky, and my skin mists with perspiration.

Hesitantly, I glance up at Max, his eyes are screwed shut under a deep frown, and his jaw ticks with a repetitive clench. I wish I could take it back. I shouldn't have blurted it out like that. It wasn't his fault.

"Yes," Doctor Fielding says, in a soft tone, "it must have been very frightening to see the man you love acting so aggressively toward you. Have you told Max how it made you feel?"

I wince, shaking my head and looking down at my shoes. I wouldn't want him to know how badly his aggression had affected me. He's consumed with guilt as it is, he'll only withdraw from me even more.

Doctor Fielding uncrosses his legs and sits forward, resting his elbows on the arms of the chair. "I've had many cases like this. It's human nature to protect the ones we love, but as evolved as we are as a species, we still find it difficult to talk to each other, to express our fears and emotions. We bottle them up, keeping them hidden away. But to hide them serves no purpose, eventually the ones we try to protect, become the ones we hurt the most."

Max breathes in deeply then exhales a frustrated sigh. Doctor Fielding's right, but I know Max doesn't want to share his fears with me.

"You need to talk to each other about your feelings." The doctor settles back in his chair, studying our reactions. His eyes level on mine. "Max isn't a violent man, Vivienne, but he has expressed violence toward you, and you both need to address that openly if you're to move on from this."

"I… Yes. I need that." My voice is small and shaky. I look up at Max and tug on his hand to try and get him to look at me, to relax, but he's resisting, tensing up beside me. "I want you to talk to me, but you always shut me out."

"Max?" Doctor Fielding's voice gently encourages him to engage, but I can feel him resisting, withdrawing.

Suddenly, he drops my hand. In a swift movement he stands up and strides over to the fireplace, resting both hands on the stone mantelpiece above the unlit fire.

My eyes fill with tears as his head bows down between his shoulders in a gesture of defeat. Watching him struggling with his inner demons, my heart sinks.

The doctor carefully studies him as the room falls silent.

Without thinking, I rise to my feet and walk over to him. After a moment's hesitation, I lift my hand to place it softly on his shoulder.

In a rapid movement that almost knocks me off my feet, he turns, taking me in his arms. Tugging me into his chest, burying his face in my neck, he sobs, his silent tears soaking into my skin. "Baby, I'm so sorry." The pain in his voice chokes me up.

"What are you sorry for?" Doctor Fielding asks, in a quiet, calm voice.

Max lifts his head to glare at him incredulously. "I'm sorry for hurting her."

"And what else?"

He pulls back still holding on to me, but standing up straight, almost defiantly, clenching his jaw. "There is no what else! I hurt her. I could have killed her!"

"And what about your guilt, Max?"

"What do you mean? Of course I feel guilty. I love her."

"And what about the guilt you feel about having sex with Monica."

The whole room begins to spin as the blood drains from my head and I can't seem to catch my breath. Although I can see Max's mouth moving, I can't hear a thing except the loud whooshing noise as my pulse rushes past my ears.

Max releases me and steps back, lowering his eyes to the floor. My confused gaze travels to Doctor Fielding who stands and walks toward us. It felt like an eternity had passed while my world remained on mute. Everything moving in slow motion.

"Here. Come and take a seat, Vivienne."

I stare up at Doctor Fielding in a daze. He takes my arm and walks me back to the couch. My knees buckle and I collapse into the soft cushions.

Dazed and confused I look up at Max with a million questions firing in my brain. His wide, tearful eyes stare at me, the anguish on his face turning to fury, his uninjured hand balling into a tight, white knuckled fist.

Turning his back to us both, he slams his fist down on the stone mantelpiece making the small ornaments and framed photographs jump.

"How do you feel, Max?" Doctor Fielding asks, in a soft, calm, professional voice.

He immediately spins around glaring at him, gritting his teeth, like he wants to rip his head off. "How the fuck do you think I feel?" His angry eyes flick over to mine, then slide away with shame darkening his features.

I'm so confused, and I still can't catch my breath.

The doctor studies Max for a moment, then calmly makes his way back to his chair. His shrewd eyes flick over to mine briefly, then back to Max. "You're angry," he says, with an almost smug tone to his voice.

Max doesn't answer but his rage is pulsing through every muscle and vein. His body solid with tension like a tightly wound spring ready to unleash its force.

"You're angry." Doctor Fielding repeats, almost goading him. "Talk to me. Tell me how you feel."

Max turns to face him with fire burning in his eyes. "Yes! Okay? Yes! I'm *fucking* angry!"

Doctor Fielding doesn't flinch. "Why are you angry?" The calmness of his voice is a total contrast to the torrent of emotions coursing through Max.

He remains silent, his body still wound tight with anger, his hard face glaring at the doctor.

"Answer the question, Max… Why are you angry?"

A kaleidoscope of emotions pass through his eyes until finally, Max's muscles relax and the tension begins to dissipate. "Because…" His sad, apologetic eyes find mine then slide away. "Because she made me come."

My heart lodges in my throat as my mind filters his words. Closing his eyes, he sinks to his knees with his head in his hands, like a man beaten into submission by the force of his own guilt.

The doctor checks my reaction before pushing him further. I'm stunned and speechless, watching Max dissolve into tears right in front of me.

In a soft, calm, professional voice, Doctor Fielding pushes Max for an answer. "Who did, Max? Who made you come?"

He doesn't answer, his face still buried in his hands.

"Answer me, Max…Who made you come?"

Stiffening with fury, every muscle hardens in his body as he bites out his response. "Monica! That fucking bitch! She made me come!" Lifting his head, his tortured face glares angrily at the doctor, resenting him for pushing him this far.

I knew she'd done something terrible to him, and now it all seems so obvious. I feel sick at the thought of her laying her hands on him, but I won't let her tear us apart. Not again.

Like a broken man, he's on his knees, his body curled over in defeat. With his head in his hands, he cries his heart out repeating the words, 'I'm so sorry,' over and over again.

A deep compulsion has me rising to my feet.

"Wait!" The doctor says, eyeing me with concern.

But I can't wait. Ignoring the doctor's warning, and the shakiness in my legs, I walk over to Max and kneel down in front of him, like I did that first time in his room of guilt. I pull at his hands desperate to see his face, but he resists. "Max, please. Don't shut me out. She's gone. She can never hurt us again unless you let her. I'm here, Max. I love you. I need you. Please don't shut me out."

I pull on his hands again and this time he slowly lets me drag them away from his face.

"I'm so sorry." The pain in his voice and the shame in his eyes crushes me.

"No, Max. No more apologies. You have nothing to apologise for. Just talk to me, don't shut me out. We can get through this together."

In a swift movement, he pulls me into his chest, burying his face in my hair. The weight of his love all around me as he holds me close, crushing me to him.

The sound of Doctor Fielding's voice breaks us apart. "Finally!" he smiles. "I've been waiting for this breakthrough all week."

Max's nervous eyes slip away from mine. Kissing me on the forehead he helps me to my feet, then we take our seats.

He rests his hands on his thighs, rubbing the sweat from his palms. I reach across and take his hand in mine, still feeling the reluctance in him. We have so much to talk about and I know that frightens him. He doesn't want me to know all the things that haunt him, but unless we get it all out in the open it will only fester inside putting us back to square one.

"Vivienne, how do you feel hearing the news that Max had sex with Monica?"

"No! It wasn't like that!" Max blurts, angrily. His hand crushes my knuckles until he realises he's doing it and then he releases the pressure.

Doctor Fielding carefully studies him for a moment. "Then what was it like. What did she do to you?"

I stare up at him wide-eyed waiting for his response. Max huffs out a heavy sigh. His tension is building again, so I offer him a reassuring smile and bring his hand across to rest on my thigh. I'm shaking and anxious, but I need him to tell me everything. "Please, Max. It's okay."

His worried eyes search mine, then slide down to the locket I'm nervously toying with. "She… Oh, god…"

I squeeze his hand a little tighter. "It's okay. You need to talk about this. It'll be okay, I promise. Just take your time."

His jaw clenches and his eyes close as the pain of his dark memories crawl across his face. When his eyes open again they're hard like stone, focused only on Doctor Fielding. His nostrils flare as his lips twitch into a hard line. Pulling his hand out of mine, rubbing the sweat against his jeans, he balls it into a fist.

"The waiter followed me down to the cabin. Monica was sitting on our bed, I was so shocked to see her there… I don't know what happened after that, someone knocked me out, but I remember being on a small boat for a while, I don't know, it's all a little hazy."

The doctor writes some notes, nodding at Max to continue.

"When I woke up again, I was in a warehouse. Those bastards beat the shit out of me… It was brutal… I couldn't move, the pain was unbearable."

He swallows, pausing for a moment to compose himself. I can hear how painful this is by the tone of his voice.

"I don't know how long I was there, I kept passing out. And when I woke up again, I was somewhere else. I didn't know where the hell I was, it was so dark, it felt like a tomb."

His eyes, now lowered, occasionally flick up to the doctor but he hasn't once looked at me.

Doctor Fielding watches him closely but doesn't speak, waiting patiently for Max to continue.

"The pain kept making me pass out, and Monica kept giving me this vile liquid which made me sleep. I don't know how long I was there, hours, days, weeks? … She kept disappearing. I don't know how, I couldn't see any doors or windows."

Swallowing several times, his body stiffens, his fist tightening against his thigh.

"I felt someone slapping my face. When I woke up, she was naked sitting on top of me, …touching me, trying to get me hard."

He pauses to swallow again as sweat begins to bead on his forehead.

"I had no strength to push her away. I didn't want her touching me. I couldn't stand it, but I couldn't stop her."

The faraway look in his eyes and the emotion in his voice,

tells me how hard this is for him to relive. My heart clenches, but I resist the urge to reach for his hand. I'm frightened he'll clam up and shut down.

"Did you become hard for her?" Doctor Fielding asks.

Max flinches and my eyes close at his question.

"...Yes."

"Did you penetrate her?"

"Stop!" His body tenses up immediately, every muscle flexing and hardening under his skin. "I didn't want her! I didn't want—"

"Did you ejaculate?"

"...Yes." His answer is barely a whisper. The shame in his voice and the guilt in his face, brings tears to my eyes and a rock to my throat.

"And what happened when you ejaculated?"

The hard lines return to his jaw, his eyes darkening, flaring with anger as he grits his teeth. "I hit her! I swung my arm around and I hit the fucking bitch on the side of the head. She fell on the floor, crying and screaming. But she kept coming back for more." Screwing his eyes shut, forces a tear down his cheek. He can barely cope with this.

I knew she had done something terrible to him. I knew deep inside she was the cause of his behaviour. It hurt me to know he was still carrying this guilt around with him, perpetuating her hold over us.

I look to Doctor Fielding for approval. He offers me a small reassuring nod and then I reach across and take Max's hand again. He resists, but I persist until he finally relaxes enough to let me hold it in both of mine.

"Max... It's okay. Everything's—"

Suddenly wrenching his hand out of mine, he rises and without a word, he marches out of the room.

Watching him leave, I have a strange feeling I'll never see him again.

I stand up to follow him, but Doctor Fielding asks me to sit down and give Max some space. Reluctantly, I take my seat, wiping the tears from my cheeks, keeping one eye on the door.

"Are you okay, Vivienne?"

I nod. My throat is too tight to speak.

"I know you probably don't appreciate it right now, but that was a breakthrough for Max. I've been trying to get him to confront this issue all week and he's finally talking. I've read his file. His guilt issues go way back to his childhood."

I nod again. "Yes, I know."

The doctor leans forward in his seat, waiting for me to engage him fully.

"Don't worry, Vivienne. He just needs a little time," he says, softly. "His recent behaviour is primarily driven by the events of his capture. Monica, and those men, had made him feel powerless, unable to control the situation. For Max, control is very important, it's essential. Has he spoken to you about the death of his parents?"

"Yes. He told me what happened."

"Good. We've had many discussions about his parents' death, how he felt completely powerless to save his mother, it must have been very frustrating for him. Equally frustrating when Monica abducted him. Monica was effectively controlling him and he couldn't do anything about it."

He pours a glass of water from the crystal jug on the table, then hands it to me. I take it willingly, my mouth is so dry.

"We've spoken at great length, but today is the first time he's spoken about the things she did to him physically. I've never met Monica, but Max gave me a brief outline of her history, and from what I know of her recent actions, I'd say she suffered from a personality disorder, maybe some form of schizophrenia."

I nod, then flick my eyes to the door. Where is he?

"I think Max's sleepwalking is triggered by his many failed attempts to escape from that room in the chateau. Not being able to find the door that he knew was there, would have deeply upset the balance of rational thought. And while he's asleep, he feels no pain."

I nod again. That's exactly what I had thought. The doctor takes a moment to gauge my reaction. Everything he's saying makes sense.

"The aggression he expressed toward you, Vivienne, is a bit more complex. It's not you he wants to hurt. But sadly, Monica's attempts to have sex with him have unfortunately blurred the lines somewhat."

I wince, I hate the thought of Monica putting her hands on him.

"When he becomes sexually aroused it triggers the memories of Monica forcing him to ejaculate. Rape and sexual assault are heinous acts, the psychological effects are no less for men than they are for women."

An involuntary shudder snakes up my spine. I know how it feels to be violated.

"All that is bad enough, but he also feels an overpowering sense of guilt, Vivienne. He thinks he's betrayed you, and *that* is what lies at the core. But," he smiles, warmly, "he's not a hopeless case, he just needs—"

I stand quickly when I sense Max standing at the door. I can't read him, his eyes are lowered to the floor, but his body seems relaxed.

"I'm sorry, Doctor Fielding, I had to throw up."

My whole body wilts with relief and I collapse back down to the couch patting the cushion beside me. Max walks over to join me, taking my hand in his. His fresh minty breath blows over my cheek as he leans over to kiss my temple.

Doctor Fielding checks his watch then reaches for his tablet.

"You've made great progress today, Max. I'd like to see you again in a few days, and I think it's important that you and Vivienne talk. It's also important to stick with your medication until you've settled into a regular routine, we don't want to set you back unnecessarily."

Once the doctor has left, an uncomfortable silence ensues. I still feel a distance between us, and I have to reach out and take his hand to make a connection.

"I'm so glad you told me, Max. It makes sense of everything now, and you should never feel guilty. You haven't betrayed me. You never would."

The look of hope in his eyes floors me.

"It's such a relief to get it off my chest. Doctor Fielding has been pushing me all week, but I couldn't… I didn't want…." He exhales deeply, tightening his grip of my hand and clenching his jaw. "I *never* wanted you to have those thoughts in your head."

I smooth my fingers down his cheek, then raise his chin with my finger until our eyes meet. "I don't. Monica's gone. And every shitty, hurtful thing she's ever done to us has gone with her… Come home, Max. Come home where you belong."

His eyes search mine and I can see the tempest of emotions in his beautiful blues.

"I just need one more night. I need to be sure that…" He takes a deep breath, releasing a tired sigh, then he pulls me into his lap, groaning at his painful ribs. "I'll be home tomorrow, I promise."

Bringing his hand to my belly, I lay mine on top of it, resting my head against his shoulder. "Okay. One more night."

THE PRINCESS AND THE PAEDO

Leaving Max was difficult, but I felt like we'd made a breakthrough and he promised he would come home tomorrow.

"Are we going home now, Ma'am?" John asks, as I slide into the rear seat of the Range Rover.

"Actually, can we pop round to my mum's house, I just want to check on her. It's on our way."

"Sure. No problem."

After finding out Mum's poor health was going to rob me of her way too early, and after Greg had turned up at the dinner the other night, I felt the need to go and see her. I had called her several times but as usual, our conversations were never easy.

The lift is out of order, so I walk up the four flights of stairs to her flat. Opening the door with my own key, I call out to let her know I'm here. "It's only me."

I walk through the cluttered hallway to the living room, where I expect to find her sprawled out in the chair with the television blaring and an empty bottle of Vodka in her hand. But as I enter the living room, she smiles up at me from the armchair. She's flicking through a magazine. She looks surprisingly sober.

"Mum! You're sob… Ah…You look great."

She looks thin and pale. The dark circles under her eyes and the years of addiction and neglect have taken their toll, but she looks better than I've seen her in a long, long time.

I cast my eyes around the room. It's tidy. It's never this tidy.

"I wasn't expecting you tonight, was I?"

"No, I was passing so I thought I'd pop in to see you."

The sight of my mother smiling, chokes me up. I rarely get to see her like this and I've missed her so much.

"Come and sit down," she says, patting the chair beside her. "I've just been admiring you and your handsome beau in this magazine." She tilts the page toward me so I can see what she's looking at. It's the photo of me and Cole on the red-carpet at the Foxx-Glove Foundation dinner, it takes up the whole page.

Gazing down at the photograph, she sighs wistfully. "Max is very handsome, and you both look so in love."

I don't bother to tell her that it's not Max in the photo, but as I study the image of me and Cole with his hand at the small of my back and me gazing up at him, I realise that's exactly what we look like. It makes me blush.

Mum gives me a strange look. Her brow furrows then she squints at the photograph placing her finger on a burly man standing just behind us. His face is slightly out of focus. "Is this him? It's been a long time, but it looks like him to me." Scowling, she taps her finger on the photograph. I lean in to take a closer look, then realise who it is. "Well?" she asks in a firmer tone. "Is that Greg?"

"…Yes." I answer, suddenly feeling angry.

Mum shakes her head, dropping the magazine to the floor. "He's an abuser, Vivienne. A paedophile. Why haven't you outed him? Why is he allowed to breathe the same air as you?" Her eyes level on me with such anger in them, filling with tears. "Oh, god. It's all my fault. I've let you down so badly. That man…" Her words get caught in her throat.

Kneeling down in front of her, I rest my hands on her

spindly knees. She lunges forward hugging me with such a force, but her skinny body feels so fragile.

"It's okay, Mum. It's okay."

She sobs against my shoulder, but my tears don't come. I've cried bucket loads over the years because of what Greg Taylor did to me, but I'll shed no more.

"Why haven't you called the police?" she sniffles. She leans back, drying her tears with her sleeve.

"I can't, Mum."

"Why not?"

"...Because I haven't told Max about him, or what he did to me."

Her wide incredulous eyes search mine. "What? But—"

"Mum... Greg is one of Max's clients. If I tell Max what he did to me... He's very protective. He'll do something stupid and I can't lose him, Mum. I can't." Now, my tears begin to flow. We hug each other again, Mum sobbing into my shoulder as we rock from side to side.

"Oh, god. I could really use a drink."

I sit back on my heels and glance over my shoulder at the drinks cabinet, usually stocked full with bottles of booze. It's empty. I'm shocked.

"Don't tell me you've given up drinking?"

She pulls a huge joint from her handbag and proceeds to light it, then she takes a long, deep, satisfying draw. Closing her eyes at the relief it gives her, she leans back in her chair puffing out a long stream of smoke. "I'm not promising anything, Vivienne, but I do want to see my grandchildren before I die."

My heart clenches. "Yeah... I'd like that too."

Seeing my mother and being able to have a proper conversation with her is long overdue. I'm delighted she's made an effort to sober up. I know how hard it will be for her to stick to it, and I won't hold my breath, but at least she's trying.

~

John drives me home and brings me up to the penthouse.

"Oh, by the way, Ma'am, Vinnie called while you were

visiting your mom, they'll be home on Monday."

"That's great. Did they manage to sort everything out up in Scotland?"

"Yes, I believe so. Well, goodnight, Ma'am."

"Goodnight, John."

The lift doors close and John heads down to his quarters.

I open the penthouse door to the sound of high pitched female giggling. A smile spreads across my face as I remove my coat and walk toward the living room.

By the sound of it, Cole has finally come to his senses and found a girlfriend. I couldn't be happier. He needs someone. Someone nice and fun and— *Oh, bollocks!*

Cole and Fiona are huddled together on the sofa. Her shoes are off, she's practically in his lap with her legs curled underneath her, and her arm is draped around his shoulders fussing with his hair.

Shit! Why her?

"Hi, Viv," Cole says, looking up at me. "You remember Fiona?" Dipping his head, he nibbles at her earlobe. That sets off her pathetic giggles again which really fucks me off. Of all the women Cole could have brought home why did it have to be her?

While Cole's face is buried in her neck, she raises her eyes to mine. Her coy smile replaced with a smug gloat. "Vivienne."

"Fi." *Well that's the pleasantries out of the way, now fuck off!*

I can't watch them canoodling anymore, so I stomp into the kitchen before I throw up. Her being here is really pissing me off. And why is Cole being such a dick? Bringing her here is totally out of order. Why can't he shag her at her place?

The remnants of a takeout lay strewn across the island, so I start to tidy up, throwing the empty Chinese cartons away. I'm in a mood, and slamming the dirty plates into the dishwasher turns out to be very therapeutic. After that, I pour myself a glass of non-alcoholic wine.

Staring out the kitchen window with my wine in hand, and stewing over Cole's poor taste in women, I feel a hand on my waist.

"Hi, long time no see," he says, leaning over my shoulder to drop a kiss on my cheek.

"And who's fault is that?" I couldn't help the snippy tone.

"I've got to pop down to the office, could you pour a glass of wine for Fiona, I'll be back in a few minutes."

"What?" I spin around but he's already on his way out of the kitchen, then I hear the penthouse door closing behind him.

"Oh, great!" I grumble under my breath. "Now I'm her sodding waitress! Where does Jan keep the laxatives?"

I couldn't find any laxatives, so I pour her a glass of the cheap stuff. I had bought it months ago but nobody had dared to drink it.

Throwing my shoulders back, I paste on a fake smile as I walk into the living room and place her glass a little too far away for her to reach without having to move. It's childish, but it makes me feel better.

I take a seat opposite and kick off my heels, curling my legs underneath me. I want her to see that this is my home. Then I watch her reach for her glass, smirking when she has to get up for it.

Her eyes travel from my face down to my heart-shaped locket. She's seen it before but never commented on it. Her envious gaze makes me smile inside.

"Isn't it beautiful?" I gloat, reaching up to fondle the locket. "Max is so romantic."

Clearly miffed, she slides her eyes away glancing around the room. "Hmm, I always wondered what Max's home would look like," she says, taking a sip of her wine, its vinegary taste obviously unpleasant.

Tilting my head, I raise an eyebrow. "Don't you mean Cole's home?"

"Oh!" she blushes. "Yes, of course." She laughs, but I keep a straight face. In my head, I'm shoving her out the door, throwing her Manolo's at her as I slam the door in her face.

"Vivienne," she starts, eyeing me with curiosity. "You seem a little tense. Is everything okay with you and Max?"

Bingo! And there it is. Her real interest in Cole, is getting closer to Max. She knows we've been living separately recently, and I'll bet she's praying that we are going to split up.

I take a sip of my non-alcoholic wine wishing it was the real thing, not for courage, just so I can blame my impending attack on the drink.

"Fiona, just because you've been invited back for drinks and a meaningless shag, don't get comfortable. You're not welcome here, and you won't be invited back. Not if I've got anything to do with it."

She blushes, her smile slowly sliding from her face. I think I may have pooped all over her party.

"I've never liked you, Fiona. And in case you haven't noticed my subtle hints, let me spell it out for you. You're about as welcome here as a bad case of the shits. I wouldn't piss on you if you were on fire. And when Cole comes to his senses, he'll see you for what you really are. A vapid waste of space, waiting for Max to notice you. He won't. And with Cole? Your time is limited."

Her indignant scowl pleases me.

"You're hanging on by the skin of your teeth and your overpriced acrylic nails. Don't get me wrong, Princess, you're beautiful on the outside. You'll never be short of admirers, so why don't you peddle your wares somewhere else. Cole deserves better."

Her eyes level on mine with much more determination than I had anticipated.

"Who?... You?"

She's caught me off guard with that remark and her now smug expression throws me a little, but I stare back at her defiantly.

"Oh, Vivienne. Anyone can see that Cole's in love with you. He doesn't stop talking about you. But you can hardly blame him, you've been leading him on since Max disappeared."

Her smug smile reminds me of Monica, sending a shiver up my spine. I glare at her still a bit confused as to why she hasn't caved in yet. My insults seem to have bounced straight off her without even denting her pride. She's still staring at me like she's holding all the cards.

"Pff! You don't know what you're talking about."

"Really? I think I do."

I can feel my cheeks flush which pisses me off. She's wrong.

"Oh, my god! It's true!" Her laugh fills the open space of the living room. Sitting forward she searches my face with her smug eyes. "You and Cole!... You've had something together, haven't you, Vivienne? It's written all over your face."

I shake my head trying to remain aloof, but inside I'm fuming, which just makes me look guilty. She's spun this around on me, and although she's wrong, I'm rapidly losing the upper hand. That's not how I saw this going.

"It's not like that Fiona, and you know it."

She leans back as her self-satisfied smile irritates the hell out of me. "Well, well, well. What a dark horse you are. What would Max say if he knew you had feelings for his brother?"

"I don't!" An unfortunate blush warms my cheeks.

Her eyes rake over me with antipathy. "It's just as well he hasn't married you yet, he'll save himself a fortune. I can't imagine he'll take the news very well, but at least he'll have me to comfort him. I've been waiting a long time for this opportunity, Vivienne. Thanks for handing him to me on a plate."

Her smug, arrogant smile widens across her face. I know she's trying to goad me and the fact that I'm letting her get to me is making things worse.

Slamming my glass down on the table, I unfurl my legs from underneath me, trying to control my temper without much success. "You're wrong!"

She calmly settles back, draping an arm over the cushions, smirking at me with a nonchalant shrug. I glare back at her wondering how the hell I've managed to fuck this conversation up.

"I don't think so," she says, saluting me with her wine.

"Hmmf, you should see your face, Vivienne. Guilt has never looked so good."

I'm just about to respond when I hear the penthouse door opening and Cole comes striding in. He comes to a standstill when he sees my face and the tension in my body.

"What's the matter?" His eyes ping-pong between us.

"Nothing! I'm going to bed." I don't bother to look at either of them, and I can't get up the stairs quick enough.

Fuming mad, I slump down on the edge of the bed, angry with myself for letting that bitch get the better of me. Fiona has always irritated me, and now she's wormed her way into my inner circle, into my home. I feel like I've been invaded.

I know she wants Max, and I know that will never happen, but I care about Cole too much to see him end up with another manipulative woman who's only using him to get to his brother. Cole would never survive another scenario like that. He's too good for her anyway.

ENDANGERED HEART

It took me ages to get to sleep last night. I had come home feeling positive about our session with Doctor Fielding and Max's homecoming. My mother's sobriety had been a bonus I wasn't expecting. But Fiona had managed to piss all over that.

Max and Cole are undoubtedly the sexiest men on the planet. Their masculine beauty and wickedly hot bodies attract admirers both male and female everywhere they go, but they also have a knack of attracting women like Monica and Fiona. Tenacious women. Dangerous women, who never take their eye off their target.

Fiona wants Max. She's using Cole to get closer to him. And I wouldn't be surprised if she's already tried to contact Max to tell him that me and Cole are having an affair.

Well, let her, I have nothing to hide. She doesn't know that we shared a kiss, and that's all it was anyway, a stupid kiss. Well, okay, two kisses, but she can't hurt me. She could hurt Cole though, he's vulnerable.

He won't admit it, but he's been deeply wounded by Monica. Sadly, Fiona's just as likely to treat him the same way, and that awful thought has kept me awake all night.

I decide to lie in longer than usual and I take my time to get ready. I don't want to bump into little Miss Fuck-Face. Her gloating smugness is the last thing I need.

I heard her annoying, giggly voice well into the night, so I assume Cole was stupid enough to shag her and let her stay. He's working this morning so I expect she'll leave when he does.

I check my phone and see that Max has left me a text:

```
Hey, beautiful,
I won't be home until after lunch.
Jimmy had a fall, nothing serious
but I want to make sure he's ok
before we leave.
M
X;-)
```

His text makes me smile. He's finally gone back to using the smiley face kiss at the end, which means he's feeling much more confident and happy about coming home. He had stopped using it when everything had gone pear shaped.

I change the sheets and tidy the bathroom, then I get dressed in something pretty. As I walk out to the top of the stairs, I stop to listen. It's all quiet, so I make my way downstairs. The living room is empty. Fiona's shoes are no longer strewn across the rug, and the wine glasses have been cleared away.

I wander into the kitchen and put the kettle on for a cup of tea, then I open the fridge and take out the bacon for breakfast.

"Hey."

Cole's voice makes me jump. I swing around to see him walking into the kitchen, he's dressed in an elegant dark blue suit with a white shirt and a blue tie which matches his eyes perfectly. He looks gorgeous, as always.

"Any chance I could have one of those? What do you call it a 'buddy'?"

"It's a butty, bacon butty."

Glancing at the digital display on the oven, I notice it's ten o'clock, he usually leaves at eight. I turn the grill on and lay the strips of bacon onto the rack. "Aren't you working today?"

"Yeah, I've got a meeting but it's not until lunchtime." He

takes a seat at the island, flicking through the morning paper.

I turn back to the grill and set the dial, then I grab the bread and start buttering a few slices. "Do you want ketchup?"

When he doesn't answer, I turn to face him. His eyes are shrouded in a serious frown. "Vivienne, I know you have feelings for me. I saw the look on your face last night when you walked in and saw Fiona. You were jealous."

A sinking feeling hits my stomach. "No… Cole, you don't understand." I look away and finish buttering the bread. My hands are shaking.

"I didn't sleep with her. We had a few drinks, a few laughs, and then I sent her home. She wasn't too pleased about that, but I don't want her. I want you... I'm in love with you."

My body stiffens and I stop spreading the butter, staring down at the bread. "Cole, please, we've been through this a million times."

His arms cage me in against the counter as he moves in behind me, not touching, but very close. Too close. My heart races in my chest. His warm breath grazes my cheek and I can feel the heat of his body against my back making my stomach tighten.

"Cole, please don't do this. It's not what you think. I don't like Fiona, I never have. She wants Max, and she's using you to get to him." I turn around to face him, he's so close that I have to lean back. "Why can't you see that she's using you? I don't want to see you get hurt, that's all."

His blue eyes blaze down at me as a prickle of awareness travels over my skin making me feel awkward. I try to move away but he holds me there, caging me in.

"I don't care about her, Vivienne. I care about you. You're choosing the wrong guy. I'm good for you. I'm safe. You'd never need to worry about me hurting you. I'd never do that. I love you, Vivienne. And I know you feel something for me, I can see it in your eyes."

The intensity of his stare leaves me breathless, but I try to stand my ground. "No. You don't. We've been through all this before. I love Max." Tears spring into my eyes. It's flattering that he thinks he's in love with me, any girl in their right mind would be lucky to have his love, any girl but me. I don't want to be the one who hurts him.

I try to push against his shoulders but he won't budge. His watery blue eyes, full of emotion, burn into mine with such intensity I can't look away.

"He'll hurt you, Vivienne. Jesus! He nearly killed you the last time you were together. I would never do that. You know how I feel about you. I'm crazy about you."

His eyes blaze with heat, searching mine for answers he'll never find. I stare up at him wishing I could take away all his hurt and make him see what I see. But as he lowers his mouth to mine, I react sharply, and slap his face.

Releasing me immediately, he steps back, the shock, and my hand print, reddening his cheek.

"Oh, god, I'm sorry." Tears brim against my lashes. The rejection on his face crushes me.

He steps back a few paces, still reeling from the sting of my slap. Resting his hands against the edge of the island, he leans back against it, his head bowed down to his chest.

I feel awful. I've handled this all wrong and now I don't know what to do to put it right. "Cole…" I take a step toward him, and then another. Then I place my hands either side of his face and pull his chin off his chest and his eyes up to mine. The look on his face breaks my heart.

"I do love you, Cole. Not in the way you want, but I do care about you, very much. I'll always be grateful to you for getting me through the hardest days of my life. I couldn't have done it without you."

His watery eyes close.

"But this isn't about me, or Max… Cole, I know it's hard, but you have to grieve for your loss. You have to grieve for her, and then let go."

His sad eyes open, searching mine in confusion.

"Your feelings for me aren't real. You know as well as I do that you're using me, and your brother, as an excuse to run away from what really lies at the heart of all this… You loved her… She broke your heart, and now she's gone…it's just—"

"I hate myself for that," he blurts. "But I still miss her. I miss the girl she used to be. The girl she was before she— I loved her so much."

His small, fragile voice and the shame in his eyes, puts a lump in my throat. The Monica I knew was evil and twisted, but Cole's heart had been captivated by her long before that version of her ever existed. Somewhere along the line her heart had turned black, but by then it was too late. She'd left an indelible imprint that Cole has never been able to discard. I smooth away a tear from his cheek. "I know. And it's okay."

His face hardens, his eyes darkening as he clenches his jaw. "No. It's not! I hate her for everything she did. For Charlie. You. Even Max. But I still…"

He doesn't finish his sentence and the look of shame and sadness in his eyes kills me. I was right all along. As fucked-up as Monica was, she had both stolen and broken Cole's heart and he's never recovered.

My heart clenches as I blink away my own tears. Cupping his face in my hands, I pull his gaze up to mine. For such a striking and powerful man, his sad eyes make him look so vulnerable.

"Cole, someday soon, if you let it happen, someone will come along and make you forget all your pain. You're funny, kind, and ridiculously gorgeous. You're too special not to be loved. But you deserve the love of a woman who will love only you. Unconditionally. Irrevocably. Completely. Someone who will curl your toes and melt your bones with her smile."

"You do that to me." His eyes search mine and it takes all my strength not to cry.

"Cole, trust me. You're just using me as a substitute for Monica, as I did with you as a substitute for Max. It's far from ideal, or kind, but I think it's some kind of survival instinct that we've both been using to get through our heartache. I love Max. I always have and I always will."

His eyes tell me he understands, but I can also see his pain.

"This is all my fault. When Max was gone I needed you. I

was selfish. I leaned on you so much that you're confused. You were my substitute for Max, that's why I know your feelings for me aren't real."

He lowers his watery eyes in defeat. He knows I'm right but he's hurting.

"Cole, somewhere out there is a wonderful woman waiting for you to find her. It's not me. And it's *definitely* not Fiona. You just have to be strong enough to let go of the past and look forward."

I can see the hurt in his eyes, and I hate that it's me who has made him feel this way, he deserves so much more than this.

"Come, on," I say, pulling him toward me and giving him a cuddle. His arms circle my waist, giving me a tight, almost desperate hug. Wrapping my arms around his neck, I stroke his hair as we rock from side to side for a long silent moment.

"How did you get to be so wise," he whispers against my neck. "I'll always love you, Vivienne."

The break in his voice is heart wrenching.

"And I'll always love you."

"Get out!"

Cole and I break apart at the sound of Max's angry bark. My heart jumps in my chest and the look on Max's face alarms me. Then I realise why. Fiona has indeed done her worst. She's standing behind Max in the kitchen doorway, a ridiculously smug smile all over her face.

I had feared she would use last night against me, but I hadn't counted on it being quite so soon. Cole had sent her off with a flea in her ear, and a woman scorned is a dangerous thing. But I've done nothing wrong, and neither has Cole.

I start to walk toward him. "Max it's—"

"Don't!" His watery, hard, steely eyes pin me to the spot.

John enters behind Fiona looking confused, then he disappears with Max's luggage. Cole moves toward his brother with his hands in the air in a gesture of surrender. "Hey, man. It's not what you think."

Squaring his shoulders, Max flicks his brother an evil glare.

He's seething with anger, fighting with himself to contain it as it hardens every muscle in his body. "I said, get out! Both of you!"

The blood drains from my head and I falter, feeling sick to my stomach. The smell of burning bacon fills my nose, churning my stomach even more. The anger in Max's eyes because he thinks I've betrayed him, cripples me. I can't breathe. I can't think. And my heart breaks that he could think I'd ever do that to him.

But my shock and incredulity soon turns into anger, surging through me like a wildfire. "Why?" I ask indignantly. "Because you're listening to her?" As I point at the smug bitch standing behind him, a fleeting moment of doubt enters his eyes, until he lifts his chin re-establishing his fixed, obstinate stance. The heat of his anger now rippling through every sinew, making him look incredibly dangerous.

Defiantly, I walk over to him until we're almost touching. He flinches, frowning down at me, his eyes are on mine the whole time. Dark, angry eyes, stewing with doubt, fear, and sadness, all rolled in to one. I hold his gaze determined to make him see. "Ask me, Max. Look me in the eyes and ask me," I say, softly, straightening my back and daring him with everything I've got.

Confusion flutters across his face. He's always been able to read me so well. He sees everything through my eyes, I could never lie to him without it showing. He knows I would never challenge him with that unless I was absolutely sure I wouldn't fail.

In my peripheral vision, I see Cole stepping forward, reinforcing Max's wariness. His chest inflates and his face hardens as he gives Cole the mother of all death stares. His uninjured arm stiffening into a rod of bulging muscles as his hand clenches into a white knuckled fist, ready to strike any second.

Cole raises his hands defensively. "Easy brother," he says, with a silly smirk on his face. "Can you dial down the crazy for just one minute?" he adds, stopping two feet away from him.

"Look, I don't know what Fiona has told you, but there's nothing going on behind your back. I'll admit, I love your woman. But she's your woman, Max. And she's done nothing wrong. She loves you, although I can't see why. But hell, even I love you."

Max physically growls when he hears Cole admitting that he loves me, and I can see he's dangerously close to the edge.

"And hey," Cole adds on a shrug. "It was just a stupid kiss."

What? No!

Max grits his teeth so hard, I can practically hear his jaw cracking under the pressure, and his eyes briefly close, while mine widen in horror at Cole's big mouth. I don't look at her, but I can feel Fiona's triumphant smile burning into me.

I have to admire Cole for his honesty but his timing stinks, and now he's forced my hand. It's time to bite the bullet and lay my truths bare. I owe it to Max. I owe it to all of us.

With a surprisingly steady hand, I reach up and cup my palm against Max's face. His eyes fly open, still wild, cautious, and heartbreakingly sad. I feel him resisting me, but I make him stay engaged so he can read my eyes and see the truth.

"Max, when you were taken from me, I died inside. I was so lost without you. Every minute of every day was torture. Cole was the closest thing I had to you. Every time I looked at him, I saw your face. Every time he spoke, I heard your voice. I wanted him so desperately to be you because I couldn't bear to live without you." I reach up and touch my locket like it's some kind of safety net. "No me without you, remember?"

His expression remains hard, eyes searching mine with deep intensity, I can tell he's listening to every word, even though my voice is barely audible. My emotions are crippling my words, saturating my eyes with hot, stinging tears.

"I leaned on Cole for support, probably too much. But I couldn't have survived those days that you were gone without him. He was my lifeline. My strength. I don't know where I would be without his help."

Max's brow twitches but he never once removes his eyes

from mine.

"The kiss was my fault. My doing. I thought you were lost to me forever, and I couldn't bear it, I was so desperate to hold on to you."

I swing my watery eyes over to Cole.

"And I'm sorry, Cole. Truly sorry. I should never have used you like that. It was selfish, cruel, and unkind. But I so desperately needed you. If it hadn't been for you, I would never have survived. If it hadn't been for you, we might never have found Max."

Silence hangs like a heavy cloud all around us. I swing my eyes back up to Max, unable to read him, unable to sense whether I've just made the biggest mistake of my life.

The overhead smoke alarm brings an end to the unbearable silence, blaring out its piercing tone. Cole walks over to the grill and switches it off, then fans the smoke with a cloth before resetting the alarm.

Max never breaks eye contact but his eyes are a furious storm of emotions, searching mine for the truth he so desperately needs. His jaw pulses, clenching tightly. His chest rising and falling with shallow breaths. And as he stares down into my eyes, I can't help but feel the pull of his magnetic gaze. Even clouded by anger and uncertainty, he has the most beautifully engaging eyes that I fall into every time I look at them.

They gradually begin to soften, and finally, I see recognition taking hold.

"Get out!"

N…No! His hostile command floors me. I've totally misread him! My heart drops to the depths of despair, my knees buckling at his words, and I'm shocked and pained by them as sure as if he'd stabbed me in the heart.

With his eyes still burning into mine, he suddenly wraps me in his arms, pulling me tightly to his chest. Turning to face Fiona, he hits her with a venomous glare. "I said, get out! And don't come back!"

Fiona stands motionless, her cheeks flushing, her mouth

open, gaping at us. The shock of Max's command has stunned her. The crashing failure of her ill-advised scheme has backfired monumentally. I couldn't be happier.

John returns, his eyes flicking between us trying to catch up. He must feel like he's just stumbled into the middle of a play.

"No!" Fiona says, in a high pitched wail. She steps forward, reaching out to Max, but John quickly moves in front of her to block her path. "Max, listen to me. She's lying. She's slept with Cole. She doesn't deserve you."

With a disgusted expression, Max turns away from her. "John, throw her out, and make sure she leaves the building. Tell security she no longer has access."

"Yes, Sir. Copy that."

John takes her elbow, wasting no time in ushering her out. Her pleas and insults muted by the closing of the penthouse door behind her.

The tension finally flows out of Max's muscles and he lowers his head nuzzling my cheek. "I'm sorry, baby. She filled my head with all kinds of shit. It's just… I couldn't… Goddammit woman! I've been going crazy without you."

Fisting my hand into his hair, I pull his head back so I can gaze into his eyes. "Max, I would never do that to you. Never. I love you."

His eyes blaze, scorching me with a look I can never get enough of. "I love you more, baby."

Rising onto my toes I kiss him hard, possessively, the only way I know how. His lips devour me and for a moment, we're the only two people in the world.

"Okay," Cole says, walking past us to leave. "I'll see you later."

Max breaks the kiss. "Not so fast," he growls, and I feel his muscles hardening again.

Cole breaks his stride and turns to face him. Lowering his shoulders, he raises both hands in surrender. "You want to punch me out? Take your best shot big guy, I won't stop you. The kiss was worth it."

I thought I had seen the mother of all death stares, but the way Max is glaring at his brother now, puts the last one to shame. I can literally hear Max's teeth grinding together and his arms have become concrete around me.

"Don't love my woman," he growls. His short but concise message, delivered through gritted teeth, makes Cole smile. I cringe knowing that's probably not wise.

"Then don't make it easy for me." Seemingly unfazed, he smirks then arches a brow. "Sort your shit out, Max. Don't hurt her again, and don't keep disappearing. She needs you. And as crazy as it sounds, so do I. You're not the only one Monica fucked-up."

Cole walks off with his words hanging above Max like a heavy rain cloud.

He turns to me with cautious eyes. "He's right. I can't fuck this up. I don't want to lose you."

I reach up to smooth his anxious brow. "You won't. We'll just have to take things slow and deal with each little problem as it comes along. But we can only do that if we talk to each other." I raise both eyebrows. "I know that's a whole new concept for you, but maybe you should give it a try."

His eyes soften and his mega-watt smile followed by his scorching hot kiss, has my body responding in its usual way. I'm powerless to the effect he has on me, and that's something I would never want to change.

Breaking the kiss, he stares down at me with love bursting from his eyes. His hand slides down my back and around to my belly. Looking down at my baby bump in wonder, he gently runs his fingers around our nuggets. "You look beautiful."

I gaze up at his gorgeous face, a face far more exquisite than my own and drink him in, marvelling at his handsomeness. Perfection has been lovingly carved into every edge and plane of his face and body without blemish or flaw. Even his scars, created by guilt but driven by love, merely enhance the beautiful soul within.

He sees me as beautiful but he is the prize, in all his forms, and I cherish his love more deeply than I ever thought possible.

Pulling him down to me, I rise up to kiss his lush lips. I'm so hot for him right now and desperate to get him naked. "Do you want to take this upstairs?" I whisper.

"No."

Before I can respond, he clamps his mouth over mine, his hands are all over me, and we stagger around the kitchen until my back hits the island. I tug at his shirt to release it from the waistband of his jeans, then I run my hand underneath it to feel his skin, digging my nails into his back as his kiss stirs my desire to a fever pitch.

He breaks the kiss panting hot breaths across my lips, his hand fisting in my hair and pulling my head back. Scorching me with his eyes he fills my senses with need and longing. His solid erection stands between us, a clear sign that he's as turned on as I am. I reach down to unbutton his fly but he grabs my arm to stop me. "No," he whispers. "Not without someone here."

My eyebrows shoot upward. "What? You want a threesome?"

He tilts his head, arrogantly arching his brow. "I don't share. Especially not you." I smile and shake my head, feeling his possessive love all around me.

Searching my eyes for a long moment, he leans his forehead against mine and murmurs, "One step at a time."

He's right, as much as I want to rip his clothes off and fuck his brains out, we need to be sure he's not going to flip out again, especially as we're on our own.

"Max?"

"Mmm-hmm?"

"I could always…" I blush and shake my head.

"What? What is it, baby?"

"Well, I was just thinking. I could always tie your hands… like we did before, remember?"

Max pulls back hitting me with his grinning face. "How could I forget?"

I blush and cringe, it wasn't the sexiest thing I had ever done. Having to get Vinnie to cut him out of the handcuffs was particularly embarrassing.

Another idea suddenly pops into my head. "How about a nice bath?"

He nuzzles my neck, breathing in my scent. "I had one this morning. Mmm, you smell good."

His lips brushing against the soft skin just under my lobe, sets my nerve endings alight with tingles. I tilt my head to give him better access as my fingers weave into his hair. My breathing deepening as a warm flourish dances in my belly. "How about we go up—"

"How about we have some breakfast and you can tell me all about your mom, and what's been going on at work."

I lean back, waiting for his eyes to find mine. When he sees the expression on my face his eyes drift downward. I'm glad he's home and thrilled that his hands are on me, but he feels distant. I know why, but it scares me.

"Are you ever going to touch me again?"

"I'm touching you now aren't I?"

"That's not what I mean."

He stops nibbling and straightens, then he runs his fingers down my cheek, gazing down at me with sadness in his eyes. "I just don't want to fuck this up. I couldn't live with myself if I hurt you again."

I reach up, catching his hand in mine, then I drop a soft kiss into his palm. "You won't. It's all in here." I tap my finger against his temple. "We'll figure this out." I rise up to kiss him gently on the lips. "Besides, I've had a lot of time to think about it, and I've come up with some pretty ingenious ideas."

I move out of his arms and walk over to the grill to sort out the charred remains of the bacon.

"Really?" he asks, his smile evident by his tone. "Do I want to know what they are?"

I giggle, "Oh, I think you do. But all in good time, Mr. Foxx. All in good time."

Max settles into one of the chairs at the island, flicking

through the paper while I set about making a full English breakfast, probably the only thing I can cook.

Once I've served two huge plates of food and poured myself a cup of tea, we slip into an easy conversation about my work, and how well Ed and Casper have been doing in my absence.

"See?" he smirks. "I said you'd make it work, didn't I?"

"You did. And I'm very grateful for the opportunity."

His scowl pauses the fork to my mouth. "…What?"

"You don't need to be grateful, Vivienne. You're a strong, talented woman, you did it all on your own."

"Pff, if you'd seen me a few weeks ago, I don't think you'd have thought of me as strong then. I was a complete wre—" I stop talking, realising I'd said that out loud.

His eyes cloud over with hurt and sadness. Placing his fork on the side of his plate, he reaches for his mug of coffee but doesn't pick it up. His eyes are cast down and the atmosphere has changed dramatically.

"All this time…" He shakes his head, still staring at his coffee mug. "All this time I've been so consumed with what I had been through. I should have been there for you when I came back. I'm so sorry, Vivienne… I'm an asshole."

Tears prick my eyes. I stand up and walk around the island to wrap my arms around his shoulders and rest my chin in the crook of his neck. "Yes, but you're my arsehole, and I love you." I kiss his cheek then wander back to my seat eyeing him warily. The poor man has been through so much, he shouldn't be worrying about me.

"Eat," I command, softly. "You're going to need your strength," I add, with a cheeky smirk. He smiles and starts eating again.

"So," he says, around a mouthful of bacon. "What was that all about earlier with Cole? He said something about Monica fucking him up?"

"Yes, I feel sorry for him. He's been putting on a brave face, but even after all this time, he's never really got over her."

His surprised expression tells me he had no idea his brother still had feelings for her. They had stopped talking years ago, when Cole and Monica got married, and it was only recently when Charlie died that they'd started communicating again. There was so much they had to catch up with.

"When we went to identify Monica's body, Cole was devastated. I could tell he was still in love with her, despite all she'd done. And now that bitch Fiona is trying to latch on to him too, only to get to you of course. But she's doing the same thing Monica did. It's cruel. He deserves so much better."

Max remains silent for a moment. I can see something's bothering him.

"Baby, after what I did to you… did you ever…did you ever wish you were with Cole instead of me?"

I lower my fork and look him directly in the eyes. "No. Never. There were many times I wished Cole was you, if that makes any sense."

His sad eyes slide down to his plate which he pushes away. He's still struggling with this.

"Max, he got me through some very dark times. I love Cole, as family. But I love you with everything I am, and everything I have to give. There is no me without you."

Wary eyes meet mine. "So… if I asked you to marry me again… you'd still say yes?"

"No." I answer softly.

His brow twitches as hurt enters his expression.

I smile. "I'd say, with all my heart and forever, yes."

ONE STEP AT A TIME

Max and I spend the rest of the afternoon snuggled up on the sofa watching old movies and talking. Not about anything deep or meaningful, just talking. It had been a long time since we'd been so close and so relaxed with each other.

Before Max had been abducted, touching one another had always been a strong element in our relationship, now it was essential. Experiencing those days when he was gone had made me realise how unbearable my life would be without him. Being apart had made us both suffer. It's funny, I had always thought of myself as strong and independent, but without Max, I was lost.

I show him the photographs of Lucy and Dan's wedding. We laugh at how tanned and healthy we looked from our holiday, a complete contrast to how we both look now. Weeks of stress and worry have definitely taken their toll.

In the photos, we were happy and completely oblivious to what lay ahead. It was also weird to see how much my baby bump had grown in the last few weeks.

It's strange, when I first found out I was pregnant, apart from the initial shock that it was even possible for me to become pregnant, the focus of our attention revolved around our bright and hopeful future. But when Max was abducted, being pregnant had taken a back seat. All I could focus on was getting him back. Without him, a future seemed pointless.

As we lie entangled on the sofa, Max lays his head back closing his eyes. I know he isn't asleep because his fingers keep circling our nuggets, but it affords me some time to gaze at his handsome face.

His ribs, although very tender, seem to be healing properly now, which still makes cuddling into him precarious, but a lot easier than it has been. And his new, blue, flexi-wrist-wrap is much lighter than the cast, which allows him more freedom of movement. He seems more content now too, but my cautious brain still prods me with questions.

For me, despite the risks, having Max home again has calmed me. I couldn't bear the distance that had grown between us. Living separately wasn't something I dealt with very well.

For Max, I fear it could be the reverse. Coming home brings new challenges for him. His biggest fear is that he could re-enact his nightmares again and hurt me or the babies. It's a valid concern which can't be ignored, but it also can't be allowed to break us apart. We're both aware of the risks, which gives us a fighting chance to avoid them, but if he were to do it again, I worry that he'll withdraw completely and I couldn't handle that.

Opening an eye, he smirks at me. "Don't you know it's rude to stare?"

Leaning up on my elbow, I trace my fingers across his chin. "I can't help it, you're so pretty."

Opening his other eye, he gives me the eyebrow. "Pretty?"

"Yes… Pretty."

He closes his eyes and shakes his head while his lips curl into a roguish smile. "Sheila has a lot to answer for." His expression shifts. "You haven't spoken about your mother, how is she?"

With a weary sigh, I absently trace my fingers across his chest. "I don't know… The last time I saw her she was sober, she'd thrown out all her booze." I roll my eyes realising how futile it is to pin any hopes on her remaining sober. "It won't last, and she's running out of time, but I hope she lives long enough to meet her grandchildren. I hope she..." The words get stuck in my throat.

"We'll take care of her," he says, softly. "We'll give her whatever she needs."

I lean into his palm and close my eyes to keep the tears from falling. His thumb tenderly brushes across my cheek and when I open my eyes, his loving gaze calms me. His eyes are a panacea. They tell me how much he loves me.

"I've missed you so much, baby. Being away from you kills me."

"Yeah, me too... No one can ever accuse us of living a dull, uneventful life."

"Any regrets?" His gaze holds mine, waiting for the truth.

"None."

That familiar pull draws me toward him, his scent, his eyes, the love in his heart, drawing me in as I surrender to his will with no objection. His kiss takes me over, possessing me, urging my need to the surface, arousing all my senses.

As I slide my leg over his hips, I feel his erection straining against his jeans. But as soon as my hand begins to slide down his body, he breaks the kiss.

"No."

That was all he said, and it was barely a whisper, but it stopped me in my tracks. For a moment, I felt put out that he was denying me what I wanted, what I needed. It was hard for me to hear him saying no. But we are still at the beginning of a long unchartered road, and I know we'll have to take things slowly. Max has made it clear, he won't take any risks, and I need to respect that.

Ignoring the tension which has suddenly built up between us, I try to change the subject. "I forgot to ask you. How's Jimmy?"

"What?"

"Jimmy. You said he had a fall."

His confused expression becomes apologetic. I search his

eyes trying to figure him out until the penny finally drops.

"He didn't have a fall, did he?"

His lowered gaze, answers my question. My cautious, analytical brain finally working it out. "You came home early… Oh, good grief. You were trying to catch me out with Cole, weren't you?"

He sighs and to his credit, he knows he hasn't got a leg to stand on. "I'm sorry, baby. Fiona called me late last night from Cole's phone. I thought it was him calling, I wouldn't have answered it otherwise. She told me she had proof that you and… that you…"

I pull back and launch the eyebrow. "That I was having an affair with your brother?"

He nods sheepishly. "She said Cole was in love with you. I didn't want to believe her, I knew you'd never do that to me, but… I wasn't sure about Cole."

"But you did believe her. You told me to get out."

Remembering the look on his face when he saw us together in the kitchen, puts a shudder up my spine. At that moment, he really had thought I was capable of that.

His eyes search mine, looking for forgiveness. He knows he's hurt me by taking Fiona's word for it, but I can hardly blame him for doubting me, it wasn't that long ago that I had thought he and Fiona had something going on too.

"I'm sorry, baby. I didn't really believe it until I saw you two together." He exhales a deep sigh. "And let's face it, Cole and I have been there before."

I stare down at him, frowning and shaking my head. "I warned you about her, didn't I?"

"You did. Duly noted."

He pulls me down to him for a kiss. His lush lips tenderly brush over mine, then his tongue gently teases me with soft licks until he slips it inside my mouth. His soft moan and the intimate trade of tongues and lips sends tingles all over my skin, heating me right to my core. Any angry thoughts are quickly replaced with the sensations his kiss evokes. Butterflies dance in my belly and then…

We both break apart staring at each other with wide eyes, eyebrows raised, mouths agape.

"Was that?… I felt something against my side. Was that one of the nuggets?" he asks, blinking up at me. His hand goes straight to my belly.

"I hope so! If not one of my kidneys is bouncing around loose in there."

The soft kick happens again, right under his hand. The look on his face makes my heart burst as nerves and excitement flutter through me on the wings of a million butterflies. It's the first time I've felt them move.

A wave of pride rolls over me. This was never supposed to be possible for me, but here they are, sending me a little reminder that they're very real.

"Hey! Keep it down in there. Your mother and I are having a moment," he chuckles. "Did you feel that, baby? Did you feel them kick?" His voice is full of wonder. I arch a brow at his dumb question, but the awe and joy played out in his eyes, and the huge beaming grin on his gorgeous face makes me so happy.

"They'll be here soon enough," I whisper. "Let's get back to our moment."

~

The hazy light of early evening filters in through the windows as the setting sun casts long shadows across the living room. We've been blissfully entwined on the sofa pretty much all afternoon and I've enjoyed every wonderful, contented minute of it.

Running my hands through his luxurious hair, I twist the soft silken strands between my fingers before letting them go and repeating the process.

"How do you feel? Being home again, I mean?"

He heaves a sigh and looks deep into my eyes. "I only left to protect you, Vivienne. I hated every minute we were apart." He lays his hand over my heart. "This is where I belong." My eyes begin to fill, blurring him a little. "But I won't take any chances, Vivienne. There's too much at stake. If I fuck up again…it'll ruin us."

My stomach slides with apprehension and I could kick myself for bringing the mood down to the low we both now feel. Racking my brain, I try to think of something to change the subject. "When do you have to take your pills?"

"Shit!" Max sits bolt upright almost rolling me off the sofa. "Arrgh!" Wincing and flinching, he slowly lowers again, his eyes screwed shut from the pain in his ribs. I untangle our legs and give him some room to settle his breathing.

"What time is it?" he asks, his teeth still clenched in discomfort.

I check the time on my phone. "It's nearly six." I hadn't realised it was so late.

"Shit! I've missed my afternoon pills." His breathing evens out, and he settles back into a more comfortable position. "I'd better take them now, but I should take them with food."

I open the bag of medication he'd left on the table, there are several boxes of tablets all with long unpronounceable names. "The pills you missed, what were they, painkillers?"

"No," he says, reaching out for the bag, so I hand it to him. "They're to help me sleep."

"Isn't the afternoon a little early?"

"I started taking them yesterday. I need them to be in my system so the last pill of the day will help me sleep through to the morning without…" He trails off, but I know what he was going to say. I try to ignore the possibility that Max is still potentially dangerous and act as nonchalant as possible.

"Okay, I'll set an alarm for you on my phone."

Max looks uncomfortable, and as he heaves another weary sigh, I can tell that he's worried he'll repeat what he did before. But neither of us knew what was going on then, at least now we both know what the risks are.

He calls out the details of his various prescriptions, and I type them into my phone reminder. While Max is separating the pills he needs to take now, I scoot into the kitchen to get him some water. When I return, I sit on the edge of the sofa while he pulls himself upright and makes himself comfortable.

A funny thought pops into my head. "Hmm, maybe I should get myself a little nurse's outfit."

He laughs, cocking an eyebrow. "I wouldn't bother. Sheila's totally destroyed any fantasy I may have had about that."

I can see why. Sheila's a natural comic with a very dry wit. Her strong personality and the fact that she isn't one to pussy foot around her patients, makes her very formidable. "Fair enough."

I watch him take his pills, frowning as each one goes down. I sense relying on his medication isn't enough for him. He's nervous of what he's capable of. So am I. But we haven't survived this far to give up now.

Cupping his face, I lean in for a kiss. "We'll get through this, Max. You and me together. You promised me forever, remember?"

His eyes sadden for a moment, all hope lost as they search mine. He's unsure, nervous. Questioning his ability to fulfil that promise. But I know he can. He has to. I won't let him give up.

"Right," I say, ignoring his anxiousness and planting a chaste kiss on the tip of his nose. "I'll order something to eat, what do you fancy?"

He hits me with his mega-watt smile. "You!"

"Obviously," I smirk. "But do you want fries with that?" Inelegantly scrambling up from the sofa, I look down at his grinning face. "No really, what do you want?"

"You. Hold the fries."

Rolling my eyes, I turn away. His warm hand smooths over my behind as I bend over to pick up my phone from the table, it makes me jump and giggle.

"Well, that's a sound we haven't heard around here for a long time."

We both look up at Cole striding into the lounge.

"Cole! I was just going to order something for dinner, what do you fancy? Pretty-boy here can't make up his mind."

Cole laughs. "Pretty boy? Oh, that's a keeper." Loosening his tie, he takes a seat in one of the leather chairs.

Max sits up throwing his brother the condescending eyebrow. "I don't know what you're laughing at, Sheila calls you Stud-Muffin."

Cole's eyebrows raise as he nods, happily contemplating his new handle. "I can live with that."

I sigh wearily, placing my hands on my hips as I wait for them both to answer me with their choices for dinner. But their banter continues with each of them trying to outdo the other's jovial quips. It's weird. They're identical twins, they both look exactly the same, but they obviously see each other very differently.

Throwing my hands in the air, I begin to march off to the kitchen. "Fine! I'm ordering mac n' cheese from Barney's, you'll just have to like it or lump it."

"Fine by me," they both say in unison.

Their conversation continues as I leave the room, it's mostly about work but it's nice to hear them talking. It's almost like they'd never been estranged at all. Cole seems much more relaxed too. After our conversation this morning, when he'd finally admitted his feelings for Monica had never died, I hoped it would be a turning point for him, where he could move on with his life. Only time will tell, but I understand why he hasn't been able to let her go.

When Max disappeared, and when I thought he was lost to me forever, I couldn't imagine a future without him. I knew in my heart I would never love anyone else. It's strange, all the logic and common sense in the world can't override what the heart wants.

As I plate up our food, Cole joins us in the kitchen fresh from his shower.

"Max, do you want a beer?" he asks, opening the fridge.

"Sure, why not?" Max places his hand on my thigh. It feels possessive, but it's also something I've missed very much.

Still leaning into the fridge, Cole turns to me. "Water, Vivienne?"

The prospect of drinking any more water brings a scowl to my face. "I'm beginning to feel like a bloody fish. I'm looking forward to wetting the babies' heads with a large glass of wine." My mouth begins to salivate at the thought of a cool, crisp, Pinot Grigio gliding across my taste buds. It's been a long time since I've been able to savour the qualities of a fine wine with my dinner. I miss it.

But as that delightful thought begins to fade, my mind begins to conjure pictures of me lying on a hospital bed with my feet in the stirrups, covered in sweat, screaming my head off. I swallow hard as my throat begins to tighten and a heated mist of perspiration floats over my skin.

So much has changed in my life recently, so much has happened. And there's still so much more to come. Child birth. Twice on the same day! Parenthood.

Today was the first time I had felt a definite movement from the babies. I'd had flutterings inside before, sometimes it would stop me in my tracks, but for all I knew it was just wind. But today, when I had felt the kick and Max had felt it too, it made me anxious.

Their physical growth and the fact that I could now feel them moving inside me seemed to bring them to life, making them real. More than just an image on a scan. My focus had been so distracted by Max's disappearance and the subsequent problems when he returned, but now the babies are front and centre. Motherhood is just a few short months away, and I'd be lying if I said it didn't frighten the crap out of me.

Max squeezes my thigh, pulling me out of my wide-eyed panic. "Everything okay?"

"Huh?" I stare up at him, his concerned eyes drifting over my face. "Oh, yes. I'm fine." Pushing my fork around my plate, I eventually attempt a mouthful, but I'm not hungry anymore.

"So, what's the P.O.A. now you're home?" Cole asks, reaching for his beer. His question is directed at Max and I'm grateful of his timely distraction. But Max doesn't answer, he's just staring down at his food. Something's worrying him, it's written all over his face.

"What do you mean?" I ask, taking up the reins.

Cole turns his attention to me. "Well, I mean, you can't sleep together, right?"

"Of course we can, he's on medication now." I look over to Max for agreement, but his face tells another story. The atmosphere has become thick with uncertainty and a silence has grown out of Max's hesitation. His eyes stay on his food as he pushes it around the plate.

"He's right," Max says, without looking up.

"What?" I ask, hating that look of defeat on his face. "But why?"

Raising his eyes to mine, the resignation in them, and the clench of his jaw says what I had feared. "You know why, Vivienne. And it's not up for debate. I'll be sleeping in the guest room until we know if these pills work."

There's a moment of silence as the elephant makes himself comfortable in the corner of the room.

"What about your sleep walking?" Cole asks, seemingly oblivious to the tension in the air. "Do we need to baby gate the top of the stairs?" He's smirking like it's all a big joke, but his insensitivity pisses me off.

I drop my fork down to my plate, the loud clink draws his attention. "Cole, if you don't have anything constructive to add, then just—"

He raises both hands in surrender. "My bad." To his credit he's no longer smirking. "Hey, I'm sorry. I'm just trying to think of all the variables, to keep us all safe. You don't want him falling out of a window, right?"

Cole's right. If Max starts wandering around in his sleep he could quite easily fall down the stairs. But if he's locked in his room overnight, surely that will just fuel his torment at not being able to find a way out. That would be like putting him back in the cell Monica had confined him to.

Max pushes his half-eaten plate away. "The pills should knock me out and stop me from sleep walking, but Sheila told me that I was still having nightmares. Even last night I had one, although she said it didn't seem as dramatic as the others."

His expression is full of woe. I know he's anxious at the prospect of repeating his behaviour now he's home.

I reach over and rub the back of his hand. "We'll just take it one step at a time."

He smiles, but it completely misses his eyes.

ADJUSTING

After dinner, which only Cole managed to finish, we retire to the living room where the boys enjoy a brandy. Cole brings Max up to speed on all the developments at work, and I sit and listen, until I tune them out and start to mull everything over in my head. With Max and my mother, there's a lot to think about.

"Is that alright with you, Vivienne?"

I suddenly realise Cole is staring at me waiting for my response. I had obviously zoned out for a moment and I have no idea how to answer that.

"...Sorry?"

"The G.T Corporation have asked Max to speak at their gala ball on Saturday. And they also want you to do their aerial shots to advertise the project... weren't you listening?" Cole asks, shaking his head at me.

"Sorry, I was just...When is it?"

"The gala's next week, but I've already spoken to Casper and the only day you have free for the aerial shots is tomorrow, but it's Sunday tomorrow, is that alright with you?"

"Um, yes, fine." I had no other plans, other than taking care of Max, so it won't make any difference to me. "But why aren't you giving the speech, it's too soon for Max to be worrying about fulfilling any public engagements, he needs to rest."

Cole's mood instantly changes, his eyes sliding from mine and falling to his fidgeting hands. "I won't be here," he murmurs softly. "I'm taking Monica's body back to the States for burial. Her service is on Sunday."

I could kick myself for not remembering. In all the time we've been home, I haven't once asked him about Daryl's trial or Monica's funeral. Judging by Max's expression he hasn't either, he looks as surprised as I am.

"I'm sorry, Cole. If there's anything we can do."

He exhales a deep sigh and forces a smile, then he rises from his seat rather abruptly. "I'm off to bed." He gives Max a sideways glance. "Sleep well, brother." Then he walks over to me, bending down to kiss me on the cheek. "Goodnight Vivienne. Sweet dreams." Pressing his soft lips against my cheek in a longer than necessary kiss, he then runs his fingers down the side of my face. I can feel Max's eyes on us the whole time.

Once we are alone, I snuggle into Max resting my head against his shoulder. "Do you want to take a bath before we go to bed? It might help you sleep."

"And have you naked right in front of me? What are you trying to do, kill me?"

I smile, leaning in to kiss him on the cheek. "Max, we can't spend the rest of our lives never seeing each other naked. *That* would kill *me*."

His concerned expression remains in place. It worries me that he's letting this dominate him.

"Look, Max, I know you're worried. I am too. But it's all in your mind. She's gone now. She can never hurt us again. You have to find a way to let it go."

"You think I don't want to let it go?"

"That's not what I meant… You've been deeply traumatised, you've had one week of therapy, and we've only spoken openly about it once. Maybe we should talk about it now."

"No," he says, adamantly, heaving a deep sigh. "I don't want to keep talking about it. It's bad enough that woman can ruin a good night's sleep, I don't want her in my head when I'm awake."

I know he doesn't want to talk about it and I can understand why, but my curiosity is piqued. When I found out Monica had wanted Max to make love to her, my initial reaction was jealousy and disgust. My brain had gone into a tail spin conjuring up all kinds of awful imagery. But then I began to wonder if it was more than just lust on her part. Was she trying to get Max to make her pregnant? He wanted nothing to do with her, but if she was the mother of his child, would he have wanted to protect her?

"Max, when she was trying to have sex with you—"

"Vivienne, please! I don't want to talk about it."

The finality in his voice halts my line of questioning, and the look on his face makes me feel bad for pushing him. As his eyes slide away from mine, his expression becomes cautious and I can feel the tension building in his body.

"Does he always kiss you like that?"

"Who?"

"Who do you think." The tone in his voice and the arrogant curve in his brow makes me pull back to fully appreciate his mood. "I've seen the way he looks at you, Vivienne. I don't like it."

A flurry of nervous butterflies enters my stomach. I don't want the brothers at loggerheads any more, especially not over me. "Max, Cole's been very good to me. He was my rock when you were gone, it was hard for both of us. You saw how affected he was about Monica's death. As cruel and messed up as she was, she got under his skin, and I don't think he's ever recovered from it. His feelings for me are just misplaced, that's all."

Max shakes his head, exhaling loudly, clearly unimpressed with my explanation. "I love my brother, and I promised my mom I would always look after him… But I don't trust him. Not with you. He's hated me since we were kids. He only married Monica to hurt me. And he has absolutely no fucking right to love you. You're mine, Vivienne. I won't let him do that to me again. Not with you."

I can see the pain and desperation in his eyes and I melt inside. "Max, you're wrong."

"Am I?" he says, on a sideways glare.

I smooth the worry furrows from his brow with my fingers and pull his moody face toward me so I can look him square in the eyes. "Yes, you gorgeously neurotic man. Completely wrong. Cole doesn't hate you, he admires you. He was jealous because you were so strong and independent and everything he wanted to be. He didn't marry Monica to hurt you, he was in love with her from the very beginning but you took her away from him. And Monica fucked him up because she knew how he felt about her, but she still chose you. She manipulated him. She manipulated you both to get what she wanted."

He looks at me with a dubious scowl, then he looks away, his brow sinking lower.

"And before you go getting your knickers in a twist, he may have said that he loves me, but he's never once overstepped the mark. He wouldn't."

Angry eyes fly up to mine. "He kissed you. I'd call that overstepping the mark, big time!" The uncertainty in his eyes makes my heart ache. I had wondered when this conversation would be resurrected. It shames me to know that I've hurt them both with my selfishness.

Holding his face between my palms, I wait for his sad blue eyes to meet mine. "Max, he kissed me because I kissed him first. I regret it with all my heart, but I was so desperate to hold on to you. I was falling apart. I thought I'd lost you forever and I couldn't bear it." Tears prick my eyes, but I hold them back. "I hurt him deeply that night because of that kiss. In a way, I had done to Cole what Monica had done to him all those years before. I used him to appease my aching heart, but he was vulnerable and grieving. If anyone over stepped the mark, it was me."

He flinches at my admission, it can't be easy for him

picturing Cole and I kissing. "At Charlie's funeral, he told me he hated her. Why the sudden change of heart?"

I ghost my fingers over the furrows in his brow. I don't want him doubting me or worrying about his brother. "Of course he hated her. He was in love with her but she picked you. Despite every terrible thing she's ever done, he hasn't got over her. And I know he feels guilty about that because of Charlie. It took you long enough to get her out of your system and you are way stronger than Cole is."

I can see him thinking it over and as his eyes soften and his body relaxes, I know he finally understands what I'm saying.

"Max, you've spent years avoiding each other, maybe it's time you two got reacquainted."

I can see the notion taking hold in his mind. I know it's not easy for Max to talk about his feelings, but if he and his brother are to move forward, they're going to have to air all their grievances.

We sit in silence for a while, both of us lost in our own private thoughts.

Max squeezes my shoulder dropping a kiss on the top of my head. "Come on, you need to get some sleep, you've got a busy day at work tomorrow." He kisses me chastely on the tip of my nose. I want to throw my arms around his neck and snog his face off, but I don't want him to go to bed with an erection when there's no prospect of us sleeping together. I hate the fact that we'll be in separate rooms, but we can't rush this, for both our sakes.

I stand and offer him my hand. Lacing our fingers together, he rises and we take a slow walk up the stairs.

At the top landing he stops, gazing down at me with warm, loving eyes. "It won't be like this forever," he whispers, kissing me lightly on the lips.

My body craves his touch, his scent alone is driving me wild. I rise to deepen the kiss, but when I feel him pulling back, I rein in my lust and drop back down to my heels, trying not to show my disappointment. I know this is hard for him, I don't want to make it any worse.

"I love you."

"Love you more, my beautiful temptress. And never forget, I'll always protect you, even if it's from me. No one will ever hurt you, Vivienne. No one. I'll kill anyone who tries."

My heart twists as his words sink in. A clear and absolute warning that if he hurt me again, he'd withdraw completely and I'd lose him forever.

He waits until I've closed my bedroom door before going to his room. It pains me to see him standing there alone. I can see he's nervous of what the night will bring, and I fear his recovery is going to take longer than I had hoped.

Lying in bed, staring up at the ceiling, I feel the familiar knot of dread tightening my chest. My phone vibrates on the bedside table. It startles me, until I see that it's Max calling.

"I just wanted to hear your voice before I go to sleep. I want my dreams to be only of you."

Tears pool in my eyes. "Oh, Max. I miss you." It sounds so ridiculous but it's how I feel. He's home, he's in the next room, and yet he feels a million miles away.

He chuckles softly then I hear him take a deep breath, exhaling a long, heartfelt sigh. "I miss you too, baby. Dream of me holding you, kissing you, gazing into your beautiful eyes. I want to see a big smile on your face in the morning."

A tear rolls down my cheek as a smile plays out across my lips. His velvety rasp begins to soothe me. "Sweet dreams, Max."

"You too."

He ends the call and as his face fades to black on the screen, I curl around his pillow praying and hoping we both sleep peacefully tonight.

A VEILED THREAT AND A TICKING CLOCK

"Morning, sleepy head. Time to get up."

I stretch, then peel my eyes open to the smiling face of my gorgeous boyfriend, gloriously naked from the waist up. My customary white rose is lodged between his teeth making me smile as my sleepy eyes trail lazily over his handsome face and magnificent chest. His bruises are almost gone with just the remnant smudges of purple dotted here and there, and his eyes seem to have regained their sparkle.

Placing a cup of tea on the bedside table, he sits on the edge of the bed gazing down at me with that familiar twinkle in his eyes. He looks decidedly happy, unusually so. A remarkable difference to how he looked last night.

I hadn't slept very well last night, I was on tenterhooks most of the time. I crept across the hallway to check on him several times, but each time he was fast asleep. His sheets looked undisturbed and he didn't even stir when I lay down with him for a few minutes stroking his hair. He looked so peaceful and relaxed, I wanted to stay there all night, but I knew I shouldn't take the chance, so I forced myself to go back to my own room.

Still half asleep and dazed by his handsomeness, I reach up

to take the rose from his mouth and smell the fragrant petals, then I curl around his pillow and gaze up at him breathing out a contented sigh. "How did you sleep?" I ask, yawning.

"Better than you by the look of it," he chuckles. "I slept very well, and I don't think I dreamt at all, at least I don't remember having any nightmares."

I sit up in a rush. "So, the pills are working?"

"It would seem so, yes."

Throwing my arms around his neck, I hug him tightly as tears fill my eyes.

"Hey, why are you crying?" He tries to peel me off him but I don't let him.

Burying my face in his neck, I strengthen my hold, sobbing like an idiot. "Oh, Max, I'm so happy. This means we can—"

"We'll see," he interrupts softly. I lean back a little miffed at his reticence. Swiping the tears from my eyes, I search his face and see his caution has returned in bucket loads. My elation completely vanishes when I realise I may have been jumping the gun. But regardless of his pessimism, this is good news and I'm grateful to hear it.

"Drink your tea," he says, peeling me off him with ease. "I've made you some breakfast and John is waiting for you downstairs to take you to work."

I sag when I remember I had agreed to work today. I'd rather stay home with Max and test out the other obstacles in our love life, but he's right, that will have to wait.

~

Grabbing a piece of toast, I kiss Max on the lips and rush out of the penthouse to meet John. He drives me to the airfield where Benny is waiting for me. My assignment today is at the G.T Corporation on the other side of town, which has its own heli-pad in the grounds of the thirty-two-acre site.

The G.T. building is very impressive. A round, modern, smoky glass and white steel structure, rising from the centre of a lake, joined by an ornate mosaic walkway. The lake is punctuated with small fountains and sculptures, and the surrounding gardens add an abundance of colourful decoration and texture.

We're met at the heli-pad by a woman who introduces herself as Rita. "Good morning, Miss Banks, I'm Rita. Welcome to the G.T. Corporation. We're so glad you could fit us in at such short notice." She shakes my hand, then gestures for me to go first. "Your work is very impressive, Miss Banks."

"Oh, please, call me Vivienne."

Her smiling eyes and soft Irish accent put me at ease straight away as she escorts me to the main building for a briefing with Brendan, the head of P.R.

Rita shows me to an office on the ground floor. The bright modern interior is very pleasant and spacious, it looks and smells very new, and the colourful mosaic floor design continues throughout. I take a seat in one of the white leather chairs gazing out at the fountains on the lake.

"Would you care for some tea or coffee?" Rita asks politely.

"No thanks, I'm fine."

When I left the penthouse this morning, Max had sent me off with a lunch box and a flask of tea. I laughed out loud when he patted me on the head and told me to play nice with the other kids. His good night's sleep had completely changed his demeanour and it was nice to see him so relaxed and happy.

As I wait for Brendan to show me around, I check my equipment.

"Miss Banks? I'm Brendan. Thank you for coming at short notice."

I rise, turning to face the voice behind me. Brendan is a tall slender man with a rather gangly appearance. "Hi. Please, call me Vivienne." We shake hands then Brendan informs me that only the exterior aerial shots are required today, which pleases me as it means I'll be home sooner than I thought.

Brendan walks with me back to the helicopter. "Miss Banks, once you've finished, if you could make your way back to the office before you leave, I'd appreciate it."

"Yes, certainly."

Brendan waits for me to enter the helicopter, then he closes my door. As Benny starts her up, the down force from the rotor blades almost blows the poor man away.

The morning weather has been kind to us, making it possible for me to take some great shots of the building, lake, and gardens. In no time at all we're back on the ground and I make my way back to the office I had met Brendan in before.

Rita is at her desk outside the office and moves quickly as I approach. She knocks, opens the door, then stands aside for me to enter. "He's expecting you," she says, with a smile.

"Ah, Vivienne. How nice to see you again."

His voice sends an arctic shiver up my backbone. I stumble to a halt, rooted to the spot as Rita closes the door behind me. *G.T. Corporation… Shit!*

As I stand face to face with Greg Taylor, I feel sick and lightheaded. His eyes are fixed on mine and the crooked smile on his face takes me hurtling back to the night he savagely ruined my childhood.

Because of him, I've spent the last fourteen years living with the thought that I would never be able to have children. For fourteen years I've battled with the nightmares and the guilt that somehow, what he had done to me, was my fault. I had let him get away with it. His threats and bullying had terrorised me, frightening me so much that I had kept his dirty little secret.

In the years that followed, I realised I should have said something. I was ashamed that I hadn't. He had probably done it again to some other young girl. He'd got away with it once, why wouldn't he? And now he has money and power, he's lived a good life by the look of things, all down to me not having the strength to point the finger at him.

But it's too late now. The consequences of outing him are too great. I lost that chance the moment I fell in love with Max.

The words Max spoke to me only last night, echo in my mind. 'No one will ever hurt you, Vivienne. No one. I'll kill anyone who tries'. My arms wrap tightly around my stomach in a defensive stance. I feel sick. I want to run away, but I know he's brought me here for a specific reason and photography certainly isn't it.

"What do you want?" I snap, failing to control the tremor in my voice and I flinch when he rises from his chair.

Rounding his desk, he walks toward me but he stops short, standing a few feet away from me with shrewd assessing eyes raking all over my body. With an arrogant smirk, he holds up his hands in a gesture of surrender. The cocky laugh and smug smile riles me as he backs up and moves to his desk, taking a seat on the corner of it. He gestures toward a chair beside his desk. "Please, sit down, Vivienne."

"I'll stand, thanks." My patience is wearing thin, there's only so much of this bastard I can stomach. The room is starting to feel very small and the air is tainted with his presence.

"Vivienne, I'm not going to beat around the bush. I know you don't like me—"

"Pff! I don't like Marmite. You! I loathe!"

He shrugs as if I've said something obvious. His irritating smile as he surveys me up and down makes me want to smash his face in.

Smug eyes land on mine, that smarmy smile of his getting wider. "I understand congratulations are in order. Max tells me you're engaged… and pregnant. He's smitten, he doesn't stop talking about you. Neither does Cole, for that matter."

His lecherous gaze disgusts me. Even breathing the same air as him, churns my stomach, making my hands clench into tight fists. The thought of Max and Greg even being in the same room together makes me feel sick.

"I don't need to listen to this." I turn to walk away, anger boiling my blood.

"Since I realised who you were, Vivienne, I've been reading up on you." I ignore him and keep moving toward the door, the sooner I can breathe some clean air the better. "You've turned into quite a woman. Your mother must be so proud."

It wasn't what he had said that made me stop in my tracks, it was the way in which he'd said it. It sounded like a threat.

I spin on my heel and glare at him. "You leave her alone."

He cocks his head, his expression of innocence fooling no-one. "I have no interest in your mother, Vivienne. Unless she starts shooting her mouth off." An arrogant smirk distorts his mouth. "I have some very interesting photographs of your mother. She really was quite the looker in her younger years, and so adventurous."

My heart stutters in my chest. Greg's voice is soft, almost kind in its delivery, but the threat inside those soulless eyes, betrays any kindness in his tone. And now, he has my full attention.

"I'm intrigued, Vivienne. You never told anyone, did you?. Even after we met at the charity dinner, you still kept your mouth shut. Max doesn't know, does he?"

My anxious silence answers his question. And when I lower my head, he laughs. I'm showing him weakness and I hate that. I hate the way he makes me feel. I hate the way he intimidates me.

"Well, well, well, Vivienne. Who would have thought you would be an ally."

With every ounce of will, I lift my head and fix him with a glare of contempt, but any animosity I'm trying to convey gets brushed aside by his broad and triumphant smile. A cold sweat crawls over my skin, creating goosebumps in its path.

His eyes narrow on me, that lecherous smile still set on his lips. "Oh, don't feel bad, Vivienne. You did the right thing keeping your mouth shut. Monica was quite the talker after a few drinks. I'm sure Max and his family wouldn't want his penchant for whips and razor blades to be made public. He's fought so hard to maintain his privacy and stories like that could really influence the markets. In today's business world, people can be so fickle."

I feel trapped, cornered. He's testing me. Threatening me because he's concerned that I'll tear down his empire by revealing his dirty little secrets to the world. I should. I want to. But I can't.

Clenching my teeth and fiercely struggling to hold back the

angry tears threatening my eyes, I take a deep breath. I have to swallow several times to keep the bile from rising in my throat. He's obviously thought this through and is fully prepared to use my mother and Max against me to keep my silence.

He stands abruptly, making me jump, his hard eyes penetrating mine, that smug smile wiped clean from his face. Now, all I see is his determination to win. To survive at any cost. "I know you'll do the right thing, Vivienne."

I feel so pathetic and weak. Inside, I want to scream and yell and gouge his fucking eyes out, but I just clutch my bags to my chest and quietly make my way to the door.

"Goodbye, Vivienne. Give Max and Cole my regards. Oh, and I look forward to seeing you at the gala on Saturday."

I freeze in my tracks. I had forgotten about the gala. There has to be a way we can get out of going, I never want to see this man again.

His smug chuckle slithers up my spine as I wrench the door open. Leaving it wide open, I march out of his office and head as quickly as my feet will take me, back to the helicopter. I want to run, I want to get away from him as fast as possible, but I concentrate on settling my breathing, trying to calm down before meeting up with Benny on the heli-pad. I can't let him see me like this.

"Mademoiselle?" Benny looks surprised that I have finished so quickly. "Are we done?"

"Oh, ah, yes. They've decided against doing the interiors for now."

He seems happy with that and without further ado, he hands me my headset and lifts off from the ground. I stare down at the building as we depart, my stomach churning, my mind full of worries.

John meets me at the airfield. He's also surprised to see us back so soon. After explaining the same to him, I ask him to take me to my mother's house. On the flight back to the airfield, I had a strong urge to see my mother. Somewhere in her jaded past, Greg had obviously taken advantage of her too.

He had loosely veiled the threat that he had in his

possession, some not so complimentary photographs of my mother. And it was crystal clear that Greg would go to any lengths to protect himself.

When I arrive at my mother's house, I let myself in. Cautious of what state I'll find her in, I gingerly call out to her. "Mum? It's only me."

"Vivienne, lovely to see you. I wasn't expecting you, is everything okay?"

I'm a little taken aback. She's dressed, clean and looks completely sober. The dark circles under her eyes and her sallow complexion make her look tired, but she seems well and happy.

Whether it's the sight of her, or the emotions of the morning bursting free, I pull her into a tight hug, sobbing into her neck.

"What's the matter?" Mum pulls me into the living room and sits me down. Taking my hand in hers, she sits beside me. "What is it? Is it the babies?"

"No." I take the tissue she hands me and dry my tears. "Oh, Mum… I just met Greg Taylor. He threatened me to keep my mouth shut about what he did, and I didn't want to go home yet. I can't tell Max, he'll do something stupid, I know he will. Why can't he just leave us alone."

Fresh tears stream down my face as my mother pulls me into a motherly hug, something I've missed. Something I desperately need.

"Oh, darling, you can't let him win. Just put him out of your mind and don't give him one more minute of your time. That bastard should be fucking castrated."

Mum rocks me in her arms and then hands me some more tissues, patiently waiting for me to stop crying.

"He says he has pictures of you…" I nervously glance up at her. The look on her face worries me. "Oh, god! He was telling the truth?"

"Never mind about that," she says harshly, clenching her jaw and twisting her fingers in her lap. "He can't hurt me now, and I don't want you worrying about me."

It all falls into place. When I found out that Mum had known it was Greg who had raped me, I thought she'd kept her silence because he had beaten her up that night, but now I realise, he has something else over her. Something bad enough to keep her mouth shut.

Rising from the sofa, she walks to the window and lifts a framed photograph from the window sill. She gazes at it lovingly. "You were such a beautiful child… That bastard needs to pay for what he's done." She bursts into tears. "I'm so sorry. I should have protected you, I should have been a better mother. Christ, I should have—"

"Mum, don't. Please. What's done is done." I stand behind her and wrap my arms around her frail, trembling body. Resting my chin on her shoulder, I gaze down at the photograph of me in her hands.

"Christ!" she sniffles. "I could really use a drink right now."

My heart slumps. She's struggling. How she's stayed sober I'll never know. This is so out of character for her to have lasted this long.

"How are you coping?"

She snorts out a laugh. "Good days and bad days, mostly bad. One day at a time." She pulls out of my hold and places my photograph back on the window sill. Turning to face me she takes both my hands in hers and a hard expression darkens her face. "Don't you worry about Greg Taylor. He'll get what's coming to him, you mark my words."

I nod, but I don't share my mother's optimism.

She squeezes my hands, her eyes glistening. "Just concentrate on Max and my grandchildren. I can't change the past, Vivienne. I wish I could, but your future is all that matters. I want you to be happy. God knows you deserve it after everything I've put you through."

Pulling her into my arms, I hug her tightly and my tears return. Time is running out for us. I've missed my mother all these years, it feels like I've just got her back but now the clock is ticking.

I spend a couple of hours with Mum, talking and even

laughing occasionally. We've never been able to talk like this before. Mum has never been sober before. She takes a keen interest in my work and my friends, and it really feels like we have finally connected again.

I try to convince her to take the doctor's advice and begin her course of chemo, but she's adamant. She doesn't want any treatment, and as much as it pains me, I have to let her make her own choices. The fact that she's sober means her mind is clear enough to be able to make those choices. And I have to respect that.

Just before I leave, she asks me if we've made any wedding plans. I begin to realise that if we don't make our plans soon, my mum may not be around to see me get married. I had never given it much thought before, but now, I so desperately want her to be there, and I want her to see her grandchildren too.

TRUST AND RECONCILE

John is waiting for me to take me home. "Everything okay, Ma'am?"

I smile up at him as he opens my door. "Yes… Yes, everything's fine."

Having spoken with my mother, the worries of my meeting with Greg have all been locked away. Mum's right, wasting time on him is a futile exercise that will get me nowhere. Because of his connection to Max I'm going to have to learn to live with his proximity, but I can still avoid him, and I will.

I enter the penthouse to the smell of roast chicken which makes my belly groan with hunger. I had lost my appetite for my packed lunch after I'd met with Greg, so I haven't eaten since breakfast.

Rounding the doorway to the kitchen, I see Max peeling some potatoes. I stand there for a moment just smiling at him. I didn't think he could cook.

He looks up, giving me that heart-stopping smile. "How did it go?"

I dump my bags and walk over to him. "They only wanted exteriors, so I finished early and then I went to see my mother."

He wipes his hands and opens his arms for me. I walk into

his chest, careful not to squeeze his ribs too tightly. His scent and the warmth of his body chasing away all the anxiety of this morning.

"How is she?" he asks, nuzzling my neck with his soft lips.

"She's okay, still sober… But…"

He pulls back, lifting my chin to raise my line of sight. "What? What is it?" His loving eyes search my mine.

"I'm just worried she won't live long enough to see me get married and meet her grandchildren."

"She still won't take the treatment?"

I sigh shaking my head, trying to look away as the tears prick my eyes, but Max cups my chin in his hand tilting my head back, then he kisses me softly on the lips.

"Vivienne, if there's anything I can do to help, you know I'll do it."

I gaze up at him, marvelling at the sincerity in his eyes. Rising onto my toes, I pull him down to me for a kiss. A deep, possessive, needful kiss. And as he tightens his arms around me, it evolves into a full on exchange of lips and tongues, giving and taking as our passion unfurls. His kisses cure everything.

"There is something you can do," I whisper, against his lips.

"Anything."

He takes my mouth again but I break the kiss and pull him with me toward the door. "Take me to bed."

Planting his feet, he halts me with him. The anxiousness in his eyes makes my heart clench.

"I need you, Max. I want your hands on me. I need to feel you inside me. I've missed you. Please. Take me to bed." I see the hunger in his eyes and the need pouring out of him. "Please, Max."

"What if—"

I lift my fingers to his lips to silence him. "Please."

As his body relaxes and his eyes scorch me to my core, I pull him with me and this time, although hesitantly, he comes with me.

We're already undressing each other on our way up the stairs, fumbling and tugging at each other's clothing. My belly is full of butterflies and my heart is pounding in my chest. I'm fully aroused and eager to get him naked as quickly as possible.

As we barge through the bedroom door still lip locked and stumbling, I kick off my shoes then I help him pull his t-shirt over his head, careful not to let him twist his ribs too much.

He's still unable to use his left hand properly, so I tug at his jeans and drag them down his legs, then I stand there in awe of his male nakedness. Our eyes greedily trace over every bare inch of each other. Gazing at me like it's the first time he's ever seen me naked, his eyes lovingly caress my skin.

His fingers, although a little shaky, hesitantly reach out and drag softly down my cheek. With his now hooded eyes following the movement, he trails those soft fingers down my throat, and then down to my breast squeezing the nipple between his fingers. Bending down, he runs his hot tongue over my other nipple, sucking and rolling it between his teeth as my fingers go to town in his hair.

My body is on fire. His touch sends a pulse to my sex and electric shocks all over my heated skin. Threading my fingers through his hair, I close my eyes as my head rolls back. Sensory overload has made me wet, my body aches for his touch.

His soft lips travel down to my bump, where he kisses my belly before taking me in his arms to kiss me hard on the lips. His cock is pulsing between us as I throw my arms around his neck and drag him toward the bed. I can feel him resisting me, and way before I'm ready, he breaks the kiss, pulling away from me.

I open my eyes to see the worry in his brow. "It's okay," I whisper, reaching up to stroke my fingers down his chest, then I lean in to kiss his M.F. tattoo. "Max, it's okay. You won't hurt me... I need you."

The conflict in his eyes makes me sad, but I can't let Monica control him like this. I won't let her do it.

"Wait here."

I quickly dart past him and head to the dressing room. When I find what I'm looking for, I return to the bedroom but stumble to a stop when I see him sitting naked on the edge of the bed with his head in his hands. He's given up. He has no faith in himself not to repeat his violent acts. He's letting Monica control him even after her death. But I won't. He's mine, and I'll fight for him if I have to.

"Okay soldier. On your back, you have a job to do, and I won't take no for an answer."

His eyes swing up to mine, his shocked expression beginning to morph into a big smile, even his eyes twinkle. It was exactly what I needed to see.

He laughs, shaking his head. "What are you doing?"

I twirl the handcuffs around on one finger and pull down the visor on my crash helmet. I know how ridiculous I must look standing naked, wearing a big black crash helmet, but there's no way I'm leaving this bedroom without having sex with my boyfriend. Nope. Uh-uh. Never going to happen.

I walk toward him with a grinning smile, then raise my visor so I can talk to him. He's staring up at me in stunned amusement.

"Lie back."

It's a command, not a request. And to my surprise, he does so with a big smile on his face and a hardening cock pulsing against his stomach.

"Woman! You are a crazy, gorgeous, beautiful, human being, and I love the fuck out of you, do you know that?"

"Ditto, Mr. Foxx. Now, do as you're told." I rattle the cuffs in front of him. With a broad beaming smile he does exactly what I want without question.

Wincing at the pain in his ribs, and without me having to direct him, he slowly raises both arms up above his head, then I cuff his hands to the wrought iron headboard. The cuff almost doesn't close over his wrist wrap, but he doesn't wince or make a sound as it eventually snaps closed around it.

"Baby, I hope you have a key for these, Vinnie isn't due home until tomorrow."

With a cheeky smirk, I show him the small silver key, then I pop it on the bedside table. "I got these from Nova, she said we could keep them."

Although I'm being jovial and trying my hardest to keep things fun, I constantly check his face for any sign that things are going tits-up. So far, so good.

"I won't need this anymore," I chuckle, pulling the crash helmet off my head. I rest it on the bedpost and ruffle my fingers through my hair. Gazing down at his dreamily gorgeous body, I take a moment to fully appreciate his nakedness. "Max, if you deny me this body any longer, I'll go crazy."

He smiles, and the look in his eyes as they trail up and down the length of me, makes me feel very sexy and corny as hell. I've missed that look and those gorgeous eyes. He has a way of caressing my skin with his eyes. My clit is pulsing with need, my nipples contracting into tight, hard buds. We've been apart for far too long.

Straddling his body, I crawl up and kiss him softly on the lips. I stroke my tongue over them gently at first, then plunge it deep in his mouth, my moans of pleasure intermingling with his.

Before I lose all control, I lean my forehead against his. "Max, if at any time I do something wrong, or you feel uncomfortable, you've got to tell me. Promise me." He nods in response. I pull back so I can see his eyes. "I mean it, Max, anything at all. I need to know." He nods again as his hooded, glazed eyes sink back down to my lips.

"God, you turn me the fuck on. Your body drives me crazy."

I kiss him again, harder this time. The feel of his tongue gliding over mine and the feel of his silken skin beneath my fingers triggers all my senses. I miss the feel of his warm hands gliding across my skin, and the weight of his strong arms crushing me to him, but if this is how it has to be for us to connect then so be it.

My lips trail a leisurely path down his throat, chest, and abdominals. I check his face every few moments. His eyes are on me the whole time, his body writhing and luxuriating in the attention, but I see nothing as a warning. Only pleasure.

His breathing deepens as I hover above his twitching cock. Butterflies swirl around in my belly as I lick my tongue up the length of him from balls to tip. Taking him in my hand, I stand his cock up, checking his face once more. His eyes are closed, making me hesitate for just a moment.

With a deep breath, I lower, taking him in my mouth, sucking and licking as I pump his cock in my firm grip.

"Fuck!" he hisses. "That feels so good." He groans a deep, low growl, pushing his head back into the pillow, his hands flexing and fisting as the sensations take him over. Without pause, but still watching his face, I continue, feeling the head of his cock expand in my mouth.

"Take off the cuffs." His voice is urgent, deep, and raspy. "Please, baby. Take off the cuffs. I need to touch you. I need to feel you." His eyes are open, blazing with heat and trained on mine.

After a moment's hesitation, I reach over for the key and crawl up his body to unlock his cuffs. As soon as he's free, ignoring the pain in his ribs, he flips me onto my back. Resting on his forearms, his face inches from mine, his scorching blue gaze searches my eyes with a hunger so deep he takes my breath away.

"Don't ever stop, baby… Whatever it is you do to me. Don't ever stop." He devours my lips in a passionate, possessive kiss, igniting all my senses at once. I almost have an orgasm at the intensity of it.

Breaking the kiss on a lustful moan, he gazes into my eyes like he's seeing me for the first time. "It's my turn to take care of you now, baby. I'm going to make you feel all the things you've been missing. I'm going to worship you like never before. And after I'm done. I'm going to make you come until you scream out my name and beg me to stop."

My glazed eyes gaze up at him, mesmerised and sated by his words alone. And when I gaze into those crystal blues and lose myself inside them, I know I'm safe. I know I'm loved.

He's back. My fearless, gorgeous, confident lover is back in all his greatness. Back in my bed, back in my life. Strong and powerful in mind and body. Defeated no more by the ghosts of his past. And I love him for finding his way home.

With achingly slow patience, his lips tenderly nip and lap their way down every inch of my body, lovingly torturing me with his fingers and insanely wicked tongue. Finally arriving between my thighs, he nudges them apart with his broad shoulders and nestles between my legs.

The first stroke of his hot tongue against the erotic bundle of nerves in my over stimulated clit, sends shuddering sparks through my body, making me gasp and claw at the sheets. When he begins to feast on me, I reach down threading my fingers through his hair as his tongue wages the sweetest attack on my vulnerable bud. Within moments he brings me to an earth shattering climax. Calling out his name, on a series of moans, my body arches and bucks as all the raw, erotic sensations ripple out from my core.

He slows, bringing me down from my high, smothering me in tender kisses all the way back up to my lips.

"Good girl," he whispers, kissing me softly. The scent of my arousal is heavy on his lips.

I wrap my legs around his hips and feel the head of his cock nudge at my throbbing opening then it sinks deep inside me as he hisses out a deep, primal groan. "Fuck!, that feels so good."

My muscles contract around him, my hips arching up to the wickedly hot sensation of his powerful body riding mine. If Max was going to lose it now, I had no hope of defending myself. I can't even keep my eyes open, the feelings are too strong, too perfect.

"Open your eyes, baby."

I do as I'm asked, and if ever there was proof of his love, proof that he'd never hurt me, it's right there in his eyes.

His slow luxurious strokes bring me closer to another orgasm as his scorching eyes feast on my face. "Marry me," he whispers softly.

I gasp, and now my eyes are fully open. "You already asked me, and I already answered." I thread my fingers through his hair, pulling him down to me for a kiss. His skillful moves and the look on his face have taken me past the point of no return. Writhing underneath him, I struggle to keep my eyes open.

"I need to hear you say it. Marry me, Vivienne. Be mine forever."

I hold his face between my palms as his hips continue to drive into me. "With all my heart and forever, yes."

His smile makes my heart ache then he ups his game tipping me over the edge as I claw at the sheets and cry out his name when another more powerful orgasm takes me over. With a low, primal growl rumbling in his chest, he buries his face in my neck shuddering as his body indulges in his own powerful release.

Lying on my back with Max's head resting on my boobs, I run my hands along the deep scars on his back while he circles his fingers over my belly. I'm nervous to ask him. I didn't see a flicker of hesitation this time, but I can't ignore the possibility that Max may have been covering up what he was really feeling inside.

"Max?... You seemed okay this time... are you?"

He lifts his head, looking me straight in the eye with his heart-stopping smile. "I'm more than okay. I'm with you." Reaching up with his strapped hand, he runs his thumb over my lips, his eyes dancing all over my face..

"And what about your ribs? I saw you wincing several times."

"Yeah, they're still a bit sore, but worth the pain." Kissing me softly on my breast, he pulls back with a confused frown. "So, tell me. Were the crash helmet and cuffs one of the ingenious ideas you were talking about?"

I nod with a smug smile.

"Awesome, you're very resourceful, Miss Banks. I can see a use for the cuffs in the future, but the crash helmet? Not so much."

We both giggle then he leans up on his elbow to kiss me. "I

love you, Miss Banks."

"I love you more, Mr. Foxx."

I begin to wrap my arms around his neck to lock him in for round two, until I get a whiff of something burning. "Max, can you smell that?"

"Shit! The chicken."

I pinch my lips together to stifle a giggle. He's burnt the dinner. Grabbing the sheet from the bed, I wrap it around me to go and investigate, while he hops around the bedroom trying to put his pyjama bottoms on with one hand.

As I pad into the kitchen, Cole is wafting a tea towel around to clear the smoke. He eyes my sheet and ruffled hair with surprise, then his eyes widen further when Max walks in semi naked behind me, wrapping me in his arms and kissing my neck.

Cole scowls at us with a clenched jaw. "What the fuck are you doing?"

I glance up at Max unsure of the hostility in Cole's voice.

Max squeezes me a little tighter, glaring at his brother. "None of your business."

A blush of embarrassment heats me all over. "Cole, it's okay, it's fine, Max is over it now." This feels decidedly awkward.

Cole's hurt eyes slide away from mine as he throws the tea towel onto the side. "Dinner's fucked!" he grates, stalking out of the kitchen.

Max nuzzles my neck, tightening his arms around me. "What's with him?"

"Max… can you give me a minute. I need to speak to Cole."

He doesn't say anything, but I sense Max is irritated with his brother's interest in me. As much as I don't want Cole to waste his feelings on me, I can't ignore the fact that I'm rubbing his nose in it. "Please. I won't be a minute."

Max slowly releases me from his arms and kisses the top of my head, then begrudgingly leaves me and wanders back upstairs.

Heaving in a deep breath, I tighten the bed sheet around me and pad out to the living room. I can see Cole out on the terrace looking forlorn and dejected. My heart sinks as I walk over to him.

"Mind if I join you?"

He shrugs but doesn't look at me. He's leaning over the edge of the balcony staring down at the city below.

"Cole, I'm sorry. I know you're worried about me, and I love you for that, I really do. Without you I would never have made it through these last few weeks."

He spins around to face me, his eyes are teary and sad. "I do worry about you. Jesus, Vivienne. What if he attacks you again, what if I'm not here to protect you?"

Closing the distance between us, I reach my hand up, softly running my fingers down his flawless, tearstained cheek. The look on his face melts me inside. "It's not your job to protect me. That's Max's job, and he's doing everything he can to make it right."

His sad eyes soften as he leans into my hand. Taking it from his cheek, he kisses my palm, then holds it between both of his. "You really love that fucked-up asshole, don't you."

I can only nod in response, my throat is too tight as my own tears begin to flow.

"He's a lucky guy."

"I am… Very."

We both turn to see Max walking out to the terrace. His expression is unreadable but his eyes are firmly fixed on Cole. Walking right up to me, he wraps his arm possessively around my shoulders, still with an impassive expression and yet, I can feel the crackle of tension in the air.

"Cole, you're my brother and I love you, but you're walking on thin ice. I'm sorry if you—"

"No." Cole interrupts. "You're right... I'm the one who should apologise." He drops my hand and looks his brother in the eyes. "I should never have blamed you for our parents' death, I know that now. I've known it for a long time. I was stupid and jealous, and I know I can't take it back, but I'm sorry."

I'm surprised at Cole, I hadn't sensed he was ready to face up to his responsibilities yet. But Max hasn't uttered a single word. I glance up at him but I still can't read what he's feeling, he's giving nothing away on his face.

Cole's jaw is clenching madly as he drags a hand through his hair. And I'm shocked at how emotional he seems. Lifting his chin, he takes a breath, his eyes now nailed on Max. "After the crash, those eight weeks you were in the hospital all banged up and broken, everyone was talking about you. 'Poor Max,' like you were the only one suffering. I felt cheated, left out, and so fucking alone. I had lost everything. Everyone I had ever loved, disappeared." His voice is breaking with emotion and he has to take a moment to compose himself. Max remains silent. Impassive.

"By the time you came out of the hospital, I was already in foster care and I hated it. I wanted to go home, I wanted my mom and dad back. I wanted my brother back." He takes a hard swallow. This is really hard for him. It's hard to hear.

"But you were so distant, so isolated. I felt so ashamed, but I couldn't stop myself from hating you. You left me. You just closed yourself off and left me on my own."

Tears prick my eyes as a lump jumps into my throat. Cole's confession is so emotional, so raw, it hurts to see him this way. Max never breaks eye contact with his brother, but I still can't gauge what he's thinking, how he's feeling. He seems so impassive, almost apathetic.

Cole is struggling to speak, and tears well up then spill over his lashes. "Fuck!" he blurts, his fists clenching at his sides. "You shut me out, Max! I needed you. I fucking needed you but you shut me out. You were all I had but you wouldn't talk. You didn't speak for two years. Two fucking years!"

Max suddenly grabs Cole by the collar of his shirt, and fiercely pulls him into a tight, brotherly hug. They both have tears in their eyes, and I see Max wincing at the pain of Cole's arms swinging around his body and squeezing him in a desperate, long overdue embrace. It hurts me to see the pain and sadness on both their faces, but this is what they need. They need to talk. They need to reconnect.

Leaving them to it, I quietly head upstairs.

CUPID'S LITTLE HELPER

As I'm first up, I take a quick peek into Max's room before heading down to make breakfast. Much to my disapproval, Max wouldn't sleep with me last night. Although we'd successfully conquered having sex while he was awake, he was still nervous that he would have a nightmare and attack me in his sleep.

It hurts to sleep alone knowing he's only yards away, and I pray this hold Monica still has over him will soon be gone, for all our sakes.

We had a late night last night. Max and Cole spent most of it talking. I was pleased to see them patching up their strained relationship, and at one point, Cole poured his heart out about Monica, bringing us all to tears. The brothers share a sensitive nature, but it would appear Monica had hurt Cole far worse than she'd ever hurt Max.

By the time she had shown her true colours it was too late. The brothers were not only living on two different continents, they'd also cut all ties with each other, so everything Cole revealed last night was news to Max.

We raked over every little detail of Max's abduction, it was both painful and cathartic. His distress was clearly etched on his face as I recounted all the things I had gone through after he had been abducted. He was especially annoyed that I had lied about the scars on my wrists. I'd forgotten about those.

It surprised me, but even Max came clean about the horrors he'd been subjected to during his captivity. Cole seemed physically shaken by Max's account of the things Monica had done to him.. And I found it hard to listen to, even though I had heard some of it before at our session with Doctor Fielding.

By the end of the evening we were all emotionally drained. But it was a step forward, a much needed time of bonding for them, and a weight off my shoulders now that Cole seemed to understand his place in our lives.

I'm so relieved we can all move forward. I love Cole, I'll never forget his kindness, and I'll always be grateful of his support in my darkest hour.

~

Once I've burnt the toast and hard boiled the eggs, I run upstairs to wake the boys.

"Morning, Pretty-boy."

Peeling his eyes open, his sleepy blues land on mine as he takes a tentative stretch, careful not to twist his ribs. His warm hand lands on my thigh, pushing up under my skirt to find the lace tops of my stockings. My usual reaction to his touch fires up my already overheated skin. Just seeing him naked in bed is a treat for the eyes and an aphrodisiac for my libido.

"You're dressed. Where are you going?" he mumbles, still half asleep.

"I'm going to work. Jan and Vinnie should be home today, so I'll pop in at lunchtime to say hello. Eat your breakfast." I point to the unappetising tray of overcooked offerings, cringing at my ineptitude. "Like I said, Jan is back today, so you won't have to put up with my terrible cooking anymore. Not that yours was any better yesterday. I mean, I've heard of Coronation chicken, but that was more like cremated chicken. We should have said some words and scattered its ashes in the garden of remembrance."

I lean down to kiss him on the lips. As he overpowers me

with his luxurious kiss, he pushes his hand further up my thigh, grazing his fingers over my silky undies. The heated stroke sends a pulse through my blood tempting me to stay home and appease the aching need only he can satisfy. But knowing I have a busy morning, I unwillingly drag myself away from his gorgeous lips.

"You're a very bad man," I smirk, trying to catch my breath.

He grins. "I hope so."

As unwilling as I am to leave him, I head downstairs to fetch Cole's breakfast, but he's already throwing it into the bin when I wander into the kitchen. He looks embarrassed that I've caught him out.

"Mmm-mmm," he says, way over the top. "That looked delicious, but I ate a couple of days ago."

I smile and grab my coat from the back of the chair. "I know my cooking's dreadful so there's no need to make excuses. And you'll be glad to hear Jan is home today."

"Thank God!" he says, way too enthusiastically. "Sorry," he smirks. "It's not that you're a bad cook, Vivienne. It's that you're a *really* bad cook."

"Yeah," I giggle, "I know."

Cole walks me out to the lift.

"Are you okay?" I ask, hesitantly. Last night was quite an emotional evening for all of us.

"Yeah, I'm fine. Really." His warm smile and sparkling eyes back up his statement. I'm glad, he deserves to be happy.

After dropping Cole off at his floor, I continue down to mine. As I wander through the reception area to my office, I see Casper laughing and giggling with a gorgeous beauty who has the most remarkable eyes. She's about my height, slender, with a light caramel skin, light brown curly hair, and pale hazel eyes, just like Casper's. He beckons me over to him.

"Vivienne. You're just in time, this is Hannah, my sister."

"Sister? You kept her quiet, Casper. I never knew you had a sister."

"Oh, well, I've only just come back to London," she smiles,

"I've been studying in Italy and now I'm home to open my new office." She offers me her hand.

"Italy? Wow. What do you do?"

"I'm an architect."

"You must let me know when you need any publicity shots, I'm very good at photographing tall buildings."

"Yes, I heard. Casper's told me all about you."

He nods excitedly in the background. He's clearly very proud of his sister.

"And where is your office?"

"Right here in the Foxx-Tech building, floor ten. I'm not fully operational yet, but I should be up and running in a week or so."

"Great. We'll have to meet up for lunch."

"I'd like that," she smiles. "I don't know anyone in London except for Casper."

"Oh, really? No boyfriend? Husband?...Girlfriend?"

"No," she giggles, "I've been too engrossed in my work to worry about things like that. Besides, I've been waiting for the right man to blow me away and curl my toes. It hasn't happened yet. One day my prince will come." She sighs, smiling her radiant smile. I can't stop looking at her eyes, they are beautiful. She's stunning and obviously very smart.

~

The morning goes by in a flash. Ed and I worked flat out to get everything up to date.

"These are nice." Ed says, looking at the photographs I had taken at the G.T. Corporation yesterday. A shudder bumps up my spine remembering Greg's comments, and I hate the fact that he can still make me feel so vulnerable even after all these years.

Checking my watch, I close my laptop and grab my bag. "Right, I'm heading upstairs for lunch. Jan and Vinnie are home today."

"Good," he smirks. "I guess we can tell the fire department to stand down now that you won't be cooking anymore."

I launch the eyebrow. It would appear my rubbish cooking

skills are famous around these parts.

"You're welcome to join us for lunch if you want."

"Thanks, but I'm meeting Nova in town."

I smile and waggle my eyebrows, their relationship is definitely blossoming.

As I pass Casper's desk, I lean up against it and wait for him to finish his call.

"Everything okay, Vivienne?"

"Yes, I'm just heading up to see Jan and Vinnie. Um, was that your sister on the phone?"

"Yes, she's so excited about her new venture, she's been calling me all morning."

"Do you think she'd mind if I pop in to see her?"

"Are you kidding? She'd be delighted."

The reception area to Hannah's office is unmanned and full of empty boxes. I can hear her humming along to a Shawn Mendes track at full volume through an open door, so I wander through to find her.

Hannah's office is beautiful, although, some of her furniture is still in bubble wrap. Her eye for design and colour is stunning. As I knock loudly on her open door she stops humming and spins around to face me, looking surprised to see someone standing in her office.

"Hi, Casper said it would be okay to come and see you, I hope you don't mind."

"No, not at all. Come in. It's a bit of a mess but please, have a seat." She scoops some files off one of the chairs gesturing for me to sit down.

"Wow, this place is amazing. I love the colours you've chosen."

The soft, golden, earthy tones and rich, luxurious fabrics really blend, and I can see her Italian inspiration throughout the decor.

"It's getting there," she sighs, taking a seat on the corner of her Ivory coloured, hand carved desk. Even without makeup, dressed in sweatpants and with her hair loosely bundled on top of her head, she looks stunning.

We chat about our work, my pregnancy, and the usual girlie stuff, and I realise fairly soon that we're going to get along very well. Lucy will love her. Hannah's sense of humour and sociable personality give us all a lot in common. And she's no air head either, her looks don't mean a thing to her.

Realising the time, I stand up and hand her my empty cup. "Thanks for the tea. I'd better go, I'm meeting family for lunch."

"Thanks for coming down to see me, it's nice to have a new friend in town."

An idea suddenly pops into my head. "Hey, why don't you and Casper come to dinner tomorrow night?"

She looks surprised at first, then beams a warm smile. "Yes, that would be nice."

"Great. Eight o'clock at the penthouse. I'll see you later."

On my way to the lift I text Cole.

Keep tomorrow night free.
Don't worry... I won't be cooking!
Viv
X:-)

He replies straight away.

In that case, great!
C
;-]

UNFRIENDLY FACE

Even before I open the penthouse door, I can smell something divine coming from inside. Jan, Vinnie, and Max are all seated in the kitchen, laughing and talking, and as soon as she sees me walking in, Jan rushes over to give me a big hug.

"It's so nice to see you."

"You too, I've missed you guys." It's so good to have them home again.

Jan looks me all over, her eyes glistening, her smile wide and heartfelt. "You look so well, Vivienne. You both do."

The last time Jan had seen either of us was in the hospital when Max fist came home. We both looked in need of a little tender loving care back then.

Seeing my heart-shaped locket, her eyes widen and with a warm smile and a shake of her head, she sighs. "It looks so beautiful on you, Vivienne. I knew he wouldn't be able to wait until the wedding to give you this."

"Yes," I smirk, "he is a little impatient."

Vinnie wanders over to give me a bear hug, almost squishing me in the process. "It's good to see you, Miss." When he releases me from his crushing hold he takes my hands. I notice him looking down at the faded scars on my wrists, then he gives me a knowing look. I suspect Max has brought them both up to speed on all the latest news since they've been away.

After Max has given me a cuddle, Jan sits me down to a lovely home cooked meal telling me all about their time in Scotland. Max leaves his hand on my thigh the whole time while he and Vinnie chat about guy stuff.

Once we've eaten I help with the dishes. "Jan, would it be okay to have a small dinner party here tomorrow evening? I'd offer to cook but no one would come."

"Certainly, how many?"

"Including you and Vinnie, seven."

"Oh, you're inviting us? Thank you, that would be wonderful."

"Of course, I've missed you guys and we've got so much to catch up on."

She looks touched, almost tearful. "What's the occasion?"

"Actually, there's someone I'd like Cole to meet, so it's kind of a blind date."

She smiles and winks. "Say no more."

"Baby?" Max rises from his seat with his hand stretched out for me. He walks me through to the living room and pulls me into his lap, nibbling my earlobe. "How was your day at work?"

For a moment, I'm too intoxicated to answer. His lips are a taunting pleasure that should never be interrupted by conversation.

"Baby?" he prompts on a chuckle.

I lean back to gaze into his loving eyes. "Max, you know I can't think straight let alone speak when you romance me like that."

His lips tip up into a roguish grin. "Don't forget, we've got the gala on Saturday, if you need a new dress, call Davis."

Shit! I had forgotten about that. I don't want to see Greg again, just thinking about him makes my blood boil. "Do we really have to go?"

"Don't you want to go?" he asks, brushing my hair away

from my face. I try to think of a reasonable excuse but I can't think of anything plausible.

"No. Yes. I suppose. But isn't it a little too soon to be worrying about things like that. I mean, are you well enough to put yourself through that?"

His soft fingers trace a delicate path down my cheek as his eyes gaze lovingly into mine. "You're always worrying about me. That's one of the many things I love about you."

I blush, it wasn't really him I was thinking about this time.

His eyes do their worst, lulling me into a state of lust. His kiss seals the deal rendering me wanton and needy. I always want to rip his clothes off and ravage him when he kisses me like that.

I realise I haven't asked him how he slept last night. I don't think I can take another night sleeping alone. "Did you have any more nightmares last night?"

"No. Not that I remember. Those pills seem to be working."

"So, do you think we can start sleeping together again? I hate this separation, don't you?"

His brow furrows. "Yeah, it sucks. But it's only been two days, we need to be sure that—"

"Max, I trust you." I really do trust him. Taking his face in my hands, looking deep into his eyes, I remember something my mother told me recently. "Max, don't let her take one more minute of your time. She's gone. She can't hurt us anymore. I trust you, and I love you, so much. I've missed you."

Love pours from his eyes as he leans in and rests his forehead against mine. "Me too. Love you more, baby."

"More than I love you?"

He leans back and smiles, soft fingers now stroking my cheek. "No, baby. I don't mean it like that. I mean, I love you more than the last time I said it."

My heart stutters and I become tearful. He floors me with every gesture, every golden word.

Lifting my chin with his finger, he gains eye contact. "Hey, what is it, baby?"

"You say the most romantic things."

"Only because they're true." He takes my lips with a soft, tender kiss.

Jan's polite cough intrudes on our moment. "I'm sorry, Vivienne. Did you want to prepare a menu for tomorrow evening's dinner party, or would you like me to take care of it?"

"Oh, yes please, whatever you think, whatever is easiest for you."

"Very good. Your evening meal is in the fridge, I'll see you both in the morning."

"Thanks, see you tomorrow. And Jan… it's good to have you home."

She smiles, blushes, then winks at me cheekily as she turns to leave.

When I turn back to Max, he's looking at me quizzically. "Are we entertaining tomorrow night?"

"Yes. Just a small gathering, it'll be fun."

"Are Lucy and Dan coming?"

"No, they're not back until midweek. Oh, that reminds me, if we must go to the gala, can we invite Lucy and Dan?"

"I've already arranged it. It'll be nice for you to spend some time together."

I gaze up at him in wonder, he's always so thoughtful. Kissing him chastely on the lips, I stand up and smooth the wrinkles from my dress. "I'd better get back to work. What are you doing this afternoon?"

He walks me to the door. "I've got Bill coming over to start my physio, I need to get back into shape."

I stop, turning to face him, dragging my eyes up and down the length of him. He has the perfect male physique, he couldn't be more toned and gorgeous if he tried.

Running my hands up his chest, I reach up to kiss him on the lips. "Don't overdo it, I want to take advantage of you when I get home from work."

He raises a cheeky eyebrow as a smile dances on his lush lips. "I'll be waiting."

When I get back to my office, I fill Casper in on my meeting with Hannah earlier this afternoon, tell him about dinner tomorrow night, and then I set about tackling the photographs of the G.T Corporation. I've got a good mind to delete everything and tell Greg to fuck off. It's very appealing, but I resist the temptation and email a set of proofs to Rita.

I'm just about to leave, when Casper buzzes through. "Vivienne, I have a gentleman here who insists on seeing you. He doesn't have an appointment and he won't give me his name. He says he's a friend of yours."

Who the hell?... Mike. "Okay, send him in."

As soon as Casper opens my door, Mike barges past him, marching straight into my office. I had wondered when I would hear from Mike. It took longer than I had expected.

"I'm sorry, Viv. I didn't think you'd see me. I just need to talk to you, please," he says, looking very agitated and twitchy.

Casper glares at him then looks at me, waiting for my command. "Shall I call security?"

"No, it's okay, Casper. He's not staying."

Casper hesitantly leaves closing the door behind him.

I lean back in my chair and look up at him with cool indifference. Where once I would have felt some connection toward Mike, some fondness. Now, all I feel is disgust. "What do you want?"

He steps closer to my desk, halting abruptly when I raise both hands to stop him advancing any further. I'm shaking with adrenaline but I'm in no mood to play nice with him today.

His pleading eyes meet my harsh glare of indifference. "Viv, I'm sorry. I just wanted you to understand why I did what I did. I love you. I never meant to hurt you, I promise."

"Mike, what you did was unforgivable. I thought our friendship meant something to you, but clearly I was wrong."

"No! Viv I—"

"I don't want to hear it, Mike."

A pained wince contorts his face, his eyes begging me to forgive him. But I'll never do that. What he did to me, made that impossible.

"You know, Mike, nothing you could say to me would ever excuse what you've done. And we could have remained friends, but you sealed your fate when you lied to me. Helping Monica was a big mistake. Huge. You're dead to me now. Get used to it. I don't want to see you, or hear from you ever again."

My office door suddenly bursts open and Max strides through it with fire in his eyes and a brooding, grim expression snarling across his face. The muscles in his arms and chest are bulging through his t-shirt. And his uninjured hand is clenched into a tight, white knuckled fist as he lands a punch straight on Mike's nose sending him sprawling to the floor. I hear the bone crunch and the fear in Mike's high-pitched voice as he yelps out in pain.

With a blood spattered face, Mike looks up at me with pleading eyes looking for me to help him, to save him from Max's deadly fist. And part of me doesn't want to protect him. He deserved that. But when I look up at Max, I fear that Mike may not survive another attack, because Max has flipped. The growl rumbling in his chest is savage, his hard, wild eyes firmly fixed on Mike as he takes a threatening step toward him, drawing his heavy arm back for another punch. I've never seen him look so deadly. So dangerous. Mike wouldn't stand a chance against him.

"No!" My command halts him in his tracks, his confused eyes begging me to let him finish the job. "No, Max. He's not worth it."

I round my desk and lay my hand on Max's heaving, rock hard chest, gently but firmly pushing him away from Mike, then I curl my other arm around his waist. His body is taught and solid, powerful and dangerous. Every muscle, sprung and ready for action. But as much as Mike deserved that, I'm not willing to let Max risk everything over a man I care nothing about.

"Get out, Mike." My voice is harsh and direct, my glare of contempt, severe.

The defeat and sadness in Mike's watery eyes would normally pull at my heart, but not anymore. I'll never forgive him for betraying me.

"You heard me, Mike. Get out and don't come back. I never want to see you again."

I can feel Max pushing against my hand, his muscles straining, longing to be unleashed. And his jaw is set in a hard clench. Mike scrambles to his feet cupping his hand over his bloodied nose. He doesn't look at me again, his eyes are set on Max, fearful, wary. And as he hesitantly takes a wide berth, he finally scurries out of my office.

I breathe a sigh of relief but Max is still wound so tight and the look in his eyes is savage.

"Hey, look at me," I whisper, smoothing my fingers down his cheek and pulling his face toward me. His stormy eyes gradually swing down to mine, and I feel the hardened muscles in his chest eventually beginning to relax beneath my palm.

"Are you okay?" he asks, searching my face with so much concern that his eyes remain a little wild.

"Yes. I'm fine. How did you know he was here?"

His eyes lose their darkness and he runs a hand through his hair as the last of his tension softens. "I got an alert when the face recognition camera picked him up in the elevator. Jesus! He should never have got this far." Max pulls me into his chest, kissing the top of my head and rocking our bodies. "I told you, baby. No one will ever hurt you again. I'll kill any fucker who tries."

I pull back to look at him. The fierceness in his eyes has returned and it scares me. I hate to think what could have happened if I hadn't been here to stop him. But he also looks incredibly sexy all pumped up and protective.

"Hey," I smile, reaching up to smooth the wrinkles from his worried brow. "Max, I'm okay." I give his arm a reassuring squeeze but his muscles are still wound so tight with aggression. I kiss him on the lips. "Come on, my savage beast, let's go home and put all this frustration to good use. I know the perfect way to relax those muscles."

That gets his attention, and I'm delighted to see his devilishly sexy smile returning with a vengeance.

PANIC ALARM

Cole hands me a glass of non-alcoholic wine as we wait for our guests to arrive.

"So," he says, with a quizzical expression. "What's all this in aid of? Why did I have to dress smart for dinner? Is it someone's birthday?"

"No, I just thought it would be nice to have dinner with Jan and Vinnie now they're home."

Cole gives me a confused frown as he takes the seat beside me on the sofa. "They're already here, so who are we waiting for?"

"Casper…and Hannah, his sister."

"Your p.a.?" He turns to Max. "Is our p.a. coming?"

Max grins shaking his head. I had already told Max that I wanted to introduce Cole to Hannah. He had met her once before and agreed with me, they would probably hit it off very well.

Cole eyes me suspiciously. "What's with you two, you're both grinning like a couple of Cheshire cats."

The doorbell chimes and Vinnie emerges from the kitchen to open the door. I don't turn to face our guests as Vinnie brings them into the living room, I want to see Cole's reaction when he sees Hannah for the first time.

Mumbling under his breath, Cole's wary eyes leave mine and judging by the expression on his face, Hannah has met with his approval. His reaction to her beauty is exactly the same as mine was. Feeling very pleased with myself, I rise to greet my guests, then I make sure Hannah takes my seat next to Cole.

Vinnie disappears into the kitchen to fetch some drinks, so I grab Casper's arm before he has the chance to sit down and I lead him out to the terrace. "You really should see the view from up here, Casper, it's beautiful." Giving Max a subtle nod, he joins us.

My plan to leave Cole on his own with Hannah seems to have worked. Judging by her carefree laughter, and the fact she hasn't noticed we've left the room, tells me she's happy in his company.

Jan, as usual, presents a delicious meal and the wine and conversation flows all night. Jan and I had previously colluded to make sure Cole and Hannah would be seated together, and Vinnie and Max have kept Casper occupied with stories and questions, so everything is running as planned.

With my non-alcoholic wine in my hand, I glance around the table feeling a deep sense of pride. I wish Lucy and Dan were here, I miss them, and I can't wait to see them on Saturday at the Gala.

My mother's face springs into my mind. I worry our time together is so short, and I intend to make the most of the time she has left.

As my eyes drift around the table, I can't help but smile. My gorgeous, handsome paramour, the love of my life, is back where he belongs, smiling, laughing, and finally reconnected with his brother.

Jan and Vinnie, two of the most loving and supportive people you could ever meet, are now like family to me.

Cole, my saviour in my darkest hour of need, seems to be finally breaking free from the bonds Monica had constrained him with, opening his eyes to a bright new future. His attention has been on Hannah all evening and I'm delighted to see her enjoying his company too.

Our miracle nuggets, now five months, make everything complete. I have good friends, and people around me who love me. Lucy is like a sister, and even Casper and Ed have proved to be solid, reliable friends, going way beyond their duty.

Everything I would ever want or need is already in place. I couldn't be happier.

Leaning over to Jan, I clink our glasses together. "This is what it's all about, isn't it? Family, friends, loved ones. You've been a good friend Jan, I'm very grateful to you and Vinnie for everything you do for us. I hope you know that."

She gives me a tearful smile. "Likewise, Vivienne. We're both very fond of you." She begins to sniffle. "Oh, dear. You'll have me in tears. I'd better get the dessert." Dabbing her eyes with her napkin, she heads off to the kitchen to organise dessert.

As soon as she leaves the room, Vinnie quickly rushes over and crouches down beside me. His eyes are nervously trained on the door as he reaches into his jacket pocket. Opening a blue velvet ring box, he shows me the ring he's chosen for Jan with a big beaming smile on his face.

"Do you think she'll like it?"

My eyes widen on the beautiful diamond engagement ring and the whole room falls quiet. "Oh, Vinnie, she'll love it. It's gorgeous." Throwing my arms around his neck, I give him a tight squeeze. "When are you going to propose?"

He rises, putting it back in his pocket. "Tomorrow. The Governor's kindly offered to fly us out to Rome. I'm taking her to the Trevi Fountain and then we're going for dinner at a swanky restaurant in the mountains. Wish me luck."

"You won't need it. I'm so happy for you." Tears fill my eyes as I watch Max stand up to shake his hand, then he pulls him into a manly, back-slapping hug. Those two are so close, it's lovely to see.

Max never said a word about this. As he takes his seat and the chatter resumes around the table, I reach for his hand and catch his eye, gazing at him lovingly. He really is a remarkable human being. With a firm squeeze of my thigh he throws me an unusually shy smile.

When Jan returns with a tray of dessert, I can tell she senses a different atmosphere in the room especially now we've all got silly grins on our faces.

Cole comes to the rescue. "Jan, I'm so glad you're home. It's nice to finally have a meal which tastes how it should and doesn't require fire retardant gloves, a stomach pump, and an open mind." We all burst out laughing and Jan remains none the wiser to Vinnie's plans for tomorrow.

The Eton Mess dessert is delicious. As I scrape the last spoonful from the bowl, I get excited when I hear Max suggesting to Hannah that she should come to the gala on Saturday.

"I could introduce you to some people who could help you with your business. You should start networking as soon as possible," he says, squeezing my thigh and slipping me a cheeky sideways glance.

She blushes. "Oh. Um, yes, that would be wonderful. Are you sure?"

"Yes, of course. You can be Cole's plus one."

I can see the idea of escorting Hannah sits well with him, but then his eyes lower to the table and his brow furrows with a resigned frown.

"I won't be here," he says, quietly. "I'll be in New York, remember?"

Damn. Monica. I forgot he was taking her body back to the U.S.

Without missing a beat, Max answers him. "I've already arranged for her to be flown out tomorrow. Benny and Tracy can fly you over in the new jet on Sunday morning for the service, if that's okay with you?"

I marvel at Max's generous and thoughtful mind, but then I get a pang of unease that Cole may not be happy about Max taking over. I can't read Cole's expression and he doesn't respond straight away, which compounds my anxiousness.

"You'd let me use the new jet?" he asks.

"Sure. They found the problem with the on-board computer, and it's passed all its flight safety checks. It's yours if you want it."

When Cole smiles then turns to Hannah saying, "Then it's a date," my shoulders relax, and I get a warm fuzzy feeling inside.

After dinner, Jan and I take Hannah out to the terrace to take in the view while the boys enjoy a brandy in the living room. Casper and Vinnie have the brothers laughing out loud with their witty one liners and they all look very relaxed and happy.

Cole and Hannah's body language has been off the charts all night, and I'm dying to know if she has any plans to take their relationship further.

"So, you and Cole seem to be getting along very nicely, what do you think of him?" I'm trying not to be too direct but I'm dying to know.

She blushes, glancing coyly between me and Jan. And then a small frown invades her brow, making me think she's not as into Cole as I had hoped she'd be. My heart sinks a little.

"Can I be honest?" she asks, hesitantly.

"Honesty is always the best policy, dear," Jan says with an encouraging smile.

"Well, he's not really my type. Men with looks and money don't usually have a personality worth a damn." Her eyes drift over to Cole who's laughing at one of Vinnie's jokes. And the look in her eyes makes me smile. "But he's different," she says, with almost a hint of surprise in her voice. "He's funny. Normal… I really like him." Her eyes lower, then sheepishly travel back to mine and there's a rosy glow in her cheeks. "He's nice… Very nice."

I can't help my grin. "Yes, he is. And I think he might just be the prince you've been waiting for."

~

After insisting that Jan leaves me to tidy up after her lovely meal, we say goodnight to our guests. The boys offer to help, but I usher them out of the kitchen and get stuck in.

Once the last dish has been put into the dishwasher and I've wiped the worktops down, I wander into the living room a little pooped.

Cole and Max are sitting comfortably on the sofas, each with another brandy in their hands. I stand and watch them, a contented smile growing on my face. The view from the terrace is stunning, but my view right now of these two gorgeous creatures, two of sexiest men on the planet, takes my breath away.

Smiling up at me, Max pats his thigh, so I kick off my shoes and curl into his lap. His soft lips find mine, giving me a lingering kiss which curls my toes, then he pecks me on the tip of my nose. "That was nice, we should do it again when Lucy and Dan are home. And we really need to invite Anne and Paul over one night too."

I nod against his shoulder, too tired to speak.

"Okay you guys. Was this a set up?"

Lifting my head, I face Cole, trying not to look guilty. "What do you mean?" His smirk and raised eyebrow makes me blush. "But you do like her though, don't you?"

"Are you kidding?" he says, grinning like an idiot. "She's gorgeous, and smart too." He suddenly looks pensive. "Did she… I don't suppose she… Did she say anything about me?"

Bingo! I love it when a plan comes together.

"Like what?" I ask flippantly, trying with all my might to dial down my excitement.

"I don't know," he shrugs, now positively squirming. "Do you think she might like me too?"

Max and I exchange a knowing smile then I try to control my idiot grin before turning back to Cole. "Yes. She likes you too. She thinks you're very nice."

"Yeah, so don't fuck it up."

Max's comment makes him scowl. But then his scowl merges into a beaming smile. "Hmmf," he says, looking very pleased with himself. "She likes me... Good."

As I settle back down to Max's shoulder, my eyes begin to

droop.

"Hey, come on sleepy head. It's time for bed, you look exhausted."

I lift my head to look him in the eye. "Only if you're coming with me. I don't want to sleep alone."

His eyes become sad. "Baby, I don't think it's safe yet. What if I—"

"Max, please. I trust you. I need you."

His anxious eyes slide over to Cole who shrugs, holding his hands up. "Hey, don't look at me! It's her life you're playing with. Have you taken your medication?"

Max nods but he still looks anxious.

Looking thoughtful for a moment, Cole rises from his seat and wanders into the kitchen, returning with a small blue object in his hand. "Here, take this." He hands it to me. "It's a panic alarm. It's Jan's I think, I found it in the drawer yesterday."

Max and I look at the object, then at each other before smiling up at Cole. "Thanks," Max says, a little bewildered at Cole's thoughtfulness.

"No. Thank you, brother. For taking care of me when I didn't deserve it. For loaning me the jet. For Hannah, for lots of things." He looks embarrassed and emotional. Turning sharply on his heel, he heads upstairs to bed. "I'm only down the hall if you need me," he calls out over his shoulder.

Staring down at the alarm, I swing my legs off Max's lap reaching my hand out to him. "Come on, Pretty-boy. Let's go to bed."

~

As I snuggle in beside him, resting my head on his shoulder, tracing my fingers over his M.F. tattoo, he lets out a deep sigh.

I look up at his face. His eyes are closed but his jaw is set in a nervous clench.

"Are you okay?"

"Are you holding the panic alarm?"

"Yes."

"Then I'm okay."

I lean up on one elbow and stroke my fingers through his hair. "Max, you're so tense. Just relax, you won't hurt me. I trust you."

His eyes open, landing on mine. Fear lurks within them making my heart ache. This isn't how it's supposed to be.

"I don't want to hurt you, Vivienne. Ever. But I'm—"

"You won't. Just relax and get some sleep. And remember, I love you."

His sad eyes burn into mine. "Your love is the only thing that keeps me going. Love you more, baby."

I snuggle back down to his shoulder and close my eyes. Gripping the panic alarm between my fingers, I hope with all my heart that I won't have to use it.

THEM'S THE RULES

With a sudden jolt, I wake from a dreamless sleep as I feel the bed move and something heavy pining my hands above my head and bearing down across my body.

Oh, my god! No!

My eyes fly open to see Max's smiling blue eyes staring down at me.

"Good morning, beautiful."

Rolling his hips into mine, he leans down to kiss me tenderly on the lips. Without hesitation I raise my head off the mattress to try and steal another kiss. I can feel the panic alarm held tight in my firm grip, even though my arms are held above my head. Opening my fingers, I let it fall to the bed as he begins his sensual journey down my body.

When he releases my arms, I lower them to weave my fingers into his luxurious silken hair as he kisses his way over every inch of my heated skin before nudging my thighs apart with his broad shoulders. It doesn't take long for me to come. His tongue is like an electric shock swathed in velvet, and his skillful expertise at drawing out the most amazing orgasms is something I relish. Every lick, probe, and tease of his expert tongue always culminates in the most explosive, shuddering climax sending erotic charges all over my body.

"You know how much I love you, don't you, baby?" he asks, trailing kisses all along my inner thigh, heating my skin with every kiss.

I sigh, unable to open my eyes as the euphoria of my mind blowing orgasm still controls all my senses. "I know."

"Then please try to remember that while I'm fucking you like I don't."

Before I have the chance to come down from my erotic cloud of bliss, he flips me over pulling my hips up and back toward him. I kneel, arching my back as he takes me from behind, grinding and thrusting into me with an urgent primal force which makes me claw at the sheets, cry out his name, and come all over again with another mind blowing orgasm.

Gripping my hips, he pummels into me, growling and moaning as his own orgasm shakes his body, tensing his muscles, thrusting him forward until his chest is pressed flat against my back. Panting deep breaths across my cheek, he wraps an arm around my stomach then sits back on his heels with me held tightly against his chest. He nips at my shoulder, my head rolling to the side as he trails his soft lips up my neck to that soft spot just beneath my ear.

"That was amazing." I sigh, turning my head to take his mouth.

"No, baby. You are amazing," he whispers against my lips. "Marry me."

I pull back to look at him with a smirk on my face. "You know I will. I said yes, remember?"

"Today. Now." His serious expression confuses me. I turn myself fully to face him, kneeling between his thighs, and cup his face between my hands. "Max, we'd have to give notice at the registry office. You can't just walk in and get married straight aw—"

"I did that already. I have all the paperwork organised, you just need to sign a sworn affidavit that you're free to marry." His concerned eyes search mine. He's worried I'm trying to stall, but I'm not, I'm just confused.

"That's it? I just need to sign that one document?"

"That's it, baby." He smiles his bone-melting, heart-stopping smile, still searching my eyes waiting for an answer.

I look away as a small frown settles into my brow. He's leaving himself wide open. I can't let him do that.

"What is it?" he asks, lifting my chin to raise my line of sight.

"No, Max, it's not right."

He flinches, his eyes searching mine in confusion.

"Max, you haven't mentioned a pre-nup. I won't marry you without one. You can't leave yourself unprotected. If anything changed, if anything went wrong between us… As long as you take care of our children, I don't want your money."

"No!" he says, a look of disgust staring back at me. "No, Vivienne. I don't believe in all that bullshit! Are you having second thoughts?" He runs a finger along the furrow in my brow. "Is that what this is?… Doubt?"

I reach up and pull his hand down from my face, then I lay it over my heart. "Max, I've never loved anyone the way I love you. I'd die if I lost your love. There is no me without you… But in a few months, when I'm waddling around the bedroom with bloated ankles and stretch marks, and then a few months after that, when I'm cranky from the night feeds, and a few years after that when I'm overweight and wrinkly, will you still feel the same way about me?"

He smiles down at me with a cheeky smirk. "Are you trying to turn me on here, lady? Because it's working."

"Max, be serious."

Holding my face in both of his hands, he tilts my head back, hitting me with both barrels of his beautiful blue eyes, misted and glistening and shining with love.

"Baby, I wish you could see what I see, and feel what I feel. And I don't mean what's on the outside, beautiful as that is. I love you, Vivienne. I fell in love with you the moment I saw you, even before I knew who you were. And when I got to know you, I loved you even more. And I always will. In all your forms, with all your weaknesses and strengths, all your perfect imperfections. I want you to be mine, Vivienne. I need you to be mine…forever."

My eyes fill with tears as he leans in kissing me tenderly on the lips, sucking out all my fears, filling my heart with his love.

~

After a long, hot shower and some more toe curling sex, Max had exhausted himself, so I left him to rest on the bed while I headed off to work. I was so happy to have him back in our bed and delighted to know that his medication was helping him overcome all the obstacles of late.

Cole had left a note outside my bedroom door asking me to find out what flowers Hannah likes, which put a big smile on my face. I'm glad he's moving on in such a positive way. He deserves happiness, and unless Hannah turns out to be a raging loony crazy-pants like Monica, I think he may have already found it.

Lucy and Dan are coming home today and I can't wait to see them.

Max and I briefly discussed the options for our wedding. Initially he wanted to rush down to the nearest registry office to get married straight away, and I was quite happy with that, I was even dialling Casper to postpone my morning appointments. But then he changed his mind, he wants to carry out the plans he had made previously at his paradise island.

Either option suited me fine, I just wanted to marry him. Whether it's a quiet, low-key, official affair in an office. Or a lavish, over the top event on a sun-drenched beach, all I will see will be him, so it makes no difference to me.

He's given me three weeks to organise my friends and find a dress of my choice, so I'm off to see Davis this afternoon after work.

As I wander into the kitchen, Jan has prepared a light breakfast for me.

"Good morning, Vivienne."

"Wow, you look nice, going anywhere special?" Jan's hair is elegantly coiffed in a chignon and her face is glowing. Underneath her apron she's wearing a very smart shift dress and killer heels too.

"I'm not sure. Vincent's taking me out today and then we're going for an early dinner, but he won't tell me where."

I can't help the silly smile spreading across my face as excited butterflies swirl around in my belly. Vinnie's taking her to the Trevi Fountain in Rome, it's something she's longed to see but has never been to. He's going to propose to Jan this evening and I'm so excited for them.

There's so much love in this house, it's almost infectious.

"Well, wherever you're going, you look stunning, and I'm sure you're going to have a wonderful time." I give her an emotional hug, trying not to let myself become teary or she'll wonder why.

"Thank you, Vivienne. I've left you some meals in the fridge."

"Okay, thanks." I take a slurp of my tea and grab my bagel. "Oh, by the way, Max and I have set the date. Three weeks this Saturday, so you may want to go shopping for a new hat."

"Oh, how marvellous."

I giggle and smirk my way out of the kitchen then head down to my floor. Casper rises from his desk and walks with me to my office. "Thanks for last night, Vivienne. It was lovely of you to invite us for dinner, we had a great time."

"Yes, me too, I'm glad you could come. Oh, could you do me favour? I need some wedding invitations. I'll email you some suggestions for the design but I don't know the details yet, I'll have to—"

His grinning face stops me mid-sentence. "Yeah, that's already been taken care of. Mr. Foxx sent me a memo this morning."

"Oh, okay, but we'll need to shuffle some commitments around, I'll be taking a few weeks off for our honeymoon."

He shifts on his feet, cringing. "Yeah, we kind of sorted that out too. In fact, as far as I'm aware, all that's required of you is to show up looking fabulous. Congratulations, Vivienne." Pausing at the door, he smiles down at me with those pale hazel eyes. "I'm very pleased for you." Pushing my door open, he stands aside to let me enter.

I'm not surprised Max has swung into action. He's very keen for us to be married, and I quite like the idea that there will still be some surprises for me.

"Casper, before I forget, what's Hannah's favourite flower?"

"Zantedeschia."

"Huh? Never heard of it."

"Calla Lily. But they've got to be pink."

"Okay, thanks." I throw my bag on the desk and unbutton my coat. "Is there anything urgent this morning?"

"Yes, the G.T. Corporation have sent you an email approving the proofs, they will need the files by lunchtime today."

Just the mention of Greg Taylor's name leaves me cold, but I try to ignore how he makes me feel or he's going to ruin a perfectly good day.

Ed is already in his studio and pops his head around the door when he hears me. "Hi, babe, I'll be with you in a sec' I just need to finish this ad banner for Bookem and Riskitt, it's a new entertainment agency in the East End."

"Okay, no rush."

I quickly send a text to Cole naming Hannah's favourite flower, then I scroll through my schedule. I was going to mark the dates that will need to be postponed for the wedding but I can see Casper has already done that.

After checking my emails, I forward the files to Rita at the G.T. Corporation. With any luck that's the last I'll hear from them, and anyway, even if I do, I will be going out of my way to swerve Mr. Taylor in future.

I skip lunch so I can clear my desk but by mid-afternoon I'm starving. Lucy and Dan are home from their honeymoon and I had contacted her earlier to arrange a meet this afternoon, so I close down my laptop and head off to Java's.

"John, I'll be about an hour-ish and then I've got a five o'clock appointment with Davis for my wedding dress."

"Copy that, Ma'am. I'll wait for you here."

Lucy is already at Java's when I walk in. Estelle greets me in her usual fashion as I wander over to Lucy's table. She looks tanned and glowing, like a new bride should, and she's practically vibrating with excitement.

After a long, affectionate hug we take our seats and Estelle delivers our hot chocolates with all the trimmings. As I'm removing my jacket, Lucy's eyes zone in on my locket and she gasps in awe of its dazzling beauty. "Holy cow! Now that is some gorgeous spangly shit." Reaching forward to feel the weight of it in her hand, she beams a big smile. "Jesus, Viv. That must have cost squillions."

I smile, feeling the pride it always seems to give me, not from its value, but from its sentiment. Opening it up, I show her the little diamond nuggets inside.

"Oh, my giddy Aunt. That man thinks of everything." She sighs, momentarily bedazzled by my boyfriend's wonderful taste in jewellery, and then she cocks both eyebrows. "Well? You said you had amazing news, so spill the beans I'm dying here." Her face beams with an excited grin and she's practically bouncing in her seat. And now, I'm grinning from ear to ear too. I can't help it, her enthusiasm is catching.

"We're getting married in three weeks."

"What!?" Lucy's yelps of excitement get everyone's face turning our way. "Oh, good grief, at last!" she grins. "You're finally going to marry that man. I'm so happy for you, Viv. So happy." Reaching across the table she gives both my hands a thorough squeeze and we both end up in tears, happy tears.

"So, when is it? Where is it?"

"I don't know exactly, but he wants to marry me in the place he had originally planned. It's his own private island somewhere in the Caribbean, that's all I know."

With tears in her eyes, she gasps bringing her hand to her mouth. "Oh, Viv. I was sworn to secrecy the last time, so I can't tell you anything. But it's going to be amazing. So romantic. I can't wait."

"So, you'll be my maid of honour?"

"I'd better be!" she says, laughing with happy tears in her

eyes. "Oh, Viv. This is it. You finally get to complete your fairy-tale and I couldn't be happier for you." Her happy smile begins to flatten. "What about your mum," she asks, hesitantly. "Is she still in the hospital?"

My smile also fades and I suddenly feel very conflicted. I'm over the moon for myself, but I'm sad for my mother. I wish she would take the treatment. I wish we had more time. "No, she discharged herself."

Lucy shakes her head, but instead of throwing out one of her usual snarky quips about how useless my mother has been, she reaches across the table and squeezes my hand. "How is she?"

"I don't know. She seems okay, and she's surprised me, if I'm honest. She's refused any treatment for her Cancer, and as soon as I heard the news, I expected her to kill herself on a wild drinking binge, but every time I've seen her recently, she's been completely sober."

"What?" Lucy sits back in her chair, frowning at me big time.

"Yes. I told you I was surprised."

"Fuck me! I don't think I've ever seen your mum sober. But that's a good thing, isn't it?"

"Yes. At least she'll be around to see me get married and hopefully, she'll be here long enough to meet her grandchildren." The thought of her not being here brings tears to my eyes.

Lucy squeezes my hand a little tighter, offering me a reassuring smile. "I'm sure she will, Viv. If she's making the effort to stay sober, she's doing it with that in mind. What do you know? She's finally doing right by you."

She looks thoughtful for a moment. "So, now William's gone, who's going to give you away?"

I'd never thought about it. Vinnie would have been my choice, but he's Max's best man. "I don't know Luce, but I'm not worried about having a traditional wedding. As long as all my loved ones are there, that's all that matters."

"Well, you can count on me. I wouldn't miss your wedding

for all the wine in France."

Lucy and I discuss the gala on Saturday. Max had already emailed her to give her the details, so she was keen to tell me what she's going to be wearing. Max had also said he will be sending a car for her and Dan on the night, which excited her immensely.

I fill her in on Jan and Vinnie's imminent engagement, all the latest news involving Cole and the issues we had worked through, and then I tell her about all the problems Max and I have recently overcome. Including getting rid of Fiona.

"Jesus, Viv. You certainly don't lead a dull life, do you? But you should have told me about the problems you and Max were having. And all that shit with Fiona. I hate that you went through all that on your own."

"Luce, we'd already fucked up your first honeymoon. I wasn't about to let us fuck up your second one!"

She grins. "Well, let's hope we've had our quota of fuck-ups."

We say our goodbyes and then John delivers me to Davis.

Just as I'm about to get out of the car, I get a text from Max.

```
No peeking!
Them's the rules.
M
X;-)
```

I smile at the text, unsure of its meaning, but I'm sure I'll find out in a moment.

"Vivienne, dah'ling. You look positively radiant." Davis kisses me on both cheeks before ushering me through to the changing rooms. Sitting me down in one of the cream Chesterfield armchairs, he then signals to the young girl standing behind him. "Bring in… The gown," he says, dramatically.

"The gown?" I ask with raised eyebrows.

"Dah'ling," he simpers, daintily smoothing his coifed hair. "Your handsome groom and your dear friend had already designed and commissioned a gown for your wedding, before all that unfortunate business in France. It would be remiss of me not to show it to you now. Of course, Mr. Foxx has left clear instructions that the final choice must be yours."

He smooths a sculpted brow with his fingertips, looking very smug. "But I have to say, your groom and your friend have created what can only be described as, perfection."

I stare at him a little bewildered. I knew Max and Lucy had designed a dress for me, Vinnie had already told me that. But I have no idea what to expect, and now I'm twenty-three and a half weeks pregnant, I don't even know if it will fit.

Davis looks me up and down, humming and hawing as he inspects my baby bump with his assessing gaze. "Shouldn't be a problem," he mutters to himself. "Don't worry, we've made alterations."

He disappears through a white curtain in a flurry of waving hands and mutterings about his tardy, lack lustre staff. "Good grief, girl. If you moved any slower, I could trace around your feet with a pencil." A few moments later he comes bursting through the curtain holding up a long, white suit bag on a padded velvet hanger, with the girl scurrying behind him looking a little flustered.

I haven't seen the dress yet, but judging by the slender outline of the suit bag, I instantly like the fact that it's not a meringue with billowing skirts and fussy bows. I prefer simple elegance to the extravagance of a crinoline and too much structure.

Davis walks it straight through to the changing room, and then returns holding out his hand. "If you'd care to follow me, Vivienne."

Leaving my bag and coat on the chair, I take his hand and follow him into the changing rooms. As I enter and look around, I don't see the dress hanging up. "Davis?"

"Oh, not yet my dear. I shall help you dress, but you mustn't look until you've got it on. Apparently, them's the rules."

I shake my head and smile, now understanding Max's text.

After I've undressed down to my white satin underwear, I call out to Davis. Moments later, he pokes his head around the door. "I'm afraid you'll have to remove your bra, Vivienne." With that he disappears again, so I quickly unsnap it and throw it onto the chaise.

"Okay, I'm almost completely naked. Now can I try the dress?"

"Certainly, but close your eyes, and no peeking."

Shaking my head on a smile, I do as he asks.

I hear Davis enter the room. It's tempting to take a sneaky peek but I decide to abide by Max's instructions and let him surprise me. I steady myself by resting a hand on Davis' shoulder as he helps me step into the dress. The cool, soft fabric glides up my thighs and snugly rounds my behind, then Davis pulls it up, guiding my arms into the straps.

It feels amazing, figure hugging and weighted. I'm dying to open my eyes, but I wait patiently while Davis zips and hooks me into it.

"Okay, don't open your eyes until I tell you," he says, pulling the train out and smoothing the skirt.

Butterflies invade my belly. It feels wonderful, but then I start to worry that if I don't like it, I'll hurt Max and Lucy's feelings. I feel Davis' hands resting on my shoulders and his soft voice is very close to my ear. "Oh, my. You bring a tear to my eye, Vivienne… Okay, you can open your eyes now."

I pause for a second, my heart is fluttering in my chest, and the butterflies in my belly are having a right old rave up. I breathe in, and when I open my eyes and gaze at myself in the mirror, the vision standing before me makes me weep. The gown really is perfection. And a testament to the love Max and Lucy have for me, they understand me so well.

Tears bunch against my lashes as I gaze at every stunning inch of my beautiful wedding gown. From the front, the dress is a slender silhouette of white silk satin, with a seductive flare at the bottom. The thin shoulder straps and empire waist are intricately detailed with tiny white rosebuds, lace, and crystals, and the neck line is a deep-v plunge showing a healthy but elegant amount of cleavage. The lines are simple yet so very elegant.

As I slowly turn to see the back view, the deep-v drop to the small of my back with a sheer lace inlay, decorated in tiny white rosebuds, lace, and crystals, looks stunning and reminds me of the red dress I wore on the night Max proposed.

The short train of intricate lace over silk satin, white rosebuds and crystals, complete the gown to perfection. The cut and style of it enhancing all my curves, even my baby bump.

"Would you like to try on any more dresses, Vivienne?" Davis asks, softly.

Dragging my watery eyes away from the gown, I look up at him through the mirror. "No... No, this is perfect... Except for one thing."

After I've picked out the underwear and shoes for my wedding day, Davis and I say our goodbyes and I head home. I'm starving. I haven't eaten today, apart from the bar of chocolate Davis kindly gave to me once I was safely away from the dress.

As I bound through the door of F1 in an excited mood, and march through to the living room, I gradually stagger to a stop when I see Max standing out on the terrace. He's leaning on his forearms against the balcony, staring out at the city with a faraway look in his eyes. He looks distant and sad.

I wander up to him, dump my bags and curl my arms around his waist, leaning my cheek against his back. "What's the matter?"

He straightens and turns, pulling me into his chest. Kissing the top of my head, he rests his cheek against it letting out a deep sigh. "...I went to Charlie and my father's grave today."

My heart sinks, I wanted to go with him, and I feel bad he had to go on his own. "Why didn't you say? I would have come with you."

I see the sorrow in his eyes but he's trying to hide it. "I know. I just wanted to talk to them, to tell them that I..." He looks down, shaking his head. "That's crazy, right?"

A lump jumps into my throat and tears prick my eyes. "No, Max." I raise his chin off his chest and gain eye contact. "No, it's not crazy. It's lovely. And both William and Charlie always knew how much you loved them. We all do. We only have to look in your eyes."

He smiles, and kisses me tenderly on the lips. "And do you know what I see in your eyes, baby?"

"Love, I should imagine. Love for you."

"Yes, so much love. And I also see my future, and my happiness. All in those big, beautiful, blue eyes." He crushes his mouth against mine, fierce, soft, powerful, tender, all the ways I can't resist. "So," he says, dragging my bottom lip through his gentle bite. "Do we have a gown for the wedding?"

"We do."

"Is it—"

I silence him with my finger across his lips. "You'll just have to wait and see, Mr. Foxx. Like every other groom out there."

A frown slips into his brow, but his eyes are still smiling. "Baby, you know how impatient I am. I don't know if I can wait."

"Well, I'm afraid you'll have to, Mr. Foxx. Them's the rules."

"And what if I can't wait?"

I bat my lashes, teasing him with a seductive smile as I pick up the small Victoria's Secret lingerie bag at my feet. "I already thought of that and bought a little something to distract you with." I hold it up and balance it on my index finger.

Shaking his head with a wicked grin, he seals his lips over mine, all thoughts of the dress now a distant memory as something a little more urgent takes over.

~

After Max and I have tossed the bedsheets into disarray, and after receiving yet another orgasm in the shower, we head downstairs for dinner.

I heat up one of Jan's pre-cooked meals and scoot up onto the chair next to Max at the island. Before forking in another mouthful, a thought comes into my head. "Do you think

Vinnie's proposed to Jan yet, or is it still too early?"

Max checks his watch. "Anytime now I guess. Hey, that reminds me. Vinnie's chosen not to be my best man. He and I spoke about it last night. He thinks Cole should do it now that we're being civil to one another, and he also asked me if I thought you might like him to give you away when we get married."

I'd be delighted for Vinnie to give me away, but I would hate to take anything away from Max. Vinnie's very special to him. "How do you feel about it?"

He looks thoughtful for a moment, then shrugs. "Vinnie will always be the best man, but I guess Cole is my brother. It took a lot of guts to apologise for what he did, and I never realised how much I had shut him out when our parents died. It would be nice to have him at my side when we get married.... Anyway, now my father's gone, I can't think of anyone better to give you away than Vinnie, and I know it would please him. It would please me too, but it's your choice, baby."

"I'd like that. I'd like that a lot."

"Good. Then it's settled."

~

Max and I spend the rest of the evening snuggled up on the sofa, stroking our hands over each other and just talking. He'd had another physio session with Bill today, and he has another session with Doctor Fielding tomorrow, but his whole attitude and demeanour has brightened considerably since he's been home. Especially since we've been sleeping in the same bed again. I hated the separation. I'll do anything to keep that from happening again.

"Mom's coming home tomorrow with Olivia. I think I'll go and see them after my session with Doctor Fielding."

I lift my head off his shoulder. "Do you want me to come with you. I can take the afternoon off."

"No, it's okay. Besides, we'll be discussing a few wedding plans, so I don't want you listening." His lips tip up with a roguish smile. "Them's the rules."

I tilt my head and smile back. "Max, whatever you have planned, whatever you think you have to do for me. I appreciate it, and I know it will be lovely, but all I want, all I need, is you."

He smiles his dazzling, heart-stopping smile. "Ditto, baby."

BLACK TIE - RED FACE

Max pulls me across his chest as we lay panting and sweaty from another mind blowing sex-a-thon. Although his ribs are still tender and his wrist is still bound in a protective wrap, his injuries don't seem to inhibit his sexual prowess. That man has skills which completely blow my mind.

As accustomed as I am to his handsome face, I never tire of looking at it and I'm completely addicted to his sinfully hot body. The man has sexy in his DNA. It goes right to his core.

We had a little blip a few nights ago. Max woke me up in the middle of the night, he was sweating, writhing around, and muttering to himself. It scared me at first, but he wasn't dreaming about Monica. Thankfully, he hasn't suffered any nightmares about her for a while now. He was dreaming about his dad, William.

In his dream, Max was trying to save him. It broke my heart that he had been denied the chance to say goodbye to the man who had meant so much to him. I'm sure William's absence at our wedding will hit him hard.

His sessions with Doctor Fielding keep him talking about the things that worry him, so as long as he keeps venting and doesn't hold it all in, I'll be happy.

His physio sessions have helped immensely. His strength is

returning and I can vouch for his stamina.

Jan accepted Vinnie's proposal, which I hadn't doubted for a minute. Apparently, he had her in tears when he flew her out to Rome to visit the Trevi Fountain, and it was there that he had proposed on bended knee.

After accepting his proposal, he wined and dined her at the same restaurant Max had taken me to on our first date. It sounded charming and romantic, and Jan was positively glowing when they returned.

Vinnie took me to one side and broached the subject of him giving me away. I accepted without hesitation which put a warm, happy smile on his rugged face, and although he tried to hide it, he had tears in his eyes.

Cole was shocked when Max asked him to be his best man. I'm sure he must have thought that he had lost that honour because of the way he'd treated Max all these years. His eyes teared up when he accepted, and I was pleased to see the brothers solidifying their relationship. They seem to be growing closer every day. I know their reconciliation will make Sylvie happy too. All she wants is for her boys to be settled and happy.

Cole has been on another date with Hannah since they first met. She seems smitten, despite the dip-shit sending her the wrong colour lilies. They're seeing each other again tonight at the gala ball, and I'm looking forward to catching up with Lucy and Dan. It'll be fun, despite the ball being hosted by Greg Taylor.

I've rehearsed my fake smile, and I don't intend to be spending any time with him. If he stops by our table, I can always make my excuses and disappear to the toilet until he's gone.

My mum seems to be hanging in there. Every time I've called her or popped round to see her, she's been sober, I can't believe she's managed it on her own. Max has offered several times to send her to rehab, but she's adamant she doesn't need it. And so far, she seems to be coping extraordinarily well. She still insists on smoking her joints, which means I have to limit my time with her, or I end up leaving her flat as high as a kite.

I haven't seen her for a couple of days and today, much to my disappointment, we are attending the gala ball hosted by Greg Taylor. I don't want to go but Lucy's very excited. She's even insisting that I go to her salon for my hair and makeup.

~

Wriggling out of Max's arms, he kisses me dressed only in a towel slung low around his hips. His chest is still wet from our shower and his scent is stirring my hormones. "Max, I have to go. If you insist on going to this gala ball at this swanky hotel, then the least I can do is look fabulous for it. I'll be back in a couple of hours. Miss me."

"Always do," he murmurs pulling me back for another kiss.

At this rate, I'll be late for my appointment. *Oh, who cares.* I fling my arms around his neck and kiss him back. His lips are an opiate and way too kissable to be ignored. And pretty soon, I start to feel boneless in his arms.

He breaks the kiss and puts me at arm's length, smirking his roguish grin. "You're going to be late."

I sway when his hands release me. I'm sure he does that on purpose, he loves to watch me melt and then have to reconstruct myself after his intoxicating charms have rendered me useless.

As he smiles at me, then walks past me, I quickly snatch the towel away from his gorgeous arse. "I just wanted to take something with me," I smirk, dragging my eyes all over his fine, naked body. I didn't really, I was just checking that my kiss had given him an erection. It had. And knowing I had the same power over his body that he had over mine, put a big smile on my face. Resisting the urge to flick the towel at his peachy bum, I head off to Lucy's salon.

~

As usual, Maggie and Trevor cast their magic on my hair and makeup, and I leave the salon looking fabulous. Although, with Lucy telling us every detail of her honeymoon, it had taken a little longer than anticipated, so I only have enough time to get home and get dressed.

Max is standing in the dressing room buttoning up his shirt as I walk in to the bedroom, but he's struggling to do up his cuff-links with his injured wrist, so I dump my bag and do it for him.

"Hmm, you smell good," he says, bending down for a kiss. "And you look amazing." It takes all my willpower to resist his innate sexual pull, and I move away from him before I lose the control, or the will, not to take things further.

I sit him down on the corner of the bed, so I can finish tying his bow tie, he's too tall for me to do it standing up. His hands skim up and down my hips and thighs, he's playing a dangerous game, he looks so sexy and handsome but we have no time to fool around. Max in a Tux is one of my guilty pleasures, and right now he's hitting all my hot buttons.

"Max, behave. I have to get dressed."

"Mmm, watching you dress and undress are two of my favourite things."

I sigh and shake my head, the look on his face right now is playing havoc with my self-control, I could quite easily push him back on the bed and have my wicked way with him, but there's no damn time.

Stripping off all my clothes, I leave them in a heap on the floor, then scoot into the bathroom to freshen up. When I walk back into the bedroom, Max is still sitting on the corner of the bed watching me with a wicked smile on his face.

I step into my thong then open up a new pack of stockings.

"Leave the panties off tonight," he says, in a low, raspy voice. I smile to myself, avoiding eye contact, but I do as he asks and take them off again. As pushed for time as I am, I slowly pull each stocking up my legs so as not to ladder them. I can hear Max's lustful growl and I can see his eyes following the path of my silk stockings. He loves them.

Once they are on, I slip into my heels and walk over to the dress rail. As I reach up to take it off the hanger, a warm breath heats my cheek and his warm hands circle my waist, one hand skimming down my belly to cup my sex. My body reacts to his touch by arching into him as my head rolls back against his shoulder.

His hot lips nip at my neck as his fingers invade my opening. I reach up and grab his hair in my fingers as his circles of pleasure initiate the warm flurry of excited nerve endings pounding in my clit.

Rolling my hips to each of his strokes, increases the quickening until it builds to a peak where I have no control and it bursts out in a wave of erotic charges all the way down to my silk covered toes.

"Good girl," he whispers nibbling at my lobe, his voice, raspy and dangerously seductive. "That was so fucking sexy."

He renders me speechless when he seduces me like this. I can't talk, I can barely stand, especially when he moves away from me. As he walks out of the dressing room, my glazed eyes drag all over him.

"Baby, we're going to be late," he says, smirking over his shoulder. "You'd better hurry up. What's keeping you?"

"You! You're keeping me. I would have been dressed by now if you hadn't manhandled me… Fiend." Grumbling to myself, I retrieve my dress and step into it, then I start to smile, at least I can go out tonight without feeling all sexed up and frustrated.

As we settle into the rear of the Bentley, Max flips me a scowl.

"What?" I ask in all innocence. "What have I done."

"You've given me a goddamn woody, that's what you done. I'll probably have it all night too, until I get you home." Grumbling under his breath, he repositions his uncomfortable bulge.

I smile, cocking a super-smug eyebrow. "That's your fault, Mr. Foxx, I'm feeling very satisfied."

He shoots me a disgruntled scowl which morphs into a sexy smile as he reaches for my hand. "Well, at least one of us does. You look beautiful by the way." Lifting my hand to his lips, he kisses my fingers.

I pull his hand to my lips to kiss his fingers, and as I do, I can smell my arousal on them. "Max! You didn't wash your hands."

His super-sexy smile makes his eyes sparkle. "Damn right. If I can't fuck you at least I'll be able to smell you all night."

There's something very sexy and romantic about that statement which brings a wicked smile to my lips.

Luckily, Max's erection subsides by the time John delivers us to the limo drop off zone. The press go wild, as usual, demanding our attention and throwing out rapid fire questions, none of which Max pays any attention to.

We present ourselves in front of the advertising board for the usual customary shots, and then, without warning, Max swoops down and kisses me full on the lips. His kiss hits all the usual hot spots and when he's finished blowing my mind, he nuzzles my ear. "I shouldn't have done that, the blood is starting to rush to places it shouldn't until I can get you home."

I smile up at him, shaking my head.

With his hand on the small of my back, Max leads me into the main hall. I immediately spot Lucy and Dan talking to Cole and Hannah at our table. Cole has obviously done all the introductions and strides over when he sees us. He shakes his brothers hand then kisses me on the cheek. "Where have you been? You're twenty minutes late."

I blush, smirking up at Max. "That's his fault."

"No," he says moodily. "It's your fault for wearing those sexy stockings and fuck-me shoes."

Raising an eyebrow, Cole tilts his head. "Viv, the man's got a point."

I roll my eyes and start toward Lucy and Hannah but Max pulls me back.

"Baby, I have a little surprise for you. Come." Taking my hand, he walks me to our table. Lucy and Dan are staring up at me with big smiles on their faces as we approach, and then I spot the woman sitting between Lucy and Hannah.

"Mum! What are you doing here?" I'm shocked to see her sitting there. I almost didn't recognise her, she looks so different, so beautiful.

"Max invited me. I hope you don't mind," she says, sheepishly.

I glance up at Max with teary eyes and then I look back to my mother. "Of course not, it's great to see you, Mum. Really great." I give her a tight hug, fighting back the tears pricking my eyes. I'm so happy to see her.

"Lucy did my hair and makeup and her mum kindly lent me this dress," Mum says, looking down at her elegant, black, cocktail dress. I'm literally gob-smacked. She looks amazing.

Walking us to our seats, Max places his hand on my thigh under the table.

"Thank you," I whisper, placing my hand over his, squeezing it gently.

As Lucy becomes the centre of attention, telling everyone about her and Dan's honeymoon, I feel Max's hand pulling my skirt up under the table. I try to stop him but I'm no match for his strength. His warm hand skims up my thigh, higher and higher until it reaches my stocking tops. I snap my knees together, trapping his hand between my thighs, then I smirk up at him with raised eyebrows and a tight lipped whisper, "My mum's here."

He hits me with his arrogant eyebrow and crooked smile. "And your point is?"

When I realise he's not going to play fair, I shake out my napkin and lay it over my lap in an attempt to cover up Max's wandering hand. He pulls it out from between my thighs and drags it over my bare flesh right up to my exposed pussy.

A ripple of excitement heats my skin and the wicked sensation of his thumb stroking my clit stirs my senses. Instinctively, I open my legs a little wider to accommodate him. He smiles and whispers, "Good girl."

My breathing deepens and my eyes glaze over as he circles my sweet spot over and over. The erotic bundle of nerves building momentum with each stroke. I look up at him, but he's looking across the table at Lucy like he's listening to every word. He even smiles when everyone else does. I couldn't tell you what she was saying, my focus is all downstairs.

Breathless and trembling with desire, I reach for my water glass as my impending orgasm builds to its peak, afraid that if I don't distract myself, I'll just throw my head back and moan out with pleasure.

His relentless strokes bring me to the point of no return, tipping me into free fall over the edge. Tilting my hips to increase the pressure, I grip the water glass with my right hand and the edge of my seat with my left hand as my orgasm shudders through my throbbing sex, rippling out to all my extremities.

Grateful of a timely burst of laughter around the table, I gather my senses and place my hand onto Max's arm as he slows and dips his thumb inside me.

With his seductively hooded eyes on mine, he pulls his hand away and sucks the end of his thumb with a salacious grin. My cheeks heat, feeling sure everyone must know what we were doing, but they all seem oblivious until Lucy stares straight at me.

"Viv are you alright? You look a bit flushed."

"What? Oh, ah, yes, I'm fine, it's just hot in here." I fan my face with my napkin to back up my lie.

Max chuckles, throwing me his sexy smile. "It's getting hotter every minute."

Luckily, the waiter comes around with the Champagne taking the focus from me and my embarrassingly flushed cheeks. I see my mum eyeing the glasses as the waiter fills them and I begin to tense up. Mum is surrounded by booze and it's all free. But when she pours herself a glass of water from the jug on the table, I let out the anxious breath I seemed to have been holding, and relax.

Because Mum is here, and because I'm anxious that she might struggle with all this alcohol around her, I had completely forgotten about Greg Taylor. When he shows up at our table just as dinner is being served, I feel myself physically recoil when I hear his voice coming from behind me.

The rough pads of his fingers grazing the bare skin of my shoulder, sends goosebumps crawling all over my flesh, but when he leans down to kiss me on the cheek, my whole body stiffens. Max is oblivious to this as he turns away from me to stand and shake his hand.

"Greg, good to see you."

"You too. I hope you have a pleasant evening, enjoy your meal." Greg returns his hand to my shoulder, squeezing it once before walking away. The feel of his rough skin on mine, repulses me.

I rise from my seat in a rush. "Excuse me."

Max looks up at me. "Is everything alright?" he asks on a concerned frown.

I try not to show how I'm feeling and force a smile to pacify him. "Just popping to the ladies' room, I'll be back in a minute."

"I'll come with you, dear." Mum rises from her seat and follows me out to the toilets.

As I push the door open and rest my hands against the basin's edge, trying to control the swirling sickness in my stomach, my mum walks in behind me and closes the door. We are on our own, but I don't suppose it will be for long.

"That was him, wasn't it?" she asks, staring at me through the mirror. I nod. Speaking isn't an option until I can settle my stomach.

"That fucking bastard!"

"Mum, please, not here. Not now… I can handle it. Don't go near him. Don't talk to him. Just leave it, Mum. Please."

She's struggling to understand why I continue to protect him, but it's not Greg I want to protect.

As the nausea passes, I blot the perspiration from my top lip, fanning my face to cool down.

"Vivienne. That man is walking around free as a bird because I did nothing."

I spin around and grab her by the shoulders. "Mum. Listen to me. Just leave it. Promise me."

Her angry eyes soften and I feel the tension relaxing in her arms as she sags and nods her head. Someone walks in, so I quickly drop my hands and usher my mum out of the toilets, back to our table.

"Everything alright?" Max asks, placing his hand on my thigh.

"Yes, everything's fine."

His eyes swing over to my mother. Her face is pinched, she looks upset. I begin to worry that she may do or say something tonight that could affect us all.

I lean into Max's ear. "She's struggling with all the alcohol here. It's difficult for her."

He gives me a squeeze. "We'll help her. Don't worry."

I've completely lost my appetite but I eat enough so as not to cause any suspicion. Mum picks at her meal and sips at her water. Without making it obvious, I watch her as she sifts through the many faces in the room. She's looking for Greg. She won't let this go.

After dinner, Max takes to the stage to deliver his speech. As he hits the podium and the spotlight lights him up, you can hear all the women in the room twittering in adoration. His elegant grace, commanding presence, and cool, self-assured delivery captivates his audience immediately. And his raspy, velvety voice and winning smile heats the room a few degrees.

I marvel at him. He looks so poised, confident, and downright sexy in his Tux. I feel privileged that I'm the focus of his desire. I'm the only woman in this room who sees him naked, who hears his giggle when I hit his tickle spot with my tongue, and who can arouse him with just a look. The man is gorgeous, powerful, sexy, and best of all, he's all mine.

"Hey, Viv?" Lucy whispers across the table. "Where's your mum?"

"What?" I glance over at Mum's empty chair, I hadn't noticed her leaving the table. I quickly look around the room, but I can't see her anywhere. "She's probably gone to the loo. I'll be back in a minute."

Grabbing my clutch, I push up from my seat and quietly make my way through the tables toward the ladies' room. When I get there it's empty, so I check outside but she's nowhere in sight.

Making my way back toward the main hall, I suddenly hear raised voices coming from the small lounge bar in the lobby. When I recognise my mum's voice, I stumble to a halt, then back track.

"Mum! What are you doing?"

Her hands are fisted in Greg's lapels and she's hissing expletives into his face. Greg's stormy eyes land on mine. "You tell this fucking bitch to back off," he snarls grabbing her wrists in a painful hold as he wrenches her hands free from his jacket. She whimpers at the pain and her knees buckle.

"Leave her alone!" I snap. "She won't say anything. Just leave her alone."

He pushes her away from him.

With my wary eyes still on Greg, I rush over to her trembling form as she leans against the bar rubbing her wrists.

Greg strides away, smoothing his jacket and huffing under his breath.

I quickly look around us, grateful to see we're alone. "Mum, what the fuck do you think you're doing? You're going to ruin everything. Just let it go. Please!"

Her watery eyes look up at me with such hurt and sorrow. Her fragile wrists are red and she looks utterly defeated. "Viv… Just one drink."

Her pleading eyes rip me apart. But I'll never give her what she craves. If she wants it bad enough that's a choice she'll have to make, and execute, on her own.

"Mum, please. Don't go down that road again, you've come so far. Don't let him win."

She bursts into tears. "He's fucked us both, Viv. He's won already."

Holding her frail body in my arms, and nervous someone will see us, I try to calm her down. "Come on, I'll get John to take you home."

She reaches up, to cup my cheek with her shaking hand. "I'm sorry, Viv. I'm sorry I never protected you. I'll find a way to make it right. It may be the last thing I ever do, but I will make it right, I promise."

Tears pool in my eyes and my voice is now trapped inside my tightening throat. Walking her out to the front of the hotel, I call John.

"Ma'am? Everything okay?"

"Yes, my mum has a headache, I wondered if you could take her home."

"Sure, I'm right outside. I'll pull around to the front entrance."

"Thanks."

A few seconds later John arrives in the Bentley. As he comes to a stop, Mum grabs my arm. "Vivienne. Please, don't let him ruin your life. Break free from him. Find a way and break free." Her sad eyes and pleading voice put fresh tears in my eyes and an ache deep inside.

"I will, Mum. I promise. Just let me deal with it, okay? Don't get involved."

She nods, but her eyes still look so sad.

I help her into the car and wait until John's driven out of sight before I turn to head back inside wiping the tears from my cheeks. When I see him, I stumble to a standstill.

"Who was she talking about?"

"Cole! Um, no one. She's not feeling well."

I start to walk off but Cole grabs my arm, stopping me in my tracks.

"Viv, you're upset. I heard your mother—"

"It's nothing!" I blurt, trying to shut him down.

"But, Vivienne, I—"

"Cole, please! Just leave it."

"What's going on?"

Max's deep, angry voice has both our heads whipping around. His wary eyes are on Cole's hand gripping my arm. He lets me go and I start to walk away.

"Not so fast." Max holds out his hand to stop me. I can see the controlled anger simmering in his eyes. "What's going on, Vivienne?"

"It's nothing. My mum couldn't cope with all the alcohol flying around so I sent her home, that's all."

I flick my eyes up to Cole. I can tell by his expression, he knows something, he heard something, but he's not sure why I'm keeping it from Max.

Lifting my chin with his finger, Max stares deep into my eyes. "Did John take her home?" He's looking to see if I'm telling him the truth. I am, sort of, she did want a drink. Maybe that's why he believes me. His eyes soften, then he curls his arm around my waist and walks me back to the main hall. I don't look back, but I sense Cole's eyes on me.

As we walk back to the table, Max looks down at me squeezing my waist. "What did you think of my speech?"

When I look up at him, I realise he's studying me, watching my reaction so I force a smile. "I thought it was very good. You certainly had everyone in the palm of your hand."

"But not you, apparently. You walked out half way through."

I blush. I wish I could control that response but I can't. He's suspicious, I can see it in his eyes.

"Max I—"

"I saw that look between you and Cole. Like you had a secret."

My stomach rolls and twists. That's the last thing I need, for Max to think Cole and I are up to something behind his back.

I stop walking, place my hands on his chest, and gaze up into his eyes. "I'm sorry. I didn't want you to know that Mum was playing up. She wanted a drink, I refused to give her one and we had an argument. That's why I sent her home. Cole found me, he could see I was upset and I snapped at him because I was embarrassed, that's all. I've been on edge all night because my Mum was here, but you'd done such a nice thing inviting her. I felt bad."

His eyes soften then he pulls me into his chest, kissing the top of my head. "I'm sorry, baby, I overreacted. And I should have realised it would be difficult for your mom. I just thought it would be a nice thing for you and her to spend some time together."

I stroke my fingers along his jaw line. "It was nice. And thoughtful."

He kisses me on the lips then we continue back to the table.

"Where's your mum?" Lucy asks as I take my seat.

"She wasn't feeling well so John's taken her home."

"Oh, that's a shame. Are you alright? You look pale."

I can tell by the way Lucy's looking at me that she knows something's wrong, so I give her one of our coded looks, the one that says, 'not now, talk later'. "Yes, I'm fine, fancy a dance?"

Lucy drags Hannah up with her and we head to the dance floor. Dan is already out there busting his moves, it's a wonder he doesn't put his back out. As we bounce to the beat, I see Max and Cole talking, it makes me nervous until I see them laughing which settles my nerves.

After a few tracks, my beautiful shoes are starting to pinch, so I head back to our empty table and pick up my bag, then I head off to the loo to fix my makeup and to call my mum, I just want to check on her.

As I walk down the corridor toward the ladies' room, I'm suddenly lifted from my feet and yanked into a small brightly lit room.

"Max! What are you doing?" He throws the lock then pushes me back against the door, burying his face in my neck, nipping and kissing and biting me on a growl of carnal lust. "Max! This is the disabled toilet, we're not supposed to be in here. What if someone really needs to come in here?"

"You're going to be walking with a limp when I've finished with you, no one will notice." His hands pull up the skirt of my gown, instinctively I throw my arms around his neck and my legs around his hips locking my feet at the ankles.

"My turn," he growls. "You've had two orgasms and I've had none." He bites my shoulder, nudging his erection at my opening. My hands take fistfuls of hair as I smash my mouth against his, and on a deep grunt, he sinks into me, shuddering as he impales me to the hilt. My head flies back against the door and he takes my lips in a forceful kiss, pumping into me with his urgent lunges.

"I've waited all night for this," he rasps, the strain of having to hold back all night showing in his voice. "You're so fucking horny in that dress, I can't wait any longer." His thrusts become deeper, his pace much faster, and the friction of him rubbing against my tender bundle of nerves brings me to that moment when my eyes close, my muscles contract around him, and I cry out his name as the pleasure takes me over.

Stifling my moans with his mouth sealed over my lips, he growls out his own moans of pleasure as he comes with a force pinning me to the door.

I feel boneless and shaky when he lowers me to my feet and straightens my gown. Staring down at me with those gorgeous blue eyes, he takes my face in his hands. "Why can't I leave you alone? You're like fucking air. I need to have you all the time. Whatever it is you do to me, baby, I like it. I like it a fucking lot."

I gaze up at him feeling exactly the same way.

A sexy, seductive smile curls his lips. "You want to kiss me now, don't you."

"I always want to kiss you," I sigh, smiling back at him.

A light tapping at the door has us both staring at each other with wide-eyes. We start to giggle, then I quickly clean up and check my face in the mirror before Max opens the door.

The man in the wheelchair looks up at us with a confused expression as we emerge from the toilet rubbing our hands with sanitising spray, trying not to smirk.

Max smiles down at the man and takes my hand. "Sorry, she suffers from pissyphobia," he says, with a perfectly straight face. "It's a fear of peeing on your own. Women, eh? What can you do?" Stifling a giggle, we head back to our table.

~

We spend the rest of the evening dancing and talking, and apart from Mum and Greg spoiling the evening, it wasn't a bad night. Lucy, Dan, Cole, and Hannah were very good company and we laughed so much my cheeks hurt.

Greg had the good sense to stay away from me for the rest of the evening too, so I felt much more relaxed.

Cole hadn't said any more about what happened with Mum earlier, and he obviously hadn't mentioned anything to Max, but his occasional knowing looks alerted me to the fact that he would still pursue the issue, but maybe not tonight.

Cole and Hannah make an early exit as he has a five-a.m. flight to New York. He's doing as he promised. He's attending Monica's funeral. It's sad because he'll be the only one there. She has no friends or family who care enough about her to say goodbye. But I respect Cole for carrying it through, and hopefully, especially now that he's found Hannah, when he says goodbye to Monica tomorrow, he'll be able to close the door on her once and for all.

I asked Max if he felt the need to attend her funeral, without hesitation he shook his head and said no. He doesn't understand why Cole is even bothering. As far as Max is concerned the only good thing about Monica had been Charlie, and she had destroyed him too.

~

Walking into our bedroom with my shoes in my hand, I drop them to the floor and throw my bag on the bed. Max starts to undo his bow tie as he walks to the dressing room but I grab his arm, stop him in his tracks, and move in front of him. Running my hands up his chest, I drag my eyes all over his gorgeous face.

"You know, one of my favourite things is you in a Tux. Stripping you out of it is another."

He smiles down at me with heat in his eyes and a salacious grin. "I'm all yours, baby, have at it."

"Oh, I will," I smirk, pushing his jacket from his shoulders. "Besides, I owe you one."

"You owe me two."

"Two it is!" I push him back to the bed and make him sit on the edge. "Unzip me first, then brace yourself, Mr. Foxx. Because tonight, I'm only going to use my teeth to strip you naked."

BAFFLED AND CONFUSED

I'm dreading it. I've been awake for three hours and I've picked up my phone umpteen times to call my mum, but each time I've bottled it. I know she'll be drunk and probably high on God knows what after last night's showdown with Greg.

When I spoke to John last night as he drove us home from the gala, he confirmed my suspicions when he told me Mum had asked him to drop her off at the corner shop at the end of her road. He tried to talk her into going straight home but she insisted, so he did as he was told.

Apparently, after he had turned the Bentley around to come back to the hotel, he got held up at the traffic lights and saw my mother leaving the shop with a plastic carrier bag. I assume she had stocked up on booze and would have binged on it as soon as she got home.

I feel guilty. Last night's outing has triggered her drinking again and it's all my fault.

As I pace up and down the terrace, twitchy and anxious, I realise I'm going to have to bite the bullet and go to see her. She could be lying in a pool of vomit by now.

Max is visiting his mother this morning, John has the day off, spending it with Julie, so I grab my keys and head down to the basement garage.

~

As I park up outside Mum's block of flats, I sit in the car for a moment mentally preparing myself for the worst case scenario. Lord knows what state she's in now. I just hope I haven't left it too long.

Hesitantly, I let myself into her flat. The radio is on in the kitchen and I can smell toast or crumpets. "Mum?"

"I'm in the kitchen, love. You're just in time. Kettle's on."

What the... I walk in to see Mum fully dressed, hair still styled from last night, lippy on, buttering some crumpets. She turns the radio down and hands me a plate.

"Tuck in, they're fresh out the toaster," she says, pouring the tea. "Still milk, no sugar?"

"Wh, ah, yes, thank you."

She stops pouring and gives me a funny look, then she pulls a stool out at the breakfast bar. "Take your coat off and sit down, you make the place look untidy. And eat your crumpets while they're still hot."

Still a little gobsmacked, I remove my coat and lay it over the back of the chair, then I take a seat and bite into my crumpet. I used to love these when I was a kid. It was always a treat after swimming lessons at school.

As I'm chomping my way through it, I cast my eyes over her, trying to figure her out. I was so sure she would have been completely shit-faced by now.

She sits opposite me, holding her tea cup in both hands, with a raised eyebrow. Resting her elbows on the table, she nods toward the living room. "They're in there, if you're wondering. On the table. I didn't touch a drop."

Placing her tea cup on the table she pulls a joint from the ashtray and lights it up, then she moves to the back door, opening it wide to let some fresh air in and the smoke out.

I'm confused, she's addled my brain. "Why didn't you?"

She huffs a sarcastic laugh, and leans back against the kitchen counter, staring out in front of her. "Oh, I wanted to. I even opened one up and poured a glass."

Her hand is shaking as she brings the joint to her mouth,

taking another draw.

Curiosity gets the better of me, so I rise from the breakfast bar and wander through to the living room. Standing in the doorway, I see two large bottles of Vodka sitting in the middle of the teak effect coffee table. One of the bottles is open. A short tumbler sits next to them with an inch of Vodka in the glass.

I'm surprised and confused. I had fully expected her to be pissed out of her head. The temptation must have been incredible, but she hasn't touched it. I screw the lid back on the bottle and pick up the glass.

"I told you," she smirks as I walk into the kitchen. But her confident expression falters as soon as her eyes land on the shot of vodka in my hand.

As I pour the contents of the glass down the sink and rinse out the glass, I can almost feel her flinching as I do it. "I'll get rid of them for you, Mum," I say, unscrewing the lid from the bottle of Vodka, so I can pour that away too.

"You will not!" she snaps, stubbing out her joint in the ashtray. "I'm saving them for a special occasion."

"Mum, you're trying to do this all on your own, it's too hard. You should go to Alcoholics Anonymous, they can help you."

"Pff, A.A.'s for quitters."

I turn to face her, angry that she's making a joke out of it. "Mum, please. Let me get rid of them, it's too tempting to have them here."

She sits back in her chair, sipping her tea. "No, you leave them be. When the time is right, I'm going to need them."

The wavering fear in her voice makes my heart ache. Although she's putting on a brave face, she must be frightened about when and how the Cancer will claim her life. I wish she would let me help her. I wish she would take the treatment. But maybe she deserves to have a back-up plan. Something to take the pain away when it finally becomes too much. With a heavy heart, I leave the bottles on the side.

"I'm sorry about last night," she says, sheepishly, "I

shouldn't have caused trouble, it's just… That fucker deserves to suffer for what he did to you. If it was up to me, I'd cut his cock off and shove it down his throat!"

"Mum, please. Leave it alone. I told you, I'll handle it."

She gives me an unconvincing smile then a silence falls between us.

"So, tell me about your wedding dress. What does it look like? Do you have any photos?"

"I do, but you're going to see it on the day anyway." The look on my mum's face confuses me. "You are coming aren't you, Mum?"

Her eyes dart away from mine. "Yeah! Yes, of course I am. But mum's usually get to see their daughter's wedding dress well in advance." She smiles, but it completely misses her eyes and I start to wonder if maybe the symptoms of her Cancer have already begun. What if she's not well enough to make it to my wedding?

I open my phone and find the photograph Davis had taken in the changing room. Handing Mum my phone, I watch her reaction. "It's not the best picture, but it gives you an idea of the shape and style."

Her hands are shaking, her eyes begin to water, and her chin quivers. "Oh, Viv. It's beautiful. You, are beautiful. Can I have a copy of this?"

"…Yes. I'll get one printed for you." A sadness comes over me. It feels like she already knows she's not going to be there.

"What colour are your bridesmaids dresses?"

"I'm only having one. Lucy. Her dress is pale yellow."

"And your bouquet?" She hands my phone back.

"White roses and buttercups."

Her smile lights up her face, even her dark circled eyes sparkle. "You always did like those. As a child you would pester me to buy them for you, do you remember?"

I do remember. That was a long time ago, before Mum started drinking, before Dad started working away. When our lives were happy and uncomplicated.

"Mum, why are you asking about my dress and the flowers?

Are you not coming to my wedding?"

She laughs, turning away from me to get another joint from her bag. "Of course I am, I wouldn't miss it for the world. I'm the mother of the bride. I just wondered about the colours, so I could buy an outfit that was appropriate, that's all… I still want that photograph though." She lights up her joint, draws deeply on it and seems to find instant relief in its effects. But something in her eyes makes me anxious.

~

I stayed with her for a couple of hours, I was glad she was okay but I was nervous to leave her. Mum was acting like everything's fine, like we have all the time in the world. Her conversation was light and airy, and she clearly hadn't been drinking, but she asked me so many questions about Max, the babies, our wedding, our friends, it was like she was hungry for knowledge.

Maybe it was because we'd never had a proper relationship? Maybe she was trying to catch up? Maybe it made her feel better? I don't know. To me it felt forced, almost urgent, like it was now or never.

I offered to take her shopping for some clothes, but she said she'd prefer to order something from the catalogue and I didn't want to argue, so I let it go.

We promised to call, giving each other a tight hug, but I left feeling baffled and confused.

LUNCH AND THE THIRD DEGREE

The Monday morning madness at work has kept me busy right through to lunchtime. Max had gone back to work this morning too. Still a little tender, and still sporting his wrist support, he's healthier and much fitter now.

I was worried he was going back too soon, but I could see how much he had missed the exhilaration of being in his command centre. The ruthless cut and thrust of business deals and acquisitions were what drove him, and he drove the company, onward and upward, increasing his empire and revelling in the rewards and successes of his hard work.

Max had offered Cole senior executive status within the company, should he choose to stay and settle here in London. And there was every likelihood of that now that he had reconciled with his brother, and especially since he met Hannah. But he has yet to give his answer, telling Max he will discuss it with him upon his return from Monica's funeral.

Cole returns today, and I suspect he'll want some answers from me about what happened at the gala on Saturday night. My belly churns every time I think about it.

I need to find out what Cole overheard before I go blurting out the truth, and then I need to figure out what lies I'm going to tell him.

I scoot into my private bathroom to check my hair and makeup. Max and I are having lunch together, although, I would much rather forfeit lunch and take him home to bed so he can repeat what he did to me this morning, it makes me smile every time I think about it.

My phone vibrates with a call from Max, putting a salacious grin on my face.

"I was just thinking about you and the wicked things you did to me this morning. You're a very bad man, Mr. Foxx, I'm wet just thinking about you."

"Really? We were wondering why he had such a big smile on his face this morning. Oh, you're on speaker-phone by the way, and Max is blushing his ass off right now. How are your cheeks doing?"

"Oh, shit!" I hear several chuckles in the background and my cheeks are glowing crimson. "Cole? I didn't know you were back. Oh, my god! I'm sorry, Max, I didn't, I just—"

"It's okay," he chuckles. "You're off speaker-phone now. And these assholes are all just jealous. Pay no attention."

I hear the smile in his voice and some more jeers and chuckles in the background. I'm so embarrassed.

"I'm sorry baby, the reason I called is to tell you that I can't make lunch. I need to go over the schematics for the new jet, but Cole said he'll swing by your office and pick you up, you can have lunch with him and Hannah. Is that alright with you?"

"Yes, okay. But don't work too hard. I'll see you in the tub at six."

"Yeah," he chuckles, "I'll be the one holding the loofah."

I smile, rolling my eyes. "You're such a tease."

Ten minutes later Cole arrives and we head downstairs in the lift.

"When did you get back?" I ask, interrupting him texting.

"About an hour ago." He looks up, smiles, then returns to his text. He looks okay, but he's like his brother, very good at disguising his emotions when he needs to.

"How did it go?"

"It was quick. There was no one there to mourn her, just me. But maybe that's all she deserved after the things she'd done." His voice and expression are not giving anything away, he's almost too calm and collected.

"And how do you feel?"

When his eyes reach mine there's just a flicker of emotion and then it's gone. "It's like you said, Vivienne. I just needed to let go. I said goodbye and I did just that, I let her go. And I'm okay. Really."

He returns to his text, finishes it, hits send then puts his phone away. The lift doors open and I realise we've sailed straight past Hannah's floor and are now in the lobby. Taking my elbow, Cole escorts me to the main doors.

"What about Hannah? Is she meeting us there?"

"Ah, yeah. I thought we'd go to Ruby's." He steers me out through the main door and across the street to a small restaurant I've never been to before.

As we enter, we are greeted by a smart looking man in a formal suit. "Mr. Foxx, good to see you again, table for two?"

"Yes. Thank you, Philip."

Philip escorts us to a small table away from all the other diners. It's obvious Hannah won't be joining us and I start to feel a little panicky. Cole obviously wants to talk, and as much as I'm not looking forward to it, we need to have this conversation.

Philip pours us some water, hands us the menus, then leaves.

Cole peruses the menu for a moment then lays it down clasping his hands in front of him on the table. "So, how are things with you and Max?"

His question takes me by surprise. I look up at him and squirm a little under the intensity of his stare. "What do you mean?"

"Vivienne, please. Let's not tap dance around the truth. I heard your mother on Saturday night. She was asking you not to let him ruin your life. She wanted you to break free from him. And you told her not to get involved, that you would handle it yourself.... Handle what? Was she talking about Max?"

"No! Cole, please, you don't understand."

"For Christ sake, Vivienne. You're getting married in two weeks, if he's forcing you to marry him, or if he's hurt you again I'll—"

"No!" I quickly reach across the table, placing my hand over his. "It's not him, it has nothing to do with Max."

The concern on his face deepens. "Then who was she talking about? And why the hell are you keeping it from Max?"

Butterflies swirl around in my belly and I have to look away from his penetrating eyes. I don't know what to tell him.

"Vivienne, I'm not an idiot and neither is my brother. You were very upset on Saturday night, and your mom was clearly concerned about you. Now, either you tell me what's going on, or I go and speak to your mother."

Tears prick my eyes and my stomach churns. I take a sip of water, stalling for time, but my hand is shaking badly and Cole notices that.

Philip returns to our table but Cole silently waves him away and we are once again left on our own. Anxiety knots in my chest as I try to come up with a plausible explanation. I need to give him something, but what?

"I've got all day, Vivienne," he sighs, leaning back in his chair. "But we're not leaving here until you tell me who your mother was talking about."

"Cole, please. It's personal and complicated. But it has nothing to do with Max. I promise."

"Okay..." he says, drawing the word out sarcastically. He's nodding at me, raising an eyebrow, his eyes still nailed on mine. "So, whoever this person is who has a hold over you, and who your mother wants you to break free from, as long as it's not Max, I shouldn't worry? Is that what you're telling me?" His sarcasm isn't helping, and it's blatantly obvious he's not going to let this go.

I meet his gaze, trying to hold it without looking guilty or blushing. I fail miserably on both counts. "Cole, just leave it, please. My mum doesn't know what she's saying half the time, she's a drunk."

With a look of disappointment, he shakes his head, still searching my eyes with his assessing gaze. But when his eyes narrow on me and recognition seeps across his face, I panic even more.

"Greg Taylor...," he murmurs thoughtfully, his eyes drifting away from my face. "He came up to our table..." I flinch and squirm, powerless to stop him putting it all together. And when his eyes return to mine, I can see he's almost there. "Your mother looked angry when he put his hand on your shoulder, you didn't seem to like it much either... What does he have to do with all this?"

My head feels hot and fuzzy and I feel sick. There's no air. What the fuck am I going to say? *Think! Viv. For fuck's sake, think!*

Cole patiently waits for me to talk but I have no idea what I'm going to tell him until I open my mouth and take that first breath. "Greg and my mother have history," I say, trying to push the emphasis onto my mother.

Cole's eyebrows shoot up in surprise.

"Look, Cole, it was a long time ago, and...well, it's personal."

He raises an arrogant eyebrow, then he leans back in his chair, folding his arms across his chest. "Keep talking."

I rack my brain for more, but I'm struggling and I start to fidget.

"Go on, Vivienne," he prompts.

Stalling for time, I take another sip of water while my brain is running like the clappers trying to formulate an answer. Anything to get Cole to back off.

"Greg has...intimate photographs of my mother."

His brow lowers but his eyes are still nailed on mine and as he doesn't speak, I realise I'm going to have to elaborate further.

A nervous smile can't be avoided, so I shrug and throw my hands in the air. "Pff, it's so stupid. She's worried that if they end up on the Internet it will ruin my life. She's just being paranoid that he'll use them against her, or me, that's all."

Cole's narrowed eyes search my face for a long, uncomfortable moment, ending up on my fidgeting hands. Unfolding his arms, he reaches across the table laying his hand on top of mine to still them as his expression softens. "Hey, it's okay. He won't release the photographs. Trust me, publicity like that wouldn't help his credibility one bit. I'll talk to him."

My head whips up, tears spilling over my lashes. "No! Please, Cole. Just leave it. You're right. It was an empty threat. Mum had been stressing out because she's trying to go cold turkey on her own, and then she saw him and picked a fight. He was just retaliating. It's her own stupid fault."

"Does Max know any of this?"

I look away and take a breath, then I look him straight in the eye. "I don't want Max to know. I didn't want anyone to know. She's dying, Cole. The woman deserves a little dignity in her final months, don't you think?"

I went for the sympathy card, and to my utter shock, I won it. Cole seemed to understand that I was trying to protect my mother and he backed off. He promised he would keep what he had heard to himself. He also promised not to mention anything to Greg, so I left the restaurant feeling confident that I had swerved that particular banana peel.

~

I was grateful to be booked out on an aerial shoot after lunch. It took up the whole afternoon and gave me something to focus on. By the time we landed back at Foxx-Tech it had removed all the nerves and tensions from earlier.

As I stroll into the bedroom Max is already naked and has started the bath. I walk up behind him as he's removing his watch and slide my hands down the smooth skin covering the well-defined muscles on his angled sides, around his waist, and then down his stomach to his cock, giving it a firm squeeze as I press myself into his back.

"If you keep squeezing and stroking me like that you're

going to give my loofah a woody and the bath water will get cold."

"Sorry," I giggle, "I can't help it, you're so scrummy, and I've missed you."

He turns around and in between long, luxurious kisses, he undresses me then picks me up and walks me through to the bath.

Lying back against his chest, running my hands up and down his thighs, I rest my head back against his shoulder and close my eyes. I love these moments when it's just the two of us. Quiet, relaxed, skin on skin. Totally in tune with each other without having to say a word.

Folding his strong arms around my shoulders and across my chest, he rests his head back against the tub on a satisfied sigh. "How was lunch?"

Heat travels over my skin. I feel guilty about lying to Cole earlier, and I'm grateful my secret is still safe, but I especially hate lying to Max. "It's was fine. But I missed not having you there." I begin to chuckle at how ridiculous that sounds.

"What are you laughing at?" he asks, raising his head up from the edge of the bath.

I turn to face him. "I missed you at lunch, and yet, I was looking at your face the whole time."

"Please," he smirks, cocking an arrogant brow. "I'm way better looking than Cole."

"I agree," I smile, taking his lips in a gentle nibble. "And in two more weeks, you, Mr. Foxx, will be all mine."

"No, baby. In two more weeks, you'll be mine. Forever."

I giggle. "Fine by me."

As the water had started to cool and after I had played around with his loofah some more, we dried off and moved it to the bedroom.

Three orgasms later, we ended up sprawled width-ways across the bed in a tangle of sheets. Max was no slouch in the bedroom and our rampant sex life had taken the place of my runs around the park. He definitely keeps me fit.

By now I was starving, so I put on Max's shirt and went to

investigate the fridge.

~

As Max and I tuck in to Jan's stew and dumplings, I feel the babies move.

"Oh! I think we're either having footballers or tap dancers."

Max rubs his hand over my bump then looks up at me with a contented sigh. "They are quite a miracle, aren't they? Do you think we'll have one of each?"

I reach up to stroke his cheek. "That would be nice, but secretly I hope one is a puppy."

He shakes his head before taking my mouth in a toe curling kiss. I pull back to gaze into his scorching blue eyes. "One of each would be good though, wouldn't it? A little boy for you to take flying, a little girl for me to dress up."

Sparkling eyes search mine as a warm smile adorns his lips. "And would you pass on your culinary skills to our daughter?"

"Of course, she'll be ordering from Barney's by the time she can speak."

He laughs out loud and pecks me on the nose.

"What about names?" I ask, already knowing which names I would like.

He seems thoughtful for a moment, then a grin curls his lips. "You've already picked the names, haven't you?"

I shrug, trying to wipe the silly grin from my face. "Kind of. But you can pick their middle names."

"Deal," he laughs, nuzzling my nose.

I reach up to my locket, fondling it in my fingers. "On a serious note. Of course I want our kids to be happy and healthy, but I want them to be nice people too. They're being born into wealth and privilege but they'll need to learn the value of hard work. We can't just give them everything and hope for the best."

His smiling eyes gaze lovingly into mine. "I totally agree. That's exactly how William and Sylvie brought us up."

I hadn't mentioned anything to Max, partly because I'm only just over half way through my pregnancy and I still fear something could go wrong. We've been plagued with disasters since day one. But it's also partly because we had agreed not to know the sex of our children until they were born.

I'd had another scan while Max was in the hospital. Doctor Alexander had checked me out because of the drug Monica had given me, and Jean carried out another ultra sound. I tried not to, and I feel terrible about it now, but I made Jean tell me the sex of our babies and then I swore her to secrecy. So, now I know. But I'm saving it as a surprise for Max.

The incredible thing, which Max doesn't seem to have picked up on, is that the due date for our babies is the fourteenth of February, Valentine's day, but more importantly, Max's birthday. I'm not holding my breath for them to arrive on time, but it's a happy omen and I'm going to keep my fingers crossed.

TRUTH WILL OUT

"Thank God it's Friday." It's been crazy this week. With aerial assignments, fashion shows, and meetings with new clients, this has been the busiest week to date.

Ed and I make a great team, he has been my rock throughout, taking care of all the technical aspects, producing some incredible work. I don't know what I'd do without him.

Max has had a busy week too. He left early this morning in his helicopter, it's the first time he's flown since just before Lucy's wedding. I was nervous, I had to bite my tongue or I would have tried to talk him out of it. But he was itching to get back in the cockpit, and as much as it worries me, flying always makes him happy.

I had lunch a couple of days ago with Clive and Luke, it was great to catch up with them and they're both so excited about their own wedding next June. As Clive said he would, they've gone all out. The whole shebang, with knobs on. We're talking swans, aerial acts, fireworks, ice sculptures, a Bob Fosse number from a Liza Minnelli tribute. You name it, they're having it. Even the vicar will be wearing sequins.

From what Clive was telling me, after Luke had excused himself from the table to go and powder his nose, their budget is already creaking under the pressure. It sounds like their wedding will make Las Vegas look positively dull.

As I leave my office and wish Casper a pleasant weekend, I head up to the penthouse. I'm excited about tonight. Max has booked a table at a swanky new restaurant. I wanted to invite Lucy and Dan, but when I called her this afternoon she told me they can't make it as they're visiting Dan's parents.

Cole and Hannah are also busy, and Jan and Vinnie are going to the theatre, so it will just be a nice romantic dinner for two. Me, and my hubby-to-be. The sexiest man on the planet. Woo-hoo!

As I check my face in the lift mirror, I can't help but smile. In a week's time, I'll be Mrs. Maxwell Foxx. Married to the most gorgeous man I've ever seen, who has the kindest heart and the hottest body.

Excited butterflies flutter in my belly. Max has organised everything for our wedding, so I've had very little to worry about and so much to look forward to. I'm glad in a way, knowing how stressful it was for Lucy, and now Clive to organise their weddings, I can't imagine that I wouldn't be pulling my hair out by now. There's so much to think about.

It is strange though, after Max had been abducted and Vinnie had told me about Max's plans for our wedding, I pretty much know what to expect, but I still find myself chuckling when I walk into a room and everyone suddenly shuts up. I love the fact that he's still trying to surprise me. He's such a romantic.

As our reservation is at seven, we have a quickie in the shower and then I wash and style my hair in voluminous bouncing waves. With smoky eyes and red lips, I've gone for a glamorous, sultry, evening look.

Max had already asked me to wear my new charcoal-grey dress with the deep-v plunging neckline. He likes the way my boobs look in it, and I have to agree, even with my baby bump, my figure is still pretty amazing, especially now my boobs are bigger.

As usual, Max walks out of the dressing room looking jaw-droppingly handsome. My pulse leaps and my breath catches at the sight of him, it's a reaction I can't seem to control, I wouldn't want to.

His tanned, chiselled features, firmly etched mouth, and sparkling, crystal blue eyes highlighted by his dark grey suit, black shirt, and matching tie, have me pausing in my tracks so I can drink him in. The man is sexy in a towel, but in a well cut, outrageously expensive suit, knowing all that exquisite masculinity lies underneath, sexy doesn't even cover it. The man is class, elegance, raw sexual magnetism. It feels like foreplay just looking at him.

As my eyes lazily drag over every perfect inch of him, I sigh, picturing us having sweaty, sheet-clawing sex. "We could stay home and order pizza," I offer in all seriousness.

He smiles, cupping my face in his hands, his scorching eyes gazing deeply into mine as his lips curl into a provocative smile. "I love the way your eyes make love to me. I'm naked now, right?"

I just nod, I can never seem to speak when he hits me with those gorgeous eyes and that wickedly sexy smile.

He pecks me on the tip of my nose. "Get dressed, we're going to be late. We can dine on each other after dinner." Kissing me softly on the lips, he releases me and leaves the bedroom with a roguish smile. Once I've reconstructed myself after his bone-melting effects have worn off. I dress and meet him downstairs.

As I hit the bottom step, Max walks in from the terrace ending a call and placing his phone in his inside pocket. "You look beautiful," he says, halting his predatory walk to give my appearance another sweep. His appreciative smile hits all my hot buttons and if I'm honest, I'd rather we just stayed home so I could peel him out of that suit and have my wicked way with him.

"Vivienne," he smirks. "Stop undressing me with your eyes, we're going to be late."

"Too late," I sigh, utterly besotted. "Can't we stay home so I can get you naked for real."

He smiles, pecking me on the tip of my nose so as not to

ruin my lipstick, then he pivots me toward the door. "Come on, you shameless temptress. Food first, sex later."

~

Max parks up in a side street and walks around to open my door. I've never been to a restaurant in this area before. It looks very expensive.

"Where are we eating tonight?"

"It's called La Roche, at the top of The Danvers Hotel. I've never been here before, but I've heard it's very good."

We cross the main street and enter the hotel through a brass, etched glass revolving door. The stunning lobby is decorated in hues of cream and gold and the floor is a beautiful mosaic design, something I've seen before.

We enter the lift and Max presses the roof-top button. Wrapping his arms around my waist he leans down for a kiss, one of his special kisses that almost blows my knickers off.

As the lift dings our arrival, Max breaks our steamy kiss and beams down at me with a super-sexy smile while I reconstruct myself and turn to the mirror to check my lips. As the doors glide open and I turn to exit, I almost jump out of my skin when I hear "Surprise!" yelled at me by a ton of people I had no idea would be here.

"Luce! Sylvie!… Oh, my god, Mum! And Clive! What are you all doing here?" Everyone I care about is here. I look up at Max with teary eyes, realising this is all his doing.

Stroking my cheek and hits me with his dazzling smile. "I couldn't marry you without giving you an engagement-slash-hen party first."

"Oh?" A salacious grin forms on my lips. "Will there be any male strippers?"

"Nope!" he says flatly. "Never gonna happen. But I'll strip for you when we get home if that'll help?"

"Mmm," I grin. "I'll hold you to that, Mr. Foxx, I can't wait."

He waggles his eyebrows and kisses me chastely on the tip of my nose.

"Max, I don't know what to say. You really are a rare and

beautiful man." Rising up on my toes, I kiss him on the lips. "This is perfect," I whisper against them. "I love you."

"Love you more, baby."

He walks me toward my family and friends who circle around me giving me hugs and kisses. It's amazing, almost overwhelming, tears were inevitable. Even my old boss Frank and his wife are here. I had no idea Max had organised this, but it explains all the whispering.

Lucy gives me a hug. When she releases me, I give her the eyebrow. "I thought you said you were visiting Dan's parents tonight? You big, fat liar."

"I am," she chuckles. "They're over at the bar talking to Casper and his girlfriend Ellie."

"What? Oh, my days, this is so great. Everyone's here."

Lucy nods toward Ed. "Hey, who's the woman with Ed? I've never seen her before."

"Oh, that's Nova, his girlfriend."

"What?" Her eyebrows hit her hairline. "Girlfriend? Don't tell me Ed is finally settling down? I don't believe you. He has the attention span of a gnat when it comes to women."

"It's true. She's a… really nice woman." I decide not to elaborate on Nova's talents, I'll leave that bombshell to Ed.

Jan, Vinnie, Cole and Hannah are beaming as they swoop in for a hug and then my tears really flow when my Mum steps forward and gives me a cuddle. She looks great. I know someone must have helped her to look like she does, I'm guessing Lucy, Trevor, and Maggie have played a part in her appearance, and I'm so proud to see her looking so happy and more importantly, still sober.

After an hour of mingling and chatting, we're seated for dinner.

As I take my seat at the long table, I feel an enormous sense of pride looking out at all my friends and loved ones. Some of us here tonight have survived extraordinary dramas with remarkable odds. Mike is the only person missing, not that I care, but maybe Sandra deserves a place here tonight. After all, she saved my life.

~

I ate every delicious mouthful, and the witty conversation flowed all through dinner. After coffee and liquors, the DJ rocks the house with some classic floor-fillers and everyone piles onto the dance floor for a boogie. Dan almost knocks Jan off her feet with his moves, and Clive entertains us with his impersonation of Louie Spence.

As we return to our seats, Max turns to face me with a beaming smile on his lips. Reaching into his inside pocket, he produces a flat, black, velvet box. "Here," he says, his gorgeous eyes gazing lovingly into mine. "It's a, 'just because,' gift. There's no other reason, other than I love you, and I can't wait to marry you."

I blink up at him, then down at the box. He opens it up and inside is a beautiful platinum bracelet with four circular diamonds set into it and an inscription engraved inside. 'Every moment spent with you, is a moment I cherish. Love you more, M x;-)'

Tears pool in my eyes, my heart swelling in my chest. "Max, it's beautiful…I…" My throat closes around the words. Everything he does is so deeply moving.

Removing it from the box, he places it around my wrist. I take his face between my palms and kiss him softly on the lips. "Max, you're so romantic. I love you so much."

"Love you more, baby."

I begin to giggle and cry at the same time. I'm so happy.

"Hey! Banks! You gotta see this, Frank's dancing to Gangnam Style and it's hideous. We should video him and put it on Youtube." Clive grabs my elbow, hauling me to my feet. Max waves me away with a grin and I leave him talking to Vinnie.

Watching Frank attempting the dance is hilarious. Who knew he could be so much fun? Once the floor show is over, Clive notices my new bracelet then everyone shows an interest crowding around me to take a look, oohing and ahhing when I tell them what Max has engraved inside it.

As we bounce to the beat, I notice Max has left the table

and is now standing at the bar talking to someone in a dark suit. When I realise who it is, I stop moving, my body turning rigid and my skin now chilled by a cold sweat.

"What's the matter?" Lucy asks, pulling on my arm. I'm just standing like a statue staring at Max talking to Greg Taylor, wondering what the fuck he's doing here. I quickly scan the room looking for my mum, grateful to see that she's with Jan and Sylvie out on the roof garden, they seem to be deep in conversation and it would appear she hasn't noticed Greg is here. But why is he here?

I pull out of Lucy's hand. "I'm going to the loo."

"Are you okay? You look white as a sheet."

"Yes, I'm fine. The babies are resting on my bladder." I force a smile and although she still looks concerned, it seems to be enough. "Back in a minute."

I begin to shake as I make my way over to the bar. Greg has no right being here, he can fuck off. I can't understand why Max would invite him, he's only a client for fuck's sake.

As I get close enough to hear their conversation, I stumble to a halt when I see Max shaking Greg's hand, thanking him for his gift.

Gift?...What gift?

Max sees me, beckoning me over to him with an outstretched arm and a big smile. "Here's my girl," he says, wrapping his arm around my waist and pulling me into his side. "Baby, you remember Greg? He's very kindly provided all the Champagne and this beautiful venue for our party tonight, as a wedding gift, isn't that nice?"

WHAT?

Surprise, anger, confusion, and loathing, battle it out in my brain. Greg's smug smile leers down at me and I feel Max's arm tighten around my waist as he waits for my response, but I'm speechless. I don't want his fucking gifts. He's trying to manipulate me, and Max. And if Max finds out...

When Greg leans forward to kiss me on my cheek, I feel myself physically recoiling slightly but I try not to let my disgust for him show.

"Congratulations, Vivienne. You look beautiful." The touch of his lips against my cheek makes me want to vomit but when he whispers in my ear, "And fuckable." I stiffen.

Realising Max is confused at my lack of gratitude, I force myself to respond with a fake smile and a pleasant tone. "Thank you, Mr. Taylor. Your generosity is beyond belief." The words almost choke me on their way out. What I really want to say would start a war and the consequences would be devastating.

Out the corner of my eye, I see my mother heading our way with a deep set frown on her face. Turning to Max, I smile up at him. "Max, would you mind asking my mum to dance, she's heading over to the bar and I don't want her drinking. Just distract her while I go to the loo."

"Sure, baby. Is everything okay, you look a little pale."

"No, everything's fine. I won't be long."

With some difficulty, I hold my smile until he turns away. And as Max heads over to my mother, jovially whisking her around toward the dance floor, I set my angry eyes on Greg. "We need to talk. Somewhere private. Now!"

He smiles, that disgusting, lecherous, self-assured smile that sends a shiver up my spine. "Follow me, Princess."

As I stride out of the room behind Greg, I quickly glance over to Max. He's busy twirling my mum around on the dance floor, but her eyes are on me and she doesn't look happy.

Greg leads me past the lifts, the ladies' room, and down a corridor to a door marked private. He waits for me to enter then he closes the door behind him. A host of emotions quicken my heart rate and put a knot in my chest. I'm shaking like a leaf. I hate being this close to him.

Every muscle is taught with tension and the adrenaline coursing through my veins is causing a sickness in my stomach. I have to physically will myself to take deeper, slower breaths before I hyper-ventilate and pass out with nerves and frustration.

Greg chuckles, moving to his desk and taking a seat in his big leather chair. I remain standing, glaring down at him defiantly.

"You should have seen the look on your face, Vivienne. Max was all smiles and you were squirming like a worm on a hook." He laughs out loud like it's amusing to him, then he leans back in his chair with his elbows resting on the arms. Steepling his fingers together, he taps them impatiently. "Well? You wanted to talk, Princess, so talk."

Involuntary tears fill my eyes. I wanted to be strong and fearless, but he intimidates me so much. "This has to stop."

His smug smile broadens, telling me he has no intention of stopping. He's loving every minute of this.

I square my shoulders and straighten my back trying to appear more fearless than I am. And as I open my mouth to speak, I close it again when he leans forward, resting his forearms on his desk with a tilt to his head and an arrogant smile on his face. "You know, Vivienne, most people would be grateful to someone who's just thrown them an expensive party."

Anger and revulsion pulse through me. "Most people don't have parties thrown by the man who raped them as a child."

He laughs, and his arrogant, smug smile makes me want to smash his bloody face in. I don't know what I thought to achieve by talking to him, he clearly has no conscience at all.

"Look at me, Vivienne," he says, gesturing at his surroundings. "Look at what I've achieved. I'm minted. The big cheese. I'm at the top of the tree, hob-knobbing with the big boys. I have wealth, power, and status." His smile completely flattens to an angry sneer. "And I'm not going to let some stupid little girl and her drunk, whore mother take all that away from me. You need to keep your mother on a leash. If you can't control her, then I will."

His threat is crystal clear, but something inside me snaps, putting me on the attack. Placing both hands on his desk, I look him straight in the eye and lean forward with grim determination. "You may have wealth and power, Mr. Taylor. But that just means you have so much more to lose. You're nothing but a bully. You like to play games. You like to watch people squirm. That's what all this is about, isn't it? You just couldn't stay away, could you? You're sick!"

His indifferent smirk to my comment just riles my anger, driving me forward and strengthening my hatred for him.

"You've been a very lucky man, Mr. Taylor. But your luck is running out. I'm warning you, don't push it." The strength in my voice is short lived as my throat tightens around the last word.

He leans forward pushing his face closer to mine, making me take a step back from his desk. And as his dark eyes roam my face, they deliver his threat before he utters a word. "Or what, Vivienne? You'll tell Max?... I don't think so. If you were going to do that, you would have done it already."

I wince at the truth of his statement. And I hate that he intimidates me.

"But you're right not to tell him, Vivienne. I've heard Max can be very protective of the one's he loves. And he really does love you, Princess. You, more than anyone." His lecherous eyes travel lazily all over my body. "But then, who could blame him? You've turned into a very beautiful woman."

His smug smile disintegrates into a snarl. "I suggest you continue to keep your pretty little mouth shut. Because if Max comes after me, he could get himself into a lot of trouble when I sue him for assault. Especially when the press find out about his penchant for whips and razor blades. You wouldn't want that, would you Princess? Besides, it's your word, and the word of a boozed-up druggie, against mine."

Dark eyes penetrate mine as his face hardens to an ugly sneer, then he opens his mouth to lick his lips as if he's savouring the moment. I jolt when he stands abruptly and rounds his desk in a brisk movement that makes me stumble back a couple of paces. I feel trapped, like an animal being stalked.

As my foot bumps into the leather Chesterfield, I gasp, almost collapsing down into it. And when I regain my balance, I quickly move away from him wishing I had stayed near the door. "Don't come any closer!" I yell, my voice stifled by fear, my heart beating out of my chest. "Stay the fuck away from me, you bastard!"

He watches me with dark, amused eyes. His salacious grin curling his lips into a smile the devil would be proud of. And then, to my utter disbelief, he holds both hands up in surrender. "You should rejoin your party, Vivienne. Max will be wondering where you are."

A flash of relief pulses through me. He's letting me go.

I start toward the door but he beats me to it, standing in my path. Reaching his hand out as if to shake mine, I stare down at it in confusion.

"I was just trying to do a nice thing, Vivienne. That's all." He shrugs and smiles, but there's not a jot of sincerity in his face. "It's just a party."

"You're sick," I grate, refusing to shake his hand. As I scowl up at him and try to push past him to get to the door, he reaches out and grabs my arm with one hand, placing the other on my baby bump. The contact makes me feel physically sick. Sliding his rough, calloused hand down my bare arm as a sneering smile slinks across his face, I shudder with revulsion.

"You look good, Vivienne. Pregnancy suits you."

Seething with anger, I push his hands away from me and lunge for the door. Just as I open it, I freeze when he says, "I hope they are little girls, just as pretty as their mother. Two pretty little dolls."

A violent rage has me spinning around and slapping his face hard, rocking him back on his heels in shock. The sting in my palm hurts like hell, but it was worth it to see the look on his face. "Stay the fuck away from me and my family! Or so help me, I'll fucking kill you!"

I don't wait for his response, and while I still have the strength in my legs, I march straight to the ladies' room and lock myself into one of the cubicles. Trembling with frustration and adrenaline, with tears streaming down my face, I collapse down to the toilet seat with my head in my hands.

"Viv, it's me."

Shit! My mother's voice has my head whipping up in a

panic. I try to control my voice and make it sound normal. "Won't be a minute."

Quickly blotting the tears with some tissue, I organise my expression before opening the door.

I walk over to the sink with my head down and wash my hands, wondering why my mother is just standing there staring at me without talking. When I bring my eyes up to hers in the mirror, she gives me a look that frightens me.

"I have nothing left to lose, Vivienne." Her expression and voice are defiant. "I'm dying anyway, I might as well take him with me."

"What?" I spin around and grab her shoulders. "Mum! Promise me you'll stay away from him. Don't do anything stupid. You're no match for him, I mean it, Mum. You have to promise me!"

Her defiant expression evaporates as her shoulders sag and her eyes glisten. "Why are you protecting him?"

"Mum, please listen to me. I'm not protecting him, I'm protecting myself. Why can't you understand that? If Max finds out, he'll kill him. I can't lose him, Mum. I can't! Promise me you won't say anything. Please!"

Mum's sad, tortured expression slowly slips into one of defeat and resignation.

Once we've calmed down and I've managed to salvage my appearance into something a little less anxious, we leave the ladies room and head back to the party.

Max is leaning against the bar looking agitated. And as soon as he sees me, he comes striding over with a look of concern.

I take a deep breath then quietly ask my mum to go back to our table.

"Where have you been? Are you alright?" Max watches my mum walk on to our table then he turns to face me looking very anxious. "I was worried about you. Everything okay?"

"Yes," I smile, "Mum was feeling a bit weepy so we had a little chat. She's fine now."

His concerned eyes search mine, looking for confirmation, then he pulls me into his chest, kissing the top of my head.

"You owe me a dance."

I'd really like to go home now, but that would take some explaining, so I do my best to put Greg out of my mind and act normal. "Okay, one hot twerk coming right up."

He grins, obviously keen on that idea, then his eyes become hooded and seductive and he hasn't let go of me yet.

"What?… What is it?"

"Nothing," he smiles. "It's just, I hate it when I can't see you. In a crowded room, I find myself searching you out. Even if I can't touch you the way I want to in public, as long as I can see you, I feel better." His smile is bashful and so very adorable. "I know," he smirks. "It's cheesy, right? But I miss you, even if it's just for a few minutes."

I smile up at him, laying my hands on his chest. "You know, I think there's a technical term for that… It's called stalking."

He laughs then dazzles me with his bone-melting smile. Curling my hand around the back of his neck, I pull him down to me for a kiss knowing that whatever challenges I face, his kisses always soothe me.

~

Some of our guests have gone home already. Lucy and Dan, Cole and Hannah, and Julie and John, are smooching to some slow songs out on the dance floor. Max and I, and the few that are left, are enjoying a final drink out on the roof garden in the warm night air. Greg hasn't shown his face anymore, and apart from the incident with him earlier, my family and friends have made tonight very special.

Sitting comfortably in Max's lap as he strokes my thigh, I stare at my beautiful bracelet feeling happy and content.

As Jan has accepted Vinnie's proposal, the conversation inevitably comes around to their wedding plans, but when Jan tells us Greg has offered his restaurant to her and Vinnie for their wedding venue, I feel myself stiffen with anger.

"It's such a lovely gesture," Jan says, gazing up at Vinnie. He's agreeing, completely oblivious to the true nature of his old friend.

I'm baffled that someone like Vinnie, someone so good and kind could know someone so dark and evil.

"How do you know him, Vinnie?"

"We went to the same school as nippers, and we ended up in the same regiment when we joined up. I lost contact with him when his dad died. He inherited a ton of dosh, left the squad, and moved away for a while. We met up in a pub a few months ago."

"Was he a close friend?" I ask, intrigued to know what Vinnie finds so appealing about that vile creature.

"Nah, we were never besties, but he always seemed like an alright geezer, and I can't fault his generosity." He smiles giving Jan a cuddle.

I hate the fact that Greg is worming his way into our lives. But he's playing a very dangerous game and I want him gone. He masquerades as a stand-up guy, but he's a devil in disguise, a rapist. The fact that he's got away with it for all these years must make him feel invincible. But how many other lives has he destroyed? How many more will he claim in the future?

"Baby? Are you okay?"

"Oh, sorry, I—"

"Viv!" Lucy comes running out to the roof-garden with panic in her eyes. "Come quick, your mum's arguing with some bloke and I think she's been drinking."

Fuck! Scrambling out of Max's lap, I rush into the main room. My stomach rolls when I see my mother repeatedly poking her finger at Greg's chest. The snarl on her face and her body language is pure hostility. Greg is snarling down at her in disgust as he tries to push her away.

Cole comes running over, giving me a knowing look. My heart is in my mouth and my belly churns because I can't see a way out of this.

Max starts toward them but I quickly yank his arm back to stop him. "Please, just let me talk to her."

I shoot a look to Cole who thankfully chimes in with an agreement. Cole thinks I'm still trying to protect my mother's dignity and I'm grateful that he does. I don't want Max hearing anything she has to say.

Vinnie tries to come with me, but I ask him to stay with the others and wait until I've spoken with my mother. "It's okay, just let me calm her down."

Everyone is staring at me in confusion, but thankfully they all stay put and leave me to sort this out on my own.

I walk over to the bar on shaking legs. "Mum!" I hiss, grabbing her arm and trying to pull her away from Greg.

He gives me a filthy look then he knocks back a shot of Vodka, slamming his empty shot glass on the bar. "Tell your fucking whore of a mother to keep her fucking hands off me," he grates, his voice a low threatening grunt, then he turns to walk away.

Mum suddenly rips her arm out of my hands and lunges at his back. She screams at him, beating her hands against his shoulders. "Don't you walk away from me you fucking bastard! You're going to pay!"

In a blind panic, I try to pull her off him but she won't stop. Greg spins around so fast my mother stops moving and even backs up a step. His eyes are hard and his teeth are gritted as he glares down at her with a savage snarl on his face. "Look at you! Embarrassing yourself in front of your daughter. Call yourself a mother! You're a fucking drunk!" He flashes me an evil glare then starts to walk off again as Mum grabs something from her bag, I'm shocked to see it's a long kitchen knife.

"And you're a fucking paedo!" she screams. "You should be castrated for what you've done."

The blood drains from my head, leaving me breathless and shaking. I stand there, unable to move, unable to breathe, watching the whole horrific scenario unfolding in front of my eyes. Everything I had tried so hard to protect is slipping through my fingers at an alarming rate and I'm powerless to do anything about it.

Max is beside me before I know it. Cole has his arms around my mother's shoulders pulling her back. And now that he has an audience, Greg is straightening his suit, doing his best to bluff his way out of it.

"She's a fucking drunk!" he grunts. "She's always been a drunk. She's probably high on crack as well! Pff, she doesn't even know what day it is!"

"I'm sober!" Mum yells, defiantly. "I haven't touched a drop for twenty-four days."

I suddenly realise she is sober. Her voice is steady and crystal clear, and her eyes, although filled with tears, are fully focused.

Greg fidgets and shifts on his feet, his eyes swinging nervously between us. Although bound by Cole's arms, Mum still tries to lunge at him with the knife. The look Greg gives her unleashes my anger, but as my mother continues to speak, the anger rapidly becomes fear.

"She was only ten years old. Ten! And you put your filthy fucking hands on her. You ruined her life, you ruined all our lives! You took away her smile, her innocence. You're a fucking monster!" She lunges for him again but Cole holds her back.

I didn't even feel him move, but Max is on Greg in the blink of an eye. One hand, his injured one, has him by the throat, the other fist bearing down on him with bone crunching force, beating him to a pulp.

"You're fucking dead you son-of-a-bitch!" I don't even recognise Max's voice bellowing down at him, and the crazed look on his face terrifies me.

Blood splatters everywhere as Max relentlessly hammers his fist into Greg's face over and over again, forcing him to the floor.

"Stop! Please stop!" I scream, frantically looking to Cole for help but he's struggling to hold my mother back. I turn to Vinnie who's whispering something to Julie, she nods and quickly disappears, then he comes running over to me.

"Stop him, Vinnie. Please! Oh, my god, he'll kill him!"

With a calm, controlled voice, Vinnie gives an order to Cole. "Julie will be back soon, put Carol in the Range Rover with Sylvie and Hannah. Julie will take them back to the penthouse, then come back here. Go!"

As Cole drags my mum away, Vinnie tries to stop Max from beating Greg to death, but Max is relentless, he won't stop pounding into him. The dark rage in his eyes is terrifying. He's tripped, there's no stopping him.

Hearing my screams, John comes running into the room looking confused at the scene, then immediately he springs into action helping Vinnie. Eventually they manage to haul Max off of Greg, but it takes all their efforts.

Fear strangles my heart when I see the look on Max's face and Greg's lifeless body lying at his feet in a pool of blood. John drags Max away, holding him back while Vinnie checks Greg's pulse. He turns to look up at me, letting out a relieved sigh which puffs out his cheeks. "He's alive."

With utter relief, I sag and collapse to the floor in a heap of wailing sobs.

"Vivienne!" Max jerks out of John's hold and scrambles over to me, pulling me into his arms, burying his face in my neck. "I'm so sorry."

I don't know what he was apologising for, but I'm so relieved he hadn't killed him. He pulls my head back, holding it in his hands, looking down at me with tortured, watery eyes. "Why didn't you tell me?" His choked, incredulous voice breaks my heart. I never wanted him to know. I shake my head, unable to speak through the emotion crippling my vocal chords.

"…I'm sorry."

He looks devastated, then he kisses me hard on the lips, wrapping me in his arms and crushing me to his chest.

We both look up when Greg groans loudly, rolling onto his side coughing and spluttering. Blood is gushing from his broken nose and the cuts to his lip, jaw, and cheekbone. Pushing himself up onto one elbow, he throws us a filthy look of contempt. I can feel Max's muscles turning to stone beneath my hands.

"Please, Max! No more!"

He sighs deeply, angrily, and I see the struggle in his eyes. I know what he wants to do. He wants to finish the job, he wants to kill him. But I can't let him do that. I won't. Eventually, on an aggravated sigh, the tension slowly leaves his muscles, although, none of the hatred has left his eyes.

Vinnie helps Greg to his feet. He's wobbly and unsteady on his feet but Greg pushes Vinnie away defiantly, and spits out some blood to the floor, gingerly feeling his broken nose with his shaking hands.

"Get the fuck out of my restaurant!" he yells. And with a contemptuous glare, he staggers out of the room.

Vinnie moves toward us as Max helps me to my feet, his angry eyes still on Greg's back as he walks away. I feel his arms releasing me, he wants to finish the job, but Vinnie blocks him and holds him back. Max strains against Vinnie's hand spread firmly against his chest, his jaw tightly clenched, his eyes dark and full of rage as every muscle turns to stone.

"Guv'! Think about Vivienne and the babies. Now isn't the time. That cunt will get what's coming to him, but right now, I want you out of here."

"Did you know about him, and what he did?" Max asks, his jaw pulsing madly.

Vinnie looks offended. Standing his ground, he straightens his back and lifts his chin. "Do you even have to ask me that?"

Max lowers his head and his voice. "I'm sorry."

Taking a deep breath, he reaches down for my hand, gripping it tightly, almost painfully. I turn to see Jan, Hannah, Lucy and Dan staring at us with wide eyes and open mouths, then Julie arrives with Cole following on behind. She gives Vinnie a knowing look which he returns. It's like they're having a silent conversation.

"Sylvie and Carol are in the car," she says, still looking at Vinnie. "Shall I take Lucy and Dan home too."

He nods. "Yeah, everyone back to the penthouse. Don't hang about, no detours."

After another exchange, they break eye contact. She gives John a knowing look, then she ushers Lucy and Dan out to the lifts. Cole takes Hannah's hand and starts to walk her out too until Vinnie calls out to him stopping him in his tracks.

"Straight back to the penthouse, quick as you can." Vinnie then walks over to Jan, reaching down for her hands he gives her a tender kiss on the lips. As they break apart, I see him handing her something which she slides into her handbag. After another quick embrace, Jan follows the others.

"Okay, Guv'," Vinnie says, striding toward us. "We'd better go."

The Bentley is waiting for us at the front of the building. Cole opens the passenger door, giving Hannah a quick kiss before she enters the vehicle. After we're all inside, he walks around to the driver's seat.

Max pulls me into his lap, still tense and rigid with anger. His bruised and bloodied hand travelling up and down my arm as he holds me close.

As I glance out the window, I can hear Vinnie talking to John in a low voice as they approach the car. "No. I'm going to drive the DB9. I'll be right behind you. I'll see you back at the penthouse. Go straight there, no stopping. And keep your eye on the Governor, under no circumstances let him leave. He's too volatile right now."

"Copy that."

As John enters the car and Vinnie slams the door shut, Cole pulls away from the kerb following the Range Rover.

WHO DARES…

The atmosphere on the way home is thick with questions nobody dares to ask. Poor Hannah seems a little shell-shocked by it all, but Jan squeezes her hand, silently reassuring her.

As we enter the penthouse in silence, everyone pairs up and heads straight for the living room to take a seat. I'm glad to see my mum has calmed down and is helping Sylvie to one of the comfortable chairs.

Dan and Lucy head for the kitchen to organise some drinks, teas and coffees, and Max walks me straight through to the study, closing the door behind us.

Taking me in his arms he buries his face in my hair, releasing a long, weary sigh against my skin. His face has been a mask of anger all the way home, he hasn't spoken, and he's covered in Greg's blood.

After a few moments, he pulls back, holding my face in his hands, searching my eyes with his sad, watery gaze. "Why didn't you tell me, Vivienne? I'd never have let him near you if I'd known what he'd done to you. Jesus, Vivienne! Why wouldn't you tell me about something so important!"

I'm lost for words. Staring into his sad, tortured face, I burst into tears.

"What he did to you… He's the reason you thought you'd

never have kids, isn't he?"

"I'm sorry." Heavy sobs inhibit my ability to say anything else.

Pulling away from me, he begins to pace, dragging his hands through his hair. Fear and anxiety curdle my stomach because the look on his face scares me.

"No!" he says, shaking his head. "I can't let that cock-sucker get away with it. I'm going to fucking kill him!" He starts toward the door but in a panic, I block him putting my hands on his chest, trying to hold him back.

"No, Max! Please!"

He stares down at me with a torrent of emotions colouring his face. His eyes burning into mine with a need to make this right. "Move out of the way." His voice is low and measured as he tries to control his anger.

"No! Please, Max. He's not worth it!"

"Vivienne… Move out of the way."

He's beyond angry, beyond control. I know I'm pushing my luck but I can't let him leave. He'll either play right into Greg's hands, or he'll kill him. Either way, I'll lose Max.

Something inside me triggers, giving me an inner strength. A protective instinct, maybe a maternal instinct, whatever it is, it kicks in empowering me to take control. Looking him straight in the eye, I reach my trembling hand up to his cheek. My voice is strong and determined, focusing his attention.

"Max. I won't lose you over that man. I know you want to make him pay, but I can't, and I won't let you do it like this. That's why I didn't tell you. I won't spend the rest of my life without you."

Dark, turbulent eyes blaze down at me and the hollows in his cheeks pulse with anger. "Vivienne, please. I need to do this."

"No. You don't. I know about anger and revenge. I've hated that man for fourteen years, but he's not worth it. None of that matters now. We have each other, we have the babies. We'll make him pay, but not like this."

I know he understands, but I can see the furious struggle

within him. I begin to fear that my words have had no impact, but then, to my utter relief his shoulders sag, he lowers his head, releases a long, deep sigh, then presses his forehead against mine. "What did I ever do to deserve your love?" he whispers in a choked, broken voice.

Pulling back, he cups my face in his hands, his watery eyes blazing with love. "You're so strong. I should have been protecting you, but you're always protecting me. Putting me first… Why?"

I gaze up at him, letting my eyes revel in the love pouring out from his beautiful blues. "Because I love you. Because there is no me without you. Because you promised me forever."

His lips crush into mine with an urgent kiss, a hungry kiss, unfurling all the feelings held deep inside me. I kiss him back with a raging passion, eager to possess the one thing I could never live without. The one thing I will protect to my last breath.

When we walk out of the study hand in hand, everyone falls silent for a moment just staring at us, and then the chatter resumes as Max walks me over to the sofa to sit with my mum and Sylvie.

"I'll be back in a minute."

Panic grips me. "Why? Where are you going?" I ask, eager to keep him in my sights.

"I'm going to change out of these clothes. I need to get his stink off me."

I watch him walk away and head upstairs. I'm still fearful that he'll try to go back to the restaurant to find Greg. He's trying to disguise it but I can see the simmering anger in his eyes.

Sylvie squeezes my hand, distracting me. "Your mother has told me everything, Vivienne. I'm so sorry sweetheart, I had no idea you'd been through so much at the hands of that vile bastard."

I take a seat next to my mum. With watery eyes and a weak smile, she takes my hand, squeezing it between hers. "I'm so sorry, Viv. I never meant to cause all this trouble. I just couldn't stand to see that bastard manipulating you like that. But we can go to the police now. We can tell them everything. We can put that fucker behind bars where he belongs!"

The hope in her eyes, makes my heart ache. I squeeze my mother's hand, trying hard not to cry. "Mum, we have no proof. It's Greg's word against mine."

"But I can testify."

"No, Mum. Don't you remember? The night it happened you were passed out. And the social services have it on record that you were abusing drugs and alcohol, Greg's lawyers will just throw it out of court. It's not worth it. Besides, I don't want the press to find out about this. They'll slaughter us."

Mum caves into my shoulder sobbing. "Oh, Viv, I'm so sorry. I've been such a shit mother."

Sylvie reaches across and pats my mum's knee. "Carol, come on now, dry your tears. You're here now, and tonight you stood up for your daughter, you fought for her. Don't waste what precious time you have left together."

I reach over and squeeze Sylvie's hand. Her words have moved me and she's right, no one can change the past, but we can all make a better future.

Leaving my mum and Sylvie, I head to the kitchen to get a glass of water and something to settle my swirling stomach. I also want to speak to Vinnie, he must be feeling awful knowing he was the one who had brought Greg into our lives.

As I walk toward the kitchen, I glance into the dining room and see Julie sitting at the table staring down into her laptop. Whatever she's doing is taking all her concentration. John appears out of nowhere making me jump, I hadn't realised he was in the room with her.

"Can I get you anything, Ma'am?"

"Oh, ah, no, I'm okay."

"Your friends are in the kitchen." He gestures behind me and I get the distinct impression I'm being moved on.

Lucy and Dan are sitting at the island with Jan, Hannah, and Cole. They've all got a drink and right now, I could use one too. As I check my watch, I realise I haven't seen Vinnie return yet. I wander over to the fridge and grab a bottle of water, then I take a seat next to Cole. "Jan, where's Vinnie?"

"Oh, he's not back yet." Her brow is creased with a nervous frown and she's wringing her hands. When our eyes meet, she offers me a weak smile, but she's clearly worried about something, there's fear in her eyes. "He's probably caught in traffic," she adds, her voice trembling slightly. "I'm sure he won't be long. Are you okay? How are you feeling?"

"A little nauseous, but I'm okay."

I do feel better knowing I'm no longer burdened with the secrets and lies of my past, but it's not over yet. Dread still lurks in my chest like a stone. Greg will want to retaliate in some way, bullies always do.

He's suffered a humiliating defeat in his own restaurant, in front of his own staff. And I know Max and Cole will do whatever it takes to terminate any deals they've made with him. They'll make sure he's blacklisted all over the city and God knows what Max will do now. His protective nature will demand he does something. No, this is far from over.

Cole reaches across the island taking my hand, his expression brings fresh tears to my eyes. "You should have told me the truth, Vivienne. Christ! I made you work for that fucker! How do you think that makes me feel?"

"I know. And I'm sorry. But you saw what Max did to him, that's why I couldn't tell anyone."

Lucy slides off her chair and walks around the island. Standing behind me, she wraps her arms around my shoulders giving me an affectionate hug. "That fucker deserved to have his nose spread all over his face. It was a long time coming if you ask me." She kisses me on the temple then moves back to Dan who pulls her toward him for a cuddle.

I glance over at the oven. The clock says 01:53am. We arrived home at five minutes to one. Where the hell is Vinnie?

Jan looks up at the kitchen door behind me, her body physically sagging with relief. As I turn around, I see Vinnie striding into the kitchen. He walks straight over to Jan, taking her face in his big, tattooed hands, then he kisses her on the lips. A full on smacker full of meaning and intent, I've never seen them so emotional before.

I look away, but in my peripheral vision I notice Jan handing something to him. When I look back, Vinnie's sliding his phone and ID card into his jacket pocket. As he does so, Jan grabs his wrist, and the fear is back in her eyes.

"Vincent! Where's your cuff link?" Her voice is hurried and panicky. Staring into her eyes, he subtly shakes his head, then reaches up to stroke her cheek. No words are exchanged but he's telling her a mouthful with his eyes.

"Oh, good! Your back."

We all turn to face Julie. I notice her and Vinnie exchanging another one of those knowing looks. "Upload complete," she says, quietly, then she walks away.

What's going on?

"Where's the Governor?" Vinnie asks.

Cole shrugs. "Last time I saw him he was heading upstairs to change."

My body turns rigid when I realise he's been gone for ages. "Oh, no!" Sliding off my stool, I bolt for the stairs. I run up them two at a time and burst into the bedroom. He's not here but his clothes are strewn all over the bedroom floor. I race into the bathroom, the steam and droplets of water still cling to the glass panels of the shower. "Max! Where are you?"

I run back out through the bedroom and check the guest rooms, but he's vanished. Standing in the corridor, panicked and shaking and gasping for breath, I hear a repetitive thudding noise coming from the gym.

As I hesitantly open the door and walk in, I see Max naked, punching the hell out of the gym bag. He's not wearing any gloves, and he's using both hands. His injured hand must be killing him, but I know why he needs the pain. This is what he does. He's punishing himself.

"Stop! Please!"

Hearing my voice, he stops punching the bag and holds it still between his bloodied hands. Bowing his head between his shoulder blades, he tries to hide his tear stained face.

"Please, Max. You don't need to do this… Not for me."

Vinnie and John barge through the door behind me. "Thank fuck for that!" Vinnie huffs, then they both quietly back track, leaving us alone.

Seeing him like this breaks my heart. I walk over to him pulling his injured hand away from the punch bag. His knuckles are red, swollen, and bleeding. The blue wrist wrap, soaked from his shower and spotted with blood.

"Come on, let's get you cleaned up." I tug on his arm but he resists me and when he raises his head, his sad, tortured, watery eyes find mine.

"I should have protected you, Vivienne. I should have—"

"You do protect me. No one has ever loved and protected me more. But what you're doing right now, Max. Seeing you like this?… It hurts. It really fucking hurts. Please don't hurt me anymore, Max. Please." I tug on his arm and this time he moves so fast, I gasp as he pulls me into a tight, desperate hug.

We hold each other for a long while, both of us in tears, both of us needing the connection. He's quiet and introverted, but he lets me lead him into our bedroom. After I've cleaned up his bruised and bloodied knuckles, I change his wrist wrap for a dry one. The firm outer shell has protected him well but his wrist is very swollen, as are his hands.

He doesn't want to go to the hospital so after I've patched him up and helped him dress, we go downstairs to join the others.

As we hit the bottom step the doorbell chimes. I look up to Max. "Who's that at this time of night?" He shrugs shaking his head, but his eyes are fixed on the door and his muscles begin to tense.

Vinnie strides out of the kitchen, he stops, takes a breath, then he looks over at us with a strange expression that puts every nerve ending on alert. As he opens the door, I see a tall black man with a uniformed officer standing behind him.

I feel Max's arm tightening around me. "That fucker's brought charges."

"What do you mean? They're not going to arrest you are they?" My voice is high pitched and anxious. My heart sinking as my stomach rolls.

Max looks over to John. "Call my lawyer."

"Yes, Sir." John disappears and then Julie walks out of the dining room with her laptop under her arm. As she walks past us, she gives me a comforting smile.

Vinnie brings the officers into the living room. The tall black man extends his hand to Max for a shake, but then stops short when he sees the condition of his bruised and bloodied hands.

"I'm D.I. Langford, we met when—"

"I remember," Max interrupts sharply. "Let's just get on with this, shall we. I take it he's pressing charges?"

The D.I. gives us both a strange look. "Could we talk privately, Mr. Foxx?"

On a deep, angry sigh, Max turns toward the study releasing me from his hold.

"I want to come too," I blurt, anxiously.

The D.I. turns to face me. "That's fine." With a smile, he gestures for me to go first and we follow Max into the study. The uniformed officer waits outside.

Panic consumes me as my mind contemplates the possibility that Max will be arrested for assault, or worse. What if Greg has died from his injuries?

Max offers the D.I. a seat, then he reaches for my hand walking me to the chair at the side of his desk before taking his seat behind it. "Do I need a lawyer for this conversation D.I. Langford?"

He looks at Max's bloodied hands resting on his desk, then he looks him straight in the eyes. "You can wait for your lawyer to arrive if you wish, Mr. Foxx, but I don't think that will be necessary. I just want to ask you a few questions about your altercation with Mr. Taylor this evening."

"Shoot."

Max appears calm and in control, although, his jaw is clenching and his brow is lowered over his eyes. I, on the other hand, feel sick to my stomach.

"Some of Mr. Taylor's bar staff witnessed you giving him a pretty severe beating earlier this evening. Can you tell me what that was about, Mr. Foxx?"

Max's face hardens as his hands clench into fists on the desk. He opens his mouth to answer but I interrupt.

"He called my mother a drunk whore!" I didn't mean to blurt it out, but I couldn't help myself. I'm angry Greg is turning all this to his advantage.

D.I. Langford looks surprised at my outburst then returns his gaze to Max.

Leaning forward, Max locks eyes with the D.I. in a hard implacable stare. "Look, the guy deserved it. He's an asshole! And if you want the truth, I'd do it again. If he wants to press charges then go ahead, arrest me."

The D.I. narrows his eyes on Max. Sitting forward in his seat, he rests his forearms on his knees. He has an expression I can't quite fathom. "Mr. Foxx… Greg Taylor is dead."

I gasp, bringing my hand to my mouth as tears burn in my eyes. My worst fears have come true.

Max looks as shocked as I am. "When? How? I punched the fucker out, but he got up and walked away. He was alive when I left him."

The D.I. nods in agreement. "Yes, the bar staff said that's what happened. And the security cameras confirm it."

An overwhelming feeling of dread churns in my stomach, hardening my throat and constricting my chest until I can't breathe. "Then why are you here?" I ask anxiously. "Is Max a suspect?"

The D.I. flips me a small reassuring smile. "No. He's not."

I'm utterly confused but enormously relieved. Getting up, I walk to Max's chair and crawl into his lap as the D.I. continues.

"La Roche has the same state of the art security system as you do, Mr. Foxx. I'm assuming that because of Mr. Taylor's penchant for child pornography, he chose not to install security cameras in his personal quarters, but the entry system is exceptional. It logs every digital device entering and leaving the building, tracking its movements and logging the data. We cross referenced the security system at La Roche with your own system here at Foxx-Tech, and you were all logged in here at the penthouse long before Greg Taylor died."

Max pulls me closer. "How do you know what time he died?"

The D.I. sits back in his chair crossing his legs and resting his hands in his lap.

"Mr. Taylor was found dead in his office. He had been watching child pornography on his laptop. The laptop uses face and fingerprint recognition, and when Mr. Taylor logged on, it gave us the exact time of one-oh-three-a.m. You and your party were all logged in here at twelve-fifty-five."

Max's eyes drift down to mine for a fleeting moment as if he's trying to tell me something, then they drift back up to the D.I.

"The building's fire alarm was activated twelve minutes after Mr. Taylor logged on, which is when the staff and all the building's occupants evacuated onto the street. But there was no fire. And we suspect the person or persons involved in Mr. Taylor's death, used the chaos of the evacuation to make their escape. When the fire department and uniformed officers arrived at one-twenty-three-a.m. Mr. Taylor was pronounced dead at the scene."

Max's brow lowers over his eyes and his muscles tense up. "So, after we left…he sat down to watch kiddie porn?"

"Yes."

"Jesus!" He squeezes me tighter, exhaling a deep, aggravated sigh. "That fucking piece of shit! How did that cock-sucker die?"

For some reason, the D. I. smirks, then his eyes slide over to mine as if assessing my ability to hear the details. "He was found sitting in his chair at his desk. His penis had been severed by some kind of cheese wire, or a garrotte, and it was pushed into his mouth. Basically, he suffocated and bled out, very quickly."

I shudder, remembering my mum screaming at Greg that she wanted to castrate him. Max gives me a sideways glance when he feels me tensing up as my mind tries to work out whether my mum could have done it. But how? When? She's been with us the whole time.

"So, if you're not here to arrest me, D.I. Langford, who did this to him?"

The D.I. uncrosses his legs and leans forward. "He had a figure eight carved into his forehead with his own letter opener. Although they're not known to operate in the U.K. we believe Mr. Taylor was murdered by a gang known as 'Infinite Black.' They deal in trafficking and child pornography among other things. The figure eight is their calling card."

I recognise the name, but Max remains totally impassive.

"We recovered records from Mr. Taylor's laptop which shows he'd had recent dealings with this gang. It would appear he owed them a substantial amount of money. Does the name Infinite Black mean anything to you Mr. Foxx?"

"No." Max gives nothing away in his face, but I'm shaking like a leaf and confused as hell.

A light tapping on the door has us all looking toward it. The door opens and a stranger walks into the room wearing a suit and carrying a briefcase.

"Stan," Max says, looking up at him. "Thanks for coming… D.I. Langford, this is my lawyer, Stanley Marks."

They shake hands. "I'm afraid you've had a wasted journey, Mr. Marks." D.I. Langford turns to face me, nodding a goodbye. "I'll leave you in peace," he says, striding for the door.

"Mr. Langford?" Max rises to his feet, placing me on mine, then he curls his arm around my waist pulling me close. "If I'm not a suspect, why are you here?"

"To check your security system's entry log." He turns to leave but turns back again. "Oh, shit. I almost forgot," he says, patting his breast pocket. He digs inside it, pulling out a small, round, gold object. Walking over to us, he holds it in the palm of his hand. "One of the staff found this at the bar. It was lying in the blood on the floor after you'd beaten Mr. Taylor, is it one of yours?"

We both look down at the gold cuff link with a design of a winged dagger engraved into the top if it and the letters W.D.W underneath. I recognise the design, Vinnie has the same winged dagger tattooed on his hand.

"No, it belongs to Vinnie. Vincent Parker."

The D.I. hands it to Max with raised eyebrows. "S.A.S. Wow." With a smile and a nod, he leaves the room looking very impressed.

Max walks over to his lawyer to shake his hand. "Thanks for coming over, Stan. I guess I won't be needing you tonight."

"My pleasure, Mr. Foxx. I'll say goodnight."

Taking me in his arms, Max gently smooths his fingers over my brow to clear the confused wrinkles. "Are you okay?" he asks, softly.

I nod, too bewildered to speak, my mind is all over the place. Tonight has been extraordinary. I never knew Vinnie was in the S.A.S., but that explains a lot.

There's a light tapping at the door then Vinnie walks in with Jan who seems very anxious. "Everyone's tired, Guv'. Cole's taken Hannah home, and Julie and John are driving Carol, Lucy and Dan home too. Lucy and your mum said to say goodbye and they'll call you in the morning, Miss."

I nod, still unable to talk, and Jan's expression is scaring me. She's hanging on to Vinnie with such a fearful look.

Vinnie cricks his neck, then he looks at Max with a wary expression. "Everything alright Guv'?"

Max smiles warmly. With a knowing look in his eyes, he closes the distance between them. "Yes, my friend." He pulls him into a tight, affectionate hug. "Thanks to you."

As they break apart, exchanging another long look steeped in emotion, Max looks down at the cuff link in his hand, moving it with a confused look on his face. "Are you missing one of these?"

Vinnie looks down at it, his eyebrows rising in surprise,

then he looks over to Jan. The look of relief on her face is immediate. Puffing out a sigh of relief, Vinnie smiles up at him. "I wondered where that had gone. Where did you find it?"

Max smirks. "I didn't, D.I. Langford did."

Vinnie looks shocked for a moment, then he chuckles and a big smile creeps across his face. "He who dares…"

I look between them, utterly confused and bewildered.

"So, what does this one do?" Max asks, pressing and pulling at the top of the cuff link.

"Never you mind," Vinnie smirks. "Give it to me, you donut. You'll only cut your fingers off."

"Is that the one you used to—"

"No." Vinnie raises his left hand revealing his other cuff link, his shirt sleeve is soaked in blood. "It was Carol who gave me the idea to—" He suddenly stops talking, his nervous eyes darting over to mine and in that moment when our eyes connect, it all sinks in becoming crystal clear.

Vinnie giving his devices to Jan to log him out of La Roche's security system and into Foxx-Tech's.

All the whispering and silent exchanges with Julie, 'Upload complete.' She'd obviously hacked into Greg's laptop to plant the records which would tie him to Infinite Black.

Vinnie's commands to put, and keep, everyone in the right place at the right time. The strategy conceived at a moment's notice, but executed with stealth and a resolute will to see it through to completion, no matter the personal risk involved.

Who Dares Wins.

It was all so precise and meticulous. But most important of all, Vinnie had kept Max safely protected throughout.

I stare up at his rugged face in absolute awe that he would put himself in such a perilous position. Whether he'd done it for Max or for me, I'll never know, and I'll never ask. I'll just be eternally grateful that he cares that much.

As I stare up at him with wide teary eyes and an open mouth, Vinnie's eyes become sad and he bows his head as if in shame. Placing my hand under his chin, I lift his eyes to mine.

"No, Vinnie. Never be ashamed of loving someone so much that you'd risk everything to protect them."

RARE AND BEAUTIFUL FOXX

After the horrors at La Roche with Max and Greg, our wedding, even our future together, seemed like it was slipping further and further away. Our relationship had been beset with tragedy and upheaval since day one. And when D.I. Langford had told us Greg was dead, I had convinced myself that Max would be accused of Greg's murder, and that my worst fears would come true.

Thankfully, and all because of Vinnie's love for us, Max was in the clear, and I was free from Greg's hold over me once and for all.

I had no conscience about Greg's death, or the way in which had he met his end. He brutalised me as a child and as far as I was concerned, he got what he deserved.

According to Julie, who had hacked into his laptop, Greg had kept trophies of all his victims in the form of photographs. He was a prolific offender with a sadistic regard for those he had preyed upon.

Julie had removed the photographs of me and the compromising pictures he'd held of my mother. None of which I wanted to see, and all of which were destroyed before the police had access to his computer.

Because of Vinnie, Max and I were safe. For once our life

hadn't been derailed and our wedding would go ahead as planned. We were another step closer to our happy ever after. Another step closer to forever.

~

Two days after our ill-fated engagement party, Max brought us here, to Paradiso Volpe. His private island in the Caribbean, where we have enjoyed six blissful days completely on our own.

Paradise doesn't even cover it. The tall leaning palm trees, white powder beaches, and crystal clear turquoise waters surrounding the island, exude peace and tranquillity. The Balinese architecture of the island's only accommodation, with its dark wooden structure, vaulted ceilings, tastefully decorated open plan design, and pristine white furnishings, offer luxurious comfort fit for royalty. It's everything you could dream of and wish for.

Every evening, after dining on the rooftop terrace, or the beach, or out on the pontoon over the water watching the incredible sunsets, we've taken a leisurely stroll hand in hand along the beach, and then we have returned to our suite to while away the hours in each other's arms. Heaven.

For me, being romanced by the man of my dreams in a real life paradise, made me realise how lucky I was to have the love of such a rare and beautiful man. As stunning as Paradiso Volpe is, anywhere with Max is paradise.

Our wedding guests are being flown in this afternoon, and will then be transported to the island by boat, in time for a pre-wedding barbecue on the beach later on tonight.

I'm looking forward to seeing everyone, but for the last six days it's just been the two of us, blissfully happy in each other's company, basking in the sun, snorkelling in the coral reefs, and swimming with the dolphins and turtles.

It's been idyllic, and I've loved every single moment we've shared together. I'm the luckiest girl on the planet, but in the back of my mind a tiny niggling thought catches me out every now and again as I wonder when the other shoe will drop.

Fiona...I wonder whatever happened to her?

~~*~~

"Morning! One cup of tea, and two toasted crumpets for the bride-to-be. Oh, and these were sitting outside your door." Lucy walks in with a tray in her hands, something clamped under her arm, and a big silly grin on her face.

Uncurling myself from Max's pillow, I stretch out with a satisfied sigh and a big smile. "Morning."

Once she's placed the tray down she releases the item from under her arm.

"What is it?" I ask, taking my time to wake up properly.

"Socks. From Pretty-boy."

I knew I should never have told her Max's nickname.

She holds up the socks to show me the printing on the soles. 'In case of cold feet!'

I chuckle, sitting myself up, patting the bed for Lucy to sit down. Reaching for my tea, my eyes land on the white rose resting on the tray, courtesy of my gorgeous fiancé, and there's a note attached. Holding the rose to my lips, I inhale the fragrant petals then I pull the delicate satin bow to release the note.

Every day I spend with you,
is the best day of my life.
Love you more,
Max ;-)
X

Tears begin to pool in my eyes. He's so romantic.

"Hey, lady! Don't start with the waterworks or you'll get me going."

"Oh, Luce, this week has been so amazing, and I can't believe it. We're here. We're getting married. At last."

"Yeah, well, don't put a hex on it before you're even dressed. You and drama have a habit of coming together at the worst possible time. Knowing you, you'll trip over your dress, head-butt the Judge, and chip a tooth when you fall flat on your face."

I laugh and cringe, but she's right. If recent history tells me anything, I do seem to be a danger magnet, and it has played on my mind.

"But don't worry," Lucy says, on a scowl. "Ed is going to be recording the whole thing, so if you do fall over, at least we'll have something funny to watch while you're in the hospital… Again."

"No. Not this time." I smile, I can't stop smiling. Reaching up, I fondle my locket. "Today is going to be perfect." Pulling Max's pillow into my chest, I inhale his scent.

"Aren't you nervous?" Lucy asks, taking a bite out of one of my crumpets.

"No. Not at all." I wasn't, but I suddenly get a pang of fear, just enough to pull an anxious frown. "Why? Is he nervous?"

Lucy's smile is accompanied with an affectionate frown and her eyes begin to glisten. "Viv, that man is aching to marry you. I've never seen a man more ready to commit than he is. And if it wasn't for me and Dan keeping him occupied, I think he would have dragged the Judge in here to marry you in your sleep!"

"Did he sleep alright?"

"Well, we saw him at breakfast and he looked great, as usual. He was grumbling about not being able to sleep with you last night, and then he went for a run on the beach with Cole. I've given Dan and Cole strict orders to keep him occupied while we get you ready."

As Lucy sits on the edge of my bed talking to me, I realise there's something different about her today. In fact, I noticed it when they arrived yesterday afternoon. Even Max made a comment about her.

I don't know what it is, but there's a definite glow to her skin, more than just her tan, and there's a pronounced twinkle in her eye. I had put it down to the fact that she's only been married for six weeks and has only just got back from her honeymoon, but no, this is different, this is… *Oh!*

Shaking my head, I can't help the silly smirk spreading all over my face.

"…What?" she asks sheepishly, lowering her eyes from mine, but I can see she's trying hard not to smile, and Lucy doesn't do coy, it's not in her nature. She's hiding something from me.

"Luce? Do you have something you want to tell me?"

She lowers her head even more but when she looks up again through her lashes, her big smile and glistening eyes confirm it. "I'm pregnant."

With a happy gasp, I leap forward and throw my arms around her. "Oh, Luce! I'm so happy for you. I knew there was something different about you. Why didn't you tell me yesterday?"

She sobs and giggles all at the same time. "I didn't want to steal your thunder. Besides, I only had it confirmed by the doctor two days ago."

"Oh, you silly moo," I sniffle, pulling back to look at her. "This is great news, and far too important to keep to yourself."

Her smile slides and then her brow pulls into a deep frown.

"I'm not like you, Viv. I don't know if I can do it. I don't know if I can handle it."

I cup her cheek with my palm. "Of course you can, Luce. Millions of women do it."

A cheeky smile slinks across her face. "Pff, having the baby will be a piece of cake. I just don't know if I can go nine months without a glass of wine. And what's worse, I won't be able to defend my title at the pub. I'll have to give up my sash as 'Piss-Head Champion.' It'll be the end of an era."

We burst out laughing. I know she's only joking, but she makes a valid point. She's such a lush.

"Is Dan excited?"

"Yeah, he can't wait, he's already making plans."

I wipe the tears from her cheeks with the bed sheet. "Does your mum and dad know?"

"Yes, and Dan's parents too, but they've been sworn to secrecy until we've had our twelve week scan."

I begin to picture all the things we can do together as new mums. "How far along are you?"

"Just six weeks. I reckon it happened on our pre-wedding party night in France. That was our last shag before our wedding."

I giggle and blot my own tears. I'm so happy for her, happy for them both.

My phone rings, and I can't help the beaming smile when I see it's Max calling.

"I'll leave you to it," Lucy says, rising from the bed. "You've got two hours. I'll be back to do your hair and makeup. No tripping, banging your head, or falling over. In fact, just stay in bed until I bring the bubble wrap." She leaves, smirking over her shoulder.

Twirling the delicate white rose between my fingers, I answer his call. "Good morning, Mr. Foxx."

"Good morning, beautiful-soon-to-be-wife." His velvety rasp caresses my ear, bringing my butterflies to life. I can hear the smile in his voice.

Sighing with deep contentment, I reach for his pillow to inhale his scent. "I missed you last night."

"Yeah, me too. I hate waking up without you, and I hate all this waiting."

I smile, stretching out across the bed. Rolling onto my stomach, I rest on my elbows, kicking my feet up behind me.

"Are you naked?" he asks, lowering his voice seductively.

"No," I giggle, "But I am wearing the saucy little slip you bought me. Lucy's just been in to deliver my breakfast."

"The white one?"

"No, the blue one. The white one is for tonight." I can hear him practically growling with lust through the phone.

"Ahh, you're killing me."

"Are you naked?" The image of Max fully naked in all his magnificence stirs my butterflies and puts a subtle throb between my thighs.

"I want to be naked, with you, but every time I try to sneak over to your room, Dan is all over me like a cheap suit. He's been following me around like a parole officer."

I laugh. "I know. But he's under orders from Lucy."

Max sighs deeply. "Tell me again why we had to spend last night apart? You know how much I hate not being able to see you, let alone touch you."

I smile, rolling my eyes. "Max, it's just tradition. But I agree, I've missed you, too. I can't wait to see you. But Mum and Lucy insist that we don't do anything to hex this marriage, and the way our luck has gone in the past, I'd hate to tempt fate."

"Baby, we are fate. We belong together. I hate it when we're apart. I've waited a long time for you to come along, Vivienne. I've waited a long time to make you mine, and you know how impatient I am."

"I know, me too. Not long now, Mr. Foxx… Any doubts?"

"I've loved you from the moment I first saw you. I've wanted to marry you ever since that moment. I know what I want, baby. You're what I want, and I'll follow you wherever you go. Until forever."

My heart stutters then explodes in my chest as his words bring tears to my eyes.

"Baby, do you even know how much I want to kiss you right now?"

"Ditto, Mr. Foxx. And thank you, the rose is beautiful."

"So are you, baby. I can't wait to see you, in…one hour and fifty-six minutes. Don't be late, or I'm coming for you. I've waited long enough."

"I won't be late, I promise."

"Good. I'll be the guy with the kick-ass smile on his face."

"I love you."

"Love you more, baby."

Ending the call, I lie there for a few moments letting the love and warmth in his voice soak in. He has such a vibrant, irresistible power over all of my senses, controlling my body even from a distance. I'm instinctively attuned to him, my response is automatic, it always has been and it's something I revel in and would never want to change.

As the ocean breeze wafts into my room, billowing the white silk curtains and carrying the scent of orchids and jasmine, I feel a sense of calm and tranquillity as it softly travels over my skin like a cool breath.

Gazing out of our enormous bedroom at the amazing view of the turquoise ocean, I release a deep sigh of contentment. It's beautiful here. The air is warm, the sky is blue, and only sparsely dotted with fluffy white clouds.

Our bedroom, which is practically on the beach, opens up on three sides with huge, glass, folding doors. And it has the most amazing panoramic views of the ocean and the islands beyond.

The infinity pool a few metres away, and the beautiful gardens of tropical plants and flowers add an elegance and peacefulness to our surroundings. And the turquoise blue of the crystal clear water is the exact same colour as Max's gorgeous eyes.

A speed boat catches my attention as it slices through the water churning up a white foamy wake. The billowing white banner rippling in the wind behind it reads;

YOU = AWESOME!

ME = THE LUCKIEST GUY ON THE PLANET!

Giggling to myself, I quickly grab my camera so I can take a picture of it as it comes around for another fly by.

As I finish my tea and crumpets, a light tapping at the door has me sitting up cross legged.

"Mum. You look amazing!"

She walks in looking like a million dollars. Lucy, Maggie, and Trevor have obviously cast their magic. And Clive had somehow managed to talk her into a shopping spree before they arrived. She looks stunning in her slim fitting, pale blue sheath dress and heels, and her fascinator of tiny feathers, shimmers in the breeze wafting into the bedroom.

Scrambling off the bed, I give her a hug. "You look stunning, Mum."

"Thanks. It's been a long time since anyone said that about me." She reaches into her handbag and brings out a delicate silver jewellery box with scroll engraved detail. It looks vintage. "This belonged to Granny Banks, your father's mother. When your father died, he left instructions in his will that this should come to you when you got married." Mum's eyes begin to tear up as she hands it to me. "There's an inscription inside it. I never knew he had it done."

Opening the lid, my eyes fill with tears. Inside the inscription reads; 'To my little girl on her wedding day, always remember, I loved you first. Dad x'

"Oh, Mum, thank you. It's lovely."

"He'd have been so proud of you," she sniffles. "As I am."

"Hey! What's all this?" Lucy chides, barging into the room. "Do you really want red-rimmed, puffy eyes when you walk down the aisle?"

Mum gives me a quick hug. "I'd better go." Then she hurries out of the room.

Lucy launches the eyebrow. "You're not even showered yet. Come on, move it, lady. We've got an hour and a half to create breathtakingly gorgeous. Admittedly you are half way there, but still, we need to get a wiggle on."

"Did you remember to bring the things I asked you for?" I ask as she shoves me into the en-suite.

"I did." she says, waggling her eyebrows. "Now hurry up."

As I close the bathroom door and turn to put the shower on, I stop in my tracks. Written on the bathroom mirror in huge red lipstick are the words;

Today, I've loved you for

276 days, and counting...

Until forever, baby.

Your impatient fiancé.

X;-)

My eyes fill with tears as a big grin spreads across my face. How the hell did he come into my room without me knowing? And why didn't he wake me up?

~

As I stand facing the full length mirror, I can't help but feel the impact of my reflection. My wedding gown is stunning, a true work of art made even more special by the fact that it was designed by my best friend and my gorgeous fiancé.

The white, silk satin fabric skims my body perfectly with a slender silhouette until it flares out seductively at the bottom.

The tailoring and structure of the dress softly accentuating all my curves, and the plunging neckline, thin shoulder straps, and deep-v at the back, exposing my golden tan from our days spent basking in the sun, make me look positively radiant.

My makeup is subtle, and Lucy's done an amazing job with my hair, which is delicately caught up on one side with tiny white rosebuds. The rest is down and flowing, full with voluminous waves curling around my shoulders, the sun-kissed highlights giving my chocolate brown hair a lustrous glow.

Lucy moves to stand behind me pulling my train into position. She looks amazing in her pale yellow, floor length gown. Her blonde hair is swept up into thick, intricately latticed braids converging in a mass of curls at the nape, and decorated with tiny yellow buttercups.

With a teary look on both our faces we catch each other's eyes in the mirror.

"Viv…"

"I know," I say, softly. "I love you too, Luce." I smile at her trying not to cry. I can see how choked up she is, but I don't want either of us to ruin our makeup, at least not yet.

"I'll get your shoes."

While she heads to the wardrobe, I smooth my dress and take a deep calming breath to alleviate my butterflies, it's almost time.

"Oh, my giddy Aunt!"

The shock in her voice makes my heart beat a little faster. "What is it?" Her big beaming smile confuses me. "Luce?"

"Look!" she says, thrusting my shoes at me. "Ahh, look what he's done. He's so romantic." She turns my shoes over one at a time. Written on the sole of the left shoe is;

No

Without

Then she turns the right one over, written on the sole is;

Me

You

I gasp, bringing my hand to my mouth. "No me without you," I whisper, using all my strength not to choke up. "He's so romantic. And sneaky."

Someone taps at the door. "Is it safe to come in?" Vinnie asks.

"Yes," Lucy chuckles, "we're decent." She holds my elbow as I slip my shoes on.

Vinnie walks in looking very handsome, wearing a dark grey suit with a crisp white shirt and a tie and buttonhole matching the colour of Lucy's gown.

He falters for a moment as his eyes follow the length of my dress from the floor up, eventually landing on beaming face. His face is almost sad for a moment, even his eyes begin to glisten, but then his big smile takes over.

"Vivienne… Wow! You are a vision of beauty. Your father and William would be so proud."

I smile, holding back the tears now pricking my eyes. "Vinnie… You called me Vivienne! That's the first time since, ever."

He chuckles and blushes, shifting on his feet. "Well, as I'm giving you away, it seems more appropriate. And I couldn't feel more proud than I do right now."

Reaching inside his jacket he brings out a wrapped gift. "This is just a little something from me and Jan. We figured as you're always taking photos of everyone else, you never get any of yourself, so we had Ed take a few at your party last week."

Tears spring into my eyes as I unwrap the small leather bound photo album and open it up. Inside are candid photographs of me with Max, me with my mother, and me with all my friends and family. I'm so touched they would do that for me.

"It's perfect, Vinnie. Thank you."

Straightening his back, he holds his elbow out for me to take. "Shall we?" he grins. "There's a very impatient man who's just dying to see you."

Swallowing the lump in my throat and taking a deep breath to calm my butterflies, I take his arm.

Lucy hands me my bouquet, gives me one last inspection before nodding her approval, then she gives me the eyebrow.

"Pick your feet up, don't slouch, and don't fall down the steps."

I laugh. "I'll do my best, but I'm not promising anything."

Vinnie grins. "Should I have brought the hard hat?" Then he walks me out of the room. My stomach tightens and suddenly I'm racked with nerves.

As Vinnie walks me through the main hall which is festooned with garlands of tropical flowers, I breathe in their heady scent trying to calm my nervous butterflies.

Rafa and all his staff are lined up in their colourful uniforms, smiling at us as we pass.

Vinnie leads me down the stairs to the outdoor terrace, and then through the lavish gardens toward the beach. I can hear the buzz of people chatting and laughing, but everyone is still hidden from my view.

Vinnie comes to a standstill at the edge of the gardens, keeping us out of sight from the wedding party gathered on the beach. "We'll start walking when we hear the music," he smiles.

Excited butterflies swirl around in a chaotic fluster in my belly. "Is it the wedding march? Or Canon in D?" I ask, having no idea what to expect. Max has planned every last detail of our wedding.

Vinnie smiles, patting my hand, giving me a comforting wink. "Are you ready?"

I smile up at him, taking a deep breath. I'm nervous of being the centre of attention but I know as soon as I see Max, all my nerves will fade away and all I will see will be him.

"I'm ready. And Vinnie… Thank you. I hope you know how much I—"

"Yes, Vivienne…I know." With a smile that could light a whole city, he squeezes my hand. "Me too."

Lucy gives me a kiss on the cheek. "You look gorgeous. Don't mumble and don't forget to breathe."

The chatter dies down and then I hear the intro to a very special song. The opening notes of the grand piano, acoustic guitar, violins, and cellos, and then the velvety, breathy voice of Spencer Combs, fills me with joy. The song 'You are mine,' is one of Max's favourites, he's romanced me to it many times.

Vinnie squeezes my hand and we start to move. As we walk along the boarded pathway littered with yellow petals, we cross the white powdery sands toward our family and friends who turn to face us with beaming smiles and glistening eyes.

My stomach flutters with a million butterflies and I can feel myself gripping tightly onto Vinnie's arm as the nerves converge in my belly. But as soon as my eyes find him, my heart slows to the same rhythm of his heart and the nerves begin to ebb.

Standing together at the water's edge, side by side under the canopy of white organza and garlands of flowers, Max and Cole out shine the beauty of this tropical paradise. But Max is the one pulling me in, bringing me toward him with his innate and powerful force. Seeing him standing there, waiting for me, makes everything feel so right, so perfect, so complete.

Mine.

He looks exquisitely masculine. Elegant and devastatingly handsome as I knew he would. His blue eyes, the same colour as the ocean, sparkle like never before. His flawless face, golden from the sun, is beaming with contentment. His luxurious, inky black mane floating in the soft tropical breeze and lightly skimming the collar of his crisp, white shirt and pale grey suit, is just begging for me to run my fingers through it.

As Vinnie brings me toward him, Max's sensually lazy smile and beautiful blue eyes gaze at me in awed wonderment. I couldn't look away if my life depended on it.

His seductive smile travels up my body, finding my eager eyes, and when he engages me in his heart-stopping smile, it completely takes my breath away. As his eyes drink me in, I feel the pull of his heart drawing me toward him, and as soon as he takes my hand my world feels complete.

I feel Vinnie releasing my arm and kissing my cheek, but I can't look away from the man before me. The force of his will is much too strong and I'm so totally and irrevocably captivated by him.

"You look so beautiful," he whispers, with a velvety rasp and that crooked smile, the one that has me biting my bottom lip.

"So, do you." I can't stop smiling.

As the ceremony begins, we stare into each other's eyes, already pledging our love through our silent conversation. The one thing I would always trust, is that we speak with our eyes, and his love for me has never shone more brightly than it is right now.

How did I arrive at this point? How did I win the heart of this incredible man?

When Max smirks at me, squeezing my hand to draw my attention, I realise I had just been staring up at him and had zoned everyone else out. His effect on me is compelling, it always has been. Even knowing I have dozens of eyes on me, when he hits me with that look, his are the only eyes I see.

It's only as Cole steps forward to present our rings that I realise I hadn't heard a word the Judge had said.

Cole gives me a cheeky wink then holds the rings forward. Max picks up the platinum and diamond band showing me the inscription inside before placing it on the tip of my finger.

'Max ~ Mine Forever.'

Before placing the ring fully onto my finger, he gazes deep into my eyes and delivers his vows straight from the heart.

"Vivienne, meeting you was fate. Falling in love with you was inevitable. Do you even know how much I love you?… You make me smile like an idiot. You make my heart beat a little faster, and love so much harder. You make me so happy, and with you, my life is complete.

"I promised you forever, and I meant it. There is no me without you, Vivienne. And for the rest of my life, I promise to make you smile. To kiss you at will without notice. To love you without boundary. To wrap you in my arms and hold you whenever and wherever I please, whether it's appropriate or not. To follow you wherever you lead. To protect you, fiercely and without reservation. Because you, are my once in a lifetime love. My crazy-good love. And from this moment on, I make you mine, forever."

The audible sigh from everyone, and Lucy's sniffles behind me, make me realise I'm not the only one touched by his vows. Tears pool in my eyes as he slides the ring onto my finger, then he kisses the back of my hand.

Emotion chokes me and I fear my vows will never be heard as Cole presents me with Max's ring, I look inside for the inscription I know will be there.

'Vivienne ~ Mine Forever.'

Trying desperately hard not to cry, I place the ring on the tip of his finger and smile up at his gorgeous face. Gazing deep into his eyes, I decide to abandon my pre-scripted vows and just let my heart speak.

"Max, I used to think that if Charlie had never brought you to me, that my heart would never have known your love, and that would have been the biggest tragedy of my life. But I know, that had Charlie not brought us together, my heart would still seek you out. That somehow I'd find you and make you mine, because there is no me without you.

"My heart is yours, without question, fear, or doubt, because I know you'll never break it. And until my last breath, I'll cherish your love, because I could never live without it… And I promise to let you kiss me at will without notice. To let you love me without boundary. To let you wrap me in your arms, whenever and wherever you please, whether it's appropriate or not. Because you, are the love of my life. A rare and beautiful man. And until forever, I will love you right back, with all my heart."

His eyes glisten with tears and burn with love. I slide the ring onto his finger and before the Judge has the chance to conclude the ceremony by pronouncing that we are man and wife, Max honours his vow by taking me in his arms, pulling me close to his chest, and devouring my lips in a hot, deep, passionate kiss.

The cheers and whistles fade into the background as his love consumes me.

Breaking the kiss, he leans his forehead against mine. "I've waited a lifetime for you, Mrs. Foxx. I love you so much."

I smile, trying to open my eyes. His kiss still has my body in rapture and my senses in a tail spin. "I love you too, my darling husband, and now that it's official…"

I nod to Lucy and she quickly removes the opaque top layer of the train of my wedding dress revealing the crystal lettering beneath. The words I had added to the dress in secret. 'M.F. His Forever.'

His eyes gaze down at the train of my dress in stunned awe, then as his smiling eyes return to mine, he unbuttons his suit jacket holding one side open. In the satin lining, the words; 'V.F. Hers Forever,' are embroidered into the fabric.

We burst out laughing and before we have the chance to throw our arms around each other, we're surrounded by our family and friends hugging and kissing us as they usher us toward our wedding feast.

MINE FOREVER

As we sway to the only contribution I made to this wedding, a beautiful song for our first dance by Ruelle, appropriately named, 'I get to love you,' Max rests his cheek against mine, holding my hand against his chest, with his other arm wrapped around my waist, holding me close. Sighing deeply with content, he gives me a loving squeeze.

Tears begin to form in my eyes. Happy tears. Joyous tears. We've been through so much and we've survived it all. Being in his arms is, and always will be, my happy place.

"Max?"

"Yes, baby?"

"There were so many times I thought we'd never get here."

He smirks, raising an eyebrow. "Yeah, it's been a crazy ride."

"You make everything so special. I'm the happiest girl in the world."

He leans back hitting me with those beautiful blues and his heart-stopping smile. "Baby, the happiest day of my life, is any day I spend with you. We belong together, and I think we've proved that no one can tear us apart. Until forever, remember?"

He floors me with every word and every gesture. "Until

forever," I whisper, rising up to kiss him on the lips.

"I'm glad you liked your dress, you look amazing in it, and I love your message on the train."

I gaze into his eyes. "I love my dress. You know me so well. And underneath it, I have a little surprise for you."

His eyebrows raise in a cheeky smirk. "Can I see it now?"

We're surrounded by dozens of smiling faces all eagerly staring at us, so I smile and shake my head. "For your eyes only, Mr. Foxx. Them's the rules."

"Hmm," he purrs. "All I can think about now is your underwear. You drive me crazy, you know that?"

"Crazy good?"

"Always." Nuzzling my neck, he releases a hot sigh of contentment, then he pulls back, smiling down at me with his dazzling, heart-melting smile.

"...What?" I ask, unable to contain my own smile.

"Nothing, it's just, I can't stop smiling. Everything's so perfect. I have a beautiful wife, and two little nuggets on the way..." He takes a deep breath, releasing another contented sigh. "You make me so happy, baby. And I can't wait to get you naked."

Gazing down at me with those seductive eyes with a look that always stirs my senses, I smile up at him, holding his cheek in my palm.

"Ditto, Mr. Foxx. I love you."

"Love you more, baby."

As our beautiful song ends, Lucy comes dashing over with the pre-arranged items I had asked her to bring with her to the island. "Here, you go," she says, her face beaming with a silly grin as she hands me the small, neatly wrapped box.

We're standing in the middle of the dance floor, but when the music doesn't continue, Max begins to look increasingly wary and all eyes are on us.

"Max, there's something I need to tell you... or rather, show you."

His concerned eyes stare down at me, searching my face as I hand him the neatly wrapped box. "Baby, you shouldn't have bought me a gift. You're all I'll ever need."

The sincerity in his eyes makes my heart sigh. "Oh, Max, you say the sweetest things." I pull him down to me for a kiss. "Open it, the contents aren't really for you, but the sentiment is."

He gives me a questioning frown then he tears the paper open and stares down at the white cardboard box. An excited crowd have gathered around us and Lucy, who is the only other person who knows what's inside the box, is cuddling into Dan, smirking it up big time.

Max's lips tip up at the corners in a roguish smile, then he gently shakes the box. "Is it a Bugatti Chiron? Because, I'm sorry baby, I've already got one on order."

I laugh, shaking my head as excited butterflies invade my belly. "Just open the bloody box."

He smirks, taking a quick look around the crowd who are eagerly waiting to see what's inside it, then he lifts the lid, and stares down at the contents. His smile slides from his face and I see the emotion building in his eyes. Nervous butterflies invade my belly when he takes an eternity to respond.

His watery eyes fly back up to mine with a stunned, awestruck expression on his face as his eyes gaze lovingly into mine.

Inside the box are two pairs of baby shoes. One pink, one blue. Both have the words, *'Daddy's Little Nugget'* stitched into the sides.

"Look at the soles," I urge him, prompting him out of his awed gaze. He looks at the blue pair first. They have the name, 'Charlie' stitched into the soles. The pink ones have 'Maria', his mother's name.

Before I have the chance to speak, he throws his arms around me, lifts me off my feet and spins me around with his face buried in my neck. "I thought it was impossible to love you more, baby. But I do… You are a rare and beautiful woman, and I love the fuck out of you, Mrs. Foxx." His voice is broken and raspy, and his shining eyes gaze deeply into mine as he devours my lips in a heartfelt, passionate kiss transferring his love straight from his heart to mine.

As the applause, cheers, and whistles subside, Cole taps Max on the shoulder interrupting our wickedly hot kiss.

"Erhum, I hate to break this up, but it's time," he says, smiling like a Cheshire cat. Max winks and nods at him in some secret, knowing code they both seem to share, but as I glance around at all our guests, I realise everyone's grinning like Cheshire cats.

"What did I miss?" I murmur, reaching up to fondle my locket. I feel out of step.

Max hands Cole the baby shoes, gives him a long brotherly hug, then reaches down for my hand, giving it a squeeze.

"Okay, everybody," he says, getting everyone's attention. "I hope you all know how much you mean to us. Personally, I can't thank you all enough for being here and for helping Vivienne and I celebrate such a happy, special day in our lives. I hope you all enjoy the rest of your evening, and the rest of the week is yours here on the island."

He squeezes my hand and throw me a wink.

"I'm taking my beautiful wife on honeymoon for three weeks, and when we get back, I hope to see you all at our new home for dinner... Ah, don't worry," he smirks, "Vivienne won't be cooking."

"Wait! New home?" Momentarily stunned into silence, I glance over to my Mum, Sylvie, Jan and Vinnie who are all huddled together, and if their smiling faces are anything to go by, it would appear I'm the only one who doesn't know what's going on.

Max gives me a kiss on my gob-smacked lips. "Don't worry, baby, I'll tell you all about it when we get where we're going." He nods toward a white helicopter on the beach, its engines roaring to life.

Mum rushes over, giving me a tight hug with tears in her eyes and a big smile on her face. "Enjoy yourselves," she sniffles. "We'll see you when you get back."

"Wha… Back from where?"

Max tugs on my hand, smiling his heart-stopping smile.

"Are you ready, baby?"

I stare up at him utterly dumbfounded. "But I thought… Where are we going?"

He moves in front of me, taking my face in his hands gazing down at me with love pouring out from his beautiful blues. "Do you love me?"

"With all my heart."

"Do you trust me?"

"You know I do."

I yelp as he scoops me into his arms, kissing me deeply, reverently, his eyes sparkling, his super-sexy smile lighting up his handsome face. "Then that, my beautiful wife, is all you'll ever need. Until forever."

In that moment, I knew he was right. Max is the love of my life, and he will always be all I'll ever need. My fairy-tale ending is just the beginning. And today, the happiest day of my life to date, I became his, and he became mine, forever.

~***~

LISA MACKAY

Debut novel: (Trilogy)

Sexy M.F. Series

Book 1 M.F.
Book 2 Missing Foxx
Book 3 Mine Forever

Lisa's next romance:
The Heart-Deep Series
Coming soon.

lisamackayuk@gmail.com
www.lisamackay.uk
@lisamackayuk
www.facebook.com/lisamackayauthor1/

To all my readers,
Mahoosive Thanks for immersing yourselves in Vivienne and Max's love story. And to all those of you who took the time to leave a review on Amazon, Goodreads, or any of the other platforms, love you more.
Lisa x:-)

GLOSSARY

Biccies – *Biscuits*
Bottle it – *Lose Courage*
Blower – *Telephone*
Claret – *Blood*
Comfies – *Comfortable clothes*
Deets – *Details*
Ding-Dong – *Argument/Row/Fight*
Give him a bell – *Telephone him/call him*
Gnashers – *Teeth*
Karsie – *Toilet*
Mahoosive – *Massive*
Mench – *Mention*
Mince Pies (Minces) – *Eyes*
Mo – *Moment*
On the fritz – *Broken*
Plonker/Pillock/Donut/Numpty – *Idiot*
Scooby – 'Scooby Doo' – *Clue*
Shindig – *Party/Knees Up/Event*
Shufty – *Look*
Sitch – *Situation*
Snog – *Kiss*
Squiffy – *Drunk*
Stonker/Stonking – *Major (emphasis)*
Sussed – *Guessed correctly*
Yonks – *Ages/Long time*